Also by Wright Morris

COLLECTED STORIES

Wright Morris

COLLECTED STORIES

STORIES

1948–1986

A Nonpareil Book
DAVID R. GODINE · PUBLISHER
Boston

This is a NONPAREIL BOOK published in 1989 by
DAVID R. GODINE, PUBLISHER, INC.
Horticultural Hall
300 Massachusetts Avenue
Boston, Massachusetts 02115

"The Lover and the Beloved," "Victrola," "Glimpse Into Another Country,"
"Going Into Exile," "To Calabria," "Fellow Creatures," "Country Music,"
and "Things That Matter," originally appeared in the *New Yorker*; "The
Sound Tape" in *Harper's Bazaar*; "The Character of the Lover" in *American
Mercury*; "The Cat in the Picture" in *Esquire*; "The Customs of the Coun-
try," "The Origin of the Sadness," and "Wishing You and Your Loved Ones
Every Happiness" in *The Boston Globe Magazine*.

Originally published in 1986 by Harper & Row

Library of Congress Cataloging in Publication Data
Morris, Wright, 1910–
Collected stories, 1948–1986.

(Nonpareil book ; 54)
I. Title. II. Series.
[PS3525.O7475A6   1989]   813'.52   88-45282
ISBN 0-87923-752-X

This book has been printed on acid-free paper. The paper will not yellow with
age, the binding will not deteriorate, and the pages will not fall out.

FIRST PRINTING
Printed in the United States of America

To the music of
ANTONIO VIVALDI

Late acquaintance
Constant companion

I thank Stephen Arkin for
his footwork, his suggestions,
and the bran muffins that
fuel our continuing discussions.

Contents

COLLECTED STORIES

The Ram in the Thicket

In this dream Mr. Ormsby stood in the yard—at the edge of the yard where the weeds began—and stared at a figure that appeared to be on a rise. This figure had the head of a bird with a crown of bright, exotic plumage, only partially concealed by a paint-daubed helmet. Mr. Ormsby felt the urgent need to identify this strange bird. Feathery wisps of plumage shot through the crown of the helmet like a pillow leaking sharp spears of yellow straw. The face beneath it was indescribably solemn, with eyes so pale they were like openings on the sky. Slung over the left arm, casually, was a gun, but the right arm, the palm upward, extended toward a cloud of hovering birds. They came and went, like bees after honey, and there were so many and all so friendly, that Mr. Ormsby extended his own hand toward them. No birds came, but in his upturned palm he felt the dull throb of the alarm clock, which he held tenderly, a living thing, until it ran down.

In the morning light the photograph at the foot of his bed seemed startling. The boy stood alone on a rise, and he held, very casually, a gun. The face beneath the helmet had no features, but Mr. Ormsby would have known him just by the stance, by the way he held the gun, like some women hold their arms when their hands are idle, parts of their body that for the moment are not much use. Without the gun it was as if some part of the boy had been amputated; the way he stood, even the way he walked was not quite right.

Mr. Ormsby had given the boy a gun because he had never had a gun himself, not because he wanted him to shoot anything. The boy didn't want to kill anything either, and during the first year he found it hard to: the rattle of the BBs in the barrel of the gun frightened the birds before he could shoot them. And that was what had made him a *hunter*. He had to stalk everything in order to hit it, and after all that trouble you naturally try to hit what you're shooting at. He didn't seem to realize that after he hit it it might be dead. It seemed natural for a boy like that to join the Navy, and let God strike Mr. Ormsby dead to hear him say so, nothing ever seemed more natural to him than the news that the boy had been killed. Mother had steeled herself for the worst, the moment the boy enlisted, but Mr. Ormsby had not been prepared to feel what he felt. Mother need never know it unless he slipped up and talked in his sleep.

He turned slowly on the bed, careful to keep the springs quiet, and as he lowered his feet he scooped his socks from the floor. As a precaution Mother had slept the first few months of their marriage in her corset—as a precaution and as an aid to self-control. In the fall they had ordered twin beds. Carrying his shoes—today, of all days, would be a trial for Mother—he tiptoed to the closet and picked up his shirt and pants. There was simply no reason, as he had explained to her twenty years ago, why she should get up when he could just as well get a bite for himself. He had made that suggestion when the boy was just a baby and she needed her strength. Even as it was she didn't come out of it any too well. The truth was, Mother was so thorough about everything she did that her breakfasts usually took an hour or more. When he did it himself he was out of the kitchen in ten, twelve minutes and without leaving any pile of dishes around. By himself he could quick-rinse them in a little hot water, but with Mother there was the dishpan and all of the suds. Mother had the idea that a meal simply wasn't a meal without setting the table and using half the dishes in the place. It was easier to do it himself, and except for Sunday, when they had brunch, he was out of the house an hour before she got up. He had a bite of lunch at the store and at four o'clock he did the day's shopping since he was right downtown anyway. There was a time he called her up and inquired as to what she thought she wanted, but since he did all the buying he knew that better himself. As secretary for the League of Women Voters she had enough on her mind in times like these without cluttering it up with food. Now that he left the store an hour early he usually got home in the midst of her nap or while she was taking her bath. As he had nothing else to do he prepared the vegetables and dressed the meat, as Mother had never shown much of a flair for meat. There had been a year—when the boy was small and before he had taken up that gun—when she had made several marvelous lemon meringue pies. But feeling as she did about the gun—and she told them both how she felt about it—she didn't see why she should slave in the kitchen for people like that. She always spoke to them as *they*—or as *you* plural—from the time he had given the boy the gun. Whether this was because they were both men, both culprits, or both something else, they were never entirely separate things again. When she called, *they* would both answer, and though the boy had been gone two years he still felt him *there*, right beside him, when Mother said *you*.

For some reason Mr. Ormsby could not understand—although the rest of the house was neat as a pin—the room they *lived* in was always a mess. Mother refused to let the cleaning woman set her foot in it. Whenever she left the house she locked the door. Long, long ago he had said something, and she had said something, and she had said she wanted one room in the house where she could relax and just let her hair down. That had sounded so wonderfully human, so unusual for Mother, that he had been completely taken with it. As a matter of fact he still didn't know what to say. It was the only room in the house—except for the screened-in porch in the summer—where he could take off his shoes and open his shirt on his underwear. If the room was *clean*, it would be clean like all of the others, and that would leave him nothing but the basement and the porch. The way the boy took to the out-of-doors—he stopped looking for his cuff links, began to look for pins—was partially because he couldn't find a place in the house to sit down. They had just redecorated the house—the boy at that time was just a little shaver—and Mother had spread newspapers over everything. There hadn't been a chair in the place—except the straight-backed ones at the table—that hadn't been, that *wasn't*, covered with a piece of newspaper. Anyone who had ever scrunched around on a paper knew what that was like. It was at that time that he had got the idea of having his pipe in the basement, reading in the bedroom, and the boy had taken to the out-of-doors. Because he had always wanted a gun himself, and because the boy was alone, with no kids around to play with, he had brought him home a thousand-shot BB gun by the name of Daisy—funny that he should remember the name—and five thousand BBs in a drawstring bag.

That gun had been a mistake—he began to shave himself in tepid, lukewarm water rather than let it run hot, which would bang the pipes and wake Mother up. When the telegram came that the boy had been killed Mother hadn't said a word, but she made it clear whose fault it was. There was never any doubt, *any* doubt, as to just whose fault it was.

He stopped thinking while he shaved, attentive to the mole at the edge of his mustache, and leaned to the mirror to avoid dropping suds on the rug. There had been a time when he had wondered about an Oriental throw rug in the bathroom, but over twenty years he had become accustomed to it. As a matter of fact he sort of missed it whenever they had guests with children and Mother remembered to take it up. Without the rug he always felt just a little uneasy in the bathroom; it led him to whistle or turn on the water and let it run. If it hadn't been for that he might not have noticed as soon as he did that Mother did the same thing whenever anybody was in the house. She turned on the water and let it run until she was through with the toilet, then she would flush it before she turned the water off. If you happen to have old-fashioned plumbing, and have lived with a person for twenty years, you can't help noticing little things like that. He had got to be a little like that himself: since the boy had gone he used the one in the basement or waited until he got down to the store. As a matter of fact it was more convenient, didn't wake Mother up, and he could have his pipe while he was sitting there.

With his pants on, but carrying his shirt—for he might get it soiled preparing breakfast—he left the bathroom and tiptoed down the stairs.

Although the boy had gone, was gone, that is, Mother still liked to preserve her slipcovers and the kitchen linoleum. It was a good piece, well worth preserving, but unless there were guests in the house and the papers were taken up, Mr. Ormsby forgot it was there. Right now he couldn't tell you what color the linoleum was. Stooping to see what the color might be—it proved to be blue, Mother's favorite color—he felt the stirring in his bowels. Usually this occurred while he was rinsing the dishes after his second cup of coffee or after the first long draw on his pipe. He was not supposed to smoke in the morning, but it was more important to be regular that way than irregular with his pipe. Mother had been the first to realize this—not in so many words—but she would rather he did anything than not be able to do *that*.

He measured out a pint and a half of water, put it over a medium fire, and added just a pinch of salt. Then he walked to the top of the basement stairs, turned on the light, and at the bottom turned it off. He dipped his head to pass beneath a sagging line of wash, the sleeves dripping, and with his hands out, for the corner was dark, he entered the cell.

The basement toilet had been put in to accommodate the help, who had to use something, and Mother would not have them on her Oriental rug. Until the day he dropped some money out of his pants and had to strike a match to look for it, he had never noticed what kind of a stool it was. Mother had picked it up secondhand—she had never told him where—because she couldn't see buying something new for a place always in the dark. It was very old, with a chain pull, and operated on a principle that invariably produced quite a splash. But, in spite of that, he preferred it to the one at the store and very much more than the one upstairs. This was rather hard to explain since the seat was pretty cold in the winter and the water sometimes nearly froze. But it was private like no other place in the house. Considering that the house was as good as empty, that was a strange thing to say, but it was the

only way to say how he felt. If he went off for a walk like the
boy, Mother would miss him, somebody would see him, and he
wouldn't feel right about it anyhow. All he wanted was a dark,
quiet place and the feeling that for five minutes, just five minutes,
nobody would be looking for him. Who would ever believe five
minutes like that were so hard to come by? The closest he had
ever been to the boy—after he had given him the gun—was the
morning he had found him here on the stool. It was then that the
boy had said, *et tu, Brutus,* and they had both laughed so hard they
had had to hold their sides. The boy had put his head in a basket
of wash so Mother wouldn't hear. Like everything the boy said
there were two or three ways to take it, and in the dark Mr. Ormsby
could not see his face. When he stopped laughing the boy said,
Well, Pop, I suppose one flush ought to do, but Mr. Ormsby had not
been able to say anything. To be called Pop made him so weak
that he had to sit right down on the stool, just like he was, and
support his head in his hands. Just as he had never had a name for
the boy, the boy had never had a name for him—none, that is,
that Mother would permit him to use. Of all the names Mother
couldn't stand, Pop was the worst, and he agreed with her; it was
vulgar, common, and used by strangers to intimidate old men. He
agreed with her, completely—until he heard the word in the boy's
mouth. It was only natural that the boy would use it if he ever
had the chance—but he never dreamed that any word, especially
that word, could mean what it did. It made him weak, he had to
sit down and pretend he was going about his business, and what
a blessing it was that the place was dark. Nothing more was said,
ever, but it remained their most important conversation—so important they were afraid to try and improve on it. Days later he
remembered what the boy had actually said, and how shocking it
was but without any *sense* of shock. A blow so sharp that he had
no sense of pain, only a knowing, as he had under gas, that he
had been worked on. For two, maybe three minutes, there in the
dark, they had been what Mother called them, they were *they*—
and they were there in the basement because they were so much
alike. When the telegram came, and when he knew what he would
find, he had brought it there, had struck a match, and read what

it said. The match filled the cell with light and he saw—he couldn't help seeing—piles of tinned goods in the space beneath the stairs. Several dozen cans of tuna fish and salmon, and since *he* was the one that had the points, bought the groceries, there was only one place Mother could have got such things. It had been a greater shock than the telegram—that was the honest-to-God's truth and anyone who knew Mother as well as he did would have felt the same. It was unthinkable, but there it was—and there were more on top of the water closet, where he peered while precariously balanced on the stool. Cans of pineapple, crabmeat, and tins of Argentine beef. He had been stunned, the match had burned down and actually scorched his fingers, and he nearly killed himself when he forgot and stepped off the seat. Only later in the morning—after he had sent flowers to ease the blow for Mother—did he realize how such a thing *must* have occurred. Mother knew so many influential people, and they gave her so much that they had very likely given her all of this stuff as well. Rather than turn it down and needlessly alienate people, influential people, Mother had done the next best thing. While the war was on she refused to serve it, or profiteer in any way—and at the same time not alienate people foolishly. It had been an odd thing, certainly, that he should discover all of that by the same match that he read the telegram. Naturally, he never breathed a word of it to Mother, as something like that, even though she was not superstitious, would really upset her. It was one of those things that he and the boy would keep to themselves.

It would be like Mother to think of putting it in here, the very last place that the cleaning woman would look for it. The new cleaning woman would neither go upstairs nor down, and did whatever she did somewhere else. Mr. Ormsby lit a match to see if everything was all right—hastily blew it out when he saw that the can pile had increased. He stood up, then hurried up the stairs without buttoning his pants as he could hear the water boiling. He added half a cup, then measured three heaping tablespoons of coffee into the bottom of the double boiler, buttoned his pants. Looking at his watch he saw that it was seven thirty-five. As it would be a hard day—sponsoring a boat was a man-size job— he would give Mother another ten minutes or so. He took two bowls from the cupboard, set them on blue pottery saucers, and with the grapefruit knife in his hand walked to the icebox.

As he put his head in the icebox door—in order to see he had to—Mr. Ormsby stopped breathing and closed his eyes. What had been dying for some time was now dead. He leaned back, inhaled, leaned in again. The floor of the icebox was covered with a fine assortment of jars full of leftovers Mother simply could not throw away. Some of the jars were covered with little oilskin hoods, some with saucers, and some with wax paper snapped on with a rubber band. It was impossible to tell, from the outside, which one it was. Seating himself on the floor he removed them one at a time, starting at the front and working toward the back. As he had done this many times before, he got well into the problem, near the middle, before troubling to sniff anything. A jar that might have been carrots—it was hard to tell without probing—was now a furry marvel of green mold. It smelled only mildly, however, and Mr. Ormsby remembered that this was penicillin, the life giver. A spoonful of cabbage—it had been three months since they had had cabbage—had a powerful stench but was still not the one he had in mind. There were two more jars of mold; the one screwed tight he left alone as it had a frosted look and the top of the lid bulged. The culprit, however, was not that at all, but in an open saucer on the next shelf—part of an egg—Mr. Ormsby had beaten the white himself. He placed the saucer on the sink and returned all but two of the jars to the icebox: the cabbage and the explosive-looking one. If it smelled he took it out, otherwise Mother had to see for herself as she refused to take *their* word for these things. When he was just a little shaver the boy had walked into the living room full of Mother's guests and showed them something in a jar. Mother had been horrified—but she naturally thought it a frog or something and not a bottle out of her own icebox. When one of the ladies asked the boy where in the world he had found it, he naturally said, *In the icebox.* Mother had never forgiven him. After that she forbade him to look in the box without permission, and the boy had not so much as peeked in it since. He would eat only what he found on the table, or ready to eat in the kitchen—or what he found at the end of those walks he took everywhere.

With the jar of cabbage and furry mold Mr. Ormsby made a trip to the garage, picked up the garden spade, walked around behind. At one time he had emptied the jars and merely buried the contents, but recently, since the war that is, he had buried it all. Part of it was a question of time—he had more work to do at the store—but the bigger part of it was to put an end to the jars. Not that it worked out that way—all Mother had to do was open a new one—but it gave him a real satisfaction to bury them. Now that the boy and his dogs were gone there was simply no one around the house to eat up all the food Mother saved.

There were worms in the fork of earth he had turned and he stood looking at them—*they* both had loved worms—when he remembered the water boiling on the stove. He dropped everything and ran, ran right into Emil Ludlow, the milkman, before he noticed him. Still on the run he went up the steps and through the screen door into the kitchen—he was clear to the stove before he remembered the door would slam. He started back, but too late, and in the silence that followed the BANG he stood with his eyes tightly closed, his fists clenched. Usually he remained in this condition until a sign from Mother—a thump on the floor or her voice at the top of the stairs. None came, however, only the sound of the milk bottles that Emil Ludlow was leaving on the porch. Mr. Ormsby gave him time to get away, waited until he heard the horse walking, then he went out and brought the milk in. At the icebox he remembered the water—why it was he had come running in the first place—and he left the door open and hurried to the stove. It was down to half a cup but not, thank heavens, dry. He added a full pint, then put the milk in the icebox; took out the butter, four eggs, and a Flori-gold grapefruit. Before he cut the grapefruit he looked at his watch and, seeing that it was ten minutes to eight, an hour before train time, he opened the stairway door.

"Ohhh, Mother!" he called, and then he returned to the grapefruit.

"*Ad astra per aspera*," she said, and rose from the bed. In the darkness she felt about for her corset, then let herself go completely for the thirty-five seconds it required to get it on. This done, she pulled the cord to the light that hung in the attic, and as it snapped on, in a firm voice she said, "*Fiat lux.*" Light having been made, Mother opened her eyes.

As the bulb hung in the attic, the closet remained in an afterglow, a twilight zone. It was not light, strictly speaking, but it was all Mother wanted to see. Seated on the attic stairs she trimmed her toenails with a pearl-handled knife that Mr. Ormsby had been missing for several years. The blade was not so good any longer and using it too freely had resulted in ingrown nails on both of her big toes. But Mother preferred it to scissors, which were proven, along with bathtubs, to be one of the most dangerous things in the home. *Even more than the battlefield, the most dangerous place in the world. Dry feet and hands before turning on lights, dry between toes.*

Without stooping she slipped into her sabots and left the closet, the light burning, and with her eyes dimmed, but not closed, went down the hall. Locking the bathroom door she stepped to the basin and turned on the cold water, then she removed several feet of paper from the toilet-paper roll. This took time, as in order to keep the roller from squeaking it had to be removed from its socket in the wall, then returned. One piece she put in the pocket of her kimono, the other she folded into a wad and used as a blotter to dab up spots on the floor. Turning up the water she sat down on the stool—then she got up to get a pencil and pad from the table near the window. On the first sheet she wrote—

Ars longa, vita brevis
Wildflower club, sun. 4 P.M.

She tore this off and filed it, tip showing, right at the front of her corset. On the next page—

ROGER—
Ivory Snow
Sani-Flush on thurs.

As she placed this on top of the toilet-paper roll she heard him call "First for breakfast." She waited until he closed the stairway door, then she stood up and turned on the shower. As it rained into the tub and splashed behind her in the basin, she lowered the lid, flushed the toilet. Until the water closet had filled, stopped gurgling, she stood at the window watching a squirrel cross the yard from tree to tree. Then she turned the shower off and noisily dragged the shower curtain, on its metal rings, back to the wall. She dampened her shower cap in the basin and hung it on the towel rack to dry, dropping the towel that was there down the laundry chute. This done, she returned to the basin and held her hands under the running water, now cold, until she was awake. With her index finger she massaged her gums—*there is no pyorrhea among the Indians*—and then, with the tips of her fingers, she dampened her eyes.

She drew the blind, and in the half-light the room seemed to be full of lukewarm water, greenish in color. With a piece of Kleenex, she dried her eyes, then turned it to gently blow her nose, first the left side, then with a little more blow on the right. There was nothing to speak of, nothing, so she folded the tissue, slipped it into her pocket. Raising the blind, she faced the morning with her eyes softly closed, letting the light come in as prescribed— gradually. Eyes wide, she then stared for a full minute at the yard full of grackles, covered with grackles, before she actually saw them. Running to the door, her head in the hall, her arm in the bathroom wildly pointing, she tried to whisper, loud-whisper to him, but her voice cracked.

"Roger," she called, a little hoarsely. "The window—run!"

She heard him turn from the stove and skid on the newspapers, bump into the sink, curse, then get on again.

"Blackbirds?" he whispered.

"Grackles!" she said, for the thousandth time she said *Grackles*.

"They're pretty!" he said.

"Family—" she said, ignoring him, "family *Icteridae* American."

"Well—" he said.

"Roger!" she said. "Something's burning."

She heard him leave the window and on his way back to the

stove, on the same turn, skid on the papers again. She left him there and went down the hall to the bedroom, closed the door, and passed between the mirrors once more to the closet. From five dresses—*any woman with more than five dresses, at this time, should have the vote taken away from her*—she selected the navy blue sheer with pink lace yoke and kerchief, short bolero. At the back of the closet—but in order to see she had to return to the bathroom, look for the flashlight in the drawer full of rags and old tins of shoe polish—were three shelves, each supporting ten to twelve pairs of shoes, and a large selection of slippers were piled on the floor. On the second shelf were the navy blue pumps—*we all have one weakness, but between men and shoes you can give me shoes*—navy blue pumps with a Cuban heel and a small bow. She hung the dress from the neck of the floor lamp, placed the shoes on the bed. From beneath the bed she pulled a hat box—the hat was new. Navy straw with shasta daisies, pink geraniums, and a navy blue veil with pink and white fuzzy dots. She held it out where it could be seen in the mirror, front and side, without seeing herself—*it's not every day that one sponsors a boat.* Not every day, and she turned to the calendar on her night table, a bird calendar featuring the natural-color male goldfinch for the month of June. Under the date of June 23 she printed the words, FAMILY ICTER-IDAE—YARDFUL, and beneath it—

Met Captain Sudcliffe and gave him U.S.S. *Ormsby*

When he heard Mother's feet on the stairs Mr. Ormsby cracked her soft-boiled eggs and spooned them carefully into her heated cup. He had spilled his own on the floor when he had run to look at the black—or whatever color they were—birds. As they were very, very soft he had merely wiped them up. As he buttered the toast—the four burned slices were on the back porch airing—Mother entered the kitchen and said, "Roger—*more* toast?"

"I was watching blackbirds," he said.

"Grack-les," she said. "Any bird is a *black*bird if the males are largely or entirely black."

Talk about male and female birds really bothered Mr. Ormsby. Although she was a girl of the old school Mother never hesitated, *anywhere*, to speak right out about male and female birds. A cow was a cow, a bull was a bull, but to Mr. Ormsby a bird was a bird.

"Among the birdfolk," said Mother, "the menfolk, so to speak, wear the feathers. The female has more serious work to do."

"How does that fit the blackbirds?" said Mr. Ormsby.

"Every rule," said Mother, "has an exception."

There was no denying the fact that the older Mother got the more distinguished she appeared. As for himself, what he saw in the mirror looked very much like the Roger Ormsby that had married Violet Ames twenty years ago. As the top of his head got hard the bottom tended to get a little soft, but otherwise there wasn't much change. But it was hard to believe that Mother was the pretty little pop-eyed girl—he had thought it was her corset that popped them—whose nipples had been like buttons on her dress. Any other girl would have looked like a you-know—but there wasn't a man in Media County, or anywhere else, who ever mentioned it. A man could think what he would think, but he was the only man who really knew what Mother was like. And how little she was like *that*.

"Three-seven-four East One-One-Six," said Mother.

That was the way her mind worked, all over the place on one cup of coffee—birds one moment, Mrs. Dinardo the next.

He got up from the table and went after Mrs. Dinardo's letter—Mother seldom had time to read them unless he read them to her. Returning, he divided the rest of the coffee between them, un-equally: three-quarters for Mother, a swallow of grounds for him-self. He waited a moment, wiping his glasses, while Mother looked through the window at another blackbird. "Cowbird," she said, "*Molothrus ater*."

" 'Dear Mrs. Ormsby,' " Mr. Ormsby began. Then he stopped to scan the page, as Mrs. Dinardo had a strange style and was not much given to writing letters. " 'Dear Mrs. Ormsby,' " he repeated, " 'I received your letter and I Sure was glad to know that you are both well and I know you often think of me I often think of you too—' " He paused to get his breath—Mrs. Dinardo's style was not much for pauses—and to look at Mother. But Mother was still with the cowbird. " 'Well, Mrs. Ormsby,' " he continued, " 'I haven't a thing in a room that I know of the people that will be away from the room will be only a week next month. But come to See me I may have Something if you don't get Something.' " Mrs. Dinardo, for some reason, always capitalized the letter S which along with everything else didn't make it easier to read. " 'We are both well and he is Still in the Navy Yard. My I do wish the war was over it is So long. We are So tired of it do come and See us when you give them your boat. Wouldn't a Street be better than a boat? If you are going to name Something why not a Street? Here in my hand is news of a boat Sunk what is wrong with Ormsby on a Street? Well 116 is about the Same we have the river and its nice. If you don't find Something See me I may have Something. Best Love, Mrs. Myrtle Dinardo.' "

It was quite a letter to get from a woman that Mother had known, known Mother, that is, for nearly eighteen years. Brought in to nurse the boy—he could never understand why a woman like Mother, with her figure—but anyhow, Mrs. Dinardo was brought in. Something in her milk, Dr. Paige said, when it was as plain as the nose on your face it was nothing in the milk, but something in the boy. He just refused, plain refused, to nurse with Mother. The way the little rascal would look at her, but not a sound out of him but gurgling when Mrs. Dinardo would scoop him up and go upstairs to their room—the only woman—other woman, that is, that Mother ever let step inside of it. She had answered an ad that Mother had run, on Dr. Paige's suggestion, and they had been like *that* from the first time he saw them together.

"I'll telephone," said Mother.

On the slightest provocation Mother would call Mrs. Dinardo by long distance—she had to come down four flights of stairs to answer—and tell her she was going to broadcast over the radio or something. Although Mrs. Dinardo hardly knew one kind of bird from another, Mother sent her printed copies of every single one of her bird-lore lectures. She also sent her hand-pressed flowers from the garden.

"I'll telephone," repeated Mother.

"My own opinion—" began Mr. Ormsby, but stopped when

Mother picked up her egg cup, made a pile of her plates, and started toward the sink. "I'll take care of that," he said. "Now you run along and telephone." But Mother walked right by him and took her stand at the sink. With one hand—with the other she held her kimono close about her—she let the water run into a large dish pan. Mr. Ormsby had hoped to avoid this; now he would have to first rinse, then dry, every piece of silver and every dish they had used. As Mother could only use one hand it would be even slower than usual.

"We don't want to miss our local," he said. "You better run along and let me do it."

"Cold water," she said, "for the eggs." He had long ago learned not to argue with Mother about the fine points of washing pots, pans, or dishes with bits of egg. He stood at the sink with the towel while she went about trying to make suds with a piece of stale soap in a little wire cage. As Mother refused to use a fresh piece of soap, nothing remotely like suds ever appeared. For this purpose, he kept a box of Gold Dust Twins concealed beneath the sink, and when Mother turned her back he slipped some in.

"There now," Mother said, and placed the rest of the dishes in the water, rinsed her fingers under the tap, paused to sniff at them.

"My own opinion—" Mr. Ormsby began, but stopped when Mother raised her finger, the index finger with the scar from the wart she once had. They stood quiet, and Mr. Ormsby listened to the water drip in the sink—the night before he had come down in his bare feet to shut it off. All of the taps dripped now and there was just nothing to do about it but put a rag or something beneath it to break the ping.

"Thrush!" said Mother. "Next to the nightingale the most popular of European songbirds."

"Very pretty," he said, although he simply couldn't hear a thing. Mother walked to the window, folding the collar of her kimono over her bosom and drawing the tails into a hammock beneath her behind. Mr. Ormsby modestly turned away. He quick-dipped one hand into the Gold Dust—drawing it out as he slipped it into the dishpan and worked up a suds.

As he finished wiping the dishes she came in with a bouquet for Mrs. Dinardo and arranged it, for the moment, in a tall glass.

"According to her letter," Mrs. Ormsby said, "she isn't too sure of having something— Roger!" she said. "You're dripping."

Mr. Ormsby put his hands over the sink and said, "If we're going to be met right at the station I don't see where you're going to see Mrs. Dinardo. You're going to be met at the station and then you're going to sponsor the boat. My own opinion is that after the boat we come on home."

"I know that street of hers," said Mother. "There isn't a wild-flower on it!"

On the wall above the icebox was a pad of paper and a blue pencil hanging by a string. As Mother started to write the point broke off, fell behind the icebox.

"Mother," he said, "you ever see my knife?"

"Milkman," said Mother. "If we're staying overnight we won't need milk in the morning."

In jovial tones Mr. Ormsby said, "I'll bet we're right back here before dark." That was all, that was *all* that he said. He had merely meant to call her attention to the fact that Mrs. Dinardo said—all but said—that she didn't have a room for them. But when Mother turned he saw that her mustache was showing, a sure sign that she was mad.

"Well—now," Mother said and lifting the skirt of her kimono swished around the cabinet, and then he heard her on the stairs. From the landing at the top of the stairs she said, "In that case I'm sure there's no need for *my* going. I'm sure the Navy would just as soon have you. After all," she said, "it's *your* name on the boat!"

"Now, Mother," he said, just as she closed the door, *not* slammed it, just closed it as quiet and nice as you'd please. Although he had been through this a thousand times it seemed he was never ready for it, never knew when it would happen, never felt anything but nearly sick. He went into the front room and sat down on the chair near the piano—then got up to arrange the doily at the back of his head. Ordinarily he could leave the house and after three or four days it would blow over, but in all his life—their life—

there had been nothing like this. The government of the United States—he got up again and called, "OHHhhhh, Mother!"

No answer.

He could hear her moving around upstairs, but as she often went back to bed after a spat, just moving around didn't mean much of anything. He came back into the front room and sat down on the milk stool near the fireplace. It was the only seat in the room not protected with newspapers. The only thing the boy ever sat on when he had to sit on something. Somehow, thinking about that made him stand up. He could sit in the lawn swing, in the front yard, if Mother hadn't told everybody in town why it was that he, Roger Ormsby, would have to take the day off—not to sit in the lawn swing, not by a long shot. Everybody knew—Captain Sudcliffe's nice letter had appeared on the first page of the *Graphic*, under a picture of Mother leading a bird-lore hike in the Poconos. This picture bore the title LOCAL WOMAN HEADS DAWN BUSTERS, and marked Mother's appearance on the national bird-lore scene. But it was not one of her best pictures—it dated from way back in the twenties and those hipless dresses and round, bucket hats were not Mother's type. Until they saw that picture, and the letter beneath it, some people had forgotten that Virgil was missing, and most of them seemed to think it was a good idea to swap him for a boat. The U.S.S. *Ormsby* was a permanent sort of thing. Although he was born and raised in the town hardly anybody knew very much about Virgil, but they all were pretty familiar with his boat. "How's that boat of yours coming along?" they would say, but in more than twenty years nobody had ever asked him about *his* boy. Whose boy? Well, that was just the point. Everyone agreed Ormsby was a fine name for a boat.

It would be impossible to explain to Mother, maybe to anybody for that matter, what this U.S.S. *Ormsby* business meant to him. "The" boy and "the" *Ormsby*—it was a pretty strange thing that they both had the definite article, and gave him the feeling he was facing a monument.

"Oh Rog-gerrr!" Mother called.

"Coming," he said, and made for the stairs.

From the bedroom Mother said, "However I might feel personally, I do have my *own* name to think of. I am not one of these people who can do as they please— Roger, are you listening?"

"Yes, Mother," he said.

"—with their life."

As he went around the corner he found a note pinned to the door.

> Bathroom window up
> Cellar door down
> Is it blue or brown for Navy?

He stopped on the landing and looked up the stairs.

"Did you say something?" she said.

"No, Mother—" he said, then he added, "it's blue. For the Navy, Mother, it's blue."

1948

The Sound Tape

I've lived across from the Porters most of my life. During the twenties, when it was fashionable to open developments that closed in the thirties, they built a chalet-type mansion across the road from my place. It was said to resemble something Mrs. Porter saw in France. We were not neighbors, however, as the Porter chalet was the first house in the new development, and mine was the last in what is charitably called the old. The road between us, I suppose, is a kind of Mason-Dixon line.

Although we lived in separate worlds, every morning Mr. Porter and I joined forces and rode into town on the same commuters' local, and in the late afternoon we rode home again. On occasion I found him walking home from the station and gave him a lift. I observed that he chain-smoked my brand of cigarettes, traded in his Ford coupé every second year, and checked the arrival and departure of the trains by glancing at his watch. Along with everybody else I made the observation that he led an orderly, careful life and that Mrs. Porter led a careless, somewhat disorderly one. Not that it mattered, except for the little problem of keys. When Mrs. Porter left her purse in the seat of some car or on some department-store counter, she also left, with certain unimportant matters, the keys to her house. As she did this five or six times a year, some thirty sets of keys were in distribution before Mr. Porter had the locks changed on all the doors. The distribution of the new keys, of course, promptly began. At this point Mr. Porter washed his hands of the matter—he rubbed his palms briskly together as he told me—it was *her* house, and she could do with it as she liked. Mrs. Porter solved the problem, as usual, by letting nature take its course, losing the last set of keys and entering the house through the garage. I could tell when she came home by the thump of the heavy overhead doors.

When they first moved in, I used to speculate about Mr. Porter's line. He seemed to have money, but I told myself that he worked for it. He kept the same monotonous schedule that I kept myself. He took the 8:04 in the morning, the 4:48 in the afternoon, with only Saturdays and national holidays off. It was nearly ten years before I discovered that Mr. Porter had no line—or rather that his only line was how to pass the time. But he went about it, as he did everything else, in a competent, businesslike way. He put in his eight-hour day at the club, where he applied himself to his growing tax problems and a wide range of anti-Roosevelt literature. He was the most informed man on obscure subjects I have ever known. A certain pride of class, I suppose, as one of the surviving unearned-increment boys, forbade him to apply himself to anything useful. But nothing prevented him from putting his mind to work. It was a good mind, and he worked it around the clock.

He preferred to sit alone, while commuting, but there were times when he found himself compelled to stand in the aisle or take the seat beside me. As he had paid for this seat, he always took it. Without troubling to open the discussion or indicating that he know who it was that sat beside him, he would share some of the strange lore he had stored away: the air distances between the capitals of the world, the reason for the smallness of French equestrian armor, or the meaning of the serial numbers to be found on the sides of freight cars. He spoke on all these matters with an air of authority, knowing that his listener would be poorly informed, which led most people to think that he was merely a kind of cybernetic marvel full of facts and figures, waiting to be tapped. I found it hard to explain the touch of covert sympathy I felt for him.

My knowledge of Mrs. Porter is of a different sort. What I

choose to call my knowledge began on a fine summer dawn, just twenty years ago, when I saw her out padding around in her garden in what she called a shift. An abundant woman, built along the lines of the concrete goddesses that brooded in her garden, she sometimes fancied herself a suburban Diana with a pack of sleek hounds. Draped in her shift and armed with a pair of garden shears in case some urban interloper might stop to marvel, she loved to pad around her acres with the spreadlegged gait of a big circus cat. That summer morning, as I remember, she went along making tracks in the dewy grass, stopping now and then to lift the shift and gaze at her well-turned calves. Like many big women, she was vain of her shapely ankles and small feet.

Later in the morning, a wrapper over the shift, and holding aloft a few wilted flowers, she would cross the road to my seedy lawn and call on me. Would I like a few flowers? She knew that I didn't grow my own. So we would start with the flowers, which she would drop, sometimes head down, in the highball glasses, and then we would get around to the latest pet in her house. It had usually run off, flown off, or simply rolled over and died. She had tried, over the years, nearly everything: exotic imported birds, which I could hear in the summer when the windows were open, and pedigreed dogs which I could hear whether the windows were open or not. Sooner or later the birds stopped singing, the dogs stopped whining and barking, and the cats I had seen at the windows disappeared. Our discussion usually centered on what sort of creature she should try next.

This problem puzzled me, as Mrs. Porter had a friendly, sympathetic nature, and while the pets were alive she often carried them around in her arms. "Baby," she would say—I was not that type, but she liked to believe she had that type around her—"Baby, isn't he a lover?" and scoop her dachshund, Himmel, into her arms. But there was always more than the usual melancholy in Himmel's eyes. He had learned, much quicker than I did, that when Mrs. Porter put him back on the ground, she had also put him, for the time being, out of her mind. She might forget for a day or two that she owned a dog. There were times when she forgot what the name or breed of her latest dog was.

"Did that boxer, the lover, leave me, baby?" she would ask, and it was sometimes quite a while before she found out. Missing cats were often found trapped in her enormous closets, and some of the smaller dogs were hard to hear at the back of the house. But not to smell. In the summer Mr. Porter soon found them out. I would hear him going through the house from wing to wing, opening and closing doors.

It was by slow stages, I suppose, that Mrs. Porter moved from pets to goldfish, from fish to flowers, and from flowers to the house. The house was always there. When a door was left open it did not run off. Something of the concern she felt for her pets, when they began to act distracted, now crept into her voice when she spoke of the house. As she had once said, "Baby, isn't he a lover?" and held up something for me to pet, she now called my attention to her house. From my porch we had a fine view of it. While I was getting her a drink she would move her chair around so that she faced the house. I'm not sure just when I came to know that the place across the road was something more than a house, or when she first noticed the change in its personality. She was the one to point out to me that its character had changed. She spoke of it as of a friend who had lost some endearing faculty.

"Baby," she would say, "what am I going to do about my house?" As a man would say, "what am I going to do about my wife?" I never knew. From where I sat it looked about the same. Every spring the same handyman painted the fence, whitewashed the concrete urns that flanked the doorway and repaired the holes that Mr. Porter's chains made each winter in the drive. Nor had she changed. She still left on my porch whatever she had brought along with the wilting flowers: sometimes her shoes, as she liked to cross the lawn without them; sometimes her squashed pack of menthol cigarettes. "I can't stand menthol, baby," she would say, "so I don't smoke much."

But she smoked more and more that summer, and if she left a squashed pack on my porch, she went off with my fresh pack tucked into the pocket of her gown. In August she spent a month at the shore, but when she returned it was not to my porch, and she no longer crossed the road to ask me what I thought of her house. There were also other changes; and when it was clear that Mrs. Amory Porter would soon be a mother, it was assumed that Mr. Porter had little to do with it. He had fathered the child, so to speak, by a legal transmission of the pollen, but in every matter that counted, the flower would be hers. Mr. Porter more or less said so himself. He was the first to joke about the matter; and when talk got around to the child, he would make that characteristic washing gesture with his hands, rubbing the dry palms together as if he stood before a fire. I didn't see Mrs. Porter that winter, but every day I drove past the house I felt that I observed a change in it. As a last resort, it amused me to think, Mrs. Porter had got around to changing her house by altering—insofar as possible—the inhabitants.

Eloise—as the child was named—was born in March. On the balcony, when the weather was pleasant, I sometimes saw the nurse with the hooded carriage, and I read in the paper that Mrs. Porter had returned to life—her name appeared on the usual committees and her voice was heard at the usual parties.

Mr. Porter no longer came home on the 4:48. He went in as usual, but he came home at one o'clock. Early in May I came home early myself, as there were things to do around the house, and when I reached the Porter house I saw him wheeling something up the drive—a baby carriage, the perambulator I had seen on the balcony. When I stopped—I think I stopped to ask him what was the trouble—he wheeled it up so I could peer into it from the car. Eloise, at that time, was about ten weeks old. But the connection between the child in the carriage and the man who was pushing it was more than a resemblance—I felt I was looking at Porter himself. As if time, right there before my eyes, had unraveled the old man who stood before me, layer by layer, until nothing remained but the Porter seed itself in swaddling clothes; the Porter essence there in the perambulator. Porter knew this—he had wheeled the carriage up, so to speak, in order to prove it; and all the proof he needed he found on my face. Without waiting for me to speak or to recover, he wheeled her off.

For a year or more I saw very little of him. He had taken over, as he told those who asked him, the education of his child. But the following summer when I dropped into the big market where I did my shopping, Mr. Porter and Eloise were often there. In the spacious air-cooled market, full of soothing music and educational commercials, Mr. Porter, as well as Eloise, felt right at home. In the second year, as if to meet his needs, the new shopping cart made its appearance, and he would hustle down the aisles with Eloise propped up between the handlebars. Before she could talk, and long before there was reason to believe that she understood, he described to her the contents of the cans he purchased. He pointed out the label and other important details. It was a great comfort to him to find that this child of his old age—he was then in his late fifties—had a mind that was very much like his own. Curious, precise and absolutely disinterested.

When she was five or six—and when Mr. Porter was not at home—Eloise, like one of Singer's Midgets, would sometimes cross the road and enlighten me. All of my opinions, as she knew them through her father, were woefully misinformed. The correct opinion was the one she brought along. Her great field, as was his, was politics. From Eloise I learned, in the course of several summers, more about the workings of the Administration than I would ever have mastered by myself. I have no mind for figures; Eloise had no mind for anything else. Very early we discovered—or rather Eloise discovered—the fatal flaw, the Achilles' heel, in nearly every statement I put forth. Invariably I fell back upon the word *feel.*

"Now don't you feel, Eloise," I would say, whereupon she would shriek and jump up and down. Like her father, she would rub her little hands together.

"You just *feel*," she would reply, "Daddy *thinks.*"

That, of course, was early, in the beginning, for later there was no particular need to tell me what Daddy did—or anybody else. At seven and one-half Eloise could do it for herself.

"You're always just feeling, Mr. Brady," she would say. "I *think.*"

She was right. I was always feeling, but she could think. She would come to my porch—that side of the porch where the grass and the robins had taken over—with her little head, like a worming robin's, cocked to one side, ready to pounce on the first wormy feeling I let slip out.

A thin, sober-faced little girl, with the oversized clothes her father bought for her, she seemed to be a woman without ever having been a child. As she stood there reciting, I seemed to hear many small fine wheels going around.

She went to school, but she was not popular. Neither boys nor other little girls seemed to interest her. She would do her lessons many months in advance and, using the books of the girls ahead of her, master the subjects she would be having the next year. She had the time. There was nothing else that she cared to do. On weekends she might walk across to tell me where macaroni was made or to name the city with the largest smelting works. She knew. And she never seemed to forget. If I happened to meet Porter at the A&P or coming home on the local, I could tell by the nature of his lecture what subject Eloise was now on at school. They read the same books, went over the questions carefully. Mr. Porter would pick her up at school, and I would often find them, an hour or so later, sitting in the front seat of the car that was parked in front of his house. Winter afternoons, when the days were short, the overhead light in the car would be on, and I would see Mr. Porter's head bent over some book, or the head of Eloise, nodding briskly, as she talked to him. At their backs was the empty house, a pale light burning behind the blind in Mrs. Porter's room.

In this manner he instructed her in fractions, learned something about algebra himself, and brushed up on the French he had not used for many years. In the A&P, around the frozen food locker, I would sometimes hear an excited exchange, as if a pair of expensive imported servants were debating in French the merits of stringless or French-style cut beans. Their arguments were full of a kind of heat lightning, intended to sharpen the faculties and illuminate the subject, and he would sometimes turn his back on her to conceal the pleasure on his face.

That was the fall that Harry Truman was a doomed, nearly pitiful man. Mr. Porter had never been in better spirits, and sometimes two or three times a week Eloise would come over, ring my doorbell and recite a bon mot. But just before the election I saw little of her. Then on Halloween, early in the evening, somebody rang my bell. When I opened the door, there stood Eloise. She carried a pumpkin lantern, made of orange and black paper, and on her small sober head sat a pointed witch's cap. The black sateen lining of one of Mr. Porter's coats covered her like a sheet. The effect was that of a dummy that had been dolled up. I failed to notice for a moment that her hand, the palm up, was extended toward me.

"That's a wonderful costume, Eloise," I said, carefully screening my language.

"You're supposed to give me something," she said.

"Oh," I said. "What would you like? How about a piece of cake?"

"I'd rather have money," she said, "if you don't mind."

That set me back a bit but I said, "Is it customary to ask for money?"

"Father says if *he's* elected, we'll all be begging," she said.

"Well, there isn't much chance of that," I said. "Is there?"

We stood there while she thought. I could see that she thought there was not much chance but that she had been impressed by what she had heard.

"Father says if *he's* elected, he's just going to give up."

"If he's elected, Eloise," I said, sounding quite a bit like her father, "it means that most of the people in the country voted for him. It means he may not be *your* man, but he's *our* president." When she didn't reply to that I said, "Well, how do *you* feel about it?" It was out before I knew it.

"What reason is there to go on in a world like that?" she said.

Was that her father? I wasn't sure it was. I put my hand into my pocket, took out some change, then said, "Well, here's twenty-five cents if you spend it right away," which was pretty sharp, but she settled for it. I held out the quarter and placed it in the hand with the long fingers and the small palm that snapped shut like a trap when the coin touched it. She turned without another word and walked off. Her small feet made a tapping sound on my brick walk. When she had first faced me I had thought how little like a Halloween witch she was, but as she walked off, her witch's head bowed, I wasn't so sure. It crossed my mind—just faintly, that is—that my grown-up idea of witches was silly, but her idea of a witch was one that meant business. Not foolishness.

I forgot about Eloise until four days later when I sat in my room listening to the returns. A little after midnight I stepped out in the yard to smoke a cigarette. It was a sharp but very pleasant night. The Porter house was dark, without a light burning, but out in front was the Porter car with the parking lights on. The front window was down and I could hear the radio. The voice was announcing what appeared to be a surprising trend.

That left a certain impression on me but I didn't think too much about it until the next morning, about eight o'clock. The phone rang just as I was getting ready to leave the house. It was Mrs. Porter. I could hear the bathwater spilling into the tub behind her and the blurred nasal noise from her radio.

"This you, baby?"

"This is me," I said.

"Is my little sound tape over there, honey?"

"Your sound tape—" I said, and turned to look around the room. I knew that they were making and selling such things.

"You're cute as cotton, baby," she said. "You know what I mean, *his* little sound tape. She isn't here. Is she over there?"

"Oh," I said. "Oh no. No, she isn't over here."

"Is *he* over there?"

"No, he isn't either," I said.

As there was no reply to that, I said, "I suppose you know they've elected Truman."

"*They* did?" she said.

"I mean the people did," I said.

"You think they went to an all-night movie?"

"I've no idea, Mrs. Porter," I said. "And right now I've got to run for the train."

She didn't answer.

"Well, I've got to run—" I said, and did. With the single exception of Mr. Porter, I'm usually the first car out in the morning, and I sometimes pass him on the highway where he waits for the school bus. When the weather is cold, he and Eloise sit there in the car. He was there ahead of me as usual, and through the glass at the back of the car I could see their heads leaning together bent over some book. Some lesson or problem that she had to puzzle out. When I pulled alongside, I gave a tap on the horn as I usually do when I pass them, but this time he didn't toot back. In the rear-view mirror I glanced back at them. Eloise, her head lolling to the side, was asleep on his arm. Mr. Porter's chin was resting on his chest. At that point it occurred to me that they had been up all night. They had probably sat right there in the car taking in the returns. Eloise was wearing her new school cap with the bright school colors, and the yellow tassel dangled where the sun-light streamed through the glass. I was relieved that my toot on the horn hadn't waked them. That was something I could leave to the school bus.

In the evening on my walk through the station I took particular trouble to steer clear of Mr. Porter's usual route. The election might be too much for him. I bought a paper for the late returns, went down and took my seat in the smoker, then opened the paper and stared at Porter's face—a photograph taken, I would say, thirty years ago. What struck me was how much he looked like Eloise. Mr. Porter had been found, the report said, with his only child, Eloise, in their car parked in the neighborhood in which they lived. They had died apparently sometime during the night. A faulty heater had flooded the car with poisonous gas.

Very little was said openly, but under the talk that got around to me was the feeling that Porter had acted deliberately; had per-suaded his impressionable child to go along with him. This came from people who had known him very well, who now referred to him as "poor Amory" and sometimes crossed my lawn to ask if I had any insight into the case. I said I hadn't really known Mr. Porter at all. We usually agreed that he had been a hard man to figure out.

Now that he is gone, I find he is often in my mind. I seldom board the local or back out my car without thinking for a moment of Mr. Porter, though I doubt that we ever exchanged a personal remark. Mrs. Porter, they tell me, now spends her time in France. The house across the road is empty, but not long ago a prospective tenant who had got wind of its history stepped over to ask me what it was all about. He had heard, he said, about the Porter case. He couldn't believe that a man would treat his only child like that. It made me think of that night when I had opened the door of my house, and Eloise Porter in her witch's costume had confronted me.

"It's not a matter of feeling, Mr. Brady," she said, "it's what you think."

As usual, Eloise was right. So far as I know she was never wrong.

1951

The Character of the Lover

For no other purpose, it would seem, than to accommodate Dr. Emil Hodler, the drugstore in his neighborhood put in a large table of bargain books. Publishers' remainders, as they were called. There was no clerk assigned to this table, but the young man who worked behind the notions counter would come forward and take Dr. Hodler's twenty-nine cents. It was usually for one of Dr. Hodler's books. On the jacket of the book there would be a picture of Dr. Hodler, looking like Franz Werfel, but the shock of recognition never crossed the young man's face.

"You like it wrapped?" he would say, and there was never anything in his manner to indicate that he was speaking to the author himself. He was either not very bright, or he didn't care.

This young man was called Robert by the other clerks. Dr. Hodler was familiar with the type, and there had been a time, not too long ago, when he thought all of these idle, handsome young men were snobbish customers, free to roam through the better-class men's stores more or less as they pleased. He still found it hard to believe that these casual creatures were clerks. If Robert differed from these strange young men it was largely due to the notions department, the counter piled high with electric fans, irons, and heating pads. The quality of his deliberation was also harder to define. Dr. Hodler simply felt addle-pated and foolish when he talked with him.

In something more than the clinical sense, Robert began to interest Dr. Hodler when he found that the young man took a certain interest in the world of books. In particular, those that Dr. Hodler picked out. He often asked just what such and such a book was about. With this in mind, Dr. Hodler was careful to buy only those books that would tend to develop a young man's taste. His own, for example, when they turned up, otherwise the more familiar classics.

It soon reached a point, however, when Dr. Hodler was sorely pressed to find on the bargain table something that he could recommend. In this extremity he settled for a doubtful book of his own. Doubtful, considering Robert's inexperience. The hero in *Blast*—a man somewhat taller, but otherwise not unlike Dr. Hodler—was hamstrung and helpless because of his basic sense of decency. Respect for his fellow man hampered him at every point. Like Hamlet, he was crippled by hours of fruitless analysis. Seeking to understand, to fathom, he had lost the will to act. As this would be quite a dose for Robert, Dr. Hodler let several days pass, nearly a week, before going back for a report.

"Well, how did you get along?" he inquired, which was the way Robert himself would have put it. Robert deliberated even less than usual.

"The character of the lover is not my type," Robert said.

This was not much, certainly, in the way of classic criticism, but it summed up the difference between the characters accurately.

"Ah-so—" Dr. Hodler said, somewhat at a loss for words, and looked at Robert with an eye as to what type of lover he might be. He found it hard to say. By and large he would be the silent type.

"No, he's not my type—" Robert said, and then disappeared behind the notions counter, where he wrapped a heating pad for a lady customer.

On the bargain table, that afternoon, were several reprint copies of a book that Dr. Hodler had been careful not to recommend. A book of romantic nonsense that belonged to another, now dead world. A book that the author ironically called *This Side of Paradise*. But in the light of Robert's opinion, Dr. Hodler felt just perverse enough to pick this book from the table and offer it to him.

"Is it more my type?" said Robert.

"You let me know," Dr. Hodler said, and went off. That was not at all like him, not a bit. But he was a man who expected too much from books. He expected them to mean as much to others, for instance, as they had meant to him. The feeling that Robert was rather hopeless led him to stay away for more than a week, and he even thought of buying his remainders somewhere else. But a habit is a habit, so he wandered back. Even as he entered the store he could see that something had happened to Robert, as he waved—he beckoned to him, that is.

"There you are," said Robert, "where have you been?"

"I've been pretty busy—" Dr. Hodler began, implying that some people he knew were not, but Robert was not listening to him.

"I've read them—" he said.

"You've read what?" said Dr. Hodler.

"I'm in love with her too," said Robert. "I know exactly how he feels."

"Who is this—?" said Dr. Hodler.

"Daisy," Robert said. As Dr. Hodler looked blank, Robert added, "You know, Gatsby's Daisy."

Now Dr. Hodler had once, long ago, looked into the Gatsby book. He had read it in France, in a pirated edition featuring a profile snapshot of the author, and appropriately titled, *Gatsby, Le Magnifique.* It hadn't impressed him much.

"You liked it?" Dr. Hodler asked.

"He's my type," Robert said.

"He's a little old-fashioned—" Dr. Hodler began.

"You knew him?" said Robert.

"I saw him once," said Dr. Hodler, as indeed he had, and he cleared his throat to describe that strange affair. He started—then he stopped, as it suddenly crossed his mind that Robert meant the character, not the author, of the book.

"What was he like?" Robert said, and rose to his full height, waiting for Dr. Hodler to comment on the resemblance. When he didn't, Robert said, "Will you have lunch with me?"

It startled both of them.

"I'd be glad to," Dr. Hodler said, "but as I was saying, right now I'm pretty busy."

"I'm right around the corner," Robert said, "we'll have it in my apartment," and he took from his pocket a small pigskin card case, removed one card, passed it to Dr. Hodler. *Robert Gollen,* it said, and gave his address on Park Avenue. "So we can talk," said Robert. "We can't talk here." Then he took the card from Dr. Hodler's hand and wrote a few words on the back of it, *Tuesday, the 17th, at 12:00,* returned the card to him, and disappeared behind the notions counter. What Robert had to say would have to wait for the proper time.

That Tuesday was a warm day for the season, and Dr. Hodler carried his coat as he walked in the sun on Park Avenue. The address on the card, a brownstone mansion with a reconverted schizoid air, had boards over the stairs while a few stone steps were being repaired. As he started up the stairs, he heard somebody call his name. Directly overhead, about three floors up, Robert had his head through a narrow window.

"Would you please use the door at the side?" he said, and waved his arm to indicate which one. Dr. Hodler went back to the street and around to a small door clearly labeled SERVICE EN-TRANCE, propped open with a soiled copy of *Blast.* As he stepped inside he could hear the voice of Robert. "I'm here on three," he called.

Up on the third floor, Dr. Hodler entered a hallway, and at the far end of it, beckoning, looking small in the doorway, was Robert. On the tile floor in the hallway Dr. Hodler's shoes made quite a stir. Robert stepped to one side to let him in, then closed the door at his back, and Dr. Hodler turned to face, on a low platform, an enormous rose-colored bathtub. He had seen such a tub—he had been in it—in a Victorian tourist mansion in Mexico City, and along with the tub there had been an arboretum and a pair of chained birds. At the far end of the room, like a faint blue lantern, a narrow ventilating window opened on an airwell, letting in the hushed roar of the traffic on Park Avenue. As Dr. Hodler had friends who sometimes specialized in bizarre entrances to their apartments, he thought this was merely one more of them. Or that the young man thought he might like to use the facilities. He waited, as the room was dim and he couldn't make out the other doorway, when Robert said, "You like to look over my books?"

Dr. Hodler was so sure that was meant to be funny that he turned with a smile on his face, ready to grin at another American joke. But there before him, at the foot of the tub, was a shelf of books. Dr. Hodler stood there, facing these books, while Robert went off to prepare the lunch—that is to say, he walked to the other end of the room. Dr. Hodler could hear the sound of the silver, the pat-pat of the paper plates, and the pop of the cork as a bottle was opened.

"I hope you like shrimp salad," Robert said, and Dr. Hodler turned to say that he simply loved shrimp, and see that a card table had been placed over one end of the tub. There was room for two folding chairs with stainless-steel frames and soft leather backs and seats. Dr. Hodler had seen them in a window at Abercrombie & Fitch. Over the table Robert had spread a cloth with monogrammed napkins to mark their places, and at each place was a Danish silver knife and fork. Paper spoons stood up in a Steuben glass. "Well, I guess we're all ready," Robert said, and as Dr. Hodler drew up his chair, Robert smiled and made, so to speak, just a passing remark—"I do without," he said, "until I can buy the best."

The shrimps—as Dr. Hodler remembered later—were very good. They were served with a sauce of Robert's own concoction and a bottle of Semmelweiss sauterne, an inexpensive native wine that he found, as he said, fairly tolerable. The rest of the luncheon came out of cartons as Robert simply didn't have the time, with an hour off for lunch, to prepare everything. They had strong black coffee from a Thermos, and at the bottom of his cup, when he tipped it up, Dr. Hodler observed the label of Black, Starr & Frost.

While they ate, Robert talked. Dr. Hodler missed some of the details as his interest was divided, but Robert had a way of making his points.

"You know, my name is not Gollen," he said, in a manner that got Dr. Hodler's attention; then he added, "Like Gatsby, I just picked it up. Does it matter?" he continued, when he saw the look on Dr. Hodler's face.

"Not intrinsically—" began Dr. Hodler, "but—"

"I just didn't like it," Robert said, "and now I wonder what I saw in Gollen?" He deliberated for a moment, then said, "The name I like is Nick—but that's your name."

"My name?" said Dr. Hodler.

"You know—" said Robert, "Gatsby and Nick," and Dr. Hodler, a little vaguely, remembered. It had been Nick who told Gatsby's story, so to speak. Dr. Hodler smiled, then stopped as Robert leaned forward and said, "Would you like to hear something of my story now, Nick?"

With the napkin Dr. Hodler wiped his face, then nodded his head.

Well, it was quite a little story, Robert said, as first of all his mother was an actress, and they had been on the go all of the time, on the continent. Living in Paris, Biarritz, Algiers, Monte Carlo, and places like that. He had shuffled in and out of expensive private schools. It had left its mark. His grounding in the classics was very poor. Then his mother married a Spanish count from an old family with nothing but honor, and in no time at all their small inheritance was wiped out. To make a long story short, the count, after several years of mourning his mother, died, and Robert had drifted aimlessly about on different tramp steamers, picking up experience, but little else. Nothing that would help him very much in his professional life. However, he had plans—nationwide plans to distribute ten-cent books through drugstores—but he needed someone he could trust with the literary end of it. Someone like Nick, who could fill in where his own background fell short.

He stopped there—it was where he had planned to stop. He excused himself, rose from the table, and left Dr. Hodler to puzzle out for himself if what he had heard was Gatsby, was Gollen, or was merely applesauce. A good deal of it had a familiar ring. At the far end of the room Dr. Hodler could see a large steamer trunk, well pasted with labels, and Robert appeared to be inside of it.

He was looking for a key to a small drawer in the compartment section. Dr. Hodler remained at the table, sipping his black coffee and gazing at the half-dozen pairs of shoes, in shoe trees, under the tub. In the tub, extending its length, was a narrow foam-rubber mattress with the bedclothes folded neatly over the drain.

Coming back to the table, Robert extended to Dr. Hodler a tooled morocco folder, which he opened on a large glossy photograph. It showed Robert, wearing a tourist cap with the flaps tied with a bow at the crown, standing in the midst of quantities of small luggage, several steamer trunks. Every piece of the luggage was stamped with the exotic labels of the world. Directly behind was a painted screen, meant to represent a departing steamer, from the deck of which many kisses were thrown, and others waved small flags. The photograph was a joke, one of those things country boys mailed home after a weekend in the city, but the young man in the tourist cap, the plus fours, and the rubber-soled shoes for deck tennis, gazed serenely into the camera. It was not funny. And Dr. Hodler did not laugh.

"Back from the West Indies," Robert said, and took the folder from Dr. Hodler, walked back to the end of the room, and placed it in the trunk. Then he closed the trunk with a snap, and turned to ask Dr. Hodler if he would mind passing him the silver, the knives first. Dr. Hodler was glad to, and Robert rinsed the silver under the faucet in the basin, then rinsed the glasses, placing them on a paper towel to dry. The silver Robert returned to a non-tarnish flannel case. Looking at his watch he announced that it was now one o'clock, and faced the mirror on the bathroom door to comb his hair. Then they went back down the stairs that Dr. Hodler had come up, and at the foot of the stairs, soberly, Robert shook his hand. It was clear to Dr. Hodler that he had made some kind of pact. He stood there, in the service entrance, watching Robert go down the street shoulder to shoulder with the men who set the style, but with a little more shoulder, and a little more style, than the rest of them.

As he was very busy, he didn't get around again for several weeks. Robert was not in the store the next time he dropped in. He had his own day off, of course, and Dr. Hodler didn't think anything about it until the next time, when an elderly man was there.

"Is Mr. Gollen on vacation?" Dr. Hodler inquired.

"Who?" said the clerk. "Oh him. No, he got fired."

"Robert left?" Dr. Hodler said, as a pact, after all, had been made.

"Nope, he was fired," said the old man. "Guess he slapped one of the customers."

"He what?" said Dr. Hodler.

"I didn't see it," said the clerk, "but Mr. Prewitt, the boss, saw him slap him." Dr. Hodler waited, and the old man said, "Guess it was one of these anti-Jewish books, and this fellow Gollen just refused to sell it to him. Said if he wanted stuff like that he'd have to buy it somewhere else. Now, you can't treat the public like that," the old man said.

"You say he slapped him?" said Dr. Hodler, as the lover in Dr. Hodler's book, in the continental manner, slapped the Nazi thug who then shot him.

"I guess this customer got a little peeved and made some anti-Jewish remark himself, and then this Gollen asked him to please step outside. Right out there in the street, right there on the curb, he slapped him in the face."

Dr. Hodler closed his eyes. He tried to picture it.

"He was wearin' the company jacket," said the old man, "with the name right there on the jacket." He reflected, then said, "If he'd just hit him, it wouldn't have been so bad."

Dr. Hodler thanked him, and as he said so many times in his own books, went for a walk with his thoughts. He went up Park Avenue, but he found the service entrance was locked. No copy of *Blast* now held open the door. Dr. Hodler felt responsible, somehow, as if had it not been for himself, and his bookish habits, the boy would still have his job. He felt like going back to the drugstore and explaining to the manager that this strange act had been committed by somebody else. That the youth they had hired, Robert Gollen by name, had little to do with it. But he didn't. Perhaps he wasn't too sure of it himself. Instead, he sat down and wrote a letter, addressing himself to *My dear Gatsby*, and saying that the plan he had spoken of interested him very much. He suggested the date for another luncheon, and then signed the note, *Yours, Nick.*

Ten days later, unopened, the letter came back. Across the lefthand corner, in pencil, someone had scribbled: *"R. Gatsby Gollen gone to Navy."*

That was all. That was all the news of Gatsby that he ever had. But when the war broke out, a few months later, Dr. Hodler found himself giving special attention to all the casualty lists. One of these days, he knew, R. Gatsby Gollen would turn up.

1951

The Safe Place

In his fifty-third year a chemical blast burned the beard from the Colonel's face, and gave to his eyes their characteristic powdery blue. Sometime later his bushy eyebrows came in white. Silvery streaks of the same color appeared in his hair. To his habitually bored expression these touches gave a certain distinction, a man-of-the-world air, which his barber turned to the advantage of his face. The thinning hair was parted, the lock of silver was deftly curled. The Colonel had an absent-minded way of stroking it back. As he was self-conscious, rather than vain, there was something attractive about this gesture, and a great pity that women didn't seem to interest him. He had married one to reassure himself on that point.

When not away at war the Colonel lived with his wife in an apartment on the Heights, in Brooklyn. She lived at the front with her canary, Jenny Lind, and he lived at the back with his two cats. His wife did not care for cats, particularly, but she had learned to accept the situation, just as the cats had learned, when the Colonel was absent, to shift for themselves. The cleaning women, as a rule, were tipped liberally to be attentive to them. The Colonel supplied the cats with an artificial tree, which they could climb, claw, or puzzle over, and a weekly supply of fresh catnip mice. The mice were given to the cats every Thursday, and on Friday the cleaning woman, with a broom and the vacuum, would try to get the shredded catnip out of the rug. They would then settle back and wait patiently for Thursday again.

The blast improved the Colonel's looks, but it had not been so good for his eyes. They watered a good deal, the pupils were apt to dilate in a strange manner, and he became extremely sensitive to light. In the sun he didn't see any too well. To protect his eyes from the light he wore a large pair of military glasses, with dark lenses and something like blinders at the sides. He was wearing these glasses when he stepped from the curbing, in uptown Manhattan, and was hit by a pie truck headed south. He was put in the back, with the pies, and carted to a hospital.

He hovered between life and death for several weeks. Nor was there any explanation as to why he pulled through. He had nothing to live for, and his health was not good. In the metal locker at the foot of the bed was the uniform in which he had been delivered, broken up, as the doctor remarked, like a sack of crushed ice. The uniform, however, had come through rather well. There were a few stains, but no bad tears or rips. It had been carefully cleaned, and now hung in the locker waiting for him.

The Colonel, however, showed very little interest in getting up. He seemed to like it, as his wife remarked, well enough in bed. When he coughed, a blue vein would crawl from his hair and divide his forehead, and the salty tears brimming in his weak eyes would stream down his face. He had aged, he was not really alive, but he refused to die. After several weeks he was therefore removed from the ward of hopeless cases and put among those who were said to have a fifty-fifty chance. Visitors came to this room, and there were radios. From his bed there was a fine view of the city, including the East River, the Brooklyn Bridge, part of lower Manhattan, and the harbor from which the Colonel had never sailed. With his military glasses he could see the apartment where his wife and cats lived. On the roofs of the tenements that sprawled below there daily appeared, like a plague of Martian insects, the television aerials that brought to the poor the empty lives of the rich. The Colonel ordered a set, but was told that his failing eyes were too weak.

On the table at his side were a glass of water, boxes of vitamin

capsules and pills, an expensive silver lighter, and a blurred photograph of his cats. A bedpan and a carton of cigarettes were on
the shelf beneath. The Colonel had a taste for expensive cigarettes,
in tins of fifty, or small cedar boxes, but his pleasure seemed to
be in the lighter, which required no flint. The small gas cartridge
would light, it was said, many thousand cigarettes. As it made no
sound, the Colonel played with it at night. During the day he lit
many cigarettes and let them smoke in the room, like incense, but
during the night he experimented with the small wiry hairs on his
chest. Several twisted together, and ignited, would give off a
crackling sound. It pleased him to singe the blond hairs on his
fingers, hold them to his nose. When not playing with the lighter
the Colonel slept, or sat for hours with an air of brooding, or used
his army glasses to examine the teeming life in the streets. What
he saw, however, was no surprise to him. To an old Army man it
was just another bloody battlefield.

Having time on his hands, the Colonel was able to see through
the glasses what he had known, so to speak, all his life. Life, to
put it simply, was a battleground. Every living thing, great or
small, spilled its blood on it. Every day he read the uproar made
in the press about the horrors of war, the fear of the draft, and
what it would do to the lives of the fresh eighteen-year-olds. Every
moment he could see a life more horrible in the streets, dangers
more unjust, risks more uncalculated, and barracks that were more
intolerable. Children fell from windows, were struck by cars, were
waylaid and corrupted by evil old men, or through some private
evil crawled off to corrupt themselves. Loose boards rose up and
struck idle women, knives cut their fingers, fire burned their
clothes, or in some useless quarrel they suffered heart attacks. The
ambulance appeared after every holiday. The sirens moaned
through the streets, like specters, every night. Doors closed on
small fingers, windows fell, small dogs bit bigger dogs, or friends
and neighbors, and in the full light of day a man would tumble,
headfirst, down the steps to the street. If this man was a neighbor
they might pick him up, but if a stranger they would pass him by,
walking in an arc around him the way children swing wide of a
haunted house. Or they would stand in a circle, blocking the walk,

until the man who was paid to touch a dead man felt the wrist for the pulse, or held the pocket mirror to the face. As if the dead man, poor devil, wanted a final look at himself.

All of this struck the Colonel, an old soldier, as a new kind of battleground. "That's life for you," the doctor would say, when the Colonel would trouble to point out that the only safe place for a man, or a soldier, was in bed. Trapped there, so to speak, and unable to get up and put on his pants. For it was with his pants that a man put on the world. He became a part of it, he accepted the risks and the foolishness. The Colonel could see this very clearly in the casualties brought to the ward, the men who had fallen on this nameless battlefield. They lay staring at the same world that seemed to terrify the Colonel, but not one of these men was at all disturbed by it. Everything they saw seemed to appeal to them. Every woman reminded them of their wives, and every child of their own children, and the happy times, the wonderful life they seemed to think they had lived. When another victim appeared in the ward they would cry out to ask him, "How are things going?" although it was clear things were still going murderously. That it was worth a man's life to put on his pants and appear in the streets. But not one of these men, broken and battered as they were by the world they had left, had any other thought but a craving to get back to it. To be broken, battered, and bruised all over again. The Colonel found it hard to believe his eyes— both inside and outside the window—as the world of men seemed to be incomprehensible. It affected, as he knew it would, his feeble will to live. He did not die, but neither did he live, as if the world both inside and outside the window was a kind of purgatory, a foretaste of hell but with no possibility of heaven. Once a week his wife, a small attractive woman who referred to him as Mr. Army, brought him cookies made with blackstrap molasses, pure brewer's yeast, and wheat-germ flour. The recipe was her own, but they were made by the cleaning woman. As Mrs. Porter was several years older than the Colonel, and looked from eight to ten years younger, there was no need to argue the importance of blackstrap and brewer's yeast. The Colonel would ask how the cats were doing, read the mail she had brought him, and when she had left he would distribute the cookies in the ward. A young man named Hyman Kopfman was fond of them.

Hyman Kopfman was a small, rabbit-faced little man who belonged in the hopeless ward, but it had been overcrowded and he couldn't afford a room of his own. When he appeared in the ward he had one leg and two arms, but before the first month had ended they had balanced him up, as he put it himself. He stored the cookies away in the sleeve of the arm that he wore pinned up. Something in Hyman Kopfman's blood couldn't live with the rest of Hyman Kopfman, and he referred to this thing as America. Raising the stump of his leg he would say, "Now you're seeing America first!" Then he would laugh. He seemed to get a great kick out of it. Largely because of Hyman Kopfman, there were men in the ward, some of them pretty battered, who looked on the world outside as a happy place. Only the Colonel seemed to see the connection. He didn't know what Hyman Kopfman had in his blood, or where it would show up next, but he knew that he had picked it up, like they all did, there in the streets. What Hyman Kopfman knew was that the world was killing him.

Hyman Kopfman was in pain a good deal of the time and sat leaning forward, his small head in his hand, like a man who was contemplating a crystal globe. During the night he often rocked back and forth, creaking the springs. While the Colonel sat playing with his lighter, Hyman Kopfman would talk, as if to himself, but he seemed to be aware that the Colonel was listening. Hyman Kopfman's way of passing the time was not to look at the world through a pair of field glasses, but to turn his gaze, so to speak, upon himself. Then to describe in considerable detail what he saw. As the Colonel was a reserved, reticent man who considered his life and experience private, Hyman Kopfman was something of a novelty. He spoke of himself as if he were somebody else. There were even times when the Colonel thought he was. At the start Hyman Kopfman gave the impression that he would describe everything that had happened; which he did, perhaps, but all that had happened had not added up to much. He was apt to repeat certain things time and time again. There were nights when the Colonel had the impression that he went over the same material the way a wine press went over the pulp of grapes. But there was always something that refused to squeeze out. That, anyhow, was the Colonel's impression, since it was otherwise hard to explain why he went over the same material time and again, here and there adding a touch, or taking one away.

Hyman Kopfman had been born in Vienna—that was what he said. That should have been of some interest in itself, and as the Colonel had never been to Vienna, he always listened in the hope that he might learn something. But Hyman Kopfman merely talked about himself. He might as well have been born in the Bronx, or anywhere else. He had been a frail boy with girlish wrists and pale blue hands, as he said himself, but with something hard to explain that made him likable. His father had it, but only his mother knew what it was. Hopelessness. It was this, he said, that made him lovable.

The Colonel got awfully tired of this part of the story since Hyman Kopfman was hopeless enough. Too hopeless, in fact. There was nothing about him that was lovable. It was one of the curious conceits he had. His skin was a pale doughy color, and his general health was so poor that when he smiled his waxy gums began to bleed. Thin streaks of red, like veins in marble, showed on his chalky teeth. His eyes were very large, nearly goatlike, with curiously transparent lids, as if the skin had been stretched very thin to cover them. There were times when the eyes, with their large wet whites and peculiarly dilated pupils, gazed upon the Colonel with a somewhat luminous quality. It was disturbing, and had to do, very likely, with his poor health. It was because of his eyes, the Colonel decided, that Hyman Kopfman had picked up the notion that there was something appealing about his hopelessness. Some woman, perhaps his mother, had told him that.

At a very early age Hyman Kopfman had been brought to America. With him came his three brothers, his mother, Frau Tabori-Kopfman, and the roomful of furniture and clothes that his father had left to them. They went to live in Chicago, where his Uncle Tabori, his mother's brother, had rented an apartment. This apartment was four flights up from the street with a room at the back for Uncle Tabori, a room at the front, called a parlor,

and a room in which they lived. In the parlor there were large bay
windows but the curtains were kept closed as the light and the
circulating air would fade the furniture. It would belong to Paul,
if and when he married someone. In the room were chests full of
clothes that his mother had stopped wearing, and his father, a
gentleman, had never worn out. They were still as good as new.
So it was up to the children to wear them out. It so happened that
Mandel Kopfman, the father, had been comparatively small in
stature, and his fine clothes would fit Hyman Kopfman, but nobody else. So it was that Hyman Kopfman was accustomed to
wear, as he walked between the bedroom and the bathroom, pants
of very good cloth, and on his small feet the best grade of spats.
French braces held up his pants, and there was also a silver-headed
cane, with a sword in the shaft, that he sometimes carried as he
swaggered down the hall. He didn't trouble, of course, to go down
the four flights to the street. Different clothes were being worn
down there, small tough boys cursed and shouted, and once down,
Hyman Kopfman would have to walk back up. He simply couldn't.
He never had the strength.

His older brother, Otto, went down all the time as he worked
down there, in a grocery, and returned to tell them what it was
all about. He also went to movies, and told them about it. His
brother Paul had been too young to go down to the street and
work there, so he made the beds and helped his mother around
the house. He cooked, he learned to sew, and since he couldn't
wear the clothes of Mandel Kopfman, he wore some of the skirts
and blouses of his mother, as they fit him all right. It didn't matter,
as he never left the rooms. No one but Uncle Tabori ever sat down
and talked with them. He worked in the railroad yards that could
be seen, on certain clear days, from the roof of the building, where
Frau Kopfman went to dry her hair and hang out their clothes.
From this roof Hyman Kopfman could see a great park, such as
they had known in Vienna, and in the winter he could hear the
ore boats honking on the lake. In spring he could hear the ice
cracking up.

Was that Hyman Kopfman's story? If it was, it didn't add up
to much. Nor did it seem to gain in the lengthy retelling, night

after night. The facts were always the same: Hyman Kopfman had been born, without much reason, in Vienna, and in Chicago he had taken to wearing his father's fancy clothes. Not that it mattered, since he never went down to the street. He spent day and night in the apartment, where he walked from room to room. Concealed in the shaft of the cane was a sword, and when he stepped into the dim gaslit hallway, Hyman Kopfman would draw out the sword and fence with the dancing shadow of himself.

Ha! the Colonel would say, being an old swordsman, but Hyman Kopfman had shot his bolt. He could do no more than wag his feeble wrist in the air. His gums would bleed, his goatlike eyes would glow in a disturbing manner, but it was clear that even fencing with his shadow had been too much for him. Nothing had really happened. The Colonel doubted that anything ever would.

And then one day—one day just in passing—Hyman Kopfman raised his small head from his hand and said that the one thing he missed, really missed, that is, was the daily walk in the blind garden.

In the what? the Colonel said, as he thought he had missed the word.

In the blind garden, Hyman Kopfman replied. Had he somehow overlooked that? Hadn't he told the Colonel about the blind garden?

The Colonel, a cigarette in his mouth, wagged his head.

At the back of the building there had been a small walled garden, Hyman Kopfman went on, a garden with gravel paths, shady trees, and places to sit. Men and women who were blind came there to walk. There were also flowers to smell, but they couldn't see them of course.

Well, well—the Colonel had replied, as he thought he now had the key to the story. One of the Kopfmans was blind, and Hyman Kopfman was ashamed to mention it. What difference did it make what Hyman Kopfman wore if his brother Paul, for instance, couldn't see him, and if Paul was blind he would hardly care how he looked himself. What difference did it make if he wore his mother's skirts around the house?

Your brother Paul was blind then—? the Colonel said.

Blind? said Hyman Kopfman, and blinked his own big eyes. Who said Paul was blind?

You were just saying—the Colonel replied.

From the window—interrupted Hyman Kopfman—what he saw below was like a tiny private park. There were trees along the paths, benches in the shade where the blind could sit. The only thing you might notice was how quiet and peaceful it was. Nobody laughed. The loud voices of children were never heard. It was the absence of children that struck Hyman Kopfman, as he was then very young himself, and liked to think of a park like that as a place for children to play. But the one below the window was not for bouncing balls or rolling hoops. No one came to this park to fly a kite, or to skip rope at the edge of the gravel, or to play a game of hide-and-seek around the trees. In fact there was no need, in a park like that, to hide from anyone. You could be there, right out in the open, and remain unseen. It was Paul Kopfman who pointed out that they might as well go down and sit there, as nobody would know whether they were blind or not. Nobody would notice that Hyman Kopfman was wearing celluloid cuffs and pearl-gray spats, or that Paul Kopfman was wearing a skirt and a peasant blouse. Nobody would care, down there, if their clothes were out of date, or that when Hyman Kopfman talked his wax-colored gums were inclined to bleed. It was the talking that made him excited, and the excitement that made his gums bleed, but down there in the garden he was not excited, and nobody cared. There were always flowers, because nobody picked them. There were birds and butterflies, because nobody killed them. There were no small boys with rocks and sticks, nor big boys with guns. There was only peace, and his brother Paul sat on the wooden benches talking with the women, as he didn't seem to care how old, and strange, and ugly they were. In some respects, he might as well have been blind himself.

How long did this go on—? the Colonel said, as he knew it couldn't go on forever. Nothing out of this world, nothing pleasant like that, ever did.

Well, one day his brother Otto—Hyman Kopfman said—his

brother Otto put his head out the window and . . .

Never mind—! said the Colonel, and leaned forward as if to shut him up. He wagged his hand at the wrist, and the blue vein on his forehead crawled from his hair.

A man like you, Hyman Kopfman said, an old soldier, a Colonel, a man with gold medals—

Never mind! the Colonel had said, and took from the table his silver lighter, holding it like a weapon, his arm half-cocked, as if ready to throw.

Was Hyman Kopfman impressed? Well, he just sat there: he didn't go on. He smiled, but he didn't repeat what Otto had said. No, he just smiled with his bleeding gums, then raised the pale blue stump of his leg, sighted down the shinbone, pulled the trigger, and said *Bang!* He was like that. He didn't seem to know how hopeless he was.

For example, this Kopfman had only one foot but he sent out both of his shoes to be polished: he had only one arm, but he paid to have both sleeves carefully pressed. In the metal locker at the foot of his bed hung the pinstripe suit with the two pair of pants, one pair with left leg neatly folded and pinned to the hip. Some people might ask if a man like that needed two pair of pants. It was strange behavior for a person who was dying day by day. Not that he wanted very much, really—no, hardly more than most people had—all he really seemed to want was the useless sort of life that the Colonel had lived. To have slept with a woman, to have fought in a war, to have won or lost a large or small fortune, and to have memories, before he died, to look back to. Somehow, Hyman Kopfman had picked up the facts, so to speak, without having had the fun. He always used the word "fun" as he seemed to think that was what the Colonel had had.

Night after night the Colonel listened to this while he played with his lighter, or smoked too much, but he said very little as he felt that Hyman Kopfman was very young. Not in years, perhaps, but in terms of the experience he should have had. His idea of fun was not very complicated. His idea of life being what it was, the Colonel found it hard to understand why he hadn't reached out and put his hands on it. But he hadn't. Perhaps this thing had always been in his blood. Or perhaps life in America had not panned out as he had thought. At the first mention of Chicago, Hyman Kopfman would wave his stubby arm toward the window, roll his eyes, and make a dry rattle in his throat. That was what he felt, what he seemed to think, about America. But there was nothing that he wanted so much as to be out there living in it.

The case of Hyman Kopfman was indeed strange, but not so strange, in some respects, as the case of the old man in the bed on his right. The Colonel had been failing; now for no apparent reason he began to improve. Now that Hyman Kopfman was there beside him—a hopeless case if there ever was one—the Colonel's pulse grew stronger, he began to eat his food. He sat propped up in bed in the manner of a man who would soon be up. He even gazed through the window like a man who would soon be out. Here you had the Colonel, who had nothing to live for, but nevertheless was getting better, while Hyman Kopfman, who hungered for life, was getting worse. It didn't make sense, but that was how it was. Not wanting to live, apparently, was still not wanting to die. So the Colonel, day by day, seemed to get better in spite of himself.

The very week that Hyman Kopfman took a turn for the worse, the Colonel took that turn for the better that led the doctor to suggest that he ought to get up and walk around. Adjust himself, like a newborn babe, to his wobbly legs. So he was pushed out of the bed, and the terrycloth robe that hung for months, unused, in the locker was draped around his sloping shoulders and a pair of slippers were put on his feet. In this manner he walked the floor from bed to bed. That is to say he toddled, from rail to rail, and the effort made the sweat stand on his forehead and the blue vein crawl like a slug from his thinning hair. But everybody in the ward stared at him enviously. He could feel in their gaze the hope that he would trip, or have a relapse. But at least they were courteous on the surface, they remarked how much stronger he was looking, and made flattering comments on how well he carried himself. They spoke of how fine he would soon look in his uniform. All this from perfect strangers; but Hyman Kopfman, the one who had spoken to him intimately, snickered openly and never tired of making slurring remarks. He referred to the Colonel's soft arms as chicken wings. He called attention to the unusual length of the Colonel's neck. Naturally, the accident that had nearly killed the Colonel had not widened his shoulders any, and there was some truth in the statement that he was neck from the waist up. Nor had the Colonel's wide bottom, like that of a pear, which seemed to hold his figure upright, escaped Hyman Kopfman's critical eye. Nor his feet, which were certainly flat for an army man. A less disillusioned man than the Colonel would have made an official complaint, or brought up the subject of Hyman Kopfman's two-pants suit. But he said nothing. He preferred to take it in his stride. One might even say that he seemed to wax stronger on it. It was this observation, among others, that upset Hyman Kopfman the most, and led him to say things of which he was later ashamed. It was simply too much, for a dying man, to see one getting well who had nothing to live for, and this spectacle always put him into a rage. It also considerably hastened his end. It became a contest, of sorts, as to whether the Colonel would get back on his feet before Hyman Kopfman lost another limb, or managed to die. In this curious battle, however, Hyman Kopfman's willpower showed to a great advantage, and he deteriorated faster than the Colonel managed to improve. He managed to die, quite decently in fact, during the night. A Saturday night, as it happened, and the Colonel was able to call his wife and ask her to bring a suitable floral offering when she came.

1954

The Cat in the Picture

On retiring from the service, the Captain rented a studio near the river, overlooking the harbor, and took up painting in watercolors. He arose at seven, put on the water for coffee, prepared the still life of fruit he would paint that day, then called his wife for a leisurely breakfast. The Captain's wife, a frail woman in her forties, wrote book reviews for an Indiana paper and passed the day reading and listening to classical programs on the radio. At four o'clock the Captain served tea, with either lemon or cream in the English manner, which he drank from a large china bowl that he held cupped in his hands. The steam from the tea fogged his glasses and gave a ruddy glow to his face. While the Captain relaxed, his wife would sometimes read from the book she was reviewing, as his tastes were wide for a military man. He favored travel books that touched on the places he had been. He would often interrupt the reading to point out some small error of fact. The Captain himself had traveled widely in both the Near and the Far East, but his wife had not been out of the States. He didn't care for the wives of other Army men and the lives they led. His own wife was free, as he liked to say, to go on with the book she was writing and pass the time between her home in Indiana and New York.

While his wife read aloud to him, the Captain would sit and gaze at his painting, as it was characteristic of him not to waste a moment's time. Having turned to painting so late in life, he had a lot to learn. As he lacked both talent and imagination, he had taken a lively interest in painting when he discovered these faculties were not necessary. The Captain's wife, and his friends, admired his painting as they had all worried for years about what a man of his temperament would do when he retired.

As the light was not good for painting in the evening, the Captain and his wife would visit friends or attend some theater where the better foreign films were shown. The Captain enjoyed seeing old familiar sights again. He would point out to his wife the buildings that had been destroyed. Later he would have a small glass of brandy, which he sipped while his wife was undressing, and if the night was clear he would gaze across the river at the lights of New York. When his wife spoke to him he would open the skylight and come to bed.

A sound sleeper, the Captain had learned to adjust himself to the fact that his wife, a very poor sleeper, often lay awake. She rested more than she slept. She lay on her back, her eyes focused on the stains on the ceiling, red or green according to the corner traffic light. Years ago this had troubled the Captain, as he was sensitive to small movements, and the habit she had of stroking the covers at her hips. But he had learned to tolerate that. If he now awoke from a sound sleep it was due to the fact that she had stopped moving, and lay there like a corpse, scarcely breathing, listening to something. Not long ago a bat had got into the room. On his own sweating face the Captain had felt the breath of its wings. His wife would lie there unable to move, her body stiff if he happened to touch her, and the Captain had learned there was little he could do. He accepted it, as he did the phases of the moon. So when he awoke, the first week in April, he didn't trouble to ask what was the matter, but reached for the flashlight that he kept under the bed. He trained the narrow beam around the room. He saw nothing at all at first, but he could hear an unusual noise, a soft, dragging sound, that seemed to come from the back of the room. That was where he painted, had his easel and the low table with his still life. In the basket with the fruit he now saw something move. Lights blinked on and off, like bobbing headlights far down a road. Rising on his elbow the Captain saw a large black cat coiled on the bananas.

"A cat," he said, matter-of-factly. "He probably came in through the skylight." When his wife didn't answer, he said, "You want him out?"

"How do you know it's a *him?*" his wife said.

That surprised the Captain, but he said, "He looks like a pretty big cat." The springs of the bed made a giggling sound. Was she laughing at him? "You want him in or out?" the Captain said.

"Can he get out if he wants to?" his wife said.

"If he got in," the Captain said, "I suppose he can get out," and turned the light beam on the easel, where it pointed toward the ceiling. There was a short jump from the easel to the skylight: not much for a cat.

"I think it's raining," his wife said. "He came in out of the rain."

Turning the beam on the skylight, the Captain could see that it was wet.

"Any port in a storm," he said, and went back to sleep.

Usually the Captain was the first one up, but early the next morning he heard his wife moving around. She was speaking in a high baby voice to the cat. When the Captain raised on one elbow he saw his wife, crouched like an Indian, watching the cat lap up a saucer of milk. His wife was a small, nearly birdlike woman, and the cat was long and thin with yellow eyes. He watched for a moment, then he said:

"Cats don't belong to people. They belong to places."

"You hear him purring?" his wife said.

The Captain lay back on the bed and thought over what he knew about cats. "They're not like dogs. They're very independent," he said.

"He's nice," his wife said.

The Captain recognized in himself a certain catlike independence. He appreciated this quality, respected it. He was thinking that if the cat wanted to stay it would be all right, as cats were not like dogs. Dogs made slaves of the people who owned them. Cats did not. A cat led its own life, and you were free to lead yours.

"He has the nicest purr," his wife said.

"They still don't know how they do it," the Captain replied, and put the coffee water on. As he stood there his wife called to him to come and look at the cat. "I got my hands full," the Captain said, stirring the coffee in the top of the Silex. Then he stopped stirring and waited for the coffee to come down.

"He wants to be in the picture," his wife said. "He wants to put a little life in the picture."

The Captain poured himself some coffee and came back into the room. The cat was back in the wooden bowl again, with his head resting on one of the bananas. His yellow eyes followed the string that the Captain's wife dangled above him.

"If you could paint that—*that* would be a picture," his wife said.

The Captain let the steam from the coffee warm his face. As his wife seldom commented on his painting, nothing that she said was lost on him.

"You're a bad, naughty boy," she said to the cat, picking him up tenderly, and it crossed the Captain's mind—just crossed it—that she had put the cat in the bowl herself. Not that she did, but somehow it crossed his mind.

"He's going to have to learn," the Captain said, rearranging the fruit in the basket, "that some places are all right, and some are not."

"You hear that?" his wife said. The cat made a noise. "You better learn that if you want to live around *here*," she said. His wife said this in a joking manner, wagging her finger close to the cat's nose, but the Captain's wife was not the joking type. Even the cat seemed to know it. "You've hurt our feelings," she repeated and walked out in the kitchen with it.

A moment later the Captain thought he heard her voice. "I can't hear you," he said, and cocked his head to one side as if that would help him.

"We're not talking to *you*," his wife replied. There was a note in her voice that distracted the Captain from what she had said. It was new. "We're not talking to him," she said, this time directly to the cat. "Are we?" The cat made a purring noise. When the Captain took another swallow of his coffee it was already cold.

So that the cat would be free to go in and out, a suitable gap was left in the skylight, and the Captain's easel served as a ladder, morning and night. Going out the cat made no sound, but coming in, around four in the morning, he would leap from the top of the easel to the foot of the bed. The thump always gave the Captain quite a shock. He never seemed prepared for it. Before he could get back to sleep again, the cat would curl up at the foot of the bed and wash himself. The stroking movement of the cat's head would communicate itself to the bed, the frame would creak, and there would be a sympathetic throb in the springs. Although the Captain was a sound sleeper, he was sensitive to small, persistent noises—just as his wife, a poor sleeper, seemed indifferent to them. The noises made by the cat did not trouble her. Quite the contrary. She seemed to miss it when it wasn't there. If the cat was five or ten minutes late she would get out of bed and raise the skylight, calling to him in a high falsetto voice. Sometimes he would answer. Other times there would be no sound. The Captain, who saw well at night, sometimes saw it seated on the skylight all the time his wife was calling. His wife, who was blind without her glasses, never seemed to know. Not that it mattered, as sooner or later the cat would stretch himself and come in.

All of this disturbance troubled the Captain. He passed the time gazing into the darkness. Many years of experience had taught him to lie quiet and let the storm blow over, but the night seemed very young at four o'clock. The cat would move, purring like a motor, from one spot on the bed to another, and his wife's nervous hand, sooner or later, would seek it out. The cat's fur would crackle as she slowly stroked its back. The Captain himself, unable to sleep, felt himself to be something of an intruder, a stranger in the bed whom his wife and the cat took pains to ignore. She spoke only to the cat. The cat, in turn, purred only for her.

One night, right out of the blue, like a man who dreams that he is drowning, the Captain's legs thrashed out and hurled the cat bodily across the room. But before the cat landed—as the Captain observed—his wife was out of the bed looking for him, calling to him in the high baby voice that he had come to detest. She moved about like a sleepwalker, stumbling against the furniture. When she found the cat it refused to purr, although she brought it back to the bed and held it in her arms while she stroked it. The Captain, wide awake, passed the rest of the night searching for the word to break this silence and listening to the whisper of his wife's hand on the cat's sleek coat. But he could think of nothing that would not make the situation worse. He had kicked out. It had been his own feet that struck the cat. He had heard the soft body strike the leg of his easel, but the terrible shock of what he had done failed to dull his glow of satisfaction.

The following day, while his wife was out shopping, the Captain made himself a place on the studio couch and early in the evening, a very tired man, he went to bed. His only comment was that he had to get some sleep. He mentioned no names, and let it be understood that his move to the couch was a temporary measure—he would give it up when certain details had been straightened out.

That night the Captain slept better than he had in weeks. There were no bad dreams and he did not wake up at four o'clock. In the morning, very early, he went to the city, leaving his wife a note that he had to pick up some painting supplies. He wanted her to have time to consider the problem, and figure it out. There would be less friction if she spent the day alone. As he figured it out for himself, he would make a cozy place for the cat in the kitchen, or, if she insisted, behind the screen on the studio couch. The Captain, of course, would return to his rightful place in the bed. That struck him as a very reasonable solution, but when he returned to the studio he found his wife and the cat curled up together on the bed, taking a nap. The studio couch, in the corner with his easel, had been neatly made up, and around it his wife had placed the painted Chinese screen. The Captain went behind it, lying on the couch until the evening sky had darkened and his wife, after having fed the cat, called him to eat.

Although the Captain passed a comfortable night on the couch and no longer heard the springs or felt the throbbing vibrations, he woke up, as usual, around four o'clock. Through the thin slats of the screen he could see the ghostly figure of his wife. She was very slender, nearly childlike in her loose, flowing nightgown. She would call to the cat, crouched on the skylight, and after five or ten minutes of coaxing it would climb down one leg of the Captain's easel and leap into her arms.

When his wife left the studio to do their shopping, the cat would follow her to the door, then crouch there, its back turned to the room, until she returned. At this time the Captain and the cat were in the room alone. There had been a time, of course, when the Captain ignored it, or smiled to himself with amusement, as he considered himself something of a student of animals, then go on about the business of painting watercolors in which the familiar fruit looked odd. But now he often turned from his work and stared at the cat. The cat, however, never stared back. The Captain would cough, or make the sounds in his throat that his wife sometimes made when she fed it, but the cat would remain with its back to the room, its eyes on the door. There was about this, the Captain decided, something personal. He admired independence, but the cat's indifference irritated him. The cat seemed to be unaware of the trouble he was causing, or that he might show, toward the Captain at least, a little gratitude. The Captain felt in the cat's rude manner an aloofness that bordered on snobbery. The cat's own feelings, in a catlike manner, he kept to himself.

One day, out of the blue, so to speak, the Captain picked up a paint tube and tossed it casually toward the door. When it struck the floor, the cat leaped high into the air. This reaction was something of a shock to both of them. The cat stalked the empty paint tube as if it were alive. It amused the Captain to see what a fool the cat was in such matters, and that it made no connection whatsoever between the Captain and the tube. The following day he tried this experiment again. The cat leaped again—but not so high. The third time he did not leap at all, but head thrust forward, as if listening, its long black tail switched on the floor. It still crouched, but its body was tense, as if to spring. By tossing just two or three tubes a day the Captain managed to keep him in this condition—taut as a spring, or a gun that is cocked.

"Now you know what it's like," the Captain would say, tossing another tube in the air, and the cat's long body would grow rigid as it dropped. But, unlike the Captain, the cat did not thrash out. Not openly, at least, until one tube, tossed high in the air, came down with a soft thud on the cat's back. So rapidly the Captain failed to follow the action—he thought the cat was having a fit—the cat spun around, trapped the tube, and sank in its teeth. When the Captain tried to retrieve it—the paint in the tube was poisonous—the cat growled, and struck out at him. It took all of the Captain's skill to get the tube of paint from its mouth and wipe the stain from the teeth before his wife returned. The cat continued to growl, and the hair along his arched back was up.

The following day, curious to see what the cat had learned from the experience, the Captain rolled a small tube across the floor. Not toward the cat, nor anywhere near him, but he spun around and trapped the tube, sank in its teeth, and disappeared under the bed. Nothing the Captain could do, or say, would persuade him to come out. The bed was also too low for a portly man, like the Captain, to get down on his knees and crawl under it. When he used the broom the cat would hiss like a snake, and growl. That was the situation when the Captain's wife came home. The Captain was back at his easel, painting, but as the cat was not there at the door to greet her, his wife knew that something was wrong. She demanded to know where the cat was, and when the Captain stood there, saying nothing, she got down on the floor, without removing her hat, and crawled beneath the bed. When she crawled out, the Captain didn't see her face, but over her shoulder he saw the scarlet smudges on the face of the cat. His fangs were deep red, and he seemed to have a mouthful of fresh blood.

With the cat still in her arms, his wife sat down and called the nearest animal doctor, then rushed off without waiting for the Captain to explain. Not that it mattered, as what was there to say? He had rolled the tube across the floor, and the cat had eaten it. While his wife was gone the Captain sat on the couch, staring at the painting on the Chinese screen, trying to think of what he would say when his wife returned. Every sensible angle left something unexplained. Every explanation only made the situation worse. The only thing for him to do, he decided, was to say nothing about the cat, but to speak very frankly about himself. To admit that the apartment was somehow too small for a man and a cat. If the cat were going to be part of the family—and he was prepared to admit that it was—what they were going to need was a little more sleeping space. A separate room for himself, perhaps, or one for the cat. The Captain wrote a long note to this effect, on a sheet of watercolor paper, then pinned it to his easel where his wife would certainly look. For the time being he would take a room in a nearby hotel. As he planned to be back in two or three days—the time it would take him to find a larger apartment—the Captain took nothing with him but his razor and his toothbrush. With a whole bed to himself he liked to sleep with nothing on.

As he always did after a critical decision, the Captain passed a comfortable night, and in the morning he lay in bed waiting for word from his wife. He had suggested that they might look for something together, in the afternoon. But as he had no word from her by noon, and being anxious to get the thing settled, he got up and went apartment hunting himself. He found himself talking, in fairly general terms, about his wife. What a stickler for certain details she was, and how she loved cats. It seemed to do him good to stand and chat with a perfect stranger about his wife or, more specifically, about his wife's uncanny way with cats. How she talked with them, the things they would do for her. This seemed to interest a good many women, landladies in particular, who either had, or had recently had, a most unusual cat.

The Captain found no apartment, but the many discussions had softened, in some fashion, his feelings about cats. He felt that he had not been disinterested enough. He had allowed his feelings to get the better of him. On his way back to the hotel he noticed that the light was on in their apartment, and in his mind's eye he could see his wife up there, talking to the cat. Perhaps they were lying on the double bed together, taking a nap. His wife had come to specialize in cat material, and on his way back to his room the Captain bought several postcards featuring posed photographs of cats. He planned to put stamps on the cards, and mail them to her. But when he asked the clerk at the desk for stamps, he was notified that a suitcase and trunk, the charges collect, had been delivered during the afternoon. The Captain readily recognized them as his own. On the trunk were the stickers of the celebrated places he had been. The trunk he left downstairs in the lobby, but the suitcase he carried to his room, where he pushed it, for the time being, under the bed. Although he had said nothing, the situation had taken a turn for the worse. Without troubling to take off his clothes, the Captain spent the night sprawled out on the bed, sleeping fitfully, until he awoke covered with sweat. He had dreamed the cat had leaped through the open window landing on his bed with a plop.

So much for the dream, so much for the fact that the Captain now sat facing the window—but how explain, since this was no dream, that he thought he heard the purring of the cat. The sweat covering his body seemed to turn to ice, and within his damp clothes, like something withered, the Captain had the sensation that he could feel his body shrink. His mouth hung open, but from it came no sound. When the chill had passed he lay back on the bed, too weak to move or to wonder, and as the first breeze off the river stirred the curtains at the window he fell asleep.

He awoke from the dreamless sleep strangely refreshed. He shaved, then removed the clothes that he had slept in and opened the bag that his wife had packed for him. Several shirts were neatly spread out on top. He put the shirts in a drawer, then removed the layer of pajamas, shirts, and socks, and stood there with a pair of socks in his hand gazing at the long, flattened body of the cat. The bottom side of the socks he held were still warm. The bloody scarlet color from the tube of paint was still on the cat's teeth. A practical man, the Captain wondered if the cat had died while eating the paint, or if he had been stuffed into the bag with his shirts while still alive—the living part of that picture his wife had always wanted him to paint.

1958

Since When Do They
Charge Admission

On the morning they left Kansas, May had tuned in for the weather and heard of the earthquake in San Francisco, where her daughter Janice was seven months pregnant. So she had called her. Janice's husband, Vernon Dickey, answered the phone. He was a native Californian so accustomed to earthquakes he thought nothing of them. It was the wind he feared.

"When I read about those twisters," he said to May, "I don't know how you people stand it." He wouldn't believe that May had never seen a twister till she saw one on TV, and that one in Missouri.

"Ask him about the riots," Cliff had asked her.

"What riots, Mrs. Chalmers?"

It was no trouble for May to see that Janice could use someone around the house to talk to. She was like her father, Cliff, in that it took children to draw her out. Her sister, Charlene, would talk the leg off a stranger but the girls had never talked much to each other. But now they would, once the men got out of the house. It had been Cliff's idea to bring Charlene along. She had never seen an ocean. She had never been higher than Estes Park, in Colorado.

On their way to the beach, Charlene cried, "Look! Look!" She pointed into the sunlight; May could see the light shimmering on the water.

"That's the beach," said Janice.

"Just *look*," Charlene replied.

"You folks come over here often?" asked Cliff.

"On Vernon's day off," replied Janice.

"If it's a weekday," said May, "you wouldn't find ten people on a beach in Shawnee County."

"You wouldn't because there's no beach for them to go to," said Janice.

Cliff liked the way Janice spoke up for California, since that was what she was stuck with. He didn't like it himself. Nothing had its own place. Hardly any of the corners were square. All through the Sunday-morning service he could hear the plastic propellers spinning at the corner gas station, and the loud bang when they checked the oil and slammed down the hood. Vernon Dickey took it all in his stride, the way he did the riots.

Janice said, "Vernon's mother can't understand anybody who lives where they have dust storms."

"I'd rather see it blow than feel it shake," said Cliff.

"Ho-ho!" said Vernon.

"I suppose it's one thing or another," said May. "When I read about India I'm always thankful."

Cliff honked his horn at the sharp turns in the road. The fog stood offshore just far enough to let the sun shine yellow on the beach sand. At the foot of the slope the beach road turned left through a grove of trees. Up ahead of them a chain, stretched between two posts, blocked the road. On the left side a portable contractor's toilet was brightly painted with green and yellow flowers. A cardboard sign attached to the chain read: *Admission 50¢*.

"Since when do they charge admission?" Janice asked. She looked at her husband, a policeman on his day off. As Cliff stopped the car a young man in the booth put out his head.

"In heaven's name," May said. She had never seen a man with such a head of hair outside of the *National Geographic*. He had a beard that seemed to grow from the hair on his chest. A brass padlock joined the ends of a chain around his neck.

"How come the fifty-cent fee?" said Vernon. "It's a public beach."

"It's a racket," said the youth. "You can pay it or not pay it." He didn't seem to care. At his back stood a girl with brown hair to her waist, framing a smiling, vacant, pimpled face. She was eating popcorn; the butter and salt greased her lips.

"I don't know why anyone should pay it," said May. "Cliff, drive ahead."

Cliff said, "You like to lower the chain?"

When the boy stepped from the booth he had nothing on but a jockstrap. The way his plump buttocks were tanned it was plain that was all he was accustomed to wear. He stooped with his backside toward the car, but the hood was between him and the ladies. As the chain slacked Cliff drove over it, slowly, into the parking lot.

"What in the world do you make of *that?*" asked May.

"He's a hippie," said Janice. "They're hippies."

"Now I've finally seen one," said May. She twisted in the seat to take a look back.

"Maybe they're having a love-in down here," said Vernon, and guffawed. Cliff had never met a man with a sense of humor that stayed within bounds.

"Park anywhere," said Janice.

"You come down here alone?" asked May.

Vernon said, "Mrs. Chalmers, you don't need to worry. They're crazy but they're not violent."

Cliff maneuvered between the trucks and cars to where the front wheels thumped against a driftwood log. The sand began there, some of it blowing in the offshore breeze. The tide had washed up a sandbar, just ahead, that concealed the beach and most of the people on it. Way over, maybe five or ten miles, was the coastline just west of the Golden Gate, with the tier on tier of houses that Cliff knew to be Daly City. From the bridge, on the way over, Vernon had pointed it out. Vernon and Janice had their home there, but they wanted something more out in the open, nearer the beach. As a matter of fact, Cliff had come up with the idea of building them something. He was a builder. He and May lived in a house that he had built. If Vernon would come up with the piece of land, Cliff would more or less promise to put a house on it. Vernon would help him on the weekends and his days off.

"What about a little place over there?" said Cliff, and wagged his finger at the slope near the beach. Right below it were the huge rocks black as the water, but light on their tops. That was gull dung. One day some fellow smarter than the rest would make roof tiles or fertilizer out of it.

"Most of the year it's cold and foggy," said Vernon, "too cold for the kids."

"What good is a cold, windy beach?" said May. She had turned to take the whip of the wind on her back. No one answered her question. It didn't seem the right time to give it much thought. Cliff got the picnic basket out of the rear and tossed the beach blanket to Vernon. There was enough sand in it, when they shook it, to blow back in his face.

"Just like at home," Cliff said to Vernon, who guffawed.

Vernon had been born and raised in California, but he had got his army training near Lubbock, Texas, where the dust still blew. Now he led off toward the beach, walking along the basin left where the tide had receded. Charlene trailed along behind him wearing the flowered pajama suit she had worn since they left Colby, on the fourth of June. They had covered twenty-one hundred and forty-eight miles in five days and half of one night, Cliff at the wheel. Charlene could drive, but May didn't feel she could be trusted on the interstate freeways, where they drove so fast. There was a time, every day, about an hour after lunch, when nothing Cliff could think or do would keep him from dozing off. He'd jerk up when he'd hear the sound of gravel or feel the pull of the wheel on the road's shoulder. Then he'd be good for a few more miles till it happened again. The score of times that happened Cliff might have killed them all, but he couldn't bring himself to pull over and stop. It scared him to think of the long drive back.

"Except where it was green, in Utah," said May, "it's looked the same to me since we left home."

"Mrs. Chalmers," said Vernon, "you should've sat on the other side of the car."

It was enlightening to Cliff, after all he'd heard about the population explosion, to see how wide open and empty most of the country was. In the morning he might feel he was all alone in it. The best time of day was the forty miles or so he got in before breakfast. They slipped by so easy he sometimes felt he would just like to drive forever, the women in the car quiet until he stopped for food. Anything May saw before she had her coffee was lost on her. After breakfast Cliff didn't know what seemed longer: the day he put in waiting for the dark or the long night he put in waiting for the light. He had forgotten about trains until they had to stop for the night.

Vernon said, "I understand that when they take the salt out of the water there'll be no more water problems. Is that right, Mr. Chalmers?"

Like her mother, Charlene said, "There'll just be others." Was there anything Cliff had given these girls besides a poor start? He turned to see how Janice, who was seven months pregnant, was making out. The way her feet had sunk into the sand she was no taller than her mother. With their backsides to the wind both women looked broad as a barn. One day Janice was a girl—the next day you couldn't tell her from her mother. That part of her life when she looked old would prove to be the longest, but seem the shortest. Her mother hardly knew a thing, or cared, about what had happened since the war. The sight of anything aging, or anything just beginning, like that unborn child she was lugging, affected Cliff so strongly he could wet his lips and taste it. Where did people get the strength to do it all over again? He turned back to face the beach and the clumps of people who were sitting around, or lying. One played a guitar. A wood fire smoked in the shelter of a few smooth rocks. Vernon said, "It's like the coast of Spain." Cliff could believe it might well be true: it looked old and bleak enough. Where the sand was wet about half-a-dozen dogs ran up and down, yapping like kids.

"Dogs are fun! They just seem to know almost everything."

This side of Charlene made her good with her kids, but Cliff sometimes wondered about her husband.

"How's this?" said Vernon, taking Cliff by the arm, and indicated where he thought they should spread the blanket. On one side were two boys, stretched out on their bellies, and nearer at hand was this blanket-covered figure, his back humped up. His problem seemed to be that he couldn't find a spot in the sand to his liking. He squirmed a good deal. Now and then his backside rose and fell. Cliff took one end of the blanket and Vernon the other, and they managed to hold it against the wind, flatten it to the sand. Charlene plopped down on it to keep it from blowing. It seemed only yesterday that Cliff and his father would put her in a blanket and toss her like a pillow, scaring her mother to death. Charlene was one of those girls who was more like a boy in the way nothing fazed her. Out of the water, toward Vernon, a girl came running so wet and glistening she looked naked.

"Look at that!" said Cliff, and then stood there, his mouth open, looking. She was actually naked. She ran right up and passed him, her feet kicking wet sand on him, then she dropped to lie for a moment on her face, then roll on her back. Only the gold-flecked sand clung to her white belly and breasts. Grains of sand, cinnamon-colored, clung to her prominent, erectile nipples. Her eyes were closed, her head tipped to the left to avoid the wind. For a long moment Cliff gazed at her body as if in thought. When he blinked his eyes the peculiar thing was that he was the one who felt in the fishbowl. Surrounded by them. What did they think of a man down at the beach with all his clothes on? He was distracted by a tug on the blanket and turned to see Vernon pointing at the women. They waddled along like turtles. All he could wonder was what had ever led them to come to a beach. Buttoned at the collar, Janice's coat draped about her like a tent she was dragging. Cliff just stood there till they came along beside him, and May put out a hand to lean on him. Sand powdered her face.

"It's always so windy?" she asked Vernon.

"You folks call this windy?" May looked closely at him to see if he meant to be taken seriously. He surely knew, if he knew anything, that she knew more about wind than he did.

"Get Cliff to tell you how it blows around Osage," she said. "It blows the words right out of your mouth, if you'd let it." Cliff was silent, so she added, "Don't it, Cliff?"

"Don't it what?" he answered. He allowed himself to turn so that his eyes went to the humped, squirming figure, under the blanket. The humping had pulled it up so the feet were uncovered. Four of them. Two of them were toes down, with tar spots on the bottoms: two of them were toes up, the heels dipped into the sand. In a story Cliff had heard but never fully understood, the point had hinged on the four-footed monster. Now he got the point.

"Blow the words right out of your mouth if you'd let it," said May. At a loss for words, Cliff moved to stand so he blocked her view. He took a grip on her hands and let her sag, puffing sour air at him, down to the blanket. "It's hard enough work just to get here," she said, and raised her eyes to squint at the water. "Charlene, you wanted to see the ocean: well, there it is."

Cliff was thinking that Charlene looked no older than the summer she was married. It was hard to understand her. She had had three children without ever growing up.

"If I'd known the sand was going to blow," said May, "we'd have stayed home to eat, then come over later. I hate sand in my food. Charlene, you going to sit down?"

Charlene stood there staring at a girl up to her ankles in the shallow water. She stooped to hold a child pressed to her front, the knees buckled up as if she squeezed it. A stream of water arched from the slit between the child's legs. The way she held it, pressed to her front, it was like squeezing juice from a bladder. There was nothing Cliff could do but wait for it to stop. Charlene's handbag dangled to where it almost dragged in the sand.

"That's Farallon Island," said Vernon, pointing. Without his glasses Cliff couldn't see it. Janice tipped forward, as far as she could, to cup handfuls of sand over her ankles: she couldn't reach her feet. "We hear and read so much about their being so dirty," said May.

"It's the hippies," said Vernon. "They've taken it over."

Why was he such a fool as to say so? Even Cliff, who knew what he would see, twisted his head on his neck and looked all around him. The stark-naked girl had dried a lighter color: she didn't look so good. The sand sprinkled her like brown sugar, but the mole-colored nipples were flat on her breasts, like they'd been snipped off. At her feet, using her legs as a backrest, a lank-haired boy, chewing bubble gum, sunned his pimpled face. On his hairless chest someone had painted his nipples to look like staring eyes. Now that Cliff was seated it was plainer than ever what was going on under the blanket: the heels of two of the feet thrust deep into the sand, piling it up. Cliff felt the eyes of Janice on the back of his head, but he missed those of her mother. Where were they?

"Cliff," she said.

He did not turn to look.

"Cliff," she repeated.

At the edge of the water a dappled horse galloped with two long-haired, naked riders. If one was a boy, Cliff couldn't tell which was which.

"Who's ready for a beer?" asked Vernon, and peeled the towel off the basket. When no one replied he said, "Mr. Dickey, have yourself a beer," and took one. He moved the basket of food to where both Cliff and the women could reach it. Along with the bowl of potato salad there were two broiled chickens from the supermarket. The chickens were still warm.

"All I've done since we left home is eat," Cliff said.

"We just ate," said Janice.

"We didn't drag all this stuff here," said Cliff, "just to turn around and drag it back." He took out the bowl of salad. He fished around in the basket for the paper cups and plates. He didn't look up at May until he knew for certain she had got her head and eyes around to the front. The sun glinted on her glasses. Absent-mindedly she raked her fingers across her forehead for loose strands of hair. "We eat the salad first or along with the chicken?"

None of the women made any comment. One of the maverick beach dogs, his coat heavy with sand, stood off a few yards and sniffed at the chicken. "They shouldn't allow dogs on a beach," said Cliff. "They run around and get hot and can't drink the water. In the heat they go mad."

"There's salt in there somewhere," said Janice. "I don't put all the salt I could on the salad."

Cliff took out one of the chickens, and using his fingers pried the legs off the body. He then broke the drumsticks off at the thighs, and placed the pieces on one of the plates.

"You still like the dark meat?" he said to Charlene. She nodded her head. He peeled the plastic cover off the potato salad and forked it out onto the paper plates. "Eat it before the sand gets at it," he said, and passed a plate to May. Janice reached to take one, and placed it on the slope of her lap. Vernon took the body of one of the birds, tore off the wings, and tossed one to the dog.

"I can't stand to see a dog watch me eat," he said.

"Vernon was in Korea for a year," said Janice.

Cliff began to eat. After the first few swallows it tasted all right. He hadn't been hungry at all when he started, but now he ate like he was famished. When he traveled all he seemed to do was sit and eat. He glanced up to see that they were all eating except for May, who just sat there. She had her head cocked side-wise as if straining to hear something. Not twenty yards away a boy plucked a guitar but Cliff didn't hear a sound with the wind against him. Two other boys, with shorts on, one with a top on, lay out on their bellies with their chins on their hands. One used a small rock to drive a short piece of wood into the sand. It was the idle sort of play Cliff would expect from a kid about six, not one about twenty. On the sand before them a shadow flashed and eight or ten feet away a bird landed, flapping its wings. Cliff had never set eyes on a bigger crow. He was shorter in the leg but as big as the gulls that strutted on the firm sand near the water. A little shabby at the tail, big glassy hatpin eyes. Cliff watched him dip his beak into the sand like one of those glass birds that go on drinking water, rocking on the perch. One of the boys said, "Hey, you, bird, come here!" and wiggled a finger at him. When the bird did just that Cliff couldn't believe his eyes. He had a stiff sort of strut, pumping his head, and favored one leg more than the other. No more than two feet away from the heads of those boys he stopped and gave them a look. Either one of them might have reached out and touched him. Cliff had never seen a big, live bird as tame as that. The crows around Chadron were smarter than most people and had their own meetings and cawed crow language. They had discussions. You could hear them decide what to do next. The boy with the rock held it out toward him and damn if the crow didn't peck at it. Cliff could hear the click of his beak tapping the rock. He turned to see if May had caught that, but her eyes were on the plate in her lap.

"May, look—" he said.

Her eyes down, she said, "I've seen all I want to see the rest of my life."

"The crow—" said Cliff, and took another look at him. He had his head cocked to one side, like a parrot, and his beak clamped down on one of the sticks driven into the sand. He tried to wiggle it loose as he tugged at it. He braced his legs and strained back like a robin pulling a worm from a hole. So Vernon wouldn't miss it, Cliff put out his hand to nudge him. "Well, I'll be damned," Vernon said.

Two little kids, one with a plastic pail, ran up to within about a yard of the bird, stopped and stared. He stared right back at them. Who was to say which of the two looked the strangest? The kids were naked as the day they were born. One was a boy. Whatever they had seen before they had never seen a crow that close up.

"Come on, bird," said the boy with the rock, and waved it. Nobody would ever believe it, but that bird took a tug at the stick, then rocked back and cawed. He made such a honk the kids were frightened. The little girl backed off and giggled. The crow clamped his beak on the stick again and had another try. A lanky-haired hippie girl, just out of the water, ran up and said, "Sam—are they teasing you, Sam?" She had on no top at all but a pair of blue-jean shorts on her bottom. "Come on, bird!" yelled the boy with the rock, and pounded his fists on the sand. That crow had figured out a way to loosen up the stick by clamping down on it, hard, then moving in a circle, like he was drilling a well. He did that twice, then he pulled it free, clamped one claw on it, and cawed.

"Good bird!" said the boy, and tried to take it from him, but that crow wouldn't let him. He backed off, flapped his wings, and soared off with his legs dangling. Cliff could see what it took a big bird like that to fly.

"What does he do with it?" said the girl. She looked off toward the cliffs where the bird had flown. Somewhere up there he had a lot of sticks: no doubt about that.

"Buries it," said the boy. "He thinks it's a bone."

The little girl with the plastic pail said, "Why don't you give him a real bone, then?" The boy and girl laughed. The hippie girl said, "Can I borrow a comb?" and the boy replied, "If you don't get sand in it." He moved so he could reach the comb in his pocket, and stroked it on his sleeve as he passed it to her. As she combed her hair, her head tipped back, Cliff might have mistaken her for a boy. The little girl asked, "When will he do it again?"

"Soon as he's buried it," said the boy.

Cliff didn't believe that. He had watched crows all his life, but he had never seen a crow behave like that. He wanted to bring the point up, but how could he discuss it with a girl without her clothes on?

"Here he comes," said the boy, and there he was, his shadow flashing on the sand before them. He made a circle and came in for a landing on the firm sand. What if he did bury those sticks? His beak was shiny, yellow as a banana. "Come here, bird!" said the boy, and held out the rock, but the girl leaned forward and grabbed it from him.

"You want to hurt him?" she cried. "Why don't you give him a real bone?" She looked around as if she might see one, raking the sand with her hands.

"Here's one, miss!" said Cliff, and held the chicken leg out toward her. He could no more help himself than not duck when someone took a swing at him. On her hands and knees the girl crawled toward him to where she could reach it. Her lank hair framed her face.

"There's meat on it," she said.

"Don't you worry," said Cliff, "crows like meat. They're really good meat-eaters."

She looked at him closely to see how he meant that. About her neck a fine gold-colored chain dangled an ornament. Cliff saw it plainly. Two brass nails were twisted to make some sort of puzzle. She looked at the bone Cliff had given her, the strip of meat on it, and turned to hold it out to the bird. He limped forward like he was trained and took it in his beak. Cliff caught his eye, and what worried him was that he might want to crow over it and drop it. He didn't want him to drop it and have to gulp down sandy meat. But that bird actually knew he had something unusual since he didn't put it down to clamp his claws on it. Instead he strutted. Up and down he went, like a sailor with a limp. Vernon laughed so hard he gave Cliff a slap on the knee. "Don't laugh at him," said the girl, and when she put out her hand he limped toward her to where she could touch him, stroking with her fingers the flat top of his head. The little boy suddenly yelled and ran around them in a circle, kicking up sand and hooting. The crow took off. The heavy flap of his wings actually stirred the hair of the boy was was lying there, nearest to him; he raised one of his hands to wave as the bird soared away.

"I never seen anything like it!" said Vernon.

"Maybe you'd like to come oftener." Janice picked at the bread crumbs in her lap.

"Did you see him?" asked Cliff. "You get to see him?"

"We can go now if you men have eaten." May made a wad of the napkin and scraps in her lap, put them under the towel and plates in the basket.

Vernon said, "Honey, you see that crazy bird?"

Janice shaded her eyes with one hand, peered at the sky. Up there, high, a bird was wheeling. Cliff took it for a gull. The wind had caked the color she had put on her lips, and sand powdered the wrinkles around her eyes. Cliff remembered they were called crow's feet, which was how they looked. Now she lowered her hand and held it out to Vernon to pull her up. The sand caught up in the folds of her dress blew over May and the girl lying behind her, one arm across her face.

"People must be crazy to come and eat on a beach," said May.

Cliff pushed himself to his feet, sand clinging to his chicken-sticky fingers. He helped Vernon with the blanket, walking toward the water where they could shake it and not disturb people. A bearded youth without pants, but with a striped T-shirt, sat with crossed legs at the edge of the water. The horse that had galloped off to the south came galloping back with just one rider on it. Cliff could see it was a girl. Janice and her mother had begun the long walk back toward the car. Along the way they passed the naked girl, still sprawled on her back.

"She's going to get herself a sunburn," said Vernon.

To Charlene Cliff said, "You see that bird?" Charlene nodded. "Just remember you did, when I ask you. Nobody back in Chadron is going to believe me if you don't."

"What bird was it?" asked May.

"A crow," said Cliff.

"I would think you'd seen enough of crows," said May.

At the car Cliff turned for a last look at the beach. The tide had washed up a sort of reef so that he could no longer see the water. The girl and the dogs that ran along it were like black paper cutouts. Nobody would know if she had her clothes on or off. He had forgotten to check on the two of them who had been squirming under the blanket. One still lay there. The other one crouched with lowered head, as if reading something. From the back Cliff wouldn't know which one was the girl.

May said, "I've never before really believed it when I said that I can't believe my eyes, but now I believe it."

"You wouldn't believe them if you'd seen that crow," said Cliff.

"I didn't come all this way to look at a crow," she replied.

They all got into the car, and Cliff put the picnic basket into the rear. He took a moment, squinting, to see if the crazy bird had come back for more bones. If he had just thought, he would have given the girl the other two legs to feed him.

"I'd like a cup of coffee," said May, "but I'm willing to wait till we get home for it."

Vernon said, "Mr. Chalmers, you like me to drive?" Cliff agreed that he would. They went out through the gate where they had entered but the boy and the girl had left the booth. The chain was already half-covered with drifting sand.

"It's typical of your father," said May, "to drive all the way out here and look at a crow."

Charlene said, "Wait until I tell Leonard!" They looked to see what she would tell him. On the dry slope below them a small herd of cattle were being fed from a hovering helicopter. Bundles of straw were dropped to spread on the slope.

"If I were you," said May, "I'd tell him about *that* and nothing else."

Cliff felt his head wagging. He stopped it and said, "Charlene, now you tell him about that crow. What's a few crazy people to one crow in a million?"

There was no comment.

"We're going up now," said Vernon. "You feel that poppin' in your ears?"

1969

Drrdla

The house needed painting when the Fechners acquired it, and Walter rented the equipment necessary to do it, climbing like a fireman to get at the rafters high in the gables. Inside, both the floors and the woodwork had been covered with many coats of paint. Walter removed it all to bring out the natural beauty of the wood. Light streamed through the high first-floor windows that Walter had cleaned with professional equipment. Whatever Walter undertook to do, he did professionally. In three of the upstairs rooms he installed cypress paneling obtained for a song from a demolition company, at the same time installing insulation materials that kept the summer heat out, the winter heat in. So much for first things first. In the dark months of the winter he taught himself to paint—among other things grinding his own colors—and with his wife Hanna's assistance, he took up the study of the cello. If it was largely a matter of application, Walter knew how to apply himself. He did no more than what he could, provided the day was long enough.

Hanna had "found" him in a jeweler's shop in Küssnacht, directly across the lake from Lucerne. His job had been to polish the silver and keep hundreds of cuckoo clocks cuckooing. They covered one solid wall of the shop into which Hanna had stepped to buy herself a new watchband, the pendulums rocking, the birds cuckooing, in one insane instant happening. The sight had so affected Hanna she had closed her eyes. Walter had spoken to her. Then another year passed before she returned, having made up her mind it was Walter she wanted.

One could hardly believe that to look at Hanna, a scholarly, shy-seeming, very Swiss woman. It had been her decision. Perhaps her being older than Walter persuaded him to let her make it. He was so very much the man Hanna knew that she wanted, it was not necessary for her to be his ideal woman. That proved to be acceptable to Walter because women were not one of his major interests. He liked them, but he didn't need them. What he proved to need, after six years of marriage, was an intelligent, congenial male companion. That was Herman Lewin. He had been recruited with this in mind. Lewin badly needed a place to stay while he completed his medical studies. Walter's knowledge of German was a help to Lewin, and he in turn tutored Walter in the new analytic psychology. If the war came up, as it sometimes did, it was discussed in an open, intelligent manner. Herman Lewin was Jewish. Hanna and Walter Fechner were German-Swiss. They were all agreed that German culture could not be held responsible for a few madmen, anymore than all Americans could be held responsible for Huey Long.

"I tell you what," Hanna would say, lowering her cup with a clack to her saucer. "You men are all crazy. It's a *man's* crazy world." Hanna simply couldn't help, on occasion, showing her resentment for a man-run world. In Switzerland a woman did not have the right to vote, no matter how smart she was. In America she could teach, but not look forward to the usual promotions. A doddering idiot could head the department of German literature— as he now did—if his sex was male.

Hanna was not the lighthearted, uncomplicated person that Lewin had assumed from their exchange of letters. She had her moods. They made her, surely, more interesting. Like the night light at the top of the stairs, she was either turned on, or she was turned off. Her work at the college demanded all of her strength, and she turned on for the college as she closed the door of the house behind her and walked down the steps. In the way she strode off, carrying her stuffed valise, Lewin recognized the Eu-

ropean in exile. Her pride and status tipped her slightly backward.
The American who walked behind tipped slightly forward, forging
ahead. In the late afternoon Hanna's return to the house was sig-
naled by a loud clapping of her hands. A professor might do that
to waken sleeping pupils. In this way Hanna summoned Walter
and Lewin to tea. She would have changed her dress, and her face
would be free of the light touch of makeup she wore to college.
The tea hour permitted Hanna to enjoy at home some of the plea-
sures of supervision that were part of teaching. It was Hanna who
spooned the tea from the pewter canister; Hanna who timed the
steeping; and Hanna who poured—glancing up to check with
Lewin, who sometimes varied as to the number of lumps of sugar
he wanted. Walter was allowed to slice up the *kuchen*. Hanna
judged the strength of the tea by its odor, an exercise that left a
film of steam on her glasses. Much of this vexed Walter. To avoid
the fuss, he might not appear until his tea was poured and cooling.
An unsuspected side of Hanna's nature was revealed in the way
she attacked her food. As if famished. Utterly absorbed until she
was fed. Her way of opening her mouth, wide, then closing it
with a birdlike chomp was disturbing. Later, with a finger moist-
ened at her lips, she would peck around the table picking up
crumbs, scraps of nuts, cake, and icing. Into her appetite Hanna
put a great deal of living. The strong brew of tea gave her pale
face a flush and started, as she said, "her motor running." As a
rule it would run for about two hours. This animated Hanna was
capable of "glee"—something new in Lewin's experience. She
would give herself over, quite completely, to the humor of something Lewin had mentioned, not infrequently placing her hand
on his arm, or as high as his shoulder, and applying astonishing
pressure. The violin, she said, had done much to strengthen her
hands.

Whatever Hanna believed to be so funny was invariably lost
on Walter. He would sit waiting for her fit of humor to pass.
Loose strands of her hair would cling to her lips, and tears of glee
give a shine to her eyes. "If it's so amusing," Walter would say,
"I fail to understand why you can't explain it." That she couldn't,
of course, was what she found so amusing, and made matters

worse. Minutes after such a scene at the table she might be heard giggling at the sink in the kitchen, or almost choking with laughter in her study. Walter put it down as a characteristic female symptom. Women were strange creatures, in Walter's opinion, still at the whimsical mercy of the moon's orbit. He detected, and complained of, the odor in the house during Hanna's "lunar period," during which time he took his shower in a stall he had erected in the basement. The basement smelled of nothing worse than fertilizer and hibernating plants.

Walter had a peasant's blunt directness of manner, but Lewin considered him rustically handsome. A woman might like him, although most objects were prone to bend or break in his hands. The handles snapped off cups, or broke off utensils, if Walter was asked to wash or dry them. His large-knuckled hands were those of a man half again his size. He broke off wine corks, snapped off pipestems, bent the prongs of forks as he mashed potatoes, and invariably cut so deep into the cheese board Lewin was warned to beware of splinters. In the basement, in fact, broken into fragments, were many mail-order objects he had tried to assemble. The iron legs of a new-type collapsible bed were twisted as if some monster had seized them. He snapped buttons off the collars of his shirts and the flies of his pants. It was of course impossible for him to shave without cutting himself. From the back and side his large knobby head resembled the Swiss carvings used for bottle stoppers, but his eyes were intelligent, and his voice, as a rule, pleasant. His gestures, however, in a heated discussion, were more like those of a karate expert, the flat of his hand slicing right or left, or brought down like a cleaver into his palm. It had not been easy for such a man to turn to painting, the cello, and the touch system of typing. The typing went the slowest, since the machine was usually in need of repair.

Walter's paintings were largely an excuse for making handsome frames. He drilled the wormholes by hand, and applied his own antique finish. These canvases were painted at the second-floor windows and demonstrated his mastery of perspective. No painting had been done out of the house. Walter did not like the curious gazing at him, or confusing him with some bohemian-type artist.

All he was doing was showing what a man could do if he applied himself. He gave the pictures numbers, and signed himself Fechner where the signature was not obtrusive. He meant to say no more than that he was responsible for what he had made.

Lewin was still in bed, on a Sunday morning, when Walter rapped on his door. He came in with flecks of sawdust in his hair and a thick powder of the dust on his hands. It was common to see Walter Fechner heated—by work he did with his hands or the warmth of his emotions—but Lewin had never before seen him excited. It changed the pitch of his voice. He looked both foolish and appealing. "It's there!" he said.

Lewin said, "What?"

Walter shrugged in the European manner, spreading his hands. "What is where?" Lewin repeated.

Walter replied, "The basement!" He spoke in a hushed, gruff whisper, as if someone were listening. Music thundered to a climax in Hanna's room. "It's there!" he said again, and Lewin was pleased to see, for himself, what Hanna had once seen in Walter. A boy's wide-eyed startled pleasure in a man's face. So what had happened? Walter had been at work at his bench, cutting a piece of glass. He had reached that stage where the glass had to be tapped with the tool to break it: a tingling sound is given off as it splinters. In the silence that followed this high-pitched vibration he heard a sound in the timbers behind him. That part of the basement was little more than an air space between the floor of the kitchen and the foundation. Old boards were piled there. Also a few traps in case of rats. There was no access to the basement from the yard, but Walter had found rat turds on his workbench. They were uncanny, those fellows. Walter had for them the highest respect.

His first thought was that he had caught a rat, and the creature, in pain, had made this sound. So he used a flashlight to check the traps back in the darkness. Both had been sprung, and the bait was gone. Otherwise nothing. He had stood there for some time, lost in thought. When he returned to work he picked up the glass and finished off what he had started. Once more, as the glass splintered, he had heard the sound. How describe it? Something between a peep and a squeak. So he took the trouble to clear away the boards and aim the beam of the flashlight into the corners. At the farthest point, the way a distant road sign picks up the glint of the headlights, he saw—for a moment he saw—two eyes: glass-like splinters of chill went up and down his spine. The palm of the hand that gripped the light had filmed with sweat. The primeval, ur-fears of man needed only this spinal tingle to revive them. Eyes gleaming in a cavelike darkness. Sounds that were felt as much as they were heard.

What had Walter done? At the moment nothing. He had been paralyzed. Sometime later he had aimed the beam of spotlight into the darkest corner. Walter and this creature had just stared at each other. A bat, possibly? No, the head was too large. In Walter's experience it resembled the slender loris, a bizarre creature he had seen only in books. A head that appeared all eyes. Fearing to damage eyes so long accustomed to darkness Walter had switched off the light and come straight to Lewin. What did he want? What he wanted from Lewin was advice.

That he thought he would get it from Lewin was a measure of his confusion. Lewin's feeling about anything found in basements was not one of excitement. Why else had he picked an apartment in the attic if not to get as far as possible from basements? Anything that slithered, squirmed, or dragged a tail was not, for Lewin, an object of study. But that was not yet known. Whatever it was, it had not yet moved. Lewin's advice—since Walter stood there, waiting—was to lure the creature into the open. Put down food and water. Put down anything the poor devil might eat. In a picture magazine Lewin had once seen a beast all eyes and ears, like a giant Mickey Mouse.

"That's a loris," said Walter, and in that simple manner he recovered his sense of proportion. It was not really advice he wanted or needed from Lewin—just his reassurance.

He did take Lewin's tip about the food, and put down samples of cheese, meat, and nuts, and canned fish. Also cereals, dry and cooked. What happened? Nothing. Nor did it respond to the bait of warm milk. That would have settled the matter for Lewin, but it merely increased the challenge for Walter. He prepared more fish, both fresh and canned mackerel, and pushed the tin plate of food back into the darkness. The next morning he could see that the mackerel had been licked clean of the sauce. More sauce was added, and this too licked off. Was it only the sauce that it liked, or did it lack the strength, or the teeth, to chew with? Walter asked Lewin, whose teeth were not so good. So that the creature could gum the fish, if necessary, a pulpy soup was made of the mackerel. That helped. The loris proved to have a weakness for canned fish soup.

From the basement stairs, where Walter kept his vigil, he used mirrors to keep his eyes on the food plate. A dim, indirect light, from a shaded bulb, transformed the scene into a parched, barren landscape. In this tableau a rat would loom as large as a dinosaur. At its farthest rim, all ears and popped eyes, a creature gazed toward Walter with a fish-smeared snout, then turned, like a reptile, and squirmed off. The tail it dragged was thin and long as a rat's, but covered with fur. If Walter could believe his eyes he had seen a starved cat. Fortunately for Lewin, he would have to wait until the creature had gained both courage and substance. This would take time. Lewin had to gain a little courage himself.

Walter began with liquid vitamins smeared on the fish or dropped into the saucer of canned milk. Quite simply, the creature had to learn to both chew food and digest it. Like a healthy cat choking on a fur ball, it had to swallow, and gag, then swallow again. Walter was patient. He spoke words of comfort and encouragement. In return it might make the sound suggested by the word drrrdla, with a rolling of the r's. Not a mew, or a meow, but a sound that looked forward—as Walter put it—to being a real mew someday. Drrdla. For the moment it served as a name. If Walter made a move in its direction it would squirm like a reptile into the darkness, but if he made only coaxing, catlike noises it was not disturbed. When Lewin came down for breakfast he would find Walter on the basement stairs, off the landing, a flashlight in his lap and a pair of bird glasses on a strap about his neck.

"How's your friend?" Lewin would ask.

"She's coming," Walter would reply, although the matter of sex was still undetermined. Her color, from what he could tell, had once been gray and white.

What it all came down to, in Walter's opinion, was the emergence of life from darkness. God knows where the creature had come from, or what had been the cause of its terror, but it now slowly squirmed its way from the primeval past into the present. It had managed to live, like a hibernating plant, on snatches of light. The very idea of a friendly gesture, or an upward look, had not emerged into its consciousness. What Walter found on his hands was a creature, like man, that had fallen from grace. Some blind or deliberate moment of terror had erased its mind of all experience. A *tabula rasa*. It had to begin, once more, from scratch. Would it be possible to restore such a fallen creature to normal life? If possible, Walter would do it. In that simple animal, as in man, there was a hunger for human affection: in its tiny, wounded soul it was drawn toward the light it feared. Like some people, it had lived in darkness so long it found the presence of light painful. The parallels were endless. The challenge inexhaustible. No project Walter had previously undertaken tested, at once, so many of his talents. Commitment and patience. Walter would prove to have what the challenge required. Every day he modified, in some way, the approach he used to win her over. It was the talk she liked: a very womanly aspect of her temperament. To enlarge his range Walter used a birdcall that employed a piece of metal in a wooden disk. What sounds he made! How her eyes would widen, her large, batlike ears would twitch. This could be observed from the landing of the stairs without intruding on her privacy. Lewin observed it. A head (he did not say so) like those withered specimens on women's fur pieces, with gems for eyes. Hanna preferred to wait, as she said, until it looked more like a cat than a rodent. That would take time. Out of long habit the creature crawled rather than walked.

Just living in the dark had developed, in Drrdla, faculties that most cats had learned to do without. Her eyes, for example, were not to be trusted. She relied on other, subtler signals. It was not out of the question that a room full of light would blind her as badly as total darkness. Take such a simple thing as perspective. How it was that objects, in *her* space, related to her. What was near and far, up and down. How high she could leap. How far she could fall. The blind woman, Helen Keller, had learned to live in a world that had no dimensions whatsoever. Drrdla was not so handicapped, but neither was she so smart. To make her way back to normal life she had to recover much of what she had lost, as well as discover faculties that were new to cats. If she made it, she would be a sort of cat-genius, starting from scratch. If one was fond of cats it could be depressing how dumb they were in simple situations, but it was inspiring what they could do when the going was tough. Few had ever had tougher going than Drrdla, if she proved to be tough enough.

The lyrical side of Walter's nature, not previously displayed, revealed a faculty that he had allowed to languish. Circumstance now required that he exercise it to an unusual degree, at breakfast. In these discussions Lewin had a glimpse of the rough diamond Hanna had plucked from the bed of cuckoo clocks. In these moments the knob-headed, iron-handed peasant underwent a transformation. Why not? Wasn't that just what he was pointing out? Evolution itself, he told Lewin, had surely come about in just this manner. This kind of thinking, of course, went around and around, and that was how Walter went. Around and around. Lewin watched and listened, sometimes risking what he felt to be a pertinent observation. What if this creature finally made it? Became a plain, normal cat. Both Hanna and Walter had once and for all decided not to be the victims of pets: it was pets that had people. It was pets that determined their lives. Wouldn't this cat, when it *lived* in the house, be some sort of pet? Walter said that such a prospect was so far away he hadn't given it serious consideration. One thing at a time. The thing at the moment was the basement wall.

This low cement wall, about waist-high, divided Drrdla's territory from the rest of the basement. She would come to the edge of it, no further, to nibble her fish. If Walter moved the plate to his workbench, or the floor, there it would sit through the night untouched. This wall, in short, provided her with the line that simplified decisions. From its edge she would crouch and exchange glances with Walter. What did he want? What did he now expect of *her?* This confronted Walter with a dilemma he was not in a position to answer. What *did* he want—besides just wanting her to come out? Suppose she really felt more at her ease with the life she had? Food enough, now, on the one hand: and all that privacy on the other. What—her glance seemed to ask—did he have in mind?

In Walter's opinion the problem was aggravated by the apparent increase of noise. Doors slammed. Was this something new, or had he merely not noticed it so much in the past? At his vigil in the basement these jarring blasts rattled the house like an earth tremor. Was it necessary? Hanna couldn't seem to gather what the trouble was. Had it reached the point, she asked, where entering and leaving her very own house created a disturbance? Would he like her to pad around the house barefoot, leaving her shoes at the door like a Japanese? Was it all right if she listened to music in the evening, and was awakened in the morning by her alarm? If just her living in the house disturbed his *little rodent,* perhaps she should think of taking a room elsewhere. Plainly, Walter and the cat couldn't, living, as they did, in such perfect harmony in the basement. Walter hardly knew which disturbed him more, the unpredictable and shattering slam of a door, or the tireless and deliberate way she referred to the creature as his "little rodent."

"How is Walter's little rodent?" she would ask Lewin, first making certain that Walter was within hearing. As aggravating, and even more of a nuisance, was the clattering ring of the phone. An especially loud ring had been installed so that it might be heard both upstairs and in the basement. The cat was naturally startled by the ring, and the way Walter turned and ran up the stairs. What were these calls? He was often just a moment too late to hear. Other times Hanna would like to know if there was something *they* would like at the market, fish or liver, perhaps? What could Walter do? If he allowed his irritation to show, the phone would ring ten minutes later. Both Walter and Hanna had been insistent on having an unlisted number, but now he received calls from solicitors and pollsters. The telephone company could not help

him. Hanna would not torment herself trying to learn a new number, after so many years of mastering the old one. To tell him *that*,
she phoned.

There were other things: doors were left ajar so a draft would
bang them; the thermostat was jiggled on the hot-water heater,
resulting in explosive bangs in the heating system. Lewin tried to
point out that Walter's suspicions, seen objectively, were without
foundation. Doors often slammed; anyone with a phone was
sometimes driven almost crazy by it. Circumstance—not Hanna—
had made him just a wee bit paranoid. Living in the basement, all
ears, like the cat, had given him the feeling that the house was
against him. That was almost as silly as Hanna behaving in a
jealous manner. Was she crazy?—Walter wanted to know. Jealous
of a cat? Lewin suggested that both cats and women had this lunatic
side to their natures. They were possessed, so to speak. They would
eat or not eat, hide in the darkness or spend the night wailing.
They were at once affectionate, trusting, and suspicious of every
movement. Idio-cy ruled the world of men—the personal, the separate, the distinct, et cetera—while luna-cy permeated the world
of women, their nature subject to forces, and impulses, not easily
controlled.

A student of Hanna's, Emil Lubke, who majored in German
literature and the piano, was given the key to the house so that he
could practice on the idle Fechner piano. Did Walter mind? No,
he was free to go for long walks. It took hours of patient, loving
coaxing, however, to lure the poor car, Drrdla, back to the light
after two solid hours of Rachmaninoff and Liszt. She now accepted—possibly she even needed—the merest touch of his out-
stretched hand. Her posture was wary. The tremor in her legs was
like that of a kitten with the rickets. All along her bony spine the
hairs lifted, and her ears might flatten at the slightest disturbance.
It was not unusual for her to cuff him, or with her fangs showing
make the hiss of a dragon. This involuntary behavior embarrassed
them both, but encouraged a fresh beginning. Palpable to his touch
was the muted tremor of her purr. Another thing she couldn't
help. The poor creature was torn, in Walter's opinion, between
the two great forces that move the world—including the moon.

The desire to open out, to confront what is new, and the fear that dictates withdrawal. Vulnerable. The deep fear of being vulnerable. Irresistibly she stretched toward Walter's hand, the mysterious gratification of his touch, and yet an equally compulsive force lured her back into the comforts of darkness. Walter dared not advance, nor make other moves associated with the food plate, but it was clear she *preferred,* after eating, completing her toilet while seated near him. If he remained, she would crouch and take her nap. A puzzling detail was that she always did this with her back to him, her head toward the darkness. Her ears carefully screened his movements, but it did seem a symbolic gesture. It was now Walter *and* Drrdla, against the unknown. Walter could therefore be excused the glance of witless delight he gave Lewin when she allowed him, in Lewin's presence, to scratch her ears. This silent colloquy brought to mind lovers otherwise speechless with emotion. Little wonder that Hanna never seemed to find the time to see how the pair of them were doing. Did she know? As well as she seemed to know the exact moment to startle them both out of their wits. At the electric moment that Walter's finger left the tingling chill of her nose—the phone would ring, a door would slam, or the pipes that ran along the basement ceiling would be convulsed with a pulsing throb, caused by the clever manipulation of the hot-water taps in the bathroom. If both were turned on suddenly, and full, the plumbing pounded like a sick monster. The cat, Drrdla, would disappear. Walter would sit there in the dark, his head in his hands.

If he continued to sit there long enough, however, he would hear, in the shelter of the steps, the drag of her tongue on a patch of her pelt, a sign that she had recovered and in no way held him responsible. He supplemented her diet with wheat-germ oil cunningly smeared on fresh chicken livers. She preferred canned milk to fresh cream, and liked nothing better than to gnaw on colossal-size non-pitted olives. She growled like a tiger when her teeth struck the stone. An olive rolled across the floor and caught her, so to speak, with her guard down. She leaped and pounced. Very peculiar behavior for a sick cat. Equally intimate and peculiar was her lust for the rind of a melon. Walter had left his breakfast slice on the step to gallop up the stairs and answer the phone: when he returned the rind had been chewed away at both ends. Other specialties included peanut butter, cream cheese on a bagel, and cold matzo-ball soup. Anything but mice, was Hanna's comment. There *were* a few mice—they rustled wastebasket paper and ate the nuts out of the candy on Hanna's desk—but Walter pointed out this would be taken care of when Drrdla had the run of the house. The remark slipped out. He hadn't meant to go so far, so fast. Hanna made no comment, but a day later he found the basement door propped open. She picked the following weekend to repot most of her plants. This took all of Saturday, and with the racket and confusion Walter saw nothing at all of Drrdla. Hanna also filled the house with fall leaves and dried arrangements, the doors slamming as she went in and out, not to mention the search for bowls and containers in all corners of the basement. Walter himself took one of his long, joyless walks, a McIntosh apple swelling his pocket. Now and then he could hear, wind-borne, the roar of the crowd at the Army-Navy game. The lights were on in the house when he returned, and the door of the kitchen was still propped open. To air out the smell of fertilizer two kitchen windows were propped up from the bottom. Hanna lay soaking in the tub. Walter put out a fresh plate of food for the cat while he scrambled some eggs for himself. Eggs too she liked. But that night she touched nothing on her plate. Walter coaxed her for an hour, then he took the flashlight and probed the corners she usually retired to. Nothing doing. He went from room to room and from the top of the house to the bottom. He discussed the disappearance for some time with Lewin. However improbably, it was possible that she had come up the stairs to the kitchen and gone through the door or one of the windows. What else? Walter spent the evening circling the block. It was not one of those streets with alleys, so all he could do was stop and peer up the driveways, making those sounds that caused other cats to howl and strange dogs to bark.

The following day Walter moved a cot from the basement to the kitchen. If he heard a cat mewing at the door he would be there, handy, to let the creature in. Part of each night Walter might make a tour of the house. Lying there on the cot he would think of a closet, or some nook or cranny a cat might crawl into, and having thought of it he would have to get up and look. He came up with the bizarre idea that she might have gone up the fireplace. He felt it explained the sprinkle of soot he often heard at night. Naturally, it meant no more fires were started, and at night a dish of food was left on the hearth, just in case. How was one to know just where she might be, until she reappeared? The smell of fish permeated the house. Walter felt obliged to change it daily, making sure it was fresh.

Hanna complained to Lewin that Walter's prowling deprived her of sleep. Her own door she kept locked, with a rug at the bottom, unless she heard Lewin passing. On an equal-time basis, Lewin felt obliged to listen to her side of the story. That too was a long one. Hanna had grown thinner, or rather leaner, but it seemed more appropriate to her role. Her fingers were always nervously laced together, or gripping the arm or the back of a chair. When she spoke to Walter she would always get to her feet. With a chair between them—her hands gripping its back—she would read him one of her "lectures." She was relieved, she told him, that the poor little rodent had managed to escape. It was not being saved for itself at all, but was being held a captive creature by Walter. What the poor cat hungered for was not food, but the company of its own kind. If that was not true it would still be in the basement fattening on chicken liver and Walter's attention. What it wanted, and finally got, was a chance to escape.

Lewin very much admired the way Walter would sit and listen to Hanna as if he felt he had it coming. Walter said it did her good to "blow her top." He put in his time fencing off those areas in the basement where a cat might hide. The night the cat came home Hanna was in bed with a slight flu. Lewin went down alone to the door of the kitchen, where he watched, unobserved, the shabby gray-and-white cat gulping up canned mackerel. Was it Drrdla? Spotted gray-and-white cats look pretty much alike. Her splotched white patches were uniformly soiled. Lewin seemed to recall the ears as larger, the tail longer and thinner, but in point of fact he had seldom seen her. His picture of the cat had been formed by Walter's numberless descriptions.

"It's her," Walter said, putting his finger to her head. "I can feel her mew." It was a fact that the cat proved to be curious about the basement, and seemed responsive to the name Drrdla. A final proof would have been a strip of melon rind, but melons were not in season. Walter had also stopped buying the large unpitted olives and had only the green ones, stuffed with pimentos, one of the few things she had tried to bury after sniffing it.

A place was prepared for the cat in the kitchen—a box for sleeping and a litter box for business—but when Walter came down in the morning she was gone. He searched the house. The cat was finally found asleep at the foot of Hanna's unmade bed. After eating, it was back at her door, where it howled until it gained entrance. There it was when Hanna returned from school, and she thought nothing of it. "Hello, cat," she said. She was not surprised that so smart a cat would rather sleep with her than alone in the kitchen. Why not? It merely showed how sensible she was. The litter box was then moved to Hanna's room, since the cat also preferred to spend the day there. The windows were warm and sunny. The place she loved to sleep was on old theme papers in Hanna's wastebasket. Nor did it come as a surprise to Hanna that the cat put on weight in an alarming manner, or chose the top drawer of her bureau—the one with old stockings—to bear and nurse a litter of four kittens, two of them black. During the long day Hanna was not in the room they could be heard doing what four kittens like to do. Walter was kept busy emptying the litter box, and trying to spade up frozen earth in the snow-covered garden. The names of the kittens were Eenie, Meenie, Miney and Moe. Miney and Moe were black. Hanna sometimes carried Moe to the college, in her muff, where he slept in her desk drawer, or played with an eraser. The mother cat, once her work was done, proved to be loose and immoral in her ways. She would howl from room to room, and from floor to floor, until Walter got up and let her out. A night or two later she would howl from door to door until he let her in. Why didn't Hanna complain? She seemed to think it perfectly normal behavior. Once a cat had learned what real life was like, what did Walter expect? Hadn't it been Walter's idea in the first place to help her to develop her faculties? To restore her to grace? Like some people, she had lived in the darkness so long the light of day almost made her giddy. Hanna knew how she felt.

Hanna was scandalized when Walter brought up the idea of having the mother cat fixed. What would he think of next?—she wanted to know. He helped her weigh the cat on the bathroom scale for the first alarming signs of increase. At that point she will need more riboflavin, as it says in the book. Walter was sometimes up four or five times a night letting her in and then letting her out. It is perfectly plain she now abuses his concern: what can he do? The sound of his padding up and down the stairs keeps Lewin awake. For some time Lewin has been sleeping in a larger bed, and it is Hanna who lies there beside him. Sometimes she giggles. Other times she laughs hysterically. It was this sound that led Lewin to think she was sobbing, and why he opened the door to her room. She beckoned to him. Catlike, he proved open to suggestion. If a laughing fit comes on her late at night she controls it by pressing her face to her pillow. The howling of the toms will bring a flood of laugh tears to her eyes. It is Hanna's back that Lewin feels he knows the best. After her pleasure, like a cat, she shows him her back. Lewin lets his fingers glide along her spine, which seems to him as bony as that of Drrdla, the fuzz of hair along it rising, the back arching, as when Walter first extended his hand toward the dark. If he had then withdrawn it, an unawakened, famished cat still would be captive in the basement, and neither Walter nor Lewin would have on his hands a female creature awakened to life.

1969

Green Grass, Blue Sky, White House

As I sit here, Floyd's mother mows the lawn. The whine of the mower can be heard above the noise of her grandchildren at their horseplay. If I close my eyes the sounds are like those we see in comic strips, WHAM! BAM! POWIE!, rising like balloons, or exploding like firecrackers. All in fun, of course. They are healthy, growing animals and have to work off their energies somehow. Why not with the mower? Mrs. Collins likes to mow her own lawn. Any day but Sunday, either Franklin DeSpain, or Lyle, or even Melanie would pop up from somewhere and do it for her, but Reuben DeSpain insists that his children keep the Sabbath holy. The Lord rested, and so do the DeSpains.

A farm girl to begin with, Mrs. Collins likes to get her hands on a machine that works and work it. The blades spin free when she nears a tree and uses short, choppy strokes. The whine of the mower makes its way around the house, and on the long run at the back it is almost gone. It stops when twigs from the elms catch between the blades. I can tell she likes to work around the tree trunks where the short, hard strokes set the blades to whirring. That's a sound from my boyhood. The whirring blades of a mower pushed by somebody else. I would wait for the thump as it hit the house at the end of its run. People in this country once might have been divided into those who knew that sound and those who didn't; those who liked it and those it made almost sick. All sum-

mer long, freshly cut lawn grass weighted the cuffs of my father's
pants.

One of Franklin DeSpain's boys walks by with a skateboard
he carries around looking for sidewalks. Not all the streets in
Ordway have them. The lawns slope down to bleed into the weeds,
and the weeds into the crumbling blacktop. Most of the walks in
town are of brick heaved into waves and troughs by tree roots.
The only walking people do is from the door at the back of the
house to the car parked in the drive.

The town of Ordway, in Missouri, is one where no line is
drawn between what is rural and what is urban. A cow is tethered
in the lot facing the square, where the sidewalk bristles with parking meters. I've seen no pigs, but the older residents, like Floyd's
mother, might keep a goat, or a cow, or a few fenced chickens.
Everything is here to make the good life possible. Mrs. Collins at
one point gave up the chickens but Mr. Collins missed their cackling. The silence disturbed his rest in the morning. If she forgets
to collect the eggs, they soon have an old hen with a fresh batch
of chicks. Almost an acre of lawn surrounds the house, and there
is sometimes snow in the yard till Easter, the first spears of spring
grass pale as winter wheat. At the back it's hard to tell where the
lawn ends and the fields begin.

One thing I have learned is that small-town people have a
pallor you can seldom find in the city. If they roll up a sleeve, or
tuck up a pants leg, the bit of skin that shows is white as a flour
sack. Mrs. Collins wears a pair of Floyd's unlaced tennis sneakers
on her bare feet. His sweaters also fit her. Her overalls, however,
once belonged to Mr. Collins, and the seat and knees are patched
with pieces of quilting. That makes for more comfort when she
kneels to weed, and less dampness when she sits to cut greens. A
faded gingham sunbonnet sits back on her head to let the sun
warm her face.

In the fall the yard is so bright with leaves Mrs. Collins tells
me it's almost painful to look at. They have to pull the shades at
the windows to sleep at night. Both a fact of that sort or a death
in the family Mrs. Collins reports with an appealing smile. If my
eyes are on her face I often miss the gist of what she is saying.

Her expression remains the same: a beaming smile, an affable, open good nature. If I hear her laughing, it is usually at herself. This can be disconcerting when it signals something is wrong. She laughed, her daughter tells me, when she fell and broke her hip. Of Scotch descent, with a long Quaker family background, Mrs. Collins believes "the slings and arrows of misfortunes," as she says, are as much to be experienced as anything else. Nothing has diminished her appetite for life.

The Collins house is *substantial,* as my father would have said, with a run-around porch that is tilted like a ship's deck, the spacious lawn shaded by sycamores and elms. There's a cleared spot at the back, hard as blacktop, where the trash and the leaves are burned. The two-board gap in the fence indicates a shortcut that connects the Collins house with the one across the alley. Her daughter Ruth lives there, but Ruth's three teen-age boys spend most of their time in the Collins kitchen, or roughhousing at the back of the yard. A trough is worn into the yard where a tire swings from the limb of an elm.

The Collins kitchen is big, and uncluttered with modern conveniences. Mrs. Collins makes my toast under the flame in the oven, then scrapes the char off at the sink. She does not believe in anything, as she says, "that you have to plug in." The crackle of her long hair, worn in a loose bun at her neck, is her daily assurance that her health is in order and her battery is charged. In the house she wears a simple gray frock with touches of faded lace at the wrists and throat. I've no idea if she knows how much it does for her corn-yellow hair. She prefers to stand, rather than sit, her hip inclined on the stove rail or the sink, with one of her brown freckled hands holding a loose wad of her apron cupped in her palm. She tests heat and flavor with her fingers, spits on the skillet before making hotcakes. Into the first pot of percolator coffee she puts a pinch of salt and one fresh eggshell, preferably white. I'm told that the house swarmed with cats until her daughter Ruth married and took most of them with her. Mrs. Collins says, "I don't mind having pets, but I don't like the pets having people," meaning Mr. Collins and his old dog Ruby, now dead three years. Every day in his life, which proved to be a long one, Ruby would walk

Mr. Collins to the railroad crossing, look up and down in both directions, then lead him across if it was safe. When Mr. Collins stopped making the walk, Ruby went under the house porch and refused to come out. It was the end of the run for both Ruby and the St. Louis & Troy.

Although it is fifteen years since a train entered Ordway, Mr. Collins still wears the striped overalls preferred by trainmen, and one of the high-crowned, long-billed brakeman's hats. This he leaves on his head until Mrs. Collins says, "Papa, your cap." All members of the family speak of him as Papa, but not often to his face. His skin is smooth, as if dampened and then stretched on his skull. The abundance of his hair gives the impression that his head is not fully developed, or with time has shrunk. His pale blue eyes have a focus just beyond the object of his attention. Before speaking he nervously fingers the bill of his cap. The two subjects Mr. Collins never loses sight of are Norman Thomas and the old dog Ruby. A picture of Ruby, a gourd-shaped little terrier with his head almost swallowed by his thickening neck, is among the family portraits on the sewing machine. More recent snapshots, featuring the grandchildren, Waldo, Luther, and Clarence, are on the piano. Waldo and Luther take after their father, a huge, affable man in the road-construction business. The younger boy, Clarence, is small-boned like his mother, but almost six feet tall. He has grown too fast, and his movements are those of a boy on stilts. The boys like to roughhouse and can usually be heard clopping up and down the stairs of the Collins house, chased by Clarence, or mauling like dogs at the back of the yard. Waldo has picked up such lingo as "Sock it to me!" supplemented with cries of "Wham! Bam! Powie!" The trouble starts when Clarence, wearing one of Melanie's aprons, helps her wash and dry the dishes.

It is a point of pride with Mrs. Collins that she has no keys; the house is never locked. Back in the Depression, when they took in roomers, the keys disappeared in the pockets of strangers, and Mrs. Collins has never troubled to replace them. Mr. Collins pads through my room, while I sleep, because it has always been his way to the bathroom. If he took another route, strange to his habits, he might easily stumble or bump into something. To close a door so that it clicks is to imply that you have something to hide. It has been years since the bathroom door actually latched shut. If it is closed, the draft nudges it open. During the night the light provides a beacon, and the drip in the tub is like the tick of a clock. Unless the bathroom door stands open wide, it is safe to assume there is someone behind it. Most members of the family make a characteristic sound when steps approach. Mrs. Collins hums, Melanie turns on a faucet in the bowl and lets it run. Mr. Collins, however, is absolutely silent. He sits dreaming on the stool, his brown hands on his white knees, his gaze on the leaf-clogged gutters of the porch visible from the bathroom window. An intruder need not disturb him. The boys shower while he sits there. Privacy can be had by going up one floor and using the small water closet, but the flush of the water when the chain is pulled seems designed to clean out miles of plumbing, and burps in all the sinks.

If this were not Sunday, or if the grass had been mowed, Mrs. Collins would be seated in the porch rocker. It is of wood, the rungs turned by hand, the cane seat so new it resembles plastic. Layers of green and brown paint are visible where Mrs. Collins grips the chair arms. She takes a strong grip when she rocks, as if she feared the chair might take off. The spreading legs are reinforced with baling wire still fuzzy with the hair of the Collins cats. They used to retire there to get away from Ruby, and one of the toms had his tail amputated. Never again did he set foot on the Collins porch.

At one time as many as eight or ten children ran in and out of the house, and sagged the rails of the porches. The chain swing had to be taken down to keep them from wearing a hole in the clapboards. They *had* to rock it sideways, or swing it so high the whole house leaned one way, then the other. The hooks for the swing are still there in the ceiling, but who would swing if they put it back up? Not the new generation. The porch stoop used to sag with the DeSpain children, who were too polite to use the hammock. They were noisy, but they had breeding and refused to do a lick of work on Sunday. Mr. Collins would torment them by offering them money to run down and buy him his White Owl cigar. The other days of the week they had to offer to do it for nothing. For every biscuit that was eaten at the Collins table, two biscuits went out the door with Rosemary DeSpain, Reuben's wife, along with what she loosely defined as "leftovers." She in turn donated her coffee stamps during the war, when Mr. Collins began to suffer his withdrawal headaches. He was accustomed to eight strong cups a day, and that was what he got. Sunday being the day of rest, the DeSpains like to spend it where they could watch other people work. Rosemary is gone now, but Mrs. Collins tells me she got up early to sit in the Collins kitchen, watching Ruth and Mrs. Collins prepare the Sunday meal. In case she ever had to do it, she wanted to be sure she knew how it was done.

Reuben DeSpain tells me that his wife was black and blue as a new stovepipe, but their children and grandchildren are best described as "golden oak." DeSpain claims that it comes from his French and Castilian ancestry. The boys have their father's light copper tan, but Melanie is so pale out-of-town people take her for an Italian, like Sophia Loren. She has Sophia's big, half-popped eyes and wide, full mouth. Mrs. Collins likes to tell how Floyd would ask her why his own tan peeled and Melanie's didn't. Unless she smiles, or talks, her impassive expression appears to be sullen. Melanie is inclined to be accident-prone, and wears Band-aids on her fingers and arms for stove burns. The burn soon heals, but the print of the adhesive leaves a visible pattern. Mrs. Collins says to her, "Melanie, that stove bite you again?" Melanie's chores are to cook, tidy up, make the beds, and hand-wash Floyd's dress shirts in case he dirtied any. She leaves the ironing board standing, blocking the pantry, to show that a woman's work is never done. She smokes Camels as she works, dropping the ashes on the ironing and between the sheets.

"One day you're going to burn this house down," Mrs. Collins says, and both women laugh. Melanie leaves the butts resting on the ashtrays, the edges of the bureaus, window sills, and cereal cartons, or they slow-burn holes in the oilcloth or char holes in the plastic soap dishes, or burn down till they tilt off something and drop to the floor. When Melanie laughs she turns her back and you see the top of her head rather than the roof of her mouth.

She takes shame in her dark laughter, and wipes it off her mouth before she turns to face me. Around the house, as a dust cap, she wears a shower hat in which she stores her matches and pack of Camels. Thinking up things to keep Melanie "busy" is one of Mrs. Collins's endless chores. While Melanie wanders around tidying up, Mrs. Collins prepares for her the well-balanced lunch she never gets at home. Left to herself Melanie will eat nothing but creamed canned corn and chipped beef in a white sauce. She loves diet cola spiked with a spoonful of chocolate syrup. The two women eat together, discussing samples of cloth Mrs. Collins receives from a store in Chicago. She has in mind a dress for herself and a new winter coat for Melanie.

One of Floyd's chores, when he was at home, was to pick up Melanie in the morning and get her home to make her father's supper in the evening. On arriving, Melanie calls out, "Here I am, Mrs. Collins," and waits until she is told what to do. They both have a cup of coffee while they plan her day's work.

"What'll I do now?" is perhaps the one thing that Mrs. Collins hears the most. Finding work to do for Franklin, Lyle, and Melanie gets Mrs. Collins up early and often keeps her awake. "Before I ever make a move," Mrs. Collins tells me, "the first thing I think of is Franklin and Lyle." They don't like to be idle, but they like her to tell them what to do. Mrs. Collins has never gone to some of the places she would like to, because the DeSpains take so much looking after. Especially Reuben, who can't stand to be idle now his wife is dead. This being Sunday, however, he is willing to sit in front of the barn under a new-painted sign that reads:

REUBEN DESPAIN
I buy junk and sell antiques

He doesn't buy junk, of course, he gets it all free, but one of his clients thought the remark would make a good sign. DeSpain came to Ordway in the early years of the Depression, when some of the whites, as well as the "coloreds," took their pay in milk and eggs and leftovers. His children wore the clothes the Collins children grew out of. He never complained. For twenty-five years he walked a horse and wagon—the horse wearing a bonnet to ward off sunstroke—up one street and down the other, collecting whatever people had to throw away, or believed they had worn out. After the war it began to add up. The software, so called, Rosemary DeSpain cleaned up and sold once a year in the Methodist basement; the hardware Reuben DeSpain stowed away in the Collins barn. The government didn't want it, you couldn't eat it or sell it, and it wouldn't burn. To make room for such stuff one of the Collins cars had to sit out in the yard, splattered with bird droppings, or in the freezing winter weather over one of the grease pits in the Collins service station. The other car, a Model T Ford with a brass radiator and a California top, had become so old it belonged in the barn as part of the junk. It had never actually been *given* to Reuben DeSpain but, as Floyd liked to say, it had been *ceded* to him. It had been *thought* to be junk, and if it was junk it belonged to DeSpain. A gentleman in Des Moines has an option on the car, and pays five dollars a month for DeSpain to store it for him. He doesn't seem to mind that the price of the car goes up and up. Two or three times a year a woman from St. Louis comes over in her station wagon for DeSpain's old bottles, beaded lampshades, wall and mantel clocks, oil lamps, and old records. A Philadelphia firm that makes stoves will buy anything good DeSpain lays a hand on, including the old Mayflower coke burner he warms his house with over the winter. It has a "sold" tag on it, but he is free to use it while he is still around. There's more people than DeSpain can keep track of to collect the buttons he snips off old clothes. Mrs. Collins has explained, and DeSpain has grasped, that as money gets cheaper his junk gets dearer. He lets it sit. DeSpain won't sell his records or his clocks to people who impress him as careless in such matters. Clocks run for him. Once off the premises they stop. There's an account at the bank for Reuben DeSpain that will pass on to his heirs if they can bother to be troubled. Money is something they don't understand, and have always left to Floyd. Besides Melanie, Franklin, and Lyle, there are Franklin's three children. In the mid-fifties Franklin, a year older than Lyle, took fifty dollars from the bank and went to Chicago, where he planned a new start. He left in June and was back in October. A few years later Lyle went to St. Louis, where he enrolled in a Peace Corps program. He learned to type, and returned with a machine on which he still owed thirty-eight dollars. Both boys were noncommittal, but according to Mrs. Collins they were shocked by people's behavior. They were also homesick, and tired of people who called light-colored boys black.

Finding work for them to do was a strain for Mrs. Collins until Floyd thought of installing a car wash at the back of the service station. Running the station is a family enterprise, and all members of the family contribute to it. When Floyd was at home, he ran it; and Ruth's husband runs it in the slack season for road work; and there is always Mrs. Collins, or one of Ruth's boys, to help at the pumps on a busy weekend. The car wash occupies space once used for parking, and does a good business with college boys from Mason City. Franklin and Lyle are good workers, but they seem to lack initiative. They work better when Mrs. Collins is around, and they like her to handle the accounts. Franklin's two eldest boys are very good with a wax job, but it doesn't help matters that one has the name *Floyd*. This seemed very touching when Franklin's son was born, but it led to nothing but complications. When someone hollered "Floyd," both Floyds answered. The result was that Floyd Collins would seldom answer when his name was called. He didn't mean to be rude, or insist on *Mr.* Collins, but what could he do?

From where I am seated I can't see but I can hear the hiss and spray of steam at the car wash, and the sound of the gong as a car pulls into the station. Until just recently Reuben DeSpain took care of such things as the tires, windshields, etc., but all that stooping and bending didn't help his back any, and his right arm, especially his "windshield elbow," seemed to get worse. All he had to do was pick up a rag and he would feel the twinge of pain. Mrs. Collins thought he'd better just sit and take it easy, before it got so he couldn't use his arm to eat with. There's nothing harder for Reuben to do than just sit, but that's now what he does. His platform rocker, covered with plum-colored velvet once popular on tram seats, sits under a beach umbrella in the dappled shade at the front of the barn. The arms are too low, the back is too high, and the angle is all wrong for comfort, but DeSpain has never lost his taste for elegance. His ancestors, by published account, were influential pirates and patrons of the arts. He has the nose, forehead, and melancholy eyes of the clergy painted by El Greco. He also has the style. If DeSpain is asked if he has something or other, he will reply, "I shall endeavor to ascertain it," then go and look. For seven years he was one of the servants close to Governor Huey Long. He considers the Governor one of the country's great men. Five weeks following the assassination, DeSpain and his family, on their way to Chicago, were towed into Ordway by a Mason City milkman. The car had broken down. It proved to be an Essex, of a year and a model for which parts were no longer available. Mr. Collins let them camp in the railroad station where they could use the lavatories and the drinking fountain, while Reuben DeSpain considered his next move. That proved to be into the barn behind the Collins house. In a few weeks' time Mrs. Collins hardly knew how she had ever got along without him. "Ma'am," he said, "all Reuben DeSpain aims to do is please."

Some of the younger generation think of DeSpain as a swami, thanks to his remarkable elegance of speech. He need say no more than "Consider the lilies—" to gather a group of teen-age loafers around him. On warm sultry days, between his neck and his collar he slips a clean white kerchief scented with insect repellent. He claims it keeps him free of pests while he naps. He wears a carpenter's apron with the big nail pockets full of unsorted parking-meter pennies. He gets them from the Ordway police department. Sorting them carefully by hand, he turns up the coins he sells to a collector in Independence. Real copper pennies are so close to DeSpain's color you feel they got it from the rubbing he gives them to bring out the dates.

On weekdays you can see Franklin or Lyle seated at the barn door tinkering with something that doesn't work. There is never an end. Just putting up the house screens and taking them down takes two or three weeks. Reuben DeSpain sits in his chair brushing off the rust with a whisk broom, his gesture that of a railroad porter dusting the lapels of Huey Long. In the winter he sits inside the barn and mends the holes. Mrs. Collins likes to feed her own chickens and collect the eggs (when there are any), but without

Lyle around to milk her, the cow, Bessie, won't give her milk. In the spring the sheds need to be fumigated and the fourteen trees on the lot pruned and sprayed. In the dry spells everything has to be watered, which means dragging the hoses from faucet to faucet, the pressure sometimes getting so low it won't operate the sprinkler: Franklin's boys will have to water the tomato plants with the watering can. Both Franklin and Lyle dislike spray nozzles and prefer to stand, using their thumbs, soaking up the water with their shoes and pants legs. When a toilet bowl in the house is flushed, the pressure drops and the outside water goes off.

Inside the house the drains get clogged and water stands for days in the second-floor tub. Periodically roots close the lines to the cesspool although the nearest tree is forty-eight feet away: what a root will do in its search for water defies belief. The lawn grass grows so thick right over the cesspool Mrs. Collins has to run at it with the mower, but she will not cut or use table greens from that part of the yard. Melanie has been warned not to do it, either, but somehow she forgets.

I've noticed the whole house shakes when the boys come clopping down the stairs. The pigeons kept by a neighbor, in a roost on his roof, go up on the sky like a cloud of smoke. There's always one that doesn't seem to get the swing of it, his wings flapping like a loose fan belt. Off where I can't see them, but I can hear them, Waldo and Luther are starting their horseplay. They go through the kitchen, slamming the screen, then clop around the house like cantering horses. Waldo is the one who strips the leaves off the lilac bushes as he makes the turns. These daily runs have not worn away the grass, but they have firmed it down so that it has a different color and texture, like the flattened wale of corduroy or the plush seat of a chair. Waldo is always first, a step or two ahead of Luther, and Clarence trails along like a caboose. If Luther stops suddenly, dropping to his knees, Clarence will stumble over him as if he were a bench. He never seems to learn. The green smears of grass will not wash off his elbows and bony knees. They all make about two hooting circles of the house, then Waldo heads for the clearing at the back. Where the tire swing dangles from the limb of an elm, he grasps the role to keep from collapsing. He can't seem to stop laughing. Luther is so winded he trips on his own feet, and sprawls out on his face. He lies there giggling as if he were being tickled to death. Clarence comes along so many moments later he seems part of another scene. I first thought he had tired and run down, like a spring-wound toy. But he had merely paused to pick up a length of clothesline. He straddles Luther and flails at him with the rope—but it's too long. He can't bring it around with the proper snap. Waldo is so winded he can hardly breathe, but he hoarsely yells, "Sock it to 'im! Sock it to 'im!" Clarence tries to. The sound is that of someone beating a carpet with a small switch. Luther will not stop giggling, and Clarence cries, "I'm going to kill you! You hear me?" Waldo is still hooting, but he has sagged to drape his arms around the tire. In that position Clarence is able to flail him as if he were a slave clamped in the stocks or tied to a whipping post.

From behind the house Mrs. Collins appears holding aloft one of her leather-palmed cotton work gloves. She wages it as she comes, with loping, silent strides, to where Clarence towers over Waldo. No word is spoken. Waldo and Luther are hooting, but it appears to be a scene on silent film. All my life, or so it seems, I have watched roughhousing boys interrupted in their play by the long arm of Tom Sawyer's Aunt Polly. With a practiced gesture she grips Clarence, wheels him about, and slaps him (POWIE!) with the glove. He straightens to stand like a machine with the power switched off. From his dangling hand she takes the rope and shortens it to give him a slap across the buttocks. With a hoot, he takes off. In an instant he is followed by Waldo, who lunges to avoid the swipe she gives him. Luther is last; he goes off howling with a gleeful shriek. I hear the screen door to the kitchen open and slam, and then the clop of their feet on the front-hall stairs. The house rocks. I feel it like an earth tremor in the boards of the porch. After a bout of such horseplay all three boys like to take long showers with their clothes on, then come down and sit in the lawn swing to dry off.

Mrs. Collins stands, her face to the sky, watching the whirring flight of the neighbor's pigeons. The disturbance has flushed her face with color; she idly slaps the shortened length of rope on her thigh. "My, how we all miss Floyd!" she says, coming toward me, and her smile is that of a priestess at the close of a ceremony. She feels better, the boys feel better, and she would like to assure me I should feel better. What is a little violence in the larger ceremony of innocence? She turns a gaze toward Mr. Collins, who stands in the garden, leaning on a hand plow. His straw hat is wider than his shoulders, and the wide limp brim rests on his ears. He looks more like a boy daydreaming at his chores than an old man resting. Nor does he move from his reverie until he hears the whirring blades of the mower.

On my drive down from Chicago (I was given ten days to look into the Collins case) I stopped in St. Louis for a talk with Floyd. They're holding him there, as we say, for observation. He's a good-looking, rustically handsome boy with his mother's jaw and prominent features. I see they suit a man's face better than they do hers. He has the casual, cool manner of most young people, and lets his hair grow long at the back. While we talked he preferred to sit on the floor with his knees drawn up. Off and on he toyed with a piece of cellophane from his pack of Camel cigarettes, blowing on it softly as he held it pressed, like a blade of grass, between his thumbs. The sound emitted is high and shrill, like a trapped insect or a fingernail on glass. I once made such a sound, or tried to, blowing through a dandelion stem.

To the President of the United States Floyd Collins wrote: *I am obliged to inform you your life is threatened. I am a reasonable man. It is reason that compels me to take this action. I propose to take your one life to spare the tens of thousands of innocent men, women, and children. Please stop this war or accept the consequences.*

I liked the "please." It showed his responsible Quaker breeding and will also help to commute his sentence, since no shot was fired. During my stay in Ordway, Mrs. Collins has treated me like "one of the family," and that is how I feel. One of the family. Some, if not all, of the emotions Floyd Collins has felt. I see a cow grazing, Reuben DeSpain napping, a blue sky towers above me and green grass surrounds me, and inside the white house I hear boys at their horseplay, training to be men.

"I raised Floyd to believe anything is possible," Mrs. Collins says. As it is, of course. Here in Ordway anything is possible. Not necessarily what Mrs. Collins has in mind, or Floyd has in mind, or even the town of Ordway has in mind, but what a dream of the good life, and reasonable men, make inevitable.

1969

A Fight Between a
White Boy and a Black Boy
in the Dusk of
a Fall Afternoon
in Omaha, Nebraska

How did it start? If there is room for speculation, it lies in how to end it. Neither the white boy nor the black boy gives it further thought. They stand, braced off, in the cinder-covered schoolyard, in the shadow of the darkened red-brick building. Eight or ten smaller boys circle the fighters, forming sides. A white boy observes the fight upside down as he hangs by his knees from the iron rail of the fence. A black girl pasting cutouts of pumpkins in the windows of the annex seems unconcerned. Fights are not so unusual. Halloween and pumpkins come but once a year.

At the start of the fight there was considerable jeering and exchange of formidable curses. The black boy was much better at this part of the quarrel and jeered the feebleness of his opponent's remarks. The white boy lacked even the words. His experience with taunts and scalding invective proved to be remarkably shallow. Twice the black boy dropped his arms as if they were useless against such a potato-mouthed, stupid adversary. Once he laughed, showing the coral roof of his mouth. In the shadow of the school little else stood out clearly for the white boy to strike at. The black boy did not have large whites to his eyes, or pearly white teeth. In the late afternoon light he made a poor target except for the shirt that stood out against the fence that closed in the school. He had rolled up the sleeves and opened the collar so that he could breathe easier and fight better. His black bare feet are the exact color of the cinder yard.

The white boy is a big, hulking fellow, large for his age. It is not clear what it might be, since he has been in the same grade for three years. The bottom board has been taken from the drawer of his desk to allow for his knees. Something said about that may have started the quarrel, or the way he likes to suck on toy train wheels. (He blows softly and wetly through the hole, the wheel at the front of his mouth.) But none of that is clear; all that is known is that he stands like a boxer, his head ducked low, his huge fists doubled before his face. He stands more frontally than sidewise, as if uncertain which fist to lead with. As a rule he wrestles. He would much rather wrestle than fight with his fists. Perhaps he refused to wrestle with a black boy, and *that* could be the problem. One never knows. Who ever knows for sure what starts a fight?

The black boy's age hardly matters and it doesn't show. All that shows clearly is his shirt and the way he stands. His head looks small because his shoulders are so wide. He has seen pictures of famous boxers and stands with his left arm stretched out before him as if approaching something in the darkness. His right arm, cocked, he holds as if his chest pained him. Both boys are hungry, scared, and waiting for the other one to give up.

The white boy is afraid of the other one's blackness, and the black boy hates and fears whiteness. Something of their mutual fear is now shared by those who are watching. One of the small black boys hoots like an Indian and takes off. One of the white boys has a pocketful of marbles he dips his hand into and rattles. This was distracting when the fight first started, and he was asked to take his hands out of his pockets. Now it eases the strain of the silence.

The need to take sides has also dwindled, and the watchers have gathered with the light behind them, out of their eyes. They say "Come on!" the way you say "Sic 'em," not caring which dog.

A pattern has emerged which the two fighters know, but it is not yet known to the watchers. Nobody is going to win. The dilemma is how nobody is going to lose. It has early been established that the black boy will hit the white boy on the head with a sound like splitting a melon—but it's the white boy who moves forward, the black boy who moves back. It isn't clear if the white boy, or any of the watchers, perceives the method in this tactic. Each step backward the black boy takes he is closer to home, and nearer to darkness.

In time they cross the cinder-covered yard to the narrow steps going down to the sidewalk. There the fight is delayed while a passing adult, a woman with a baby sitting up in its carriage, tells them to stop acting like children, and asks their names to inform their teachers. The black boy's name is Eustace Beecher. The white boy's name is Emil Hrdlic, or something like that. He's a real saphead, and not at all certain how it is spelled. When the woman leaves, they return to their fighting and go along the fronts of darkened houses. Dogs bark. Little dogs, especially, enjoy a good fight.

The black boy has changed his style of fighting so that his bleeding nose doesn't drip on his shirt. The white boy has switched around to give his cramped, cocked arm a rest. The black boy picks up support from the fact that he doesn't take advantage of this situation. One reason might be that his left eye is almost closed. When he stops to draw a shirtsleeve across his face, the white boy does not leap forward and strike him. It's a good fight. They have learned what they can do and what they can't do.

At the corner lit up by the bug-filled streetlamp they lose about half of their seven spectators. It's getting late and dark. You can smell the bread baking on the bakery draft. The light is better for the fighters now than the watchers, who see the two figures only in profile. It's not so easy anymore to see which one is black and which one is white. Sometimes the black boy, out of habit, takes a step backward, then has to hop forward to his proper position. The hand he thrusts out before him is limp at the wrist, as if he had just dropped something unpleasant. The white boy's shirt, once blue in color, shines like a slicker on his sweaty back. The untied laces of his shoes are broken from the way he is always stepping on them. He is the first to turn his head and check the time on the bakery clock.

Behind the black boy the street enters the Negro section. Down there, for two long blocks, there is no light. A gas streetlamp can be seen far at the end, the halo around it swimming with insects. One of the two remaining fight watchers whistles shrilly, then enters the bakery to buy penny candy. There's a gum-ball machine that sometimes returns your penny, but it takes time, and you have to shake it.

The one spectator left to watch this fight stands revealed in the glow of the bakery window. One pocket is weighted with marbles; the buckles of his britches are below his knees. He watches the fighters edge into the darkness where the white shirt of the black boy is like an object levitated at a séance. Nothing else can be seen. Black boy and white boy are swallowed up. For a moment one can hear the shuffling feet of the white boy; then that, too, dissolves into darkness. The street is a tunnel with a lantern gleaming far at its end. The last fight watcher stands as if paralyzed until the rumble of a passing car can be felt through the soles of his shoes, tingling the blood in his feet. Behind him the glow of the sunset reddens the sky. He goes toward it on the run, a racket of marbles, his eyes fixed on the FORD sign beyond the school building, where there is a hollow with a shack used by ice skaters under which he can crawl and peer out like a cat. When the streetlights cast more light he will go home.

Somewhere, still running, there is a white boy who saw all of this and will swear to it; otherwise, nothing of what he saw remains. The Negro section, the bakery on the corner, the red-brick school with one second-floor window (the one that opens out on the fire escape) outlined by the chalk dust where they slapped the erasers— all of that is gone, the earth leveled and displaced to accommodate the ramps of the new freeway. The cloverleaf approaches look great from the air. It saves the driving time of those headed east or west. Omaha is no longer the gateway to the West, but the plains remain, according to one traveler, a place where his wife still sleeps in the seat while he drives through the night.

1970

Fiona

In England, where Fiona felt free, she would tie the sleeves of a sweater about her waist, fill the pockets of her tunic with Fig Newtons, then clop for hours through a landscape green as the sea and almost as wet. She loved the pelt of rain on her hair, the splatter of it on her face. This rain did not pour. It hung like a vapor that settled on her skin and smoked in her lungs. As she trotted and walked, the drizzle steaming her face, her legs sliced with the drag and tangle of the grass, those who heard her coming or going said that she sounded like a winded horse. How that made her laugh! From these wet runs she would return to her room soaked to the skin, too exhausted to sleep, like one of the small watery cubs of Beowulf's dam, escaped from the deep. That's her own description. The one subject she never tires of is herself.

Time would prove that nothing else would arouse in Fiona such a full awareness of her flesh as a piece of nature. Sex didn't. In her opinion, strange as it seems, there was too much in sex that was *im*material. All of the sentiment, for one thing. Then all of the mess. Fiona didn't blather it to the world, but she took for *granted* the primacy of the spirit. That seemed obvious. The difficult and the beautiful thing was to make the spirit flesh. That common practice would see it just the other way around was a flaw in man, not in nature, and the major flaw in man—she would add with a guffaw—was the one she had married. A joke? That was how people took it. Including Charles, the one she had married. Fiona's strident, horsy laugh is surprising in a woman of her cultivation. Seated, she rocks back and forth, slapping her knees. One sees the teeth she has missing and the dark cave at the back of her mouth. So the gods must laugh at men, and in the same spirit Fiona laughs at the gods. Who else can be held responsible? On their last trip to the coast (they took a Pullman) the porter had assumed that the man along with her, in his cap and sports jacket, *had* to be her son. What could she do but laugh? She had learned to live with it, but what she found a strain was how his weakness seemed to give him strength. Life clung to him. He lacked even the strength to fight it off. Every day of her life it was forced upon Fiona that this hapless man she had married would survive her. The older he became the younger he looked. If he wore his tennis sneakers and went out without his hat, students at the college took him for an instructor. Some of the girls swooned to learn that he read Greek. With a few exceptions, only Fiona could appreciate the humor of her situation, the love of folly being the last, great love of her life.

Somehow the first question Fiona is asked is where in the world, and how, she met Charles. Why will take time. It is not felt necessary to ask where in the world Charles met Fiona. Perhaps he didn't. It is obvious that Fiona met him. This question is a natural at the yearly fall parties introducing new members of the department. Fiona, who is pouring tea, will be seated. Charles stands—somehow he is always standing—an erect, handsome man, scholarly, cultivated, his face little changed from the day Fiona met him thirty years ago. That can't be, of course, but it is. Charles wears caps, does not wear glasses unless he sits reading, has the attractive smattering of gray hair of a young college man. No wrinkles. A seam where his head joins his neck. He stands, thighs pressed together, holding in one cupped palm an elbow, in the other a silver-rimmed glass with three ice cubes and his first stint of daily bourbon. If any, the water comes from the ice. If witty and effusive, Charles is tight, and capable of a very misleading performance. His manner, and the Oxford accent that time has not eroded, lead people to correctly think that Fiona met him in

England. It is never easy for them to accept that Charles was born in Indiana, just thirty miles north of Pickett, where he attended a school so backward he was able to major in Greek. This had more than a little to do with his being chosen as a Rhodes scholar; being chosen by Fiona shortly followed. They were married in France.

Charles will go on to tell you—if Fiona hasn't—that in his second year at Oxford, on a walking tour with a companion, he stopped to watch two teams of girls club each other nearly senseless. The game was lacrosse. The most proficient clubber of the lot was Fiona. But at that very moment she was getting hers with a sharp crack on the elbow. For the cello (she planned a career in music) she exchanged Charles, as simple as that. Broad in the shoulders and hips, long-limbed and large-boned, a mane of chestnut hair in two pigtails, Fiona Copley personified the spirit of Sparta that seemed to be absent from the study of the classics. There is a snapshot of Charles, taken on that excursion, standing just to one side of the Amazon, Fiona, that sums up in a glance the new world that is born, and the world that is gone. His arms are folded on his chest. His finger marks the place in a book of Housman's poems. If Housman's brook proved too broad for leaping, it was not entirely Charles's decision. At the sound of the word "leap," he had leaped. Was it at that moment he first experienced, or suffered, Fiona's laugh? Uninhibited, laced with fragments of what she happened to be chewing, it is not now, nor was it then, unusual for Fiona to almost choke to death. The only cure is several thumps, with the flat of the hand, on her broad back. Both friends and colleagues not so friendly have had occasion to thump Fiona. She takes it in good spirits. It often starts her laughing again. Flushed with coughing, her face red and perspiring, she will glance up at Charles, who stands tunelessly whistling, or toying with one of the cubes in his drink.

"I believe he'd let me choke rather than thump me!" she will cry, and this often leads to another fit of coughing. It is the truth that makes Fiona laugh, never mind what it is.

Neither a pretty girl nor a womanly woman—even her abundant hair is like a barrister's wig—Fiona resembles a well-endowed but obvious female impersonator. Her feet are large, her strides are those of Piers Plowman in foot-molded shoes. If she came at the wrong time, and in the wrong country, nevertheless she came to the right school. Her music festivals attract the gifted, fussy people who consider Aspen too high, Lucerne too far, and the Berkshires too close. They have precisely the taste and quaint cultivated madness to enjoy Charles's slides of the Crusader castles, a subject on which they will admit him to be the authority. For thirty-one years he has been at work on the text. It can be idly examined in the whiskey cartons that line one wall of his study: they stack well, and he can always assume they contain something else. Scholarly books in Greek and Latin, bound in vellum, stuffed like wallets with cards and notations, occupy the table, the chairs, and the bed where Charles does his sleeping and reading. Every year, for twelve years, a scholarly press advertised the book and took orders for it, then announced a brief delay in its publication. Some scholars hold the opinion the work is published, but hard to find. The work keeps him happy. More important, it keeps him out of the way. Fiona has a lively interest in people, and will sometimes say that she *collects* men. Their wives are always told there is no reason to worry, and they don't.

Before settling down Fiona and Charles had lived everywhere one could do it cheaply. Majorca first, of course, and then the Costa Brava. After Ibiza to Rhodes, where Charles continued his exhaustive researches into Crusader castles, and from there to Corfu, to Mykonos, to Dubrovnik, then to Minorca and the Canaries, a winter in Madeira, and several summers island-hopping, in and out of known and unknown villas on which Fiona left the impression of royalty in exile. This characteristic had the effect of enlarging her past and diminishing her future. It was seldom asked where she was off to—merely where she had been. The whack on the elbow had scotched a career, but it could hardly be said it ruined her talent. On an income of less than three thousand a year, with introductions to people who sat waiting for them, they managed to be warm when it was freezing and reasonably cool when it was stifling, living with people but not strictly off them, and always remarkably independent. In those years the London office of the Oxford Press—with other offices in Bombay, Calcutta, and elsewhere—received further material on a volume that would be definitive if it was ever completed.

No matter what island, Charles was up early, Fiona slept late. Her quality showed to its greatest advantage in her mastery of leisure. She detested committees, cultivated no hobbies, and showed no interest in world- or self-improvement. Charles did his writing in the morning, and after lunch they would take a long walk together: their hosts impatiently waited for the clop of their hobbled boots on the porch. Both wore hiking shoes, carried binoculars, canes, biscuits, and bars of bitter Swiss chocolate. Chocolate kept Fiona going as she waited for Charles to determine where.

On their honeymoon—a walking tour of the Alps—Fiona had insisted on visiting the tiny village of Coppet, noted as the burial place of Madame de Staël. That seemed understandable. Fiona had much in common with a woman of her temperament and talents. Charles knew the usual things about Madame de Staël but he had not heard the story about her mother, Madame Necker. She did not have her daughter's assortment of talents, nor did she dream, like her daughter, of an enduring fame. Yet she had her dream. In some respects a very ambitious one. Madame Necker did not want to *live* forever, but she did want to survive. Not in the hearts and minds of men, like her child, but in the sweet, solid flesh on her own bones. Death she did not fear. Physical disintegration she did. To die she was willing—to turn to food for worms she was not. Over the years she had observed, like many people, that actual bodies were preserved in large stoppered bottles, where they floated in the clear, immortal broth of alcohol. If this could be done for God's smaller creatures, why not for a large one like Madame Necker? All one needed was a bottle, or a cask, big enough. So she had one made, a huge glass-lined cask large enough for both Madame Necker and her husband. It was filled with alcohol. Soon enough, it floated the remains of the Neckers, and by draining off an appropriate quantity of the liquid, room was made, in time, for Madame de Staël. It was this excess liquid—according to tradition, and as recounted to Charles by Fiona—that was used to fortify the local vintage, and make it much in demand.

On such a story such a twist was to be expected, but who

could guess that Fiona would never tire of it? Nor did her listeners, the way she could tell it. It often left her gasping and choking, tears of laughter in her eyes. Only Charles, who lacked Fiona's strong stomach, seemed to be a little sensitive about it. His comment was that the story betrayed her original but somewhat perverse ancestor worship. She had replied that it was no such thing: it was pure self-love. Nor was she the first to cherish the fat on her own bones. Self-love seemed to Fiona—as she never tired of saying—much less perverse than other forms of love with which she was familiar, a comment that diverted the discussion to other things.

I need to emphasize that Fiona's self-love has little to do with matters of the spirit. She is the first to point out that the spirit is free to shift for itself—it's her too solid flesh that gives her the willies. Into dust or worse? She won't accept it. The important point is, she no longer has to. All of that is part of the past—one large past—that she has put behind her. The discovery and perfection of the modern freezing unit—at about the time she was at school in England—made it possible for Fiona to be practical as well as ambitious. Survival in the flesh was no problem. The problems now were in the field of thawing out.

This obsession—or passion, if you prefer it—has its origin in her childhood. One winter Fiona, with her brother Ronald, skated on a millpond near the house. It's still there: one of many nuisances she refuses to give up. The first freeze of winter had left the pond ice clear as glass. Fiona didn't skate too well, as a child, and spent most of the time on her hands and knees, peering into the ice. On that day she saw, just a few inches beneath her, the wide staring eyes of a life-size doll, frozen in the ice. The lips were parted. She felt it might speak back if she spoke to it. She called to her brother and they stood there considering how to get the doll out of the ice. Ronald ran to the house, and returned with a sled and a saw that his father used to remove blocks of ice in the spring. After a great deal of effort they lugged the block home on Ronald's sled. As the ice quickly thawed in a tub of warm water, the doll's lovely hair spread out on the surface. A moment later Fiona was able to free one of the chubby pink hands. Ronald says that she shrieked like a wild bird at the touch. This doll's hand was that of a recently drowned child. It had been so perfectly preserved in the ice that Fiona believed it must still be alive. It took time to convince her. She was convinced that it merely slept, and would speak to her when it thawed. The thaw, unfortunately, soon occurred, and she watched the flawlessly beautiful eyes dissolve like ice cubes and run down the cheeks like tears.

Such an experience is not easily forgotten. For a child like Fiona it was crucial. It provided her, as she admits herself, with the key to her own nature. Survival was what she wanted: survival in the flesh. This bizarre experience had revealed to her how it might be done.

For Charles, the crucial revelation was his brief acquaintance with Madame Necker, floating in the huge cask in Coppet. There he saw for himself how well alcohol preserved the flesh. He accepted the proof, but preferred to take it internally. When the time came to die he would be so well pickled he would require only framing.

As it applied to Charles, Fiona came to be fond of the word *pickled.* Charles is pickled, she would say, to explain his occasional absence, or the way he might stand, the glass cupped in his palm, blowing softly on the ice cubes as if to thaw them, a dimpled, archaic smile on his moist lips.

For all her love of alcohol, Fiona does not drink. Neither does she smoke, but for years her health has not been good. Her hair is white, several joints are stiffening, and there will soon be little solid flesh to preserve on the bones.

For all that he drinks, Charles's health appears to be good. He is one of those men who seem to be preserved in the very liquid that destroys so many others. His teeth are white. He has a thick pelt of hair. True enough, he does have the shakes, which is why he holds the glass in such a curious manner, the cubes tinkling as he stands like a good whiskey ad with his back to the fire. It is one thing to be pickled, briefly, while alive: quite another to be pickled, and bottled, forever. It's the *forever* that bugs him, and helps explain his apparent good health.

To have nothing to fear but fear itself, Charles will tell you, is more than sufficient. For one thing, pure fear is inexhaustible. For another, the age has caught up with Charles, after so long being safely behind him. Once only alcohol would preserve what seemed to matter. Now there is dry ice. It took a few thousand years and great quantities of ice to preserve the woolly mammoth in the wastes of Siberia, but this could currently be done at small expense in a frozen-food locker. It is Fiona's idea that a huge floating freezer would have served much better than Noah's ark. In the freezer, two of every kind of creature would still be as fresh as the day they were frozen, with more than a fifty-fifty chance of being thawed and put back into circulation. In the basement of her home Fiona has her own freezer, one six feet six inches long and forty inches wide. That is large enough for her: to prove it she will stretch out in it for you, the metallic walls of the box magnifying her remarkably resonant laughter. Does she plan on just lying there forever? Why not? Just in case the power might go off during an electric storm, or an air raid, she has installed a power plant that operates on its own gasoline motor. Charles—who still looks as young as ever—will be around to supervise and keep things going. If by chance he isn't, the box is also large enough for him. One of her expanding programs, now gathering members, is concerned with continued Freezer Survival, and will supply the organization and funds necessary to keep the current flowing. Everybody knows the idea of his dying first is what keeps Charles looking so young. Fiona makes him nervous, but he is the one with the black head of hair, she with the white one. Charles has the air of breeding that makes it unnecessary for him to talk very much. He stands a good deal, his back to the fireplace, or moves about whatever room he is in looking for new or old time-pieces. He has a thing about clocks. Battery-driven ones interest him less than those activated by atmospheric pressure, or run by weights. The ticking that many find so aggravating appeals to Charles. He likes the modern clocks with the visible movements, or the older type with the pendulum rocking, perhaps a smaller dial on the face notching off the seconds. Time. What the devil is it?—Charles will ask. Since everybody knows he is a student of the subject the question is rhetorical, to say the least. It is a fiction, surely, having no meaning beyond the measurement of the past. Otherwise it is merely a form of the future tense. That simple, ticking hand of the clock indicates something that defies comprehension. Something that never was, for a moment is, and is as suddenly gone. In Fiona, for example, time ticks away in a visible, even audible, measure. In Charles, oddly enough, it appears to have stopped. An illusion, of course, as the beat of his heart can be seen in the tremor of his hand, or, when he is seated, in the wagging toe of his boot. If time is not the movement of one thing or another, has it stopped? If, indeed, a low point of freezing brings all movement to a standstill, can it be said, or proven, that time exists? Queries like that get from Fiona one of her memorable, infectious guffaws. The erosion of time can be seen at both the back and front of her mouth. Doesn't she care? She behaves like a player with the trump card. For all of her remarkable talents she sometimes seems a little simple-minded. Or on the mad side— whichever side that is. The latitude in these matters merely points up what we know to be the gist of the problem. On a subject of interest, of life and death, does anybody really know anything of importance? Just who is dying, for example, is as hard to determine as who is living. It is in the courts. We no longer know for sure when a person is dead.

Three days ago, now, Charles was found lying face up in the freezer as if he had dropped there. He was frozen stiff. That is all that can be said for certain: he is frozen stiff. Fiona will not allow the authorities to thaw him out. The one thing that is known for certain in these matters is that you can't refreeze what has once been thawed, and this is neither the time nor the place to bring Charles back for interrogation. If a better world was what he had in mind, this is not it.

Something will have to be done, sooner or later, but Fiona has threatened to sue for murder any person or persons who thaw Charles out. Until he is thawed, who can say what remains to be said? There is another school of thought on the matter, which suggests a period of watchful waiting. Why not? There is little or nothing that can happen to Charles. Ten years from now he will still be as he is. The authorities have adopted the position of watch and wait. Some believe it safe to assume, from her present appearance, that Fiona will not long survive him, and at the time of her death such legal steps as are found necessary might be taken. She is the one who laughs when she considers what they might be. I could be wrong, of course, but my impression is that Fiona is looking better than ever, now that Charles—that is, his future—has been taken care of. She looks younger. With a little persuasion she will join you for a drink.

1970

Magic

Robert could see Father in the front seat, steering. He could see Mother and the lover in the back seat, sitting. They came around the lake past the Japanese lanterns and Mrs. Van Zant's idea of a birthday party. The car stopped and Father got out and opened the door for Mother. Mother got out and pulled her dress down. She leaned back in and said, "Here we are—here we are, lover!"

"I object to your sentimentality," said Father.

"Here we are, lover," Mother said, and pulled him out of the car. His arms stuck out of the sleeves of his coat. One pocket of his pants was pulled inside out. Robert wanted to see the bump on his head but he had on his hat. "Here we are," Mother said, and turned him to look at Robert.

"This is Mr. Brady, son," said Father.

"I told you," Mother said, "Callie's boyfriend."

"Where's Callie?" said Robert.

"Callie's got her lungs full of water, baby. She's where they'll dry her out."

"He's dried out?" asked Robert. He didn't look it. There was a line around his hat where the water had stopped. Under the hat, where he had the bump, Mother said his head was shaved. "Why'd she hit him?"

"She didn't hit him, baby. He fell on it. When they fell out of the boat, he fell on it."

"A likely story," Father said. "Is that Emily?"

Robert's sister Emily stood in the door holding one of Robert's rabbits and wearing both of Callie's slippers.

"Go put your clothes on!" Father said.

"My God, why?" cried Mother. "She's cute as cotton. Why would anybody put some lousy clothes on it?"

"Don't shout!" shouted Father.

To the lover Emily said, "Did you ever hug a rabbit?"

"He doesn't want to hug a rabbit," Father said, "or see little girls with all their clothes off."

"Why not?" Mother said.

"Mr. Brady is not well," said Father. "When he fell from the boat he bumped his head and was injured."

"Where does he hurt?" said Robert.

"In his heart, baby."

"Mr. Brady has lost his memory," said Father.

"What a wonderful way to be," said Mother.

"How does he do it?" asked Robert.

Father said, "You don't *do* it. It just happens. You forget to feed your rabbits. He has forgotten his name."

"Isn't he wonderful?" Mother said. She took his hand. "You must be starving!"

"They said he had just eaten," said Father. "Where you going to put him?"

"Did Callie lose her memory, too?" asked Robert.

Mother said, "No such luck, baby—"

"She has some water in her lungs," said Father, "but she didn't lose her memory. She said she wanted you in bed."

To Emily, Mother said, "Is that the *same* rabbit? My God, if I'm not sick of rabbits."

"Can't they dress themselves without her?" Father said. "Put down that rabbit, will you? Go put some clothes on."

"Isn't she cute as cotton?" Mother said to Mr. Brady. Emily put down the rabbit and showed her funny belly button. Robert's button went in, but Emily's button went out.

"Are you going to speak to her about that?" said Father.

"Show lover your sleeping doll, pet," said Mother.

Emily rolled her eyes back so only the whites showed. Robert called it playing dead.

"I'll show him up," Father said. "Where you putting him?"

"Callie's room!" they both cried.

To Mr. Brady, Mother said, "You like a nap? You take a nap. You take a nice nap, then we have dinner."

Father whinnied. "If Callie's not here, who's going to prepare it?"

Mother hadn't thought about it. She stood thinking, fingering the pins in her golden hair.

"We could eat pizzas!" cried Robert. "Pisa's Pizzas!"

Emily clapped her hands.

"You don't seem to grasp the situation," said Father. "You have a man on your hands. You have a legal situation."

"I hope so," said Mother.

"It's your picnic—" began Father.

"Picnic! Picnic!" Emily cried.

Father rubbed his palms together. "I'll show him up. You dress the children. You like to use the washroom, Mr. Brady?" Father led him down the hall.

Their mother took off the green hat and felt for the pins in her golden hair. She took them out like clothespins, held them in her mouth, while she raised her arms and let the fan cool beneath them. Through the open French doors she could see across the lake to Mrs. Van Zant's lawn and all the Japanese lanterns. Mrs. Van Zant lay in the hammock on the porch with her beach hat on her face. Mother gave Emily her hairpins, then threw back her head so the hair hung down like Lady Godiva's. When she shook her head more hairpins dropped on the polar bear rug. These pins were for Robert. He picked them up and made a tight fistful of them.

"What was I going to say, pet?" Mother said.

"Where's Callie," said Emily.

"In the hospital, baby. She's in Mr. Brady's head. That's why it hurts him."

"He's got no memory?" said Robert.

"Who needs it, baby. Give Mother her pins." His mother sat on the stool between the three mirrors with her long golden hair parted in the middle, fanned out on her front. "Your mother is Lady Godiva," she said.

"Lady Godiva my lawnmower!" said Father. He came through the French doors with a drink and took a seat on the bed.

"You like horses, baby?" Mother said to Robert. "She was the one on the horse."

"Can you picture your mother on a horse?" said Father. "Ho-ho-ho," he laughed.

"Tell your father he's no lover," said Mother.

"Tell your mother you could all have done worse," said Father. "Her looks, my brains."

"I'm not sure he understands her," said Mother. "You think he thinks she meant to hit him?"

Father said, "Just so she didn't lose any more than he did."

"She won't like it," said Mother. "She likes to make her own bed and eat her own food. Did you see it? White fish, white sauce, white potatoes, white napkins. I thought I'd puke."

"In my opinion," said Father, "he jumped out of that boat. He tried to drown himself."

"That's love for you," Mother said. "Your father wouldn't understand."

"It's a miracle he *didn't* drown," said Father.

"See how your father sits and stares," said Mother.

"Ppp-shawww, I'm too old for that stuff," said Father.

"God kill me I should ever admit it!" said Mother.

"What I came in to say, was—" Father said, "I'm washing my hands of the whole business."

"You're always washing your hands," Mother said.

"It's no picnic," Father said. "You get a man in the house and the first thing you know you can't get him out."

"No such luck," Mother said.

"I'm warning you—" Father said.

"Tell your father he can go wash his hands!" Mother shouted.

"Eva—" Father said, "there is no need to shout."

"It's this damn house," Mother said. "Twenty-eight rooms

and two babies. An old man, and two pretty babies."

"All right," said Father, "have your stroke."

"When I do—" Mother said, "I want someone here with me. I won't have a stroke and be cooped up here alone."

"Eva—" Father said, "that will be enough."

Mother let her long hair slip from her lap and stared at her front face in the mirror. Her mouth was open, and the new bridge was going up and down. She took the bridge out of her mouth and felt along the inside of her mouth with her finger. She spread her mouth wide with her fingers to see if she could see something.

"If you just keep it up," Father said, "you're going to have a little something—"

"Where's my baby?" Mother turned to look for Emily. She was sitting on the head of the polar bear feeding fern leaves to the rabbit. "If you do that he'll make BBs," Mother said. "You want him to go around the house making BBs?"

"It's not a him," said Robert, "it's a her."

"You have to shout?" shouted Father. "We're sitting right here."

"That's why *I* have to shout!" shouted Mother.

"Don't pick her up," Father said, "put her down. It's picking her up that makes BBs. If you don't want BBs pick her up by the ears."

Emily picks her up by the ears, then puts her down.

"I swear to God you're all crazy," Mother said. "Who could ever like that?"

Father takes his drink from the floor and holds it out toward Robert. There is a fly in it. "You see that?" Robert saw it. "What is it?"

"A fly," said Robert.

"Don't let him fool you, baby."

"Son—" said Father, "what kind of fly is it?"

"Are you crazy?" said Mother.

"Not so fast," said Father, "what kind of fly is it?"

"A drownded fly," said Robert.

"A drowned fly," said Father.

"Why should he look at a drowned fly?" said Mother.

Father didn't answer. He held the glass close to his face and blew on the fly as if to cool it. It rocked on the water but nothing happened.

"You would agree the fly is drowned?" his father asked.

"Don't agree to anything, baby."

"I'm going to hold this fly under water," said Father, "while you go and bring your father a saucer and a salt cellar."

"Don't you do it," said Mother.

"Obey your father," said Father.

Robert put his mother's hairpins in her lap and went back through the club room, the dining room, the game room, through the swinging door into the kitchen. Callie's metal salt cellar sat on the stove, where the heat kept it dry. He sprinkled some on the floor, crunched on it, then carried it back through the house to his father.

"Where's the saucer?" Father said.

"They're not for flies," said Mother. She took the ashtray from her dresser and passed it to Robert. Father used his silver pencil to push the fly to the edge of the glass, then fish it out. A drowned fly. It lay on its back, its wings stuck to the ashtray.

"This fly has been in the water twenty minutes," said Father. "That's a lot longer than your Mr. Brady."

"What did you drown him for?" asked Robert.

"I got the urge," said Father. "Cost me a drink!"

"It's probably a *her*," Mother said. "If it drowns, it's a her."

Father took the blotter from Mother's writing table and used one corner of it to pick up the fly. The drowned fly made a dark wet spot on the blotter. "Mumbo-jumbo, abracadabra—" chanted Father. "Your father will now bring the fly to life!" He put the blotter with the fly on the ashtray, then sprinkled the fly all over with salt. He kept sprinkling until the salt covered the fly like snow.

"My God, what next?" said Mother.

"It is now twenty-one minutes past five," said Father, and held out his watch so Robert could read it.

"Twenty-two minutes," said Robert.

"It was twenty-one when I started," said Father. "It was

twenty-two when we had him covered. It takes a while for the magic to work."

"What magic?"

"Bringing the dead to life," said Father. He took one of Mother's cork-tipped cigarettes, lit it with her lighter, then swallowed the smoke.

"It's not coming out your ears," Emily said.

"That's another trick," said Father, "not this one." He swallowed more smoke, then he held the glowing tip of the cigarette very close to the fly. From where she sat Mother threw her brush at him and it skidded on the floor. "What we need is some light on the subject," said Father, "but more light than that." He looked around the room to the lamp Mother used to make her face brown. "Here we are," said Father, and pulled the lamp over. He held it so the green blotter and the salt were right beneath it. Robert could not see the fly. The brightness of the light made the green look blue. "Feel that!" said Father, and put his face beneath it.

"My God, you look like a turkey gobbler," Mother said.

"When you get my age—" Father began.

"What makes you think I'm going to get your age?" said Mother.

"Well, well—" Father said, "did you see it?"

"What?" said Robert.

"At sixty-two years of age," said Father, "I find my eye is sharper than yours. You know why?"

"Tell him your mother knows why," said Mother.

"You know why?" Father said. "I have trained myself to look out the corner of my eye. Out of the corner we can detect the slightest movement. With the naked eye we can pick up the twitch of a fly."

"How your father's taste has changed!" cried Mother.

Up through the salt, like the limb of a snowman, appeared the leg of the fly. "Look! Look!" cried Robert.

"Four minutes and twenty seconds," said Father. "Brought him around in less time than it took to drown him." The fly used his long rear legs like poles to clean off the snow. Using his naked eyes just like Father, Robert could see the hairs on the legs, like brushes. He used them like dusting crumbs from the table. He began to wash off his face, like a cat. "Five minutes and forty seconds so far," said Father.

"Does he know who he is?" asked Robert.

"The salt soaked up the water," said Father, and used the silver pencil to tip the fly to his feet. The fly buzzed but didn't fly anywhere. He buzzed like he felt trapped.

"How many times can he do it?" said Robert.

"A good healthy fly," said Father, "can probably come back four or five times."

"Don't he get tired?" Robert said.

"You get tired of anything," Father said, and picked up the fly, dropped him back into the drink. He just lay there, floating on the top. He didn't buzz.

"He's pooped," said Emily.

"Pooped?" said Father. "Where did she hear that?" Mother was looking at her face close to the mirror. Father pushed the fly under the water but he didn't buzz. "No reaction," said Father. He put the glass and the ashtray on Mother's dresser. "He's probably an old fly," Father said. "It probably wasn't the first time somebody dunked him."

"What's that?" Mother said. There was a flapping around from the direction of the game room.

"You leave the screen up, son?" Father said. When Robert left the screens up bats flew into the house because it was dark. They had flown so close to Robert the wind of their wings had ruffled his hair. Her golden hair fanned out on her shoulders, Mother went to the hall door and threw it open. The flapping sound stopped.

"Callie!" Mother called, "is that you, Callie?"

"You crazy?" said Father. "Her lungs are full of water. She almost drowned."

"What a lunch!" said Mother. "You ever see anything like it? If I know her she just won't stand it."

There was a wheezing sound, then suddenly music. Through the dark beyond his mother, across the tile-floored room, Robert could see the keys of the piano playing.

"My God, it's him!" said Mother. "It's the lover!"

Father got up from the bed and put the robe with the dragons around her shoulders. He used both hands to lift her hair from inside it. Mother crossed the hall, her robe tassels dragging, to where the cracked green blinds were drawn at the windows. "You poor darling!" she cried, jerking on the blind cords. "How can you see in the dark?" When the blind zipped up Robert could see the lover sitting on the bench at the player piano. His legs pumped. He gripped the sides of the bench so he wouldn't slip off. He wore his hat but his laces were untied and slapped the floor when he pumped.

"Now how'd he get in *there*?" said Father. "How explain that?"

"Go right on pumping," Mother said, "play as long as you like." She stooped to read the label on the empty roll box. "The 'Barcarole'! Imagine!"

"It's not," said Robert.

"I'd like to have it explained," Father said. "The only closed-up room in the house."

"It's not the 'Barcarole,' " said Robert.

"I know, baby," said Mother. She stood with the empty roll box at the veranda window looking at the lovers' statue in the bird bath. Kissing. One of her orioles splashed them. Across the pond there were cars parked in Mrs. Van Zant's driveway and some of the Japanese lanterns were glowing.

"If only she was here to hear it," Mother said.

Robert said, "She likes it better when you play it backwards."

"If only she was here to see it!" Mother said.

"She's seen it every summer since the war," said Father.

"Oh, no you don't," said Mother. "It's just once you see it."

"Now you see it, now you don't, eh?" said Father. He rubbed his palms together. "When do we eat? Guess I'll go wash my hands."

Mr. Brady, the lover, sat in the covered wicker chair with the paper napkin and the plate in his lap. He wore his hat. He sat looking at Mrs. Van Zant's Japanese lanterns. Out on the pond was a boy in a red inner tube, splashing. Mrs. Van Zant's husband walked around beneath the lanterns, screwing in bulbs.

"All right, all right," Mother said, "but I'm not going to sit on these iron chairs."

"They were your prescription," Father said.

"Not to sit on." Mother spread her napkin on the floor, sat on it. She spread her golden hair on the wicker chair arm.

"Listen to this," Father said, "rain tonight and tomorrow morning. Turning cool late tonight with moderately cool westerly winds." Father wet his finger and put up his hand. "Southwesterly," he said.

"Tell your father how we need him," Mother said.

"What about his h-a-t," Father said.

"Don't you think he can s-p-e-l-l?" said Robert.

"Your father never takes anything for granted," Mother said.

"I don't want him forming habits," Father said, "that he's going to find hard to break when he's better."

"I don't think he's hungry," Mother said. "He's thinking about her. I know it."

"Asked him if he'd like a drink. Said he doesn't drink. Asked him if he'd like to smoke. Said he doesn't smoke."

"What's your father mumbling now?"

"A man has to do something—" Father said.

"Which would you rather be—" said Robert, "a rabbit or a hare?"

The lover stood up and spilled his pizza on the floor.

"You can just go and get me another plate," Mother said, and gave the lover the one she was holding. He sat down in the chair and held it in his lap.

"Asked him if he played rummy. He shook his head. Asked him if he played bridge. He shook his head. Suppose you ask him if he can do anything."

"Tell your father how we love him," Mother said.

"I don't care what his field is," Father said, "whether it's stocks and bonds, insurance, or religion. It doesn't matter what it is, a man has to do something. Smoke, drink, play the ponies—he has to do *something*."

"I never heard a sorrier confession," Mother said.

Robert sang—

> "Star light, star bright
> First star I seen tonight."

"Wouldn't that be *saw*?" Father said.

"SSSShhhhhhh—" said Mother. Across the lake Mrs. Van Zant's loudspeaker was saying something. Mrs. Van Zant's voice came across the water, the people clapped, the drummer beat his drums. More of the Japanese lanterns came on.

"If I don't love the Orient," Mother said.

"You didn't when we were there," Father said. The drummer beat his drums, stopped, and the music played.

"How old is Sylvia now?" Mother said.

"You don't know?" said Father; "or you don't want to know? She's your first one, right? That makes her fifteen this summer."

Mother said, "The right time is whenever it happens. Heaven knows, I was just a little fool when it happened to me."

"I wasn't so smart myself," said Father.

"If my mother had had the brains she was born with she would have locked me in my room or shipped me off to Wellesley."

"You talking to me, by chance?" said Father.

Robert jumped up from the steps and ran up and down in the wet grass, around and around the sprinkler, and while he ran he sang—

> "Beans, beans, the musical fruit,
> The more you eat, the more you toot."

"You hear that?" said Father.

"Baby—" Mother said, "we don't sing that one."

"I *feel* it—" Robert yelled. "I feel it—I feel it."

"I know you do, baby, but we don't sing it."

"Why?" Robert cried.

"It's not couth," said Mother.

Robert stopped running around and around the sprinkler, and let the water just rain on him. Across the lake the Japanese lanterns made colors like sparklers on the water. A man sang—

> "How deep is the o-shun?
> How high is the sky?
> How great my de-voshun?
> I'll tell you no lie—"

"For God's sake," Mother cried, giving Emily a push, "go do something foolish. Go chase your brother."

Emily made a kink in the hose so that the sprinkler stopped working, letting the pressure build up to where she couldn't hold it. The water gushed like a fountain shooting up into the dark then falling like a quick summer shower. Both Mother and Father headed for the porch, but Mr. Brady just sat there till the shower had stopped.

"I'm going to drown you both," Mother cried, "you hear me?"

Chased by Robert, Emily ran into the woods, her white legs gleaming, then she ran down the gravel path to the boat pier, out to the end of the pier, where Robert caught her.

"Let go of me, you beast!" she cried.

"We're all lovers!" Robert shrieked. "We're lovers, lovers lovers."

Emily ran back up the pier and into the woods, where Robert caught her from behind and rubbed slime in her hair. Her white legs waved like arms as they wrestled. Then they stopped wrestling and lay quiet, listening. They could hear the voice of Amos talking to Andy. From where they were lying they could see the tassels on the lampshade and the open sheet music on the piano.

Across the water, first near then far—

> "You're the cream in my coffee,
> You're the salt in my stew.
> You will always be
> My ne-cess-ity.
> I'd be lost without you."

At the window of her bedroom Mother called, "You hear that, baby? They're playing your song."

Robert pulled away from Emily and ran like he was scared to the back of the house, and into the kitchen. Then he ran up the stairs into Mother's bedroom. She was seated at her table smearing gobs of goo on her face.

"What's eating you, baby?" Mother said.

Robert saw her three times in the three-way mirror. As if he were outside and wanted in, he said, "Knock, knock, knock."

"Yes, love—" Mother said.

Robert thrust his clenched fists toward the mirror and said, "Which hand do you choose?"

"If it's another frog," said Mother, "I'll kill you."

"Go on, choose," said Robert. "You've got to choose."

Mother closed her eyes and chose one of his fists.

"Open your eyes!" Robert cried, and unclenched his fist. Mother drew his hand toward her to see what he was holding.

"Is it sugar, baby? Are you turning to sugar?"

"Taste it! Taste it!" cried Robert.

Mother sniffed whatever it was, then she flicked her tongue at it. "Salt," she said. "What does your mother want with salt?" Robert just stood there with the salt in his palm. Mother picked up the brush with hairs tangled in the bristles and stroked it slowly through her golden hair. Where it fanned out on her shoulders strands of it would lift to be near the brush. Robert could hear the electricity crackle.

"Do something for your mother, baby—go sprinkle it on your father." When he turned to leave she gave him a pat on his bottom. "Mr. Brady, too, love," she said, "sprinkle both of them."

1970

Here Is Einbaum

Here is Einbaum at an open casement window, three floors above the street. On the corner just below him, barefooted, a beggar stands in the fresh fall of snow. His head is bare. He has tipped his face so that Einbaum can see his beard. Before him, in an attitude of prayer, the palms of his hands are pressed together, with a narrow slit for coins between his thumbs. He sings. Someone from a window below Einbaum has tossed him a coin. It is searched for in the snow by two shabby children and the woman who holds a third child at her hip. The head and feet of this child are bare, but it looks well fed. Einbaum has been told that these cunning beggars rent the children from people who have too many, but the woman who told him this is the one who dropped the coin. What is he to believe—that she is wrong, or merely a fool? Until he was told, he sometimes dropped a coin himself. When the beggar sang Christmas carols, the children joined in, their mouths round and dark in their pale white faces. Einbaum's delight was in the sensation that they were needy and he could help them; his torment in the certain knowledge that he was a fool. In the room behind Einbaum the ceiling is high and his sister, Ilse, sits sewing on buttons. She is paid by the button. Her scalp gleams white at the part of her hair. Einbaum steps back from the window to let the housemaid, Karina, air out the bolster and puff the pillows, and they both stand waiting, knowing that the dust will make her sneeze.

Here is Einbaum in the woods of the Wienerwald, concealed by shadows and leaves. He lies sprawled on his face; we see only the soles of his boots and the rucksack strapped to his back. One arm is crooked beneath his head. The other grips an unloaded military rifle. Einbaum is in the midst of the training exercises he enjoys much more than he does his freedom. He is good at it. He can tramp with his pack eighteen miles a day. In his group it is openly admitted that if there is war Einbaum will rise fast. He likes to serve. He likes the simple, orderly life. On him and around him glows the golden light of a melancholy Viennese fall, the leaves crushed by lovers who have been careful to stub their cigarettes.

Here is Einbaum at the Studenten Klub, seated at the window overlooking the Schottengasse: snow is falling. It blurs the Christmas lights and the spire of Stefansdom. Einbaum strains to read the time on the glowing face of a clock. The woman seated at his side is his mistress, Frau Koenig. She wears galoshes that are wet and give off an odor. He is only at his ease with her, she tells him, when they are in bed. Little if anything ever said to Einbaum, up to this moment, has pleased him so much. Einbaum the heartless rogue. Einbaum the callous sensualist. It is unimportant, for the time being, that he is also not at ease with her in bed. Part of the problem is technical. He sometimes fears he might suffocate. Her gloved hands rest on her wide matron's lap. Frau Koenig hasn't given him much pleasure, but she has given Einbaum great plans. He will be a roué. Generous matrons will support him in the manner to which he will one day be accustomed. As the snow falls he wonders what time it is. Frau Koenig will misinterpret Einbaum's glancing at his watch, which happened to be the one she gave him. Now it is Christmas. Before buying her something he would like to know what she intends to give him.

We might doubt it, but this, too, is Einbaum. He wears a bowler and carries a valise. It is heavy with books necessary to his life at the University. Two volumes of Spengler, Count Keyserling's *Travel Diary,* one book of Italian grammar, another of Italian history. There is also a separate folder of notes, written in code. Einbaum the revolutionary, the *agent provocateur*, waits on the steps of the university for a colleague from Graz, Herr L—— (Einbaum will always see it with the letters missing), who, with Einbaum, will create the disturbance initiating the new order in Vienna. The password is *Oesterreich über alles*, unlikely as it seems. While running from this scene, which proved to be a fiasco, he is pursued by a man no larger than Dollfuss, who fires a shot that turns up in the second volume of Einbaum's Spengler—a lead pellet he later attached to the fob of his watch. He liked intrigue. He considered an offer that would set him up, comfortably, in Buda. It was one of his options when something more interesting intervened.

Once more, here is Einbaum—but does it matter? Everyone has an album full of such snapshots. Few, of course, were ever taken by the camera, but they remain indelible on the lens of the eye. In the dark, as a rule, one sees them the clearest, glowing like figures on the face of a watch. Why these and not others? Einbaum often wonders. Something to do with his own life and torment. He cannot spell it out, but in these recurring snapshots the film of his life had its reruns. He studied it for clues to what later happened: some inkling, some suggestion, of emerging powers. Nothing unusual. The same vague apprehensions common to millions of German Jews. Mendelssohn Einbaum often feared for his life, but that was hardly news.

With shame he admits it, but a German first. Both sides of the family burghers in Linz, where they specialized in leather tanning. Einbaum's Jewish grandfather used to say Austria is a condition from which Germans must recover. Perhaps Einbaum did not. He was born in Vienna—his mother, Elsa Nottebaum, an actress of some importance in Hofmannsthal's plays. Einbaum's grandmother wore the family jewels on a cord between her breasts, where they acquired a patina. Is it possible to be a German and a Jew? Einbaum stands before you. Other people's clothes fit him better than his own. The way he backs into a chair, or crooks his finger into the coin slot of a pay phone, the way he nods his head, like a finger, when speaking, or juts it forward, wagging, when listening, the way his coat gapes open like a tent flap—but the impression is clearer across the room than when face to face. A German, unmistakably, and more or less mistakably, a Jew. Was it the German or the Jew in him that seemed to be the clearest that day in August 1939? The century was ten years older than Einbaum. He walked in a drizzle on Kärntnerstrasse. Where the street bends and opens on Stefansdom he stepped from the curb to make way for two ladies. The hair of one was damp. His face actually brushed it as he dipped his head beneath her umbrella. It is why a moment passes before he notes the cab pulled up beside him at the curb. From the lowered rear window a gloved hand beckons. Einbaum peers around. At the moment he stands alone, so it must be him. "Frau Koenig?" he says, sure that it must be, and he is half into the cab before he knows better. It is a fine scene: Einbaum bodily abducted in the full light of day. This woman in the cab he knows casually from the musical evenings at the Studenten Klub, and from pictures of her in the *Wiener Tagblatt* skiing in the Alps or playing tennis. Sophia Horvath had neither much money nor a title, but she had class, the unmistakable air of breeding. It is at Sophia women turn and look: forget the men. She has wrists and ankles thicker than Einbaum's, she wears hightop pumps that she laces, a scent that is both animal and mineral. It lingers in the cab as she leans to smile at Einbaum. What is this fragrance? He will come to know it as *fleur de peur.* This imposing, substantial woman, wreathed in a boa in early August, fears for her life.

So it is here, on this day that everything smells, Einbaum's story begins. The year is 1939, the city is Vienna, close as a shabby unaired museum full of aging attendants and apprehensive tourists, both living with dreams already buried. Vienna was not music to Einbaum, nor the sight of the bedding of lovers at casement windows, nor *Kaffee mit Schlag,* nor the birthplace of Mendelssohn Einbaum. In those days he used the tip of his cane to flip leaves from the sidewalk on his way to the séances of Lady Golding-Brieslau in her apartment on Schottengasse. Einbaum liked the atmosphere of anxiety, dread, and childish awe. At the ringing of bells his heart pounded. The odor of fear was stronger than the incense. Regardless of what happened, Einbaum himself felt cleansed and one of the chosen to have survived it. He felt he understood the appeal of the Mass without the nonsense of the faith. Besides elderly women, he also met people of unusual background or superior attainments.

Sophia Horvath played remarkable tennis and had a scholarly interest, like her father, in church history. She spoke, in addition to German and Hungarian, excellent English and French. With a deliberation that was characteristic she used Einbaum to practice her French, skillfully fending off his efforts to practice his English. She talked of going to Brazil. Her father had mining interests that would profit from her personal supervision. She had the cunning and assurance of a Cossack. Indoors she perspired. In the dimmed light of the séance her face gleamed like gold leaf. All the features were too small, more like those of a child than a woman, the small pointed teeth busily nibbling at her wind-chapped lips. Hardly a beauty or a charmer, she had a somewhat puzzling but magnetic attraction. Her eyes sparkled. Something to do with animal vitality. Einbaum was not alone in the thought he had given to how a man might seduce such a woman, if that was the word. Her thighs were enormous. In her frequent rages at tennis blunders she would snap the racquet in her hands like pastry. What did she want with French? She considered it the language of confidences. Einbaum's inside track, insofar as he had one, lay in his superior knowledge of the French subjunctive. The question of what to *do* with money, for instance, or jewels, seemed amusing and plausible when discussed in French. It was possible to be remarkably intimate, and yet impersonal. French novels were specific, if not up-to-date. There were also imaginary problems of travel, decisions about luggage, and questions of climate. Heat she did not like. Her favorite high place in Europe seemed to be in Gavarnie, in the Pyrenees. One could see it on a poster in the lobby of the American Express. She liked high places. She liked the white silence of a world of snow. Einbaum, in contrast, felt himself especially drawn to lower altitudes and more open space. The American Wild West appealed to Einbaum—what he had seen of it in the movies. Man and nature harmoniously blended. The savage beauty and simplicity of the Indian. In the Historical Museum, Einbaum had paused to examine the feathered headgear of the chiefs, and their bows and arrows. Remote as cavemen, yet alive at the time Einbaum's Grandfather Nottebaum came from Prague to Vienna, the Battle of Balaklava the high point of his long life.

Einbaum loved the movies and felt they were related, in a way, to the séance. One sat in the dark and waited for materializations; at the movies they occurred. To Einbaum's taste, these appearances were more gratifying than the ringing of bells, the table knockings, and the voices that Sophia found so impressive. Although a devout Catholic, she liked the reassurance of a more physical survival. The spiritual she took for granted. No doctrine justified a belief in the spirit's return to the flesh, but she felt there might be progress in this area. The purpose of religion, quite simply, was to dispense with the problem of death. A start had been made, but fulfillment would come when the spirit recovered the flesh it had lost. Einbaum saw it as part of her inheritance. It amused him that this indestructible woman seemed so concerned with her life elsewhere. She wore a jeweled cross, a scarab ring, and carried in her purse cabalistic objects to increase her luck and frighten away evil spirits. To what end? Yet Einbaum noted he felt safer in her company.

As the summer waned, Einbaum helped Sophia shop for what she might need in her travels. It was not clear where; that would be the last decision she would make. He rode about with her in taxis, holding her purchases. In the confines of the cab, if not concealed by the smell of her rubbers, or of her wet coat and umbrella, Einbaum was aware, as in a shuttered sickroom, of the odor of the patient, or the illness. This woman who smelled of money, health, and assurance also gave off the sweet-sour scent of fear. An essence—like that in stoppered bottles—puffed out of her clothes when she sagged into a chair. Was it death she feared? Was she ill with more than apprehension? The straw-yellow hair, the ice-blue eyes, the face as broad and flat as a trowel concealed from others, but not from her, the dram of tainted blood that troubled her thoughts. In diplomatic French she admitted to Einbaum that they had more in common than met the eye. In her father's blood Sophia Kienholz, a Jewess, had left the strain that his daughter, among others, thought apparent. Not anything in particular—no, nothing like that. One simply sensed it was there, as one sensed it in Einbaum. The Jewishness. The *je ne sais quoi*, as the French would say. Einbaum was quick to appreciate the confidence, and share their mutual bond and apprehension. So much for the secretly tainted! But what did this have to do with the openly tainted Einbaum?

They were in the *Kaffeehaus* frequented by musicians, on the Lindengasse. Einbaum had taken his coffee *mit Schlag,* and sat dunking the puff with his spoon. Conspiracies he liked. In French they ran smoother and promised more reward. In public Sophia frequently wore gloves to conceal the rings embedded in her fingers, but the kid leather fit so snugly it bore a clear imprint of the stones. There had been no discussion about how to conceal the jewels she could not take off. Einbaum was inexperienced, but not indifferent to the nuances and complexities of his emotions. He liked the drama. He vaguely sensed that the drama, with the passage of time, would prove to be of more interest than the crisis. With one gloved finger she pressed her lip to where her teeth could nibble a raw spot, her eyes flickering from side to side to show the charge of her thought. Einbaum was thinking somebody should paint her, regretting that he lacked the talent. This cunning blonde peasant had reason for her apprehension. What reason did she have for Einbaum?

In her opinion, Mendelssohn Einbaum bore a remarkable resemblance to her father. The same stocky frame, with no neck to speak of. The deferent, attentive manner of a good headwaiter. Also a good listener, with an almost inaudible voice. A student of Ottoman history, he spent most of his time living privately, among his books. He saw few people; outside of family friends, even fewer saw him. If Einbaum, for instance, occupied his quarters—with the knowledge of a few close servants—and went through his usual habits, or stayed in his quarters, he might not actually be missed for weeks, possibly months. That would prove to be more than enough time for Sophia and her father, traveling different routes to the same destination, to be in Brazil, Guatemala, Gavarnie in the Pyrenees, or possibly the Canary Islands, before his absence was noted. Einbaum, in the meantime, would have broken no law and his impersonation would have been purely accidental. As a friend of theirs he had been a guest on the estate. He could stay on, or he could return to Vienna. Einbaum, of course, would do this as a favor, but she would see to it that he was rewarded. One of the rings from her fingers would make it worth his trouble, if that was what it would take.

Had Einbaum forgotten that he, too, was a Jew? Perhaps he had never felt it so strongly. But he was no Horvath and had nothing to lose but his life. In August of 1939, in Vienna, it was hard to imagine who would take Einbaum's. There were laws on the statute books. High in the council of the city of Linz was an influential uncle, husband of an Einbaum. Besides, the minor risks involved appealed to him. Not for nothing had Einbaum been a student of the gangster film and the Wild West.

Einbaum himself made the boat reservations for their trip to Budapest, on the seventh of September. That was the season for river outings, and they were certain to be seen by innumerable people. For this excursion Einbaum bought himself a trenchcoat, of the sort popular with Germans, and a cane often seen at the races, with the handles forming a saddle the observer could sit on. That was not all. The metal shaft contained a glass tube for several ounces of brandy or *Kirschwasser*. When it was not in use, he wore it in the crook of his arm.

Thus matters stood on the first day of September, the day Hitler invaded Poland. Just one day later, with a servant named Rudi, who carried several pairs of skis along with other luggage, Sophia and Einbaum took a train for a ski resort in the Italian Alps. They left the train at Graz, however, and went by car to a village on the Hungarian border. Her father, perhaps without luggage, would arrive on the bus that left Pest that morning. He would take Einbaum's seat on the train; Einbaum would return to Pest and they would make new plans. The bus from Pest appeared on schedule, before midnight, but her father was not on it. A briefcase with his initials, containing a bottle of *akvavit*, two Swiss chocolate bars, and a phial of sleeping powders, was found on one of the seats. Without a word Sophia took one of her ski poles and beat the driver of the bus as she would a horse. When Einbaum tried to restrain her, she beat him. All of this was observed by the servant Rudi, from his seat on the pile of luggage. He waited both for help and for the seizure to pass. This side of her temperament was new to Einbaum, and so was her grief. Was it her affection for her father or merely the interruption of her plans? Nothing would console her. She bolted the door to her room in the inn, but her shoes were there in the morning for Rudi to polish. First things first. Later that day, inanely gay, as if drugged, her mouth frozen in the smile of an animal trainer, she appeared at Einbaum's door to tell him that marriage would simplify their travel problems. Had she lost her mind? The point seemed academic. She still had more mind to lose than Einbaum. Nothing at Einbaum's disposal had the power to deflect her will. There would be delays, thanks to complications, and Einbaum thought he read the script as a staged performance, an act of hysteria that met her needs but for which she might not be responsible later. Shock, they called it. Einbaum would come to know much about shock.

In practical terms, the novels of intrigue supplied them both with a pattern of action. Little seemed new. All of this had been done so often before. Stranger couples than Einbaum and Sophia were seen on trains out of Vienna, and their story would not surprise the porter she had generously tipped. The servant Rudi had been blessed, put on the bus, and sent back to Pest. Strange that Einbaum, rocking in a berth euphoric with *akvavit* and the rising elevation, should remark that he had seldom felt so good about the future as at the moment the lights were going out over Europe. How explain it? He was by nature a gentle, even apprehensive man.

Money got them to Spain. The plane itself, a kite with open cockpits, recruited in Gorizia, was worth less than the money they paid for the passage, but she enjoyed the flight. At a moment her fear, accumulating for hours, would release itself in exhilaration— the thrill of a child rocking the seat of a Ferris wheel. Einbaum was terrified. He sat so long with stiff, clasped hands he had no feeling in his fingers. Wind filled his ears at night. They might have flown on to Lisbon, and from there to New York, but the travel agent could find few listings and accommodations under "Skiing." Before they flew on to Brazil, where little snow fell, the Countess wanted a last winter of skiing, and a chance to reconsider her plans for the future. The war might soon be over. Privately, she feared the godless Russians more than the Germans.

With her two sets of skis and shoe skates for Einbaum—along with wool mittens and matching fur earmuffs—they went north to a village in the Spanish Pyrenees that proved to be jammed with refugee traffic. There was little skiing. There was also a shortage of rooms and beds. The rumor was that ports of exit, in either direction, were in the hands of spies or Nazi sympathizers, and all foreigners, particularly Jews, were subject to investigation, their possessions confiscated. Was it possible? Einbaum thought it possible.

Sophia Horvath, traveling alone, with the added inducement of a little jewelry, might fly off to do her skiing elsewhere. Then again she might not. Although she was fond, as she said, of Einbaum, and talked to him as she would to a priest, her feelings, as well as her affections, followed the custom of a master and a servant. Frankly, Einbaum rather liked it. It testified to her breeding, as her appearance did not. On the vantage side, for Einbaum, this proved to mean that she needed him more than he needed her. She was accustomed to a Rudi, or a Helga, or a pet—she was subject to weeping for a hound, Süsschen, that slept on her bed and licked her awake—to be there at her side, at her service, or within range of her voice. The division of the men and women made necessary by the crowding—into separate groups, occupying separate dormitories—was a greater hardship on her than the incident at the border. She could not stand the lack of privacy; she could not stand absolute privacy. Without Einbaum she lost her wits and she made a fool of herself among the women. Her ingroup, a half-dozen or more females he was never given the opportunity to study, occupied a corner of the dormitory screened off from the room with several bedsheets. Among them was a Spanish Jewess, a lean, bitter woman Einbaum later thought he saw in the movie *La Strada*—one of the faces uplifted to the performer on the high wire. A cardinal principle of Sophia Horvath was that Jews could be bought. She let it be known that she would buy her way out, preferably through France, when the winter was over. She liked the language. She would take up residence in Paris. This should have upset Einbaum or made him apprehensive, but his temperament displayed a chronic weakness: people amazed him. What would they think of next? His anger at human folly was not equal to the pleasure observing it gave him. This remarkable woman, known to him as a countess, could change her spots when the script called for it. The word "script" was Einbaum's. It seemed appropriate to the cast and the circumstances. Here in the Pyrenees, as in an ambitious movie, several thousand strangers were locked in a drama of waiting. Einbaum did not merely endure it. No, as the tension mounted, he speculated on its resolution. Along with hunches and calculated guesses, there was increasingly the question of people. Like francs, pesetas, and dollars, they were negotiable. Some would prove to cash in, others to check out. As an example, Sophia, for all her discomfort, was at her best when she *hated* something. It brought out in her a vitality, a passion, that Einbaum associated with more intimate matters. This cow of a woman aroused desire. Einbaum marked it in himself. She slept in the clothes she feared she might lose, with her valuables worn on a chain at her armpit. Einbaum had seen them, the chain green as American money, when she raised her arms to put up her hair. Someone had told her this patina would increase their value, testifying to their age. Cash money she kept in a fold of flesh at her waist.

One morning at sunrise, the village still in the shadow of the snow-capped peaks to the east, Einbaum was awakened by a boy, Alexis, and hurriedly taken to the women's quarters. Most of them slept. There had been no disturbance to wake them up. The stale air had the sickening sweetness Einbaum associated with the female period. In the favored location, for which she had paid, set off from the cots of her in-group, Sophia sprawled on her back as if stoned. A wet towel had been placed on her forehead and eyes, but her mouth stood open. In such a bulk, how small it looked. A quilt pressed between her flanks, where someone had knelt. Among other things too numerous to mention, she had lost the gold crowns to her teeth. Someone had propped open the jaws, fished them out. Einbaum had the impression of a crudely looted piece of antique statuary, known to have had rare gems for eyes and solid gold teeth. Nevertheless, the overall impression was comical. A beached and looted hulk, or ship's prow, waiting for the tide to sweep it out to sea. The ring promised to Einbaum had been cunningly cut from her finger. On her spacious behind—she had been rolled onto her face by an official who knew what to look for, and where—a spot no larger than a pinprick indicated the point where the needle had entered. Perhaps it had never left. (Einbaum had heard the stories of how they circulated like fish in the bloodstream.) This grotesque incident would not have occurred in the orderly rigor of a well-run police state, and owed its success to the relaxed confusion of the time and place. Friends and enemies were not clearly defined—a situation she had instinctively feared. The consensus was that she had been the victim of the impression she left on others. Nothing would kill her. So she had had the benefit of too great a dose. The frail and cunning were better qualified to survive.

Einbaum's health actually improved on the camp rations and absence of tobacco. The letters Einbaum might have written for himself he wrote for others in French, German, and English. Few were answered. Einbaum was not tempted to try his luck. The past so desperately cherished by others held little attraction for him. Nor did the flight to Brazil, Canada, or the United States. Confinement gratified something in his temperament. An elderly Jew, Klugmann, who asked Einbaum's help with his Double-Crostics, diagnosed Einbaum's contentment as a return to the womb of the ghetto. Here in the camp he was at home. In a condition of freedom was he ill at ease? Klugmann had practiced psychoanalysis in Prague, where the anxiety of the Jews, if they had not been dispersed by war and incineration, would have tested Klugmann's theory that fear was more productive of spiritual renewal than hope. Now it hung in the air. Klugmann talked in this way while Einbaum dozed over the gaps in Klugmann's Double-Crostics—an American entertainment supplied to him by the secretary of the American Friends Service Committee, a society of

Quakers. The Crostics came to her from a friend in New York by the name of Bettina Gernsprecher. It was Einbaum who took the trouble to write and thank her for them both.

Here is Einbaum in New York. A greeting-card salesman, he has the use of one of the company's imported Volvos. The president is a Swede, a strong believer in foreign trade. Einbaum's area is in Bucks County, where his knowledge of German is considered an advantage. His manner is friendly, but his speech is sort of muttering, and the talk slacks off. There is something annoying about Einbaum, but it goes unmentioned, being hard to define. What is appealing is obvious. Einbaum is human. He has lived, like you, an already long and pointless life. He is on the road four or five days a week, and looks forward to sleeping late on Sundays. While in the city Einbaum stays with Bettina Gernsprecher, who colors the greeting cards by hand. The outline is there, and Bettina is free to vary the colors of the lips, the hair, and the eyes. This costs the buyer extra, but it gives Bettina a steady job. It takes eight months of the year to prepare for the seasonal rushes. Bettina sits on a stool, her back arched over so the bones protrude like knuckles, her knees drawn up to support the clipboard and the card. She puts a point to the brush by twisting it on her lips. Einbaum has warned her. He has told her the story of the women who died from painting numerals on watch faces—those that glow in the dark. Bettina's cards do not glow as yet, but one day they might. On his trips to the city Einbaum brings her his laundry, and while they listen to music she darns his socks. She likes to darn. She cannot sit for long without using her hands.

Early pictures of Bettina are lacking, since they were destroyed with the ghetto in Cracow. Because she was tall for her age, a place was made for her in a brothel limited to Jewish females. This information she shared with Einbaum the Sunday they went to the Met together. Humiliation, remorse, even self-disgust are sentiments that she has dispensed with. There is skill in her hands. She received her training in a concentration camp. She paid her own way when Einbaum took her to lunch, and shared with him the lower half of her daybed. Stretched at his side, or beneath him, she was taller, but her chronic stoop brought her eye to eye with him in elevators. Einbaum saw very little of her when they walked in the street. He found himself, soon enough, either a stride or two behind her or several strides ahead and pausing to wait for her. During her formative years, she had either been led (she found it hard to remember) or pushed from behind.

It is not easily explained that a woman's age and appearance seem irrelevant. Einbaum talked a good deal; could it be said she listened? When Einbaum showered, he would find looped over the curtain rail her brassière with the padded cups: if a woman really cared *that* much, why didn't she care more? Another time he found a shirt that was not his own in the laundry he brought back from the city. A small neck size, but the arms of an ape. Einbaum returned the shirt without comment, and that was where the matter rested.

Nevertheless, in her company he was subject to puzzling sensations. Years after any woman had been seen with a bob, Bettina found it a sensible hair style. The hair in front she cut herself, and let the barber apply clippers at the back. Einbaum could not make up his mind if he thought her a new and higher form of life or a lower. Her detachment extended beyond the things of this world. It was the contrary—he felt obliged to point out—with Sophia Horvath, the other woman in his life. She had been attached to things until death and thieves took them from her. "Looted" was the word. Einbaum had frequently described the spectacle for Bettina. The puzzling thing was that these two women, for all their differences, had one thing in common. They had chosen Einbaum. It could not be said that he had actually chosen them. Sophia had all but kidnapped him in Vienna, beckoning to him from the back seat of the taxi, and Bettina Gernsprecher, sight unseen, had agreed to support him until he found work, persuading her employer with the ape-long arms to hire Einbaum as a greeting-card salesman.

So here is Einbaum—through, as we say, no fault of his own.

1971

In Another Country

Madrid was so dim and sulfurous with smog Carolyn wrote letters to five museum directors, urging them to save the paintings in the Prado while there was still time. Paintings were what Carolyn had come to see, but she actually found it hard with her eyes smarting, her sinuses clogged. Ralph had come to Spain to see Ronda, where they had once planned to honeymoon. Ralph had stumbled on it in Hemingway's bull book as the place a man should go when he bolted with a woman. They had not bolted, but Ralph had always wondered what they had missed, so now they would see. They took a plane to Seville, rented a car, and the same day drove to Arcos de la Frontera, a place hardly on the map but so fabulous Carolyn didn't want to leave. Wasn't it a commonplace that people didn't know when to *stop?* Carolyn did, and she had the premonition that after Arcos anything would be a letdown. They might not have gone on, Carolyn feeling the way she did, if there had been a room for them in Arcos, but the small *parador* was full of English dames from the nineteenth century, one, surely, from the eighteenth century, who received her advice and encouragement through a tuba-shaped earhorn. A room had been found at a nearby resort, put up in a rush to meet the tourist traffic, the cabins so new the paint seemed sticky, and the sheets on their beds actually proved to be damp.

Carolyn had nearly died, and to keep her from freezing they

shared a bed no larger than a cot. Moored at the pier on the artificial lake was a miniature paddle-wheel steamboat, with the word *Mississippi* painted on the prow. It had been too much. Nevertheless, once they were up and had had breakfast, Carolyn had this feeling that Ronda would disappoint them, the view from Arcos being one that nothing could top. Why didn't they just act smart for once and fly to Barcelona and see the Gaudís? Even Ralph liked the Gaudís, or anything you couldn't get into a museum. Why didn't they compromise, Ralph said, and go to Barcelona if Ronda let them down? They might, anyway, if Carolyn's chill turned out to be a cold, which she would rather come down with in Barcelona where they had the name of an American dentist. Whenever they traveled she lost fillings and gained weight.

Their drive to Ronda on a windless spring day was so fabulous it made them both apprehensive. Birds sang, water rippled, the bells on grazing sheep chimed in the distance every time Ralph stopped the car and somewhat frantically took pictures. Was there no end of it? Each time they stopped Carolyn would cry, "Why don't we stop here!" It was a good question, and Ralph explained how the Mormons had faced the same dilemma as they traveled west. Carolyn found the parallel far-fetched but agreed she might feel different about it if she had been raised in the Midwest, rather than in the East. Ralph was romantic in a way Carolyn wasn't and took the statements of writers personally, following their suggestions to bolt to Ronda, and what to eat and drink. Of course, she liked that about him, up to a point. Over the winter he had read all the books about Spain and tried to persuade her they should travel with a donkey, Spain being the one place in the world a stranger was safe. If it was so gorgeous, Carolyn asked him, why had his great Mr. Hemingstein left it? Ralph thought it had something to do with their civil war. In a gas station on the outskirts of Córdoba the gas attendant had thrown his arms around Ralph, and given him a big hug. He had confused him with some American he had known in the war. It had been difficult for Ralph to persuade him to accept money for the gas. Loyalties of that sort were very touching, and at the same time disturbing. If there had been a war to go to, Ralph would have been tempted to enlist.

This morning the slopes of the mountains were green right up to where the granite shimmered like a sunning lizard. In everything Ralph saw, there was some Hemingway. Admittedly, the bottle of wine he had drunk the most of also helped. Carolyn was more enchanted by the whitewashed villas in the patterned rows of olive trees. But Carolyn was a realist. She knew what they were like inside. While they sat eating lunch, a man with his ox plowed a jagged furrow maybe forty yards long, frequently pausing to glance at the sky, his own shadow, or nothing at all. Waiting for him to reach the end of the row was a strain for Ralph. He was too much of a Peace Corps pilgrim at heart to watch a man kill time like that. If he was going to plow, let him plow and get on with it. One of Ralph's forebears combined spring plowing with memorizing passages from the Bible, which replenished the stories he would tell his family all winter. The Bible he had carried in his pocket was one of Ralph's treasured possessions. Here in this earthly paradise the man seemed lower on the scale than the grazing sheep, with their tinkling bells, or the hog, hobbled in the yard, surrounded by grass plucked that morning.

Carolyn found such dilemmas boring. Couldn't he accept things as they were, and not think so much? The blazing light had brought on one of her headaches, not a little aggravated by the sight of him brooding. She sat in the car while he took more pictures. Even as he did, his pleasure in it was diminished by the knowledge that Carolyn would argue with him about the slides. In her opinion he forgot where he had been; she did not. "To hear Ralph," she would say, "you would think I hadn't been on the trip!" Actually, it was true in a way she would never admit. Those walks Ralph took while Carolyn napped were often the source of his finest shots. "I'm sure he bought that one somewhere," she would say. "I never saw such a place."

These depressing reflections, like Carolyn's headaches, often occurred on those days that "were out of this world," and indicated that they both suffered from too much light. In such euphoric situations they helped Ralph keep his feet on the ground. When he came back to the car, it was surrounded by sheep and Carolyn had run her window up for protection. He could see Carolyn speaking to him, but the bleating of the lambs drowned out what she said. Ralph was disturbed, as he was so often, by the meaning of a scene that seemed to escape him, just as her open mouth spoke words to him that he failed to hear. In this instance she would accuse him of thinking more of his silly pictures than of her safety, using as his excuse this talk about how safe it was in Spain. Carolyn didn't mean these things, she simply found it a relief to talk.

As they climbed toward Ronda, Ralph tried to recall some of the high points of Hemingway's description, but it seemed to be a large impression made up of very few details. That was the art of it. If the gorge he spoke about was a mile deep, it meant the city itself would be a mile high. There was a possibility that Carolyn, who was sensitive to heights, might feel a bit queasy and not want to eat. The actual approach was not at all exciting, but it freshly prepared them for the view from the window of their hotel. Absolutely dazzling: Carolyn stepped back from it with a gasp. Ralph took a roll of shots right there in the room so she would be able to enjoy the view later, safe at home. The altitude left Carolyn bushed, however, and she settled for a nap while Ralph peered around. Three busloads of German tourists—in buses so huge Ralph marveled how they had ever got up there—crowded the aisles of the small gift shop and gathered in clusters in the patio garden. Many of them, like Carolyn and Ralph, had come to Ronda with a purpose, which was why one saw them huddled in silence before the life-size statue of Rilke. That in itself surprised Ralph. What had ever brought Rilke to a place like this? He was one of the people Carolyn read and liked so much better than Mr. Hemingway. Rilke would never think of bolting with anybody to such a public spectacle. Ralph's pleasure at the thought of informing Carolyn that her sensitive poet had his statue in the garden was diminished by the fact that he had come here thirteen years before Ralph had been born, and ahead of Hemingway. Ronda was an old tourist mecca, really, and the English and the Germans had been coming here for ages. How had Hemingway convinced him he had more or less discovered it?

When the Germans had departed Ralph had the garden and the view to himself. More than a mile below, lamplight glowed in the windows of the farmhouses. It was like another country, cut off and remote from the one on the rim. Down there it had been dark for an hour or more; here where Ralph stood the sun flamed on the windows. Ralph took a picture of the one behind which Carolyn slept. It would be hard for her to refute something like that. Several wide brick paths crisscrossed the garden, and one went along the rim, with bays for viewing. In every direction the prospect seemed staggering. In their first years of marriage Ralph had schemed to get Carolyn, somehow, to Arizona, and by stealth, driving at night, up to Bright Angel Lodge on the rim of the Canyon. In the morning she would wake up to face that awesome sight. Her own feeling was that she had come too late for great spectacles. Fellini movies and travel pictures had spoiled it for her. Ralph couldn't seem to understand that actually *being* there, under these circumstances, merely led to a letdown. She would just as soon miss whatever it was as feel something like that.

The path Ralph followed ended so abruptly that he found himself facing a high cable fence, while still preoccupied with his reflections. The two wings of the gate were locked with a chain, but Ralph could see that the path still continued. Weeds grew over it now, and the wall along the rim had breaks here and there that made it dangerous, but in Hemingway's time—not to mention Rilke's—people who came to Ronda did not stop at this fence. They had not come all this way to be fenced in. The tourist walked in those days, he was known as a traveler, and he did not climb from a bus to sit in a bar, or spend a frenzied half-hour in the gift shop. He got out and looked around. He wanted his money's worth. Ralph was not so crass, but he had not come to Ronda to peer through a fence. He had not come with that in mind, but as so often happened that was what he was doing, his fingers hooked in the wires, his eyes at one of the holes. Otherwise he would never have noticed the figure seated on the wall some fifty yards ahead. It was warm there. The sun, in fact, had moved from his lap to his chest and shoulders. He seemed to sit for the portrait that Ralph would like to take. He wore the wide-wale corduroy, with the comfortably loose jacket, the pockets large, the back belted, that Ralph had seen on men he judged to be groundskeepers, guides, watchmen, or whatever. He gave Ralph a nod and a quick smile—free of all "at your service" intimations. Like Ralph, he was a man enjoying the scene. Ralph also thought him so rustically handsome he would like to have a shot of him for Carolyn. Among other things, it would give the scene scale. On second thought it crossed his mind that just such a picture might be available in the hotel lobby. The fellow held a stick, or a cane, in such a manner one knew it was part of his habit, tapping it idly on the hobnailed sole of his boot.

When Ralph remained at the fence, as if expecting to enter, the man rose and came toward him, flicking the weeds with his stick. He greeted Ralph in Spanish and, as if he had been asked, unlocked the chain that closed the gate. He then gestured—in the manner of a man who works with children, or clusters of tourists—for Ralph to come along with him. Concealed beneath the overgrowth was a hard stone path that he followed out of long habit, his eyes up ahead. Ralph trailed along behind him, rising slowly to an elevation once cleared but now strewn with boulders from collapsed walls. The view from here—at this hour of the day—looked south along the canyon like the sea's bottom, the upper slopes flaming with a light like the glow from a furnace door. Where had Ralph seen it before? In the inferno paintings of Breughel and Bosch. At once, that is, indescribable and terrifying. Ralph had no word for it, and apparently none was expected. His companion stood, dyed in the same flaming color, facing what appeared to be left the instant following the act of creation, while the earth still cooled. Swallows nested in the cliffs, and their cries could be heard, changing in pitch as they shifted direction. Their flight on the sky was like fine scratches on film. After a moment of silence the man turned his head and appeared to be surprised that Ralph merely stood there. His eye moved from his face to the camera on his chest.

"No pictures?"

Smilingly, Ralph shrugged. Wasn't it almost impertinent to think that anything but the eye might catch it? The canyon had darkened even as they stood there, as if filling with an inky fluid, rising on the slopes. At the bottom a sinuous road was the exact metallic color of the sky, like the belly of a snake. No, Ralph was not so foolish as to believe he could catch it on film. His companion, however, was puzzled.

"No feeelm?" he asked.

Oh, yes, Ralph had film. He nodded to indicate the camera was loaded; he was just not taking any pictures. This aroused the man's interest. He tilted his head in the manner of the querulous, credulous tourist, looking sharply at Ralph. Was he something new? If he had not come to Ronda for pictures, what then? Ralph sensed his question clearly enough, but he could do no more than stand there. His position was not easily explained. He attempted, with some strain, to indicate that he "was taking it all in with his eyes" rather than his lens. Did it help? The man continued to eye him—a good honest man, Ralph thought, but perhaps a little simple in his thinking. People came here to take pictures. Why didn't Ralph do what was expected of him?

What Ralph *did* do—to distract his gaze, to do something if not take pictures—was remove from his pocket the bar of chocolate he had brought all the way from Madrid. Swiss bitter chocolate, the best; something this sensible fellow would have a taste for. The piece Ralph offered he accepted, with *muchas gracias.* Chewing up the piece, he was led to comment that he knew Swiss chocolate, and judged it superior. The Swiss made chocolate and watches. He extended toward Ralph a thick, hairy wrist, ornamented with a watch of Swiss manufacture. The one Ralph then exposed to him received his respectful, somewhat awed, admiration. Such an object with dials and levers he had heard about, but not seen. It is a commonplace of travel experience that absolute strangers have these congenial moments—not in spite of, but rather because of, their brevity. With the second piece of chocolate his friend suggested—this was the feeling of the moment—that they take seats on the boulders and enjoy the last of the sunset. Knees high, the leveling sun in their eyes, they finished off the chocolate. Ralph observed how, as his companion peeled off the foil, he put the wad of wrapping in his pocket. Overhead were the swallows. Nearer at hand Ralph was conscious of bats. Fortunately, Carolyn was not present to destroy this moment with hysterical shrieking, believing, as she did, that bats were no more than horrible flying mice.

Four or five minutes? Ten at the most? Now and then they idly glanced at the display before them, as gods might be amused by the northern lights. On the cliffs the remarkable tints seemed to bleed and dry like watercolors. His friend was the first to rise— not without a groan—and extend toward Ralph a helping hand. Why should something so common be so memorable? In his brusque matter-of-factness Ralph sensed that the guide also felt it. He was not so simple he did not know that this moment was something special. They walked back toward the hotel, the man ahead, Ralph trailing, turning once for a last glance at what vanished as they were looking. In that instant, it seemed, the air turned cold. They continued to the gate, where Ralph, in an involuntary gesture, turned and placed his left hand on the man's shoulder, and offered him his right. His companion lowered his eyes as if to locate Ralph's hand in the darkness. Yes, he actually looked. It seemed so droll a thing to do—something you might expect from a natural comic—that Ralph actually smiled. He also reached for the hand that was partially offered, gripped it firmly, then said *Vaya con Dios*—only one of many things he would soon enough regret. The man muttered something, but Ralph was so moved by his own feelings, his own generous impulses, he heard nothing but the wind of his own emotion.

Fortunately, the gate had been opened, and he was able to turn and make his escape. *Make his escape?* Was that the first suspicion that he had misread the situation? He did not look back. The fresh smarting of his face, a warmness all over his body, was not the result of his downhill walking. No, he was blushing. He was overheated with embarrassment. So clear to him now he could only go along with his head down, thankful for the darkness, was that this man had looked to his hand for something Ralph had not offered. A payment for services rendered.

Least of all the things in this world he had expected, or wanted, was a handshake. A *handshake!* He must be standing there shaking with laughter. This Americano who offered him a handshake? Was it believable? He would now go home with empty pockets but a story, a tale, that would last forever, be repeated by his children, conceivably become a legend of sorts at Ronda. The big Americano tourist who had gripped his hand, and urged him to go with God.

From a niche behind the statue of Rilke, Ralph paused long enough for a quick glance rearward. Had he gone? No, he was still there, but the rising tide of darkness had submerged him. He was all of one color, at this distance, his face the weathered tan of his corduroy, but Ralph had the distinct impression that his teeth were exposed in a smile. That could have been wrong. Maybe he merely stood there stupefied. Ralph might have walked, unseen, into the lobby, where the lights were now on, a fire was burning, and the woman who stood before it, warming her backside, wore a mini-skirt. Was it something he could speak about to Carolyn? How would it be phrased? Would she understand his failure to grasp he was in another country? And if not where he was, *how things were?* This man had done him a service—could it have been more obvious? He had opened a gate and given him a short tour—and on the return Ralph had offered him his hand. Would it be sensible, would it be believable, that Ralph considered him an equal, such a fleeting but true friend, really, that to have offered him money would have falsified their brief meeting, and reduced something gold to something brass? Carolyn would only make one of those gargle sounds in her throat. The other thing was—a sudden chill brought it home—that what he had been thinking of all the time was the high value of his own sensations, and in this intoxication he felt these sensations would be shared with his companion. As Ralph valued him, surely he would be moved to value Ralph, a fumbling but generous tourist who in a kind of Eucharist offered him chocolate. In this brief wordless drama two illusions had suffered, but was there any doubt whose had been the greater? Both stories were good, but Ralph's would be one he kept to himself.

1972

Real Losses, Imaginary Gains

On the firm's stationery, the loose pages in disorder, sent off to me by regular mail to a previous address, my cousin Daniel writes me that our Aunt Winona has passed away. A blow to us all. A loss that found him unprepared. Among her meager effects, stored away in its box, he found the silk kimono he had brought her from Hong Kong. Money given to her she sent to missionaries. He writes me in longhand, filling the margins, using both sides of the paper, giving vent to his affection, his frustration, his helplessness. In the past he only wrote such letters to her.

I see by the date it is more than three weeks since she passed away. My father's people, protesting but resigned, still reluctantly die, or go to their reward, but my mother's four sisters have all passed away. The phrase is accurate, and I use it out of respect for the facts.

Last summer we stopped in Boise to see her, the house both crushed and supported by huge bushes of lilacs. When I put my arms around her she said, "There's nothing much to me, is there?" One day she would say, "Let me just rest a moment," and pass away.

My aunt's couch faced the door, which stood open, the view given a sepia tone by the rusted screen. At the bottom, where children sometimes leaned, it bulged inward to shape a small hole. The view framed by the door was narrow if seen from the couch.

Lying there, my aunt took in only what was passing: she did not see what approached, or how it slipped away. On the steps of the bungalow across the street children often crouched, listening to summer. In the yard a knotted rope dangled a tire swing to where it had swept away the grass. A car passed, a stroller passed, music from somewhere hovered and passed, hours and days, weeks and months, spring to winter and back to spring, war and peace, affluence and depression, loved ones, old ones, good ones and bad ones, all passed away.

"Who is that?" she asked, as the picture framed by the door altered. My aunt lay on the couch, I was seated on the ottoman at her side. We were able to share the sunlit picture and the wavering shadow it cast toward the porch. The glare of light penetrated the sleeves of an elderly lady's blouse, and took an X-ray impression of her bloomers. Perhaps my aunt knew her. Had she stopped to admire the flowering lilac, or tactfully attract my aunt's attention? Her quandary had about it something vaguely imploring, of a person hopefully expectant. If her presence in the picture gave it a moral, the word "losses" gave it an appropriate caption. Just losses, not specifying what they were.

My aunt lifted her head to call out, "Would you like to step in?" Over the years, over the decades, many people had. The very young had given way to the very old, defying all belief that they had ever been children. Perplexities of this sort might lead my aunt to place her face in her hands, as if weeping. What she hoped to contain was her laughter, not at all that of an elderly, religious woman. On my father's side all of my Protestant aunts shared a common ceremony to ease the pain of this world, uttering no word as they gathered their aprons to hurl them like tent flaps over their heads. My Aunt Winona laughed: one might think it the muffled mirth of a child. Her nephews and nieces, the offspring of God-fearing parents, had grown up to be thrice married or worse, and divorced, their belief limited to one remaining article of faith—that *she* would understand. She did not understand, not for a moment, but their belief released the resources of her forgiveness, and gave proven sinners three to four times their share of her concern and love.

Perhaps the woman in the picture, poised like a worming robin, sensed the presence of strangers. She wheeled slowly, her dangling bag brushing the tops of the uncut grass. Her bearings taken, she went off in the direction from which she had come. The picture framed by the door, empty of its previous meaning, called to my attention the loose, dangerous boards of the porch. On the lower stoop one was curled like a ski tip. Over the years these boards had been mentioned, or were invisibly present, in much of my aunt's correspondence. One of her nephews always planned to do something about them. Recently, however—in the last twenty years—they have paid her only brief, flying visits, in which there was no time to be wasted repairing porches. Also, it was the porch itself now, not a few boards, that needed to be replaced. That would require removing the ambush of lilacs, replacing both the porch roof and one wall of the house. The floor in the bathroom tilted in a manner that delayed draining the tub. A late addition to the house, it had a self-opening door, and guests had to be warned.

On our arrival we had been given glasses of well water for refreshment. It was water but resembled broth in which life was emerging. About water she was eccentric. It was her opinion that water out of pipes lay at the root of many disorders, including some of her own. Well water, however, cleansed the system of its poisons. Water coursing through miles of pipes picked up poisons. This water came from the well of a friend, who brought it to her weekly, in gallon-size vinegar bottles. From there it was poured into mayonnaise jars and stored on the bottom shelf of the refrigerator. This shelf was cool but not cold: one might as well eat raw potatoes as pour ice-cold water on the stomach. After this water had sat for a spell, cooling, a sediment collected on the jar's bottom. Pouring the water from the jar into a glass stirred it up, so that the varieties of life could be studied. My wife had seen things swimming. I searched it for some sign of polliwogs.

The windows of the house were cluttered with plants that filtered the light like cataracts. Posses of flies had their own territories, and staged raiding parties. A fly swatter was used to break up these games if they got too rough. On the wall beside the couch, tucked into a loose strip of molding, were postcards from her far-flung friends. One from Perth, Australia, featured a baby kangaroo peering from its mother's pouch. There were numberless cards of kittens playing with balls of yarn, kittens stuffed into baskets, kittens asleep with puppies. Postcards from faraway places were not unusual, with so many of her friends being missionaries of the Adventist faith.

With her father and sisters—the sisters could be seen in a photo on the bric-a-brac shelf behind her—Aunt Winona had left the plains at the turn of the century to settle on a homestead near Boise, Idaho. Her father felt the plains of Nebraska were getting crowded, and moved his family of daughters westward. The two sons had already taken off on their own. Her father and mother were shown in a photo taken in the salon in Grand Island, Nebraska, in 1884. Her father is seated, and her mother stands at his side, her right hand resting on his left shoulder, more of a bride in appearance than the pioneer mother of seven children. The husband is holding the new child in the cradle of his arm. This child is my mother. She will die within a few days of my birth.

I was a young man of nineteen before I set eyes on my aunt and other members of my mother's family. I came west from Chicago, my locker covered with the stickers of Ivy League colleges I hoped to go to. I wore a blue serge suit and my pair of Paris garters. My grandfather was old but spry, a God-fearing man long prepared for God. I saw him in the flickering glow of kerosene lamps, a second-time child to his matronly daughters. Only my mother was missing: he searched my face to recoup that loss. I slept that night in a large bed with two uncles, who assured me that my lack of Adventist faith was not crucial. The love of my aunts would be more than enough to get me into Heaven, if that was my wish.

In the morning my Aunt Winona, the only one not to marry, stood in the sunlit kitchen and watched me eat. Her first love had been the Lord, the second her father, and in this world she had found no replacement. It was him she saw when she gazed at me. She gave to this farmhouse kitchen, the light flaming her hair, the time-stopped dazzle of Vermeer's paintings. She poured milk from a bowl, threaded a needle, picked up crumbs from the table with her tip-moistened finger. She was at once serene, vulnerable, and unshakable. The appalling facts of this world existed to be forgiven. In her presence I was subject to fevers of faith, to fits of stark belief. Like the grandfather, she saw me as a preacher in search of a flock.

In a recent letter she wrote:

> When your mother died my sister Violet, who was married, wanted to take you, but your father would not consent to it. He said, "He is all I have left of Grace." O dear boy, you were the center of so much suffering, so many losses you will never know, realize, or feel. . . .

What is it I feel now, sitting here in the full knowledge of my loss? In my mind's eye I see her couch, now empty, the impression of her figure like that the wind leaves on tall grass.

No, in the flesh there was nothing much to her—she had reduced the terms by which we measure real gains and losses. "I always thought she needed me," her nephew wrote, "and now I find I'm the one who needs her." That's a miserable loss. I weigh mine each time I lift a glass of water and note its temperature, its color, and what it is that swims I can no longer see.

1973

The Cat's Meow

What were the symptoms?

No voice. A total loss of voice. Using a small pocket flash, with an intense white beam, Dr. Payne peered into the patient's throat. "Some redness," he said, and appeared to relax.

"Some redness?" Morgan repeated.

"Laryngitis. Not uncommon, you know. Does he eat?"

Oh yes, he ate very well. One might say too well. Dr. Payne turned away to make jottings on his three-by-five file card. There were two cards for the patient, both sides recording his history.

"Twice a day," said Dr. Payne, tapping pills from a jar, and counting out twelve he slipped them into a packet. They were moderate-size pills, pink in color. Both Morgan and the patient disliked large pills. Morgan wondered if their taste was minty. "If there's no improvement by Friday—" Dr. Payne continued, but Morgan was sure there would be marked improvement. The patient had never been long silent. Besides, there were twelve pills, and only a small redness. The patient, a large, fat, short-haired cat (the card recorded his weight at 17 pounds 4 oz.), mewed silently, his motor purring. Morgan turned to see if Dr. Payne had observed it. A most curious effect. "Hmmmmmm—" said Dr. Payne.

"Thought it was my hearing, first time I heard it—I mean *saw* it," said Morgan. "Gave me quite a start."

Dr. Payne smiled. He used the ballpoint pen he was holding

to scratch the skull of the patient, which seemed to please him.

"How come," asked Morgan, "you can hear his motor running, but no voice?"

Dr. Payne was long accustomed to ridiculous questions from non-patients. "This one is Bloom, right?"

"This is Bloom," replied Morgan. Hearing his name, hearing it from Morgan, Bloom lifted his tail and soundlessly meowed. Why was that so disturbing?

"Makes for quiet, I must say!" said Dr. Payne.

Actually it did not make for quiet. It made for silence.

"The big problem is the morning," said Morgan. "He comes to the door about five, give or take a few minutes. I *know* he's there, but I can't hear him. A strain for both of us."

"You complain about that?" Dr. Payne was clearing up for the next patient. A calico-type cat with glassy, rheum-clouded eyes crouched in a cage at the door to the lobby. Morgan hoped it wasn't catching. Over nine years Bloom had had many things, but no trouble with his eyes. About the soundless meow, it had ceased to be a pleasure when it became a worry. He had relied on that meow, as he did his wife's breathing. If for any reason she checked that breathing, in order to listen to something, he was awake in an instant. In the past week his sleep had been disturbed by the tick of the clock that had replaced the cat's meow. Even the luminous numerals on its face interfered with his sleep. At five o'clock sharp, give or take a few minutes, he would get up and find Bloom at the bedroom door. Morgan could not hear it, but he could sense the puzzled irritation in the cat's manner.

"If I were you," said Dr. Payne, "I'd enjoy it while it lasts. It won't be long."

Into his traveling box, with its wire-mesh top, Morgan pushed the reluctant Bloom. A marvelous cat. Reluctant but seldom stubborn. If Morgan said so, he would do it. Absolute, unerring faith in Morgan, in all for the best.

Outside the clinic, in the seat of the car, he knew that Bloom was silently mewing. He did not like cars. If he had eaten first, he always whooped it up. But what a relief it had seemed, driving over, not to hear his yawping complaint. Not a meow at all, of the usual sort, but a sound squeezed up from his innards. Now Morgan missed it. To hear nothing at all was worse.

These trips to the clinic Morgan made alone after a disastrous worming session. His wife, Charlotte, had never once imagined that they were in Bloom's stomach, and would come up the front way. It had been too much. Charlotte had disappeared into the ladies' room of the Texaco station.

Morgan and Charlotte, Bloom and Pussy-baby, lived in a hillside house under a cluster of live oaks, a heaven for cats. On the two-thirds acre there were too many birds, foolish, stupid little birds scratching under the bushes, and there were too many creatures better left unnamed that could be heard at dawn, plaintively shrieking, but Morgan had explained (he had lied, to put it bluntly) that cats were quick and merciful killers. Without cats, he soberly warned her, the place would suffer a population explosion, and Morgan had only to mention the word *rodent* to confuse her sympathies toward mice.

The other cat, Pussy-baby, a small black Manx, had a card at the clinic almost free of afflictions. He had had his shots, and he had once been wormed, but otherwise even bugs could not keep an eye on him. A tiny fawnlike creature, he had also eluded a determined search for a suitable name. He had been a baby, a pussy-baby, and after several years of futile experiments, plain names, weird names, and just plain cute names, he remained Pussy-baby. Fortunately, this was only a problem when he met people, which was seldom, or had to go along with Bloom to the clinic, where the girl at the desk, looking for his card, would cry out in the lobby, "Which one is Pussy-baby?" Charlotte had steeled herself to endure it. Morgan would stand near the door thumbing the pages of a magazine. Pussy-baby was Charlotte's cat.

In being ten weeks younger than Bloom, Pussy-baby's life and times had been predetermined. The big loutish Bloom, a friend to man, *any* man and most women, at the sight of Pussy-baby had been transformed into a cunning jungle tiger. Quite possibly, lacking experience he failed to recognize the creature as a fellow cat. Batlike ears, button eyes. A startled look or no look at all. In the first few weeks Bloom had mauled him, pounced on him, carried him about like a homeless kitten, until the problem had been partially solved by concealing him beneath food cartons. One can well imagine—Charlotte always says—what Morgan would have been like after such a childhood.

At dawn, with Bloom, Pussy-baby leaves the house to lie concealed under something, or peer down from something, occasionally returning to gulp food from the saucer in the kitchen, to reappear at dusk, as the lights come on, and assume his role as a member of the family, crouching like a sphinx on Morgan's knee, which is well scarred by his claws, or curling up with the dreaded Bloom for a snooze, or a bout of face washing. Another cat? One has to believe it. Wild rather than tame, murderous claws, inflexible tastes, indifferent alike to threats and persuasions, given to swallowing string, choking on grass, and sneaking into the garage when Morgan has his back turned. There he hides until late at night, when his penetrating mew, like an out-of-order buzzer, is instantly heard by Charlotte. There is nothing to be done, of course, but rescue him. He was once gone and given up for lost over a long Labor Day weekend, but when it was over, and the neighbors had returned, he was found in the cab of the Steyerhausers' pickup, the leather palms of a pair of garden gloves gnawed away. Morgan tirelessly wants to know what earthly good such a cat is, and Charlotte tirelessly reminds him what a cat is good for is a cat's business. There are moments, however, somewhat infrequent, in no conceivable way to be relied on, when Pussy-baby will pause, as if petrified, as he crosses a room or enters the kitchen, holding a posture only seen in the low reliefs of creatures and birds on Egyptian temples. A captured moment of time! It might last a full minute, neither Morgan nor Charlotte breathing, then the merest twitch of his stub tail would indicate the time destroyer, life itself, once again circulating in his tiny veins, starting up his motor so that he could pick up from where he had stopped. Charlotte and Morgan are agreed that these moments almost justify his endless exasperations, and that if cats were as rare as diamonds people would pay more money for them. What good is it for Morgan to remind her that they are not?

Back at the house, Morgan stands with Bloom in the grass at

the edge of the driveway, on the chance that he might have something on his mind. It had been Bloom's decision that he was Morgan's cat, both of them being outdoor types fond of peeing while the sprinklers are running. What can Charlotte do? *Her* cat is Pussy-baby, but there are times even Charlotte loses patience. Food mostly. Both cats will eat *any*thing found in the yard, but absolutely *nothing* from the table. If it is on the table, and they find it, that of course is another matter. It distresses Charlotte that after nine years Pussy-baby would rather cheat than not cheat. If he turns up his nose at the chopped kidney, just leave the can on the counter and he will gulp it. The look he gives Charlotte, licking his chops, is that he might turn on her next. That is too much: but nevertheless, that is how he is.

If Morgan lets drop that such an independent cat should *really* be independent, Charlotte will accuse him of not liking cats unless they are willing to do his bidding and are not really cats at all, but some new kind of dog. It is a fact that Bloom, since he was a kitten, either thinks that Morgan is a special kind of cat or has very uncatlike characteristics, tailing Morgan, relaxing with Morgan, driving Charlotte crazy in Morgan's absence, as if she, Charlotte, had hidden Morgan in a closet, locked him in the garage, or possibly worse. His voice and his manner on such occasions are unmistakably hostile, which is hard to believe in such an easygoing, affectionate fat cat. Both Morgan and Bloom appreciate that Morgan and Bloom are pretty unusual, but tactful in the area of making any ridiculous claims. If Morgan snaps his fingers, Bloom sometimes comes, other times he does not.

The rear view of Bloom being one of Morgan's favorites—a fat trousered harem master—they walk in tandem, Bloom leading, his tail erect and his button gleaming from the attention received in the clinic office. Charlotte stands at the door, waiting, relieved to see that the patient is walking.

"You wouldn't believe it," said Morgan. "Laryngitis."

He was right, she does not believe it. Morgan is a joker, and his jokes cost him the desired effects of a true story. Charlotte impatiently waits.

"I'm not joking," he reports. "It's laryngitis."

Passing Charlotte, Bloom glanced up to soundlessly meow, then enter the house. Charlotte followed him without comment. When Morgan insisted on his little jokes, there was nothing for Charlotte to do but wait. In the kitchen, at the patio door, she lifted and rattled the box of Friskies. Bloom soundlessly meowed. She spilled a handful into his bowl, the one farthest from the wall, where his tail would not catch in the heavy, sliding patio door. With Pussy-baby there was no problem.

"Payne gave me some pills," said Morgan. "He says it ought to clear up by the weekend."

They stand watching Bloom crunch up his Friskies. The big, loutish cat is very delicate in his eating habits. In contrast, the fawnlike Pussy-baby covers his face and the floor when he laps milk, bolts hunks of liver, whoops up half-and-half.

This little jaunt to the clinic, going and coming, plus a twenty-minute wait for Dr. Payne, has raised hell with Morgan's working schedule. He is a writer. From nine to one he sits at his desk. He leaves the packet of pills for Bloom on the counter, then walks through the house to his study. The desk lamp shines on the sheet of paper in his typewriter. Three lines have been typed. One of the lines has been canceled. To get back to where he was, to recover his thought, Morgan takes the last sheet typed from the wire basket. Near its center is a smear that has dried, to which a few black hairs are attached. Other things being equal, the hours of nine to one Bloom spends in Morgan's wire basket. That is how it has been for some years now. It is how things are. Sheets are added to the basket when he leaves for a snack, or when Morgan lifts him and slips them beneath him, accepted by Bloom as an important part of the morning's work. On occasion so little work is accomplished, and the basket sits so close to the typewriter carriage, that Bloom naps with his chin on the nob and work is further delayed until something disturbs him. On some occasions it is Morgan. The cat faces him, his eyes blinking in the desk light, and the look he gives Morgan, and Morgan returns, is not something to be lightly dealt with, or even when soberly and thoughtfully dealt with, put into words. The cat is the first to speak, and Morgan replies. There is a passage in a book by Konrad Lorenz that Morgan has read to Charlotte, concerned with the habits and cackling of the graylag goose. While the geese are strolling about, or grazing, the mated pair keep in touch by cackling, which had been translated to mean "Here am I, where are you?" Cats meowed, geese cackled, people talked. Morgan didn't want to make too much of this, but neither did he want to make too little, having shared his life, and his wire basket, with Bloom. While he had his voice he said plainly to Morgan, "Here I am!" and expected an answer.

Morgan read the last sheet, returned it to the basket, then sat for something less than a full minute waiting for the cat to come from the kitchen. He came, as usual, to the side of the desk, where the light narrowed the pupils of his eyes to slits, and reminded Morgan of the lizards in his past. Acknowledging the patient's need for special treatment, Morgan stopped to lift the seventeen pounds of cat to his place in the wire basket. It was customary for Bloom to thank him for that, but this time he said nothing.

A few summers back, a big orange tiger with the gait of a leopard, and huge white paws, liked the patio and decided to adopt them. Morgan himself was all for a *ménage à trois*—what was another mouth to feed? The handsome tiger had beautiful manners and elegant disdain for the dumbfounded Bloom. In the morning he would sidle through the patio door, eat Pussy-baby's chopped liver, share Bloom's Friskies. If Bloom left the house, there he was on the patio lounge. Morgan was at the sink, squeezing oranges, when the blood-curdling shrieking made the hairs on his neck rise. In the clearing between two fuchsia bushes—a scene they transformed into a jungle—the two big cats stood eye to eye, horribly growling, the mouth of Bloom tufted with orange hair, the mouth of the tiger with black hair, the bell-like flowers rocking wildly from the whiplike snap of their tails. In a ballet leap, they went up together, legs thrashing, then fell with a thud that Morgan actually felt in the floor. Pure fury. A spectacle both appalling, terrifying, and gratifying. In helpless shame Morgan let it go on, enthralled by the unleashing of such forces. Then he used the sink spray to douse them, which they appeared to enjoy as a cooler, before he ran to the hose at the side of the house and let them have it full blast. The tiger had to be carted to another county, where adoptions were less complicated, and Bloom had to be driven to the clinic for what was listed on the bill as surgery. Dr. Payne thought it amazing how well he had recovered. At his age (roughly sixty-three, as calculated by Charlotte) Bloom was now kept in the house until dawn to avoid further confrontations.

After giving Bloom his pill, Morgan and Charlotte went out to dinner with friends and were late getting home. It was customary for Bloom to step out for a moment, but he slept on. If there was something in the pill to put him to sleep, Morgan should have taken one of them himself. Worried about Bloom, they had ignored Pussy-baby, who had cunningly made his way into the bedroom, where the noise he made, licking his coat, was like that of an animal chewing up his neighbor. Morgan had to switch on the light to find him in the half-open drawer of the bedside table. In the top drawer he kept a loaded pistol, wrapped in a cloth scented with furniture polish. On sleepless nights, like this one, Morgan tried to recall the exact nature of its operation. He had never actually fired it. When he bought the gun he meant to drive into the mountains and shoot it a few times, just to get the feel of it, but Charlotte would not allow the pistol in the car, knowing there was a law against transporting handguns. Who were the people who were always getting shot? People fooling with guns.

Morgan's restlessness was due in part to the rich food—Charlotte's friend was a disciple of Julia Child—in part to his persistent feeling that Bloom was at the door—or at some door. There were three doors he used to enter or exit the house: the one to the patio, which was customary; the chained and bolted front door, which was a damn nuisance; and in unpredictable emergencies, the door to the deck. The deck door, as a rule, was an IN door—bad weather, large dogs, garbage trucks, meter readers—and in practical terms it was Charlotte's business. Morgan let the cats out—Charlotte let them in. Charlotte could hear the faint mew of Pussy-baby, at the door to the deck: Morgan swore he could not. If Morgan lied on this point, or stretched it a little, it was in the interest of law and order. Disturbed by a break in the routine (the sight of Morgan) Pussy-baby might take off instead of coming in. Leave well enough alone, was Morgan's rule, if it applied to cats.

This early morning, however—it was not yet four—he knew the cat Bloom was at the door, wanting out. It was not his usual time, but it had been an unusual day. To check on this impression Morgan went to the door, and there he was, silhouetted against the night light, his *back* to Morgan by way of indicating his irritation at Morgan's slowness. In tandem, Morgan trailing, they padded through the house to the patio door, where the cat made his cautious, sniffing exit. The night air chill in his lungs, and pleasurably cool on his body, Morgan might stand there until his feet were cold, sharing something of the cat's experience, the sensation of leaving a safe haven for the dark, watchful jungle of the night. The cat in Morgan at one with Morgan in the cat.

It was not unheard-of for Morgan, if he couldn't sleep, to let the cat out and then make himself some coffee, as if he meant to start the day early. He might read the morning paper, or sit there watching the sky get light. Bloom came back into the house when Morgan stepped out to empty the garbage. He was in the wire basket, curled up asleep, when Morgan left the house to turn on the sprinklers. He used the patio door, walking around the house— this little tour might take him four or five minutes—to get to the sprinkler faucet under the deck. The cat, Bloom, sat in the shelter of the deck, his customary place.

"How did this cat get here so quick?" he called to Charlotte.

"He meowed at the deck door," she replied.

"He what?"

There was a pause. "I just know I heard him meow," said Charlotte. Morgan was delighted. He stooped to stroke Bloom and praise him for his quick recovery. Bloom accepted this interest without comment.

"You sure he meowed?"

"How would I know he was there?" replied Charlotte. She had been in the bathroom, the door standing open. Even with the water running she had heard him.

This sort of thing with Bloom—never with Pussy-baby—was frequently a subject for discussion. It always amused Charlotte the way that Bloom, asleep in his chair, would know when Morgan had left the room, allow him one long minute to return, then immediately go in search of him. Was it feline ESP? Morgan didn't really think so. It was just like man, of course, to call it *extrasensory* if he didn't have it himself. It was simply that Bloom heard what he wanted to hear, and nothing else. The slightest move that Morgan made he picked up on his radar. Hadn't they both noticed how his ears tuned in even while he napped? With the house full of people, all of them yakking, Bloom would hear the drop of a Friskie in the kitchen, or the tap of a bird's beak in the feedbox on the deck. If Charlotte or Morgan were attuned like that the world would be a different place than they found it, and quieter. As for what Charlotte had heard, in his afflicted condition Bloom might well make a noise one time and not another. Morgan did not feel that the time was ripe to make an issue about it. He turned off the sprinklers, then went for the mail, a chore that Bloom observed from the top of the driveway. When he glanced up from the street the cat was gone—or perhaps he should say, not visible. From the shrubs on the left Pussy-baby, with his tailless, uncatlike canter, saw him to the house along the walk at the side, then took off like an escort who had done his duty. The fat cat Bloom was in the basket on his desk, tidying up.

Morgan went to bed early, to catch up on lost sleep, and did very well to the moment he awakened, as if called. At his side, Charlotte's rhythmical exhalation was like the wash of water in a bed of reeds. Morgan was wide awake, but without apprehension, as if he had been awakened by a familiar alarm. He felt the peace of one who, having been chosen, was spared a choice. After a few moments of this he went to the door, the curtains stirring as it opened. At full aperture not even the eyes of the cat were visible. But at the touch of the fingers Morgan extended he turned to leave, once more clearly expressing his irritation. "Cat got your tongue?" Morgan hissed at him, this being one of his little jokes. From Bloom no comment. At the patio door Morgan restrained the impulse to give him a powerful assist from the rear, Bloom pausing on the threshold, eyes lidded, to gingerly sniff the night air.

Back in bed he lay awake for some time, thanks to the caterwauling beneath the window. The cats were in good voice, and not to be rushed. One voice seemed more familiar to Morgan than the other, even shriller for want of practice. Was it unusual for a cat to lose his normal speech, but still be able to howl? Ordinarily Morgan would have leaped from the bed to throw the empty tin cans (kept there for that purpose) to where they would roll the length of the concrete driveway, arousing the Steyerhauser dog to a frenzy of barking that often silenced the cats. Now he just lay there until Charlotte leaped from the bed to clap her hands on the window sill, then shriek "Bloom! Bloom! Bloom!" as if part of a cheer. This considerable racket was followed by a silence in which they could both hear a plaintive meowing at the door to the deck. Lost in the mists of time were the reasons why Morgan let the cats out and Charlotte let them in. Now he could hear her, he could hear *them*—Pussy-baby also having entered—while she refilled their bowl of Friskies, then padded back through the house to tell him, knowing he was awake and listening, that dear, darling old Bloom, thanks to the scuffle, had recovered his voice. It was too bad that included his howl, but in these matters one couldn't be choosy, as Morgan knew.

It still proved to be early, but having once been out, Bloom was usually content to stay in. Charlotte slept like a baby, but Morgan was not free of the impression that a cat, the non-meowing Bloom, was back at the door. It could be nothing more than Morgan's apprehension, resulting from the patient's laryngitis; it could be, but Morgan was reasonably sure it was not. The presence of Bloom, his radar beaming, was there on the grid of Morgan's mind. As plain as day, when days were plain, Morgan recorded the message *Here I am—where the hell are you?* Taking care not to disturb Charlotte's sleep Morgan tiptoed to the door, opened it gently, and stooped to stroke the invisible cat. There he was, his motor purring as he arched his back. They then proceeded as usual to the patio door, when the first touch of dawn blazed on the glass: the whine of freeway traffic had displaced the music of the spheres. Morgan might have preferred a more orthodox alliance—this one was sure to cost him much sleep—but in the nature of things he could see no reason why one creature, in union with another, through affliction and affection, in sickness and in health, should not dispense with the obvious. Turning to give him a look, not a meow, Bloom took his leave.

1975

The Lover and the Beloved

Through the misty hissing spray of the yard sprinkler, through the moving screen of the hanging ferns, Paul could see Lois Casey sprawled in the porch hammock, her father's unlaced tennis sneakers on her long, narrow feet. Mr. Casey stood in the driveway hosing down his new Hupmobile sedan. At the wheel of the car sat Lois's little brother Charlie, wearing his father's streetcar motorman's hat. The noises he was making, blowing through his lips, could not be heard, because the windows were up.

The catbirds nesting in the wire baskets of ferns flew in and out of the sprinkler's range, their wings beating. Paul was unable to see, but he knew that Lois held a rabbit in her lap, one of a pair of Belgian hares he had given her for her birthday a year ago. The male of the pair had been returned to the pet store after it had eaten part of its own litter. Lois was not indifferent to the facts of life she observed in the mason jars in her bedroom, but the role of males, now that it was questioned, had not been settled to her satisfaction.

On the porch beneath the hammock, in an ice-cream carton, were two spotted long-tailed goldfish, a gift from Paul yesterday on her fourteenth birthday. Nobody but her mother believes Lois is merely fourteen. When she dances with Paul in her tennis sneakers they are eyeball to eyeball, and she is still growing. He agrees with her mother that in the past year she has grown too fast.

Beginning early this spring, Paul was no longer needed to reach for her books on top of the school locker, or to return the gravy bowl, after wiping, to the top shelf in the pantry. In the dusk of the basement, while he had both arms around her, she had put up one arm to switch off the light she previously couldn't reach. A moth fluttered around the arm she had lifted to the light cord, the elbow inwardly bent, like a drawn bow. Paul had found that disturbing, even at the time, since it confirmed that her bones were not yet fully formed.

Since last night's movie Lois seemed to have forgotten about the carton of goldfish beneath the hammock. Her attention had been diverted back to butterflies. Before he gave her the rabbits (Mrs. Casey had warned him that Mr. Casey did not like puppies or kittens), Paul had helped her catch butterflies in the park, or in the orchard of her Uncle Ed's bee farm in Urbana. The more unusual butterflies were put into mason jars with their Latin names printed on the jar labels. A long row of these jars sat on the sill of her window to catch the afternoon sun. Lois did not as yet read Latin, but she planned to take it in her first year of high school— the one coming up.

At the rear of the house, Mrs. Casey had her vegetable garden, adjacent to the Epworth League's volleyball court. A high chicken-wire fence enclosed the court, but some balls went over it into her garden. Lois's little brother Charlie would get the ball, but almost go crazy trying to throw it back over the high fence. If Lois tried to do it, throwing the ball the way girls do, it was so painful to watch her that Paul would turn away and go to the fountain for a swallow of water. Most of the time he had to go for the ball himself, using the gate on the alley. That was how they first met, even though she had lived all those years right across the street. If Paul was playing volleyball, she might sit on the porch stoop, her legs drawn up, or she might come to stand at the chicken-wire fence, her arms stretched high to hook her fingers in the wire, her nose pressed through one of the holes, as if she might just hang there till her mother came out and called her in.

The peculiar eating habits of male Belgian hares led him to present her with the long-tailed goldfish, one of which he had found would swallow lead BBs he could see as a lump in its stomach.

When Mrs. Casey first asked Paul to join them on a picnic at Uncle Ed's farm, he was shown where and how to look for glowworms and for caterpillars that would turn into butterflies. No matter what he and Lois did, her little brother spied on them. On the long drive home, Mrs. Casey confessed (Lois was in the front seat, with her father and Charlie) how relieved she was that Lois had found an older companion who shared her own interests, which included wiping the supper dishes. In her own life Mrs. Casey had found that nothing—no, nothing—ever replaced those first affections. After the grubs and caterpillars had been put into the gauze-topped jars, with the bits of twigs and leaves they liked to chew on, everyone played rummy with the joker wild, Mr. Casey and Charlie winning most of the games. Later, unable to sleep because of his sunburn, Paul saw a glow at her bedroom window, which he took to be the jar with the glowworms. The aspect of her beauty that enthralled him the most was the way she would sit, on the top step of the porch, with her legs hugged to her front, her chin resting on her knees, as far away as the Sphinx, who had a similar hairdo.

In the quiet between passing streetcars, Paul could hear water falling like rain on the Caseys' sidewalk. Mr. Casey himself, in his undershirt, sat on the steps of the porch, sprinkling the corners of the lawn. Now and then he aimed a stream of water into the trees, from where it would drip onto the walk. A tall, thin man with a truculent manner, Mr. Casey was different when you got to know him. On the previous day, for Lois's birthday, he had taken his family and Paul to see *All Quiet on the Western Front.* To make the first show they had gone without supper, and they picked up four bags of popcorn in the lobby. Lois had simply not known it was a war movie, or she wouldn't have gone. She liked Lew Ayres, the young German soldier, but in the trench scene with the butterfly she had withdrawn the hand Paul was holding. She could not control her sobbing. Mrs. Casey had led her out to the lobby. To just sit there as if he didn't share Lois's feelings made Paul miserable. The emotion he felt made it hard for him to swallow, but it was not for the soldier, or the butterfly, that he felt it.

When the lights came on, Paul went out to the lobby to be with Lois. First he looked for her in the basement near the washroom, then among the crowd of people waiting near the entrance. She liked to watch people. Almost anything some of them did made her laugh. The fits of giggling she might have in an Epworth League meeting made it embarrassing for Paul to be with her. What she had probably done now, to punish all of them, was leave the movie house and go home alone. Paul had to choose between siding with Lois and not pleasing Mrs. Casey, or siding with the family and having Lois ask him if he was her mother's new boyfriend. With her mother he already had so much in common that they discussed it while he wiped the dishes. If Lois thought they were talking about her, she would make a simply god-awful face by flattening her nose with the heel of her hand. "You're going to do that just once too often," her mother told her, and that was what worried Paul the most. In moments of excitement she could flare her nostrils like one of her rabbits when it sniffed something.

Paul found her back at the house, lolling in the hammock, with her favorite female Belgian hare in her lap. *Amos 'n' Andy* was tuned in on the neighbors' radio. On the floor beneath the hammock, where she had left it, was the ice-cream carton with the long-tailed goldfish. Paul worried about them, too, but it wasn't the time to bring it up. When the Caseys got home, Mr. Casey went inside, but Mrs. Casey stopped to say a few words to her daughter. She was especially critical of the selfish way Lois had spoiled Paul's evening and her own birthday. They all had feelings, just the same as she did, only they had the good manners to control them.

During the night, flashes of heat lightning lit up the front of the Caseys' house. It startled Paul to see it all so clearly one moment, then the next moment it would be gone. In the bright flash, he could see the mason jars, each one with something in it that would soon be something else. The white columns of the porch were ghostly in the street light, and he could read the iceman's card over the hole in the screen door. On warm summer nights like this one, the Caseys' screen would be latched but the front door left open, and he could see the night light glowing at the top of the stairs. At the front of the house, the wire that fenced off the new grass dangled strips of white rags so the neighborhood kids wouldn't trip on it. On the first step to the porch, her little brother Charlie had left a single roller skate for somebody to step on and kill himself. Not that Charlie cared. When that was pointed out it only made him laugh.

As Paul's eyes adjusted to the darkness, he saw something move on the roof of the porch. One of Lois's rabbits was hopping around in the leaves of the gutter. Straining to make out more, he saw an apparition, white as skimmed milk, on the roof just to the right of her window. A figure crouched there, the legs drawn up, the chin resting on the knees. As he gazed, unblinking, a firefly appeared to emerge from the lips. In the brief, incandescent glow, he saw her face. Unmistakably she held, and was puffing on, a cigarette. It had shamed him not to share her uncontrolled weeping at the sight of the butterfly and the soldier, or her tears for the baby rabbits eaten by their father; but for the pity he now felt for lovers, especially himself, he was grateful.

1981

The Customs of the Country

To put things in perspective, Hapke was born in a hayfield near Küssnacht where his mother had been at work with a hand scythe. To his knowledge she had never been to Zürich, looked from the window of a train, or had her picture taken. The image of her retained by Hapke is that of a small woman hugging a large loaf of bread which she struggled to slice as she drew the knife toward her, as if cutting its throat. Was it, then, to his mother that he owed his preference for American sliced bread?

A short, wide man, with hands like gnarled roots and the habit of rudely squinting at people, Hapke was offered work by Dr. Soellner, an American who liked to vacation in Küssnacht. This opportunity faced him with a moral decision: a choice between the fatherland and another country. Years later it would shame Hapke to admit that both his affections and his allegiance had shifted. He preferred Americans.

That did not confuse Hapke, as it did so many others, about his own place. Dr. Soellner's handsome wife, a native of Basel, liked the way that he addressed her as *gnadige Frau*. Over Christmas she invited him into her kitchen for *Kaffee mit Schlag* and a slice of her stollen. He had combed his hair, and he sat at the table with his cap in his lap. In those days there were no bridges over the bay to San Francisco, and many of Dr. Soellner's patients had to use the ferry. Hearing their laughter and hearty German talk, Hapke felt right at home.

Yet his reluctance to make friends, or seek out younger women, led Frau Soellner to conclude that he longed for his homeland, as she did. She persuaded Dr. Soellner to give him a year's wages and his passage back to Küssnacht. Hapke enjoyed the passage through the Panama Canal, but within the year he was back in California. In that time Dr. Soellner had retired from his practice, and he and his wife had departed for Basel. Hapke found work as a janitor and gardener at a school for younger children. What he liked especially was that as the children grew older, and he liked them less, they were sent to another school. These were the years of his greatest contentment. He was fond of children, and they were delighted with a man they called Mr. Happy, thinking that was his name. If he had been one to put his feelings into words he would have said that children were the best people.

Then a change was made, welcome to the children, but a cause of concern to Hapke. The great increase in the number of students required a change in the school's operation. The students would now remain together through the lower and upper grades, with their friends, their teachers, and of course Mr. Hapke. They all looked to him to help supervise the playground and keep an eye on the younger children.

Still, in the first years Hapke had few complaints. There was, of course, more roughhousing at recess, but that was to be expected as the boys grew older. Hapke was the first to notice the piecemeal mutilation of many shrubs and bushes adjoining the playground. Some of these had been planted by Hapke. Time after time he observed idle boys, while they were just loafing about, strike at flowering plants with sticks, or absentmindedly break off buds and twigs. They surely meant no harm, of course, but they did it.

Hapke spoke about this to the principal, Mrs. Parker, who brought some of the boys together to discuss the problem. To his astonishment one of the older boys referred to him as Popeye. Mrs. Parker shared in their amusement. To Hapke's question— who was Popeye?—she said only that boys will be boys. She then explained to the boys that Mr. Hapke had his feelings, and he felt them for the bushes and shrubs he had planted. The needless destruction of a plant he felt as a personal injury. On hearing that, some of the boys looked at him as if for the first time. What was it they saw, besides a grown man who could easily be hurt?

A few days later, as Hapke raked leaves in a shaded corner of the playground, he came on one of his shrubs so beaten and battered he could hardly identify it. It had been hacked with a stick, then trampled. Hapke was slow to comprehend what he saw. Rather than summon Mrs. Parker to see what had happened, he went to his chair in the utility room where the big ventilating fans were droning. This mindless, vibrating racket helped to calm him. It occurred to him—that in itself was unusual—that the brutal battering of the shrub was not really what the boy, or the boys, had in mind. The blows and kicks they had given the plant had been for this Popeye, whoever that person was. It further came to him that it would be a mistake to speak of this to Mrs. Parker. Several of these boys, young as they were, would soon be big and strong enough to attack more than bushes. He did not put his mind to consider what that might be.

Hapke often ate his lunch in the bright sun of the playground, where he was joined by several dogs. The big red setter, which had usually been wading, always came back to Hapke to shake off the water. One of the smaller mutts, named Max, always checked Hapke's bag to see what he was eating. Who would believe that his favorite snack was fresh orange peels? After lunch they would sprawl at his feet and bask in the sun together.

Children also came to Hapke, especially little girls, who were often moved to offer him something. Their interest might be in his wrinkled, jug-eared face, the white hair cropped so short it was like a pelt, or the gnarled, rootlike fingers just the length and thickness for a child to grasp. Perhaps they lacked a face and hands like those at home. It had startled Hapke to observe that even little children can be cruel. The victims were commonly puppies and kittens. Recently, however, there had been goldfish which they carried about in plastic pouches. How explain to a child that water was what a fish breathed? Both little boys and girls were quick to understand the occasional pinch he gave their plump bottoms, but the hurt they had received was now one they could give to something else.

At the back of the playground a creek meandered through a wide, shallow, rock-strewn basin. From where Hapke sat, in the sunlight, he could keep an eye on the younger waders. One day he saw a child, one of the preschool toddlers, crouched in the shallow stream as if responding to a call from nature. The frazzled ends of her honey-colored braids dangled in the water. Perhaps something wondrous held her attention. She did not seem aware of the two boys on the bank who were idly tossing pebbles at her. Hapke had seen both boys, just a moment before, snake through the playground on a single bicycle, one seated on the rear stand, his long legs dangling. The bike was sprawled on the creek bank, the front wheel still revolving. A canvas bag, for carrying newspapers, hung by a strap from the older boy's shoulders. Hapke knew them both. Run-of-the-mill, tow-headed American boys. The smaller boy took occasional gulps from a Coke bottle.

Hapke watched the older boy, once he had run out of pebbles, step from rock to rock in the creek bed until he stood directly over the crouched child. Perhaps she saw his reflection in the water. Her blond head tilted to peer upward just as the canvas bag fell to conceal her. A moment passed, as if the boy might be waiting, before he stooped to press firmly on the bag's center, then he returned to the bank. The smaller boy had cupped the palm of his free hand to his mouth. His companion picked up and straddled the bike, then waited for his friend to take the seat behind him before pedaling away.

And Hapke? He simply didn't believe what he had seen. He needn't believe it, of course, to take action, and he had risen to his feet to cry out hoarsely. This startled the dogs at his feet, but nobody else. The noon-hour bedlam in the playground was like the racket in a zoo birdhouse. Hapke shouted, he waved his arms and pointed, but there was little to see. A bearded jogger, his body gleaming with perspiration, paused long enough to grasp what Hapke was saying. He then ran to the creek, trailed by Hapke, and raised the limp, dripping parcel out of the water. With it he ran, through the swarm of hooting children, the three blocks down the street to the fire station. Later Hapke learned that they had done what they could, but it was not enough.

He proved to be the only eyewitness. He was quick to agree that seeing was believing, but he had not been able to believe what he had seen. He recognized and identified both boys. Only one, of course, was judged old enough to be culpable, his "prank" resulting in the child's death.

The boy's father, a prominent real-estate dealer, expressed feelings and reservations felt by many that Hapke was more to be censured than his son. Why, in God's name, hadn't he acted sooner? In his defense it was pointed out that he was strange to the customs of the country. Who would believe that a boy, with due deliberation, would take the life of a child?

At the interrogation the older boy confessed to having once tampered with parking meters. That led many to smile. Both boys were well respected by their friends and teachers, and to all intents and purposes, as Hapke read in the paper, they were well-bred, well-liked, well-behaved American boys. That was how they looked.

Coming on the child crouched in the creek bed the older boy had given in to a "prankish" impulse. Had it not crossed his mind that the child might drown? It had not crossed his mind. Had he done it for kicks? His gray-green eyes betrayed a flicker of amusement at the question. The fleshy part of his thumb was white as a wound where he pressed his gum to his teeth before he popped it. He had his models. He was himself a model for the younger boy.

One of the questioners made the comment that the boys were too young to know what they were doing. Another answered that they knew that very well: What they didn't know was what it was to be human. People were born, he said, but human beings had to be made. This person went on to say that a freedom-loving people were now free to be, or not to be, human.

On hearing this, another person shouted that "what they really wanted was to put an end to humans." By "they" did he mean these boys? That was what he meant. First Hapke could not believe what he had seen: Now he could not believe what he had heard. This incredible statement was applauded by an elderly woman who sat near Hapke. She had been harassed, and her house vandalized, by boys known and unknown. Nothing of value had been taken. They had destroyed her property for the pleasure of it. It was an effort for Hapke to control his impulse to rise and speak about his plants and shrubs. What good would it do? It might even prove to do him harm. He kept his own counsel, and later he read in the paper that the boys had been assigned to a "correctional facility" in the valley. Nothing would be gained by treating such boys as criminals.

Hapke continued to eat his lunch at the playground, but he no longer felt responsible for young waders. The big red setter still frolicked in the creek and came running to Hapke to splash the water on him. Little girls, their heads a blaze of light, still approached Hapke to peer at him closely. It set them to squealing like little pigs if he gave them a wink. How explain that? What could they know of the ways of men? Almost every day a tan-limbed youth, open-faced, open-minded, but unsmiling, hurled a Frisbee through the sun glare to a companion as like him as two peas. Compared with the short-legged, stub-limbed Hapke they were like young gods. Their parents, surely, had dreamed of such offspring, sun-dried and sun-basted on the white beaches, delivered daily to their appointed places in the spacious station wagons. They had dreamed about them, and now they had them.

Some weeks later, as Hapke left the playground, a small boy trailed along behind him. When Hapke paused to peer about, the boy also paused. He could sense that he was part of the boy's deep brooding. Would anyone believe that Hapke experienced a tremor of fear?

Some moments later he heard steps approaching, and there at his side, without hesitation, the boy put his small, soft hand into Hapke's big rough one. For a moment he held it like an injured bird. To have been singled out, after due deliberation, for such an intimate and trusting association made it difficult for Hapke to speak. But the boy had no such problem. He was overflowing with his subject, and in pressing need of a listener. Too bad Hapke heard so little of all that he said. As they walked along together, his tongue freely wagging, the boy's free hand absently plucked the leaves and twigs from the bushes they were passing. He did that as if it helped him with his thinking, as Hapke was sure that it did.

1982

Victrola

"Sit!" said Bundy, although the dog already sat. His knowing what Bundy would say was one of the things people noticed about their close relationship. The dog sat—not erect, like most dogs, but off to one side, so that the short-haired pelt on one rump was always soiled. When Bundy attempted to clean it, as he once did, the spot no longer matched the rest of the dog, like a cleaned spot on an old rug. A second soiled spot was on his head, where children and strangers liked to pat him. Over his eyes the pelt was so thin his hide showed through. A third defacement had been caused by the leash in his younger years, when he had tugged at it harder, sometimes almost gagging as Bundy resisted.

Those days had been a strain on both of them. Bundy had developed a bad bursitis, and the crease of the leash could still be seen on the back of his hand. In the past year, over the last eight months, beginning with the cold spell in December, the dog was so slow to cross the street Bundy might have to drag him. That brought on spells of angina for Bundy, and they would both have to stand there until they felt better. At such moments the dog's slantwise gaze was one that Bundy avoided. "Sit!" he would say, no longer troubling to see if the dog did.

The dog leashed to a parking meter, Bundy walked through the drugstore to the prescription counter at the rear. The pharmacist, Mr. Avery, peered down from a platform two steps above floor level—the source of a customer's still pending lawsuit. His gaze to the front of the store, he said, "He still itching?"

Bundy nodded. Mr. Avery had recommended a vitamin supplement that some dogs found helpful. The scratching had been replaced by licking.

"You've got to remember," said Avery, "he's in his nineties. When you're in your nineties, you'll also do a little scratchin'!" Avery gave Bundy a challenging stare. If Avery reached his nineties, Bundy was certain Mrs. Avery would have to keep him on a leash or he would forget who he was. He had repeated this story about the dog's being ninety ever since Bundy had first met him and the dog was younger.

"I need your expertise," Bundy said. (Avery lapped up that sort of flattery.) "How does five cc.s compare with five hundred mg.s?"

"It doesn't. Five cc.s is a liquid measure. It's a spoonful."

"What I want to know is, how much Vitamin C am I getting in five cc.s?"

"Might not be any. In a liquid solution, Vitamin C deteriorates rapidly. You should get it in the tablet." It seemed clear he had expected more of Bundy.

"I see," said Bundy. "Could I have my prescription?"

Mr. Avery lowered his glasses to look for it on the counter. Bundy might have remarked that a man of Avery's age—and experience—ought to know enough to wear glasses he could both see and read through, but having to deal with him once a month dictated more discretion than valor.

Squinting to read the label, Avery said, "I see he's upped your dosage." On their first meeting, Bundy and Avery had had a sensible discussion about the wisdom of minimal medication, an attitude that Bundy thought was unusual to hear from a pharmacist.

"His point is," said Bundy, "since I like to be active, there's no reason I shouldn't enjoy it. He tells me the dosage is still pretty normal."

"Hmm," Avery said. He opened the door so Bundy could step behind the counter and up to the platform with his Blue Cross card. For the umpteenth time he told Bundy, "Pay the lady at the front. Watch your step as you leave."

As he walked toward the front Bundy reflected that he would rather be a little less active than forget what he had said two minutes earlier.

"We've nothing but trouble with dogs," the cashier said. "They're in and out every minute. They get at the bars of candy. But I can't ever remember trouble with your dog."

"He's on a leash," said Bundy.

"That's what I'm saying," she replied.

When Bundy came out of the store, the dog was lying down, but he made the effort to push up and sit.

"Look at you," Bundy said, and stooped to dust him off. The way he licked himself, he picked up dirt like a blotter. A shadow moved over them, and Bundy glanced up to see, at a respectful distance, a lady beaming on the dog like a healing heat lamp. Older than Bundy—much older, a wraithlike creature, more spirit than substance, her face crossed with wisps of hair like cobwebs— Mrs. Poole had known the dog as a pup; she had been a dear friend of its former owner, Miss Tyler, who had lived directly above Bundy. For years he had listened to his neighbor tease the dog to bark for pieces of liver, and heard the animal push his food dish around the kitchen.

"What ever will become of him?" Miss Tyler would whisper to Bundy, anxious that the dog shouldn't hear what she was saying. Bundy had tried to reassure her: look how spry she was at eighty! Look how the dog was overweight and asthmatic! But to ease her mind he had agreed to provide him with a home, if worst came to worst, as it did soon enough. So Bundy inherited the dog, three cases of dog food, balls and rubber bones in which the animal took no interest, along with an elegant cushioned sleeping basket he never used.

Actually, Bundy had never liked biggish dogs with very short pelts. Too much of everything, to his taste, was overexposed. The dog's long muzzle and small beady eyes put him in mind of something less than a dog. In the years with Miss Tyler, without provocation the animal would snarl at Bundy when they met on the stairs, or bark wildly when he opened his mailbox. The dog's one redeeming feature was that when he heard someone pronounce the word "sit" he would sit. That fact brought Bundy a certain distinction, and the gratitude of many shop owners. Bundy had once been a cat man. The lingering smell of cats in his apartment had led the dog to sneeze at most of the things he sniffed.

Two men, seated on stools in the corner tavern, had turned from the bar to gaze out into the sunlight. One of them was a clerk at the supermarket where Bundy bought his dog food. "Did he like it?" he called as Bundy came into view.

"Not particularly," Bundy replied. Without exception, the dog did not like anything he saw advertised on television. To that extent he was smarter than Bundy, who was partial to anything served with gravy.

The open doors of the bar looked out on the intersection, where an elderly woman, as if emerging from a package, unfolded her limbs through the door of a taxi. Sheets of plate glass on a passing truck reflected Bundy and the notice that was posted in the window of the bar, advising of a change of ownership. The former owner, an Irishman named Curran, had not been popular with the new crowd of wine and beer drinkers. Nor had he been popular with Bundy. A scornful man, Curran dipped the dirty glasses in tepid water, and poured drops of sherry back into the bottles. Two epidemics of hepatitis had been traced to him. Only when he was gone did Bundy realize how much the world had shrunk. To Curran, Bundy had confessed that he felt he was now living in another country. Even more he missed Curran's favorite expression, "Outlive the bastards!"

Two elderly men, indifferent to the screech of braking traffic, tottered toward each other to embrace near the center of the street. One was wearing shorts. A third party, a younger woman, escorted them both to the curb. Observing an incident like this, Bundy might stand for several minutes as if he had witnessed something unusual. Under an awning, where the pair had been led, they shared the space with a woman whose gaze seemed to focus on infinity, several issues of the *Watchtower* gripped in her trembling hands.

At the corner of Sycamore and Poe streets—trees crossed poets, as a rule, at right angles—Bundy left the choice of the route up to the dog. Where the sidewalk narrowed, at the bend in the street, both man and dog prepared themselves for brief and unpredictable encounters. In the cities, people met and passed like sleepwalkers, or stared brazenly at each other, but along the sidewalks of small towns they felt the burden of their shared existence. To avoid rudeness, a lift of the eyes or a muttered greeting was necessary. This was often an annoyance for Bundy: the long approach by sidewalk, the absence of cover, the unavoidable moment of confrontation, then Bundy's abrupt greeting or a wag of his head, which occasionally startled the other person. To the young a quick "Hi!" was appropriate, but it was not at all suitable for elderly ladies, a few with pets as escorts. To avoid these encounters, Bundy might suddenly veer into the street or an alleyway, dragging the reluctant dog behind him. He liked to meet strangers, especially children, who would pause to stroke his bald spot. What kind of dog was he? Bundy was tactfully evasive; it had proved to be an unfruitful topic. He was equally noncommittal about the dog's ineffable name.

"Call him Sport," he would say, but this pleasantry was not appreciated. A smart-aleck's answer. Their sympathies were with the dog.

To delay what lay up ahead, whatever it was, they paused at the barnlike entrance of the local van-and-storage warehouse. The draft from inside smelled of burlap sacks full of fragrant pine kindling, and mattresses that were stored on boards above the rafters. The pair contemplated a barn full of junk being sold as antiques. Bundy's eyes grazed over familiar treasure and stopped at a Morris chair with faded green corduroy cushions cradling a carton marked "FREE KITTENS."

He did not approach to look. One thing having a dog had spared him was the torment of losing another cat. Music (surely Elgar, something awful!) from a facsimile edition of an Atwater Kent table-model radio bathed dressers and chairs, sofas, beds and love seats, man and dog impartially. As it ended the announcer suggested that Bundy stay tuned for a Musicdote.

Recently, in this very spot—as he sniffed similar air, having paused to take shelter from a drizzle—the revelation had come to Bundy that he no longer wanted other people's junk. Better yet (or was it worse?), he no longer *wanted*—with the possible exception of an English mint, difficult to find, described as curiously strong. He had a roof, a chair, a bed, and, through no fault of his own, he had a dog. What little he had assembled and hoarded (in the garage a German electric-train set with four locomotives, and three elegant humidors and a pouch of old pipes) would soon be gratifying the wants of others. Anything else of value? The cushioned sleeping basket from Abercrombie & Fitch that had come with the dog. That would sell first. Also two Italian raincoats in good condition, and a Borsalino hat—*Extra Extra Superiore*—bought from G. Colpo in Venice.

Two young women, in the rags of fashion but radiant and blooming as gift-packed fruit, brushed Bundy as they passed, the spoor of their perfume lingering. In the flush of this encounter, his freedom from want dismantled, he moved too fast, and the leash reined him in. Rather than be rushed, the dog had stopped to sniff a meter. He found meters more life-enhancing than trees now. It had not always been so: some years ago he would tug Bundy up the incline to the park, panting and hoarsely gagging, an object of compassionate glances from elderly women headed down the grade, carrying lapdogs. This period had come to a dramatic conclusion.

In the park, back in the deep shade of the redwoods, Bundy and the dog had had a confrontation. An old tree with exposed roots had suddenly attracted the dog's attention. Bundy could not restrain him. A stream of dirt flew out between his legs to splatter Bundy's raincoat and fall into his shoes. There was something manic in the dog's excitement. In a few moments, he had frantically excavated a hole into which he could insert his head and shoulders. Bundy's tug on the leash had no effect on him. The sight of his soiled hairless bottom, his legs mechanically pumping, encouraged Bundy to give him a smart crack with the end of the leash. Not hard, but sharp, right on the button, and before he could move the dog had wheeled and the front end was barking at him savagely, the lips curled back. Dirt from the hole partially screened his muzzle, and he looked to Bundy like a maddened rodent. He was no longer a dog but some primitive, underground creature. Bundy lashed out at him, backing away, but they were joined by the leash. Unintentionally, Bundy stepped on the leash, which held the dog's snarling head to the ground. His slobbering jowls were bloody; the small veiled eyes peered up at him with hatred. Bundy had just enough presence of mind to stand there, unmoving, until they both grew calm.

Nobody had observed them. The children played and shrieked in the schoolyard as usual. The dog relaxed and lay flat on the ground, his tongue lolling in the dirt. Bundy breathed noisily, a film of perspiration cooling his face. When he stepped off the leash the dog did not move but continued to watch him warily, with bloodshot eyes. A slow burn of shame flushed Bundy's ears and cheeks, but he was reluctant to admit it. Another dog passed near them, but what he sniffed on the air kept him at a distance. In a tone of truce, if not reconciliation, Bundy said, "You had enough?"

When had he last said that? Seated on a school chum, whose face was red with Bundy's nosebleed. He bled too easily, but the boy beneath him had had enough.

"O.K.?" he said to the dog. The faintest tremor of acknowledgment stirred the dog's tail. He got to his feet, sneezed repeatedly, then splattered Bundy with dirt as he shook himself. Side by side, the leash slack between them, they left the park and walked down the grade. Bundy had never again struck the dog, nor had the dog ever again wheeled to snarl at him. Once the leash was snapped to the dog's collar a truce prevailed between them. In the apartment he had the floor of a closet all to himself.

At the Fixit Shop on the corner of Poplar, recently refaced with green asbestos shingles, Mr. Waller, the Fixit man, rapped on the glass with his wooden ruler. Both Bundy and the dog acknowledged his greeting. Waller had two cats, one asleep in the window, and a dog that liked to ride in his pickup. The two dogs had once been friends; they mauled each other a bit and horsed around like a couple of kids. Then suddenly it was over. Waller's dog would no longer trouble to leave the seat of the truck. Bundy had been so struck by this he had mentioned it to Waller. "Hell," Waller had said, "Gyp's a young dog. Your dog is old."

His saying that had shocked Bundy. There was the personal element, for one thing: Bundy was a good ten years older than Waller, and was he to read the remark to mean that Waller would soon ignore him? And were dogs—reasonably well-bred, sensible chaps—so indifferent to the facts of a dog's life? They appeared to be. One by one, as Bundy's dog grew older, the younger ones ignored him. He might have been a stuffed animal leashed to a parking meter. The human parallel was too disturbing for Bundy to dwell on it.

Old men, in particular, were increasingly touchy if they confronted Bundy at the frozen-food lockers. Did they think he was spying on them? Did they think he looked *sharper* than they did? Elderly women, as a rule, were less suspicious, and grateful to exchange a bit of chitchat. Bundy found them more realistic: they knew they were mortal. To find Bundy still around, squeezing the avocados, piqued the old men who returned from their vacations. On the other hand, Dr. Biddle, a retired dentist with a glistening head like an egg in a basket of excelsior, would unfailingly greet Bundy with the words "I'm really going to miss that mutt, you know that?," but his glance betrayed that he feared Bundy would check out first.

Bundy and the dog used the underpass walkway to cross to the supermarket parking area. Banners were flying to celebrate Whole Grains Cereal Week. In the old days, Bundy would leash the dog to a cart and they would proceed to do their shopping together, but now he had to be parked out front tied up to one of the bicycle racks. The dog didn't like it. The area was shaded and the cement was cold. Did he ever sense, however dimly, that Bundy too felt the chill? His hand brushed the coarse pelt as he fastened the leash.

"How about a new flea collar?" Bundy said, but the dog was not responsive. He sat, without being told to sit. Did it flatter the dog to leash him? Whatever Bundy would do if worst came to worst he had pondered, but had discussed with no one—his intent might be misconstrued. Of which one of them was he speaking? Impersonally appraised, in terms of survival the two of them were pretty much at a standoff: the dog was better fleshed out, but Bundy was the heartier eater.

Thinking of eating—of garlic-scented breadsticks, to be specific, dry but not dusty to the palate—Bundy entered the market to face a large display of odorless flowers and plants. The amplitude and bounty of the new market, at the point of entrance, before he selected a cart, always marked the high point of his expectations. Where else in the hungry world such a prospect? Barrels and baskets of wine, six-packs of beer and bran muffins, still warm sourdough bread that he would break and gnaw on as he shopped. Was this a cunning regression? As a child he had craved raw sugar cookies. But his euphoria sagged at the meat counter, as he studied the gray matter being sold as meat-loaf mix; it declined further at the dairy counter, where two cartons of yogurt had been sampled, and the low-fat cottage cheese was two days older than dated. By the time he entered the checkout lane, hemmed in by scandal sheets and romantic novels, the cashier's cheerfully inane "Have a good day!" would send him off forgetting his change in the machine. The girl who pursued him (always with pennies!) had been coached to say, "Thank you, sir!"

A special on avocados this week required that Bundy make a careful selection. Out in front, as usual, dogs were barking. On the airwaves, from the rear and side, the "Wang Wang Blues." Why wang wang, he wondered. Besides wang wang, how did it go? The music was interrupted by an announcement on the public-address system. Would the owner of the white dog leashed to the bike rack please come to the front? Was Bundy's dog white? The point was debatable. Nevertheless, he left his cart by the avocados and followed the vegetable display to the front. People were huddled to the right of the door. A clerk beckoned to Bundy through the window. Still leashed to the bike rack, the dog lay out on his side, as if sleeping. In the parking lot several dogs were yelping.

"I'm afraid he's a goner," said the clerk. "These other dogs rushed him. Scared him to death. He just keeled over before they got to him." The dog had pulled the leash taut, but there was no sign that anything had touched him. A small woman with a shopping cart thumped into Bundy.

"Is it Tiger?" she said. "I hope it's not Tiger." She stopped to see that it was not Tiger. "Whose dog was it?" she asked, peering around her. The clerk indicated Bundy. "Poor thing," she said. "What was his name?"

Just recently, watching the Royal Wedding, Bundy had noticed that his emotions were nearer the surface: on two occasions his eyes had filmed over. He didn't like the woman's speaking of the dog in the past tense. Did she think he had lost his name with his life?

"What was the poor thing's name?" she repeated.

Was the tremor in Bundy's limbs noticeable? "Victor," Bundy lied, since he could not bring himself to admit the dog's name was Victrola. It had always been a sore point, the dog being too old to be given a new one. Miss Tyler had felt that as a puppy he looked like the picture of the dog at the horn of the gramophone. The resemblance was feeble, at best. How could a person give a dog such a name?

"Let him sit," a voice said. A space was cleared on a bench for Bundy to sit, but at the sound of the word he could not bend his knees. He remained standing, gazing through the bright glare at the beacon revolving on the police car. One of those women who buy two frozen dinners and then go off with the shopping cart and leave it somewhere let the policeman at the crosswalk chaperon her across the street.

1982

Glimpse into
Another Country

Hazlitt's wife carried a broom to ward off the neighbor's dogs as she walked with her husband down the drive to the waiting taxi. Too old now to attack, the dogs barked hoarsely from behind a screen of bushes. "I'll outlive them if it kills me," she remarked, and she stooped for the morning paper, flattened by the garbage pickup. "No ethnic food," she told Hazlitt. "You hear me? You remember what happened in Phoenix." From his shoulders, as he stooped to kiss her, she removed the gray hairs.

Hazlitt was reluctant to fly, anywhere, but he wanted something in the way of assurance—of life assurance—that he hoped to get from a specialist in New York. "If that's what you want," his own doctor, in San Francisco, had advised him, "and you can afford it, go get it." Could he afford it? He had that assurance from his wife. "You're worth it," she said.

She had made considerable fuss to reserve Hazlitt a seat at one of the plane's windows, which turned out to be near the center of the right wing. A stewardess helped him out of his coat, and held it while he felt through the pockets for his glasses. A woman with quick searching eyes came along the aisle to stop at his row, then turned to hiss at her companion. The habit of hissing at people had always dismayed Hazlitt.

The woman's hair looked as if she had just blow-dried it. The man with her, by appearance a cultivated person, wore a smart suède cap and carried their coats. His rather abstracted manner led Hazlitt to feel he might be a teacher, off to an academic meeting. As he reached her side, the woman slipped between the seats to the one beside Hazlitt, without glancing at him. She registered his presence, however, as she would a draft from the window, by shifting in the seat toward her companion. She wore knit gloves. With one hand she clutched a paperback book.

Hazlitt had not flown enough to know if her indifference to him was part of the etiquette of plane travel, where so many strangers were jammed in together: why start up something with a person who might well prove to be tiresome? He himself was guarded even with his colleagues at the university. The woman at his side had an appealing intactness, and her profile seemed intelligent. A perfume, or it might be a powder, was faintly scented with lilac.

Advised to buckle his seat belt, he observed that the palms of his hands were clammy. At the takeoff he faced the window with closed eyes. Perhaps the tilted wing spared him the vertigo that might have been part of the liftoff, and as the plane set its course he caught glimpses of the far blue horizon. The woman beside him browsed in a copy of the *New York Times,* picked up in the airport. Her interest seemed to be in the ads. At one point, he was screened off behind the paper but able to check the market quotations on his side. Finished with the paper, she stuffed it between the seats on her left, away from Hazlitt. He thought that rude, since he made it a point to share newspapers with his traveling companions. As she relaxed for a moment, closing her eyes, he was able to appraise her profile further—a little sharp to his taste, but attractive. From the pink lobes of her ears he received faintly erotic signals.

Suddenly, perhaps feeling his gaze, she turned to look directly past him, as if someone had tapped on the window. Now she would speak, he thought, but she didn't. She turned away, with a birdlike quickness, and leafed through the pages of her paperback book. Idle riffling—the sort of thing Hazlitt found irritating. At the back of the book, she paused to read a few words about the author, then turned to read the book's concluding page. That done, she read the next-to-last page, then the one before it. As she read, she nibbled at the corner of her lip.

Hazlitt was flabbergasted. He had discovered that the book she chose to read backward was *The White Hotel.* He could not fully believe what he had seen, yet there was no question he had seen it. She did manage to read most of the final chapter before turning the book back to its opening page, which she placed face down in her lap. What did she want now? Something to drink. Her husband raised his hand to signal one of the stewards.

Surely a more worldly traveler than Hazlitt would not have been so appalled by what he had witnessed. How justify this scanning of a book in reverse? Could it not be argued that a sensible person, of a sensitive nature, might want to know what was in store before making a full commitment? Perhaps, but the practice was new to Hazlitt, a sworn and outspoken enemy of speed-reading.

At the announcement that they were passing over Lake Tahoe, the woman leaned toward the window as if she might see it. Her seeming unawareness of Hazlitt had a calming effect on him. He made way for her. He was at pains not to be there. Leaning forward, she had crushed several pages of her book, but this too was a matter of indifference to her. She put the book aside to accept, from her companion, a news magazine. She leafed through the pages, then stopped to consider an article on crime, with illustrations.

"Oh, my God!" she exclaimed, crumpling the page, and turned to fix Hazlitt with an intense, green-eyed stare. Did she think him a criminal? It seemed to him that her eyes moved closer together. "There's no place to go!" she cried. "Just imagine!" She had ignored Hazlitt; now he felt cornered by her. "Where would *you* go?" she barked.

His lips were dry. He wet them, and said, "My wife and I were recently in Oaxaca—"

"*Mexico?* Are you crazy?" She saw that he might be. "There is *nowhere* . . ." Her voice trailed off. Her husband had placed his hand on her lap to calm her.

"I was at a party in the forties—" Hazlitt began.

"In the forties!" she cried. "Who lives in the forties?"

Fortunately, he divined her meaning. "The *nineteen*-forties—the party was in the East Seventies. Musicians, writers, composers, and so on. Do you remember Luise Rainer?" Clearly she did not. "At the time," he continued, "she was an actress—"

"You write?" she asked him.

Hazlitt did write scholarly articles; he asked himself if she considered that writing. "I was with a friend," he said, "a painter. We all agreed there was nowhere to escape to. The war was everywhere, or soon would be. Then one of them said, 'You know what? There *is* no *where*. All the wheres have vanished.' "

Perhaps the woman felt there was more to the story. Her lips parted, but she said nothing.

"We have friends in Buenos Aires," he went on, "but I would never go so far as to recommend it."

"It's like no *air*. That's what it's like. It's like there's less air."

"As a matter of fact—" began Hazlitt, but she had turned from him to her crumpled magazine. Carefully, as if she meant to iron it, she smoothed it out on her lap. "That book you were reading," he continued. "I've met the author. A very respectable chap." (Everything he was saying was the purest hogwash.) "I know that he would consider it a personal favor if you read his book as it was printed, from the front to the back."

What had come over him? In her green, unblinking stare he caught the glimpse of a chill that might excite a lover. She turned from him to lean on her companion, who peered over her frizzly hair at Hazlitt. The man wore tinted bifocals. His expression was mild. "My wife said you had a question?"

Returning his gaze, Hazlitt knew he had been a fool. "It's just that I happen to know the author, and took the liberty of speaking for him."

"He's crazy," said the wife. "Don't rile him."

Calmly the man removed his glasses and polished the lenses with a fold of his tie. Unmistakably, Hazlitt recognized one of his own kind. A physicist, perhaps, with those hairy fingers. Or a member of a think tank. "Theoretically," the man said, breathing on a lens, "there is something in what you say, but, as a practical matter, having bought the book my wife is free to read it as she pleases, or to ignore it. Wouldn't you agree?"

Particularly galling to Hazlitt was the way the fellow had turned the tables on him. It was usually he who was the cool one, the voice of reason in the tempest, the low-keyed soother of the savage breast. Worse yet, this fellow was about half his age.

"Of course! Of course! Stupid of me. My apologies to Mrs.—"

"Thayer. I'm Dr. Thayer."

Across the lap of Mrs. Thayer, who shrank back to avoid him, Hazlitt and Dr. Thayer clasped hands, exchanged the glances of complicit males. If there was a shred of solace in it for Hazlitt, it lay in Mrs. Thayer's full knowledge of this complicity.

"Take the filthy book!" she said, thrusting it at him. "And read it any way you like!"

Hazlitt let it fall to the floor between them. He fastened his gaze on the glare at the window. Sometime later, the stewardess, serving his lunch, had to explain to him how to pull out the tray from the seat in front of him, and pry the lid from his salad dressing.

Hazlitt would say for this woman—when he discussed it with his wife—that she maintained to the last his nonexistence. He remained in his seat until the plane emptied, then wandered about the airport. He caught a glimpse of Dr. Thayer, on one of the escalators, helping his wife into her coat. The sharpness of her elbows troubled Hazlitt. Thin and intent as a cat, she reminded him of someone. Was it his wife? She groped in her purse for a piece of tissue, pressed it to her nose.

In the taxi to Manhattan, Hazlitt was moved to chat a bit with the driver, but the Plexiglas barrier between them seemed intimidating. Through the tinted windshield, as they approached the city, the October evening skyline was like the opening shot of a movie. Hazlitt had often told his wife that if the sun never rose he might like city living. In the car lights the streets glittered like enamel. It pleased him to note, as they drew near the Plaza Hotel, the horse-drawn hacks lined up along the curb. One of the drivers was a young woman with pigtails, frail as a waif. She held a leather feed bag to the muzzle of her horse, whose pelt shone like patent leather where the harness had worn off the hair.

The hotel porter, elderly himself, took a proprietary interest in Hazlitt. He led him into the bathroom to explain that the knobs on the faucets might confuse him if he got up at night for a drink of water: they turned contrary to the usual directions. A sign of the times, Hazlitt thought.

He thanked the porter, then stood at the window listening to the sounds of the street. A warm, moist breeze stirred the curtains. The tooting horns put him in mind of the radio plays of the forties. Turning to phone his wife, he saw his reflection in the mirror on the closet door. Something about the light, or the mirror, altered the impression he had of himself. A pity his wife couldn't see it. He would call her later; it was early still in California, and such talk could make her uneasy. What she feared the most when he traveled without her was that he might do something foolish, if not fatal, and end up hospitalized where she could not get at him. As he washed his hands—taking care with the faucets—he remembered her final caution: not to walk the streets at night, but if he did, not to be caught without money. She had given him a hundred dollars in twenties on the understanding he was not to spend it, so that when the muggers looked for money they would find it.

Hazlitt meant to stroll a bit—he needed the exercise—but when he left the hotel the young woman with the pigtails and her black spotted horse were still there. Frequent tosses of the horse's head had spread oats on the street and sidewalk. Jovially, Hazlitt inquired, "This rig for hire?"

"That depends where you're going." She spoke to him from her perch in a tone of authority.

"Bloomingdale's," he said, "before it closes."

"That's where I'm headed," she replied, ignoring his playful tone, and watched him climb into the cab. Hazlitt must have forgotten the leisurely pace of a weary horse. He leaned forward in the seat as if that might urge it along. As they approached Bloomingdale's, he saw that peddlers had spread their wares out on the sidewalks.

The girl stopped the horse so that the hack blocked the crosswalk, and a stream of pedestrians swirled around it. As Hazlitt arose to step down from the cab, it teetered slightly, and he peered about him for a helping hand. One of the peddlers—a tall, swarthy fellow wearing a pointed hat made of a folded newspaper—had taken a roll of bills from his pocket to make change for a customer. This person, lights reflected in her glasses, peered up at Hazlitt with a look of disbelief. Did he seem so strange? A moment passed before he recognized Mrs. Thayer. She wore tinted horn-rimmed glasses, and a babushka-like scarf about her hair, tied beneath her chin. To take her change, while holding her purse, she gripped one of her knit gloves between her teeth, where it dangled like a third hand. The sight of Hazlitt had, in any case, left her speechless. He could think of nothing better to do than slip one hand into his coat front and strike the comical pose of a public figure welcomed by an admiring throng. The tilt of the carriage may have led him to misjudge the step down to the street. He toppled forward, both arms spread wide, and collapsed into the arms of the peddler, knocking off his paper hat. Over the man's broad shoulder he caught a glimpse of Mrs. Thayer, her hand clamped to her mouth now in either astonishment or laughter. She was gone by the time Hazlitt's feet were firmly planted on the street.

The peddler, after recovering his hat, was remarkably good-humored about it. "She knows you, eh?" he said, giving Hazlitt a leer as he smoothed the rumpled front of his coat. Hazlitt pondered the query as he selected, from the peddler's display, a French-type purse for his wife, a woman reluctant to buy such things for herself.

"Don't you worry!" the peddler added. "She'll be back. I still got her three dollars!" From his wad of bills he peeled off several and passed them to Hazlitt, giving him the smile of a collaborator. "You O.K.?" he said, and steadied the older man's arm as he stepped from the curb.

In Bloomingdale's foyer, where the doors revolved and Hazlitt felt well concealed by the darkness, he paused to spy on the peddler. There was something familiar about him—a big, rough fellow who turned out to be so gentle. In his sophomore year at college, Hazlitt had been intrigued by a swarthy, bearded giant, wearing a faded orange turban and a suit coat over what appeared to be his pajamas, who used to cross the campus directly below the dormitory window on his way to a shack in the desert wash. He walked with a limp, and carried a sack of groceries over his shoulder. As he passed beneath Hazlitt's gaze he would crook his head around, revealing his dark, hostile expression, and then beam directly at him the wide-eyed, toothy smile of a child beholding a beloved object. These extremes of temperament were like theatrical masks of contrary humors slipped on and off his face. Hazlitt learned that the man was a Sikh, one of a sect of fiercely independent warriors in India. What had brought him to California? Everything about him was out of scale and seemed disconcerting— even his smile. There were rumors that he kept his wife captive, that he trapped and ate coyotes. But what did all of that have to do with Hazlitt spying on a peddler from Bloomingdale's foyer so many years later?

Nevertheless, the incident had aroused him, agreeably. This state, he thought, might be what his younger colleagues called "having a buzz on"—an expression that had previously mystified him. He wandered about the store's crowded aisles. In the cosmetic section, the customers and the clerks chattered like birds in an aviary. They leaned to peer into mirrors as if uncertain who they were. Hazlitt paused at a counter displaying bracelets set with semiprecious stones. A young woman with dark bangs to the edge of her eyes spoke to him. She opened the case to lift out several of the items. In her opinion, they cost practically nothing—a special purchase at seventy-nine dollars. He would have guessed a price a third of that, but he showed no surprise. One by itself was very nice, she advised him, but two or more enhanced their beauty. To illustrate, she placed two about her broad wrist, above a hand with blunt fingers and cracked nails.

"Very well," Hazlitt said, feeling nothing at all, and waited as she wrote up the order. Was it cash or card? Card, he replied, and searched it out in his wallet.

"Oh, I'm so sorry," she said, "but we don't take Visa."

Hazlitt's astonishment was plain. He wondered if it might be a cunning revenge of the East on California. Would they accept his check? Of course. As he filled one out, his wife's face materialized suddenly, then receded. He wrote so few checks that she had cautioned him to make certain he did it correctly.

His driver's license was also needed, the clerk told him. Ah, he was from San Francisco? She had spent a summer with a friend in Carmel, where she nearly froze. Hazlitt explained that the summers might run cooler than the winters, which was why some people found it so attractive. She did not follow his reasoning, her attention being on other matters. "I've got to get this O.K.'d," she said. "Would you just like to look around?"

Hazlitt looked around. Having already spent so much money, he could do without further temptations. To get out of the crowded aisles he wandered into an adjoining department. Against a pillar he saw a canvas chair, apparently meant for the lover of horses: it was made with stirrups, bridles, bits and strips of harness leather. He sagged into it. Nearby, a TV screen glowed like the sun at a porthole. He made out the image of a dense throng of people moving about in a large, dimly lit building. The flowing garments of the women, the density of the crowd suggested it was somewhere in India. As his eyes adjusted, Hazlitt saw that the floor seemed to be strewn with bodies, to which the passing crowd was indifferent. Some were alone. Others were gathered in crumpled heaps. The milling of the figures among these fallen creatures gave the scene an unreal, dreamlike aspect. Were they dead? No, they were sleeping. The film gave Hazlitt a glimpse into a strange country where the quick and the dormant were accustomed to mingle. Perhaps, he thought, it was not the walkers but the sleepers who would range the farthest in their travels.

He was distracted by a stream of jabbering, excited people, most of them young, who hurried down the store aisles toward the front exit. Then, rather suddenly, the place was quiet. He delayed a moment, expecting further excitement, then came out of the shadows and returned to the jewelry counter. The clerk was not there. Other departments also appeared to be abandoned.

Through the glass doors of a side entrance he saw hurrying figures and flashing lights. A young man in shirtsleeves, with a perplexed expression, ran toward Hazlitt, waving a flashlight. He took him by the arm and steered him down the aisle. "Out! Out!" he cried. "We're emptying the building!"

"The clerk still has my driver's license," said Hazlitt, but in his agitation the man ignored him. He urged him along through the empty store to where several policemen stood at the exit.

"The clerk has my driver's license!" Hazlitt repeated.

"Don't drive," the man replied. "Take a cab."

Police vans and patrol cars blocked off the street. He stood for some time under one of the awnings waiting for something dramatic to happen. The revolving beacons on the cars lit up the faces of the crowd like torches. Several men in helmets and olive-drab uniforms entered the building carrying equipment. Hazlitt heard someone call them a bomb squad. The awareness that he had no driver's license, no positive identification, touched him with an obscure elation. He strolled along with a noisy group of young people who had just exited from a movie, and they seemed to take his presence for granted. When someone asked him the time, he said, "Nearly nine," and was reminded that he had not yet called his wife. "You won't believe this," he would say, knowing she would.

To get his call so early in her evening startled her. "Where are you?" she cried. It was his custom to report the events of the day—or the nonevents, if so they proved to be—and this time he really had a story to tell. But, hearing the note of concern in her voice, he changed his mind. Any mention of the bomb scare would disturb her rather than amuse her.

He explained—feeling the need to be explicit—that he was in his hotel room, seated on the bed, facing the partially opened window. A cool breeze stirred the curtain. He asked her if she could hear the car horns in the street below. If she had been with him, he said, they would have gone to a play—she loved the theater. As she spoke to him—how well he saw her—she would be seated at the kitchen table, behind the lazy Susan, with its clutter of vitamin bottles, and several of the squat candle glasses set out in anticipation of the first seasonal storms and blackouts. Hazlitt knew so exactly just how it all was that he could hear the sound of the wall clock—stuffed with a towel to mute the ticking—and he could read the pressure (falling) on the barometer at her shoulder. He continued to talk, in a way that soothed her, about his short ride in the horse-drawn hack (a thing they had done together), and about the swarthy peddler selling his wares on the Bloomingdale's corner—for some reason, he avoided mention of Mrs. Thayer—until she spoke up to remind him that he was phoning from New York, at his own expense, and not from his office at the college. Before he replied she had hung up.

He was aware, with the lights switched off, how the sounds at the window seemed magnified. In the play of reflections on the ceiling he glimpsed, as through a canopy of leaves, the faraway prospect he had seen on the Bloomingdale's TV—bustling figures swarming soundlessly among the bodies strewn about a station lobby. Somehow the spectacle was full of mystery for him. None of this was a dream—no, he was awake; he heard the blast of the horns below his window—but the dreamlike aura held him in its spell until those sleeping figures arose to continue their journey.

In the doctor's waiting room the next morning, Hazlitt faced a wall of brightly colored children's paintings, goblinlike creatures with popped eyes, short stumpy arms, stiltlike legs. It was his wife who once remarked that this was probably how most children saw the world—like specimens under the lens of a microscope. In the suspended time that Hazlitt sat there, he held and returned the gaze of a purple-faced goblin, preferring it to the pale, ghostly image of the old man reflected in its covering glass.

The specialist's assurance, spoken at Hazlitt's back between thumps on his ribcage, drew more from its offhand manner than from what the man said: he showed little real concern. Every hour, Hazlitt gathered, the doctor saw patients more deserving of attention. His assistant, a well-coifed matronly woman with sinewy legs and the profile of a turkey, shared with Hazlitt her opinion that "a reprieve is the best one can expect, at our age."

He was down in the street, flowing north with the current, before he sensed that he was free of a nameless burden, and seemed lighter on his feet. He crossed to Park Avenue for a leisurely stroll through the Waldorf lobby, for the pleasure of its carpet and the creak of expensive Texas luggage. Approaching Bloomingdale's again, he paused to reconsider the previous evening's scene: Hazlitt himself teetering in the hack, the dark-skinned peddler in his paper hat, and Mrs. Thayer reaching for her change, with one of her knit gloves still dangling from her teeth.

Back at Bloomingdale's jewelry counter, he found that the girl with the bangs had the morning off. In her place, an older and more professional clerk requested some further identification before she could give him his license back with the bracelets. She reminded him that one couldn't be too careful. Last night's bomb scare—a telephone call from the Bronx—proved to be without foundation, but the entire building had had to be vacated. What was this country coming to, she asked him.

Before Hazlitt could reply, his attention was distracted by a display in the case he was leaning on—a short strand of pearls on a headless bust. Was it some trick of the lighting that made them seem to glow? "These are real?" he asked the saleswoman. They were real. Would he like to see something less expensive? Her implication piqued him, because it was accurate. She took the strand from the case and let him hold it. He knew nothing about pearls, but he was dazzled. He saw them on his wife—he saw her wide-eyed astonishment, her look of disbelief. "If it's not too inconvenient," he said, "I'd like to return the bracelets and take the pearls."

He had not troubled to ask the price, and the clerk gave him a glance of puzzled admiration. "We'll just start all over," she said, "but I'm afraid I'll have to ask you once more for your driver's license."

Right at that point, Hazlitt might have reconsidered, but he did not. From his wallet he removed a second blank check, and waited for the woman to present him with the bill. The sum astounded but did not shock him. Writing the numbers, spelling the sum out gave him a tingling sense of exhilaration. Again he saw his wife, seated across the table from him, gaze at him open-mouthed, as she would at a stranger.

"This will take a few minutes," the clerk said, and went off into the crowded aisles.

Hazlitt's elation increased. He drummed his nails on the case as he peered about him. One might have thought that he had propositioned the clerk, that she had accepted and gone off to pretty up a bit and get her wrap. His exhilaration persisted as he moseyed about. In the bakery department, he flirted with the clerk, who served him a croissant he could eat on the spot.

Back at the jewelry counter, he found everything in order. Was there anything else? His wife kept her jewels in pouches, he said— would they have a small pouch? The woman found one, of a suèdelike material, into which the pearls nestled.

He was out of the building, under an awning that dramatized his own reflection in the shop window, before he again remembered the incident with the peddler on Fifty-ninth Street. He wanted to ask him if Mrs. Thayer had come back for her change, but the fellow was not there.

In the early years of their marriage, while he was doing his graduate work in the city, Hazlitt had loved to walk up Fifth Avenue with his wife for lunch at the Met. The museum itself confused and tired her; she did not like mummies, or tombs, or religious paintings. But Hazlitt liked to watch the people as they strolled about looking at objects, the stance they assumed when contemplating an artwork. Secret transactions were encouraged there, he felt, and a burden of culture was enlarged or diminished. An hour or so of this spectacle always left him so fatigued he was eager for the comforts of the dim Fountain Court lunchroom, the buzz of voices, and the splash of water.

Heading for the museum now, Hazlitt was already at Seventy-eighth Street before he was aware of the almost stalled bumper-to-bumper traffic. Passengers riding downtown in the buses and cabs made no faster progress than those who were walking. Some waved and exchanged remarks with the pedestrians. Hazlitt saun-tered along, hardly caring that it had started to drizzle. Puddles had formed on the steps of the Met, and the sleeves and shoulders of his coat were wet. He checked the coat, then strolled about in a crowd like that in Grand Central Terminal. Just off the lobby, to the right, a new book department was jammed with shoppers. Hazlitt was attracted by the displays and the brilliant lights. On one of the tables, someone had opened, and left, a large volume— Fauve paintings, as bright as Christmas candy. Across the table another browser, sniffling slightly, her face partially veiled by the hood of a transparent slicker, had paused to dip into a collection of van Gogh's letters. She read the last in the book, which she seemed to like; she tried the next-to-last, then the next. Her slicker clearly revealed the unfortunate S-curve of her posture, and the purse that she clutched to her forward-thrusting abdomen. She pressed a wad of tissue to her nose as she sneezed.

Hazlitt wore a tweedy wool hat that concealed, his wife insisted, his best features. Mrs. Thayer passed so close behind him that he felt and heard the brush of her slicker. Was it possible that she found his reappearance as unsurprising as he found hers? Then he saw her at a distance, looking at cards, and her cheeks appeared flushed. It troubled him that she might have a fever. The short-sleeved dress she wore under her transparent raincoat exposed her thin arms. Later, in one of the admission lines, he watched her remove one of her knit gloves by gripping the tips of the fingers with her teeth, then tugging on them like a puppy. Hadn't her husband explained to her about germs?

Although it was still early, and Hazlitt was not fatigued, he made his way toward the Fountain Court lunchroom. He was standing at the entrance for a moment or two before he noticed the renovation. The dusky pool and its sculptured figures were gone. The basin was now a mere sunken pit, of a creamy color without shadows, and it was already bustling with diners crowding its tables. Instead of the refreshing coolness and splash of the water, there was the harsh clatter of plates and cutlery. Hazlitt just stood there, until he was asked to move. There was a bar to his right— he could have used a drink—but the flood of creamy light depressed him. He backed away, and out of long habit found the stairway that led down to the basement.

The dark and cool lavatory in this wing of the building used to be one of Hazlitt's regular stops. The high windows were near a playground, and he could often hear the shrill cries of the children outside. He thought he heard them again now as he opened the door, but the babble stopped as he entered the washroom. Six or seven small boys of assorted colors and sizes, their arms and faces smeared with gobs of white lather, stood facing the mirror at the row of washbowls. Their wide-eyed, soapy faces seemed to stare at Hazlitt from an adjoining room. The stillness, like that of a silent movie, was broken only by the sound of lapping water. A thin film of water covered the tiles at Hazlitt's feet.

As if he found this circumstance more or less normal, he crossed the room to the nearest booth and pushed open the door. A youth, older than the others, was crouched on the rear of the fixture with his feet on the bowl's edge. With the thumb of his right hand he depressed the handle. The water spilled evenly from the rim of the clogged bowl to splash on the floor.

In the dark of the booth, Hazlitt saw little but the cupped whites of the boy's eyes. The youth raised his free hand slowly to his face as if to wipe away a lingering expression. Something in this gesture, like that of a mime, revealed to Hazlitt that the boy was stoned. In the deep void of his expanded pupils was all the *where* that the world was missing. The eyes did not blink. Hazlitt turned from him to face the mirror, and the boys, who had formed a circle around him. One had opened his shirt to expose his torso, creamy with lather. With the light behind them, all Hazlitt saw was the patches of white, like slush on pavement. Still, it pleased him to have their close attention.

The smallest boy thrust a hand toward him, its wet palm up. "Trick or treat," he said gravely. Two of those beside him hooted like crows.

"Well, let's see," Hazlitt said, and drew some coins from his pocket. He exposed them to the light, the silver coins glinting, just as the boy gave his hand a slap from the bottom. The coins flew up, scattering, then fell soundlessly into the film of water.

"Hey, man, that's no treat!" the boy scoffed, and he rolled his eyes upward.

From the pocket of his jacket Hazlitt withdrew the suède pouch; he loosened the noose and let the string of pearls fall into the boy's coral palm. How beautiful they were, as if just fished from the deep! The boy's hand closed on them like a trap; he made a movement toward the door as one of the others grabbed him. Down they both went, slippery as eels, with their companions kicking and pulling at them. They thrashed about silently at Hazlitt's feet like one writhing, many-limbed monster. He was able to leave unmolested and track down the hall in his squishy shoes.

In the gift shop off the lobby he bought a pin, of Etruscan design, that he felt his wife would consider a sensible value. Carrying his coat—the drizzle had let up, and the humid air seemed warm—he walked south under the trees edging the park to the Seventy-second Street exit. Held up by the traffic light, he stood breathing the fumes of a bus and listening to the throb of its motor. At a window level with his head, one of the riders tapped sharply on the glass. Hazlitt was hardly an arm's length away, but he saw the woman's face only dimly through the rain-streaked window. What appeared to be tears might have been drops of water. The close-set green eyes, as close together as ever, were remarkably mild, and gave him all the assurance he needed. As he stared, she put a wadded tissue to her nose, then raised her gloved hand, the palm toward him, to slowly wag the chewed fingertips. Its air brakes hissing, the bus carried her away.

1983

Going into Exile

The view from his window was so much like a painting that Coker often just stood there gazing at it. At one time he had painted a little—over the years, he had done a lot of things a little. Now he looked closely at what he saw, to try to understand why it disturbed him. Light from an unshaded bulb lit up the doorway and the red-brick front of a fraternity house. This bulb burned day and night, but only Coker seemed aware of it. The Greek letters above the door gave the house a touch of class, and the ivy clinging to the bricks a touch of tradition, but the light bulb had something ambiguous about it. In Coker's experience, only houses of ill fame burned lights in the daytime. It interested him that one unshaded bulb could make a classy sort of place look a bit shady.

The other houses on the street were still more substantial, but somehow they looked less distinguished. All had flights of steps leading up to wide front porches, but even in this mild autumn weather nobody sat on them, or raked the leaves in the yards. A neighbor had told Coker, "We don't sit and visit anymore the way we used to. We just watch TV." Coker had always envied Southern life for the good talk he had heard while he was stationed at an Army camp in Alabama more than forty years ago. People had liked to talk, and they were good at it. He thought he might have come back to Alabama now to see if the South was at all like what he remembered.

As he stood at the window, he watched a familiar black man go along the curb pulling a boy's wagon, as he did several times a week. He was of many shades of blackness, from his hat to his shoes. The tails of his dark shirt hung out of his pants. He pulled a wagon like one Coker himself had once owned, with disk wheels and hard-rubber tires. The tires were now gone—it scraped along on the metal rims—and the name had been obliterated from the sideboards. One of the front wheels wobbled so badly it made the wagon hard both to pull and to steer. If the man was headed east, down the slight incline, the box on the wagon would be empty, but if he was headed west, it was usually piled high with scraps of wood.

A woman would appear after the man had passed, ten or twelve yards back, as if she didn't know him. Coker guessed she might be either a battered thirty-eight or a well-preserved eighty-two. Today she wore a green stocking cap with a yellow pom at its peak, and an unbuttoned, shapeless sweater that dangled bulging pockets below her knees. She carried a staff, like some tribal shepherd tending her flock, and wore blue jogging shoes much too large for her feet. He had never seen her eyes in her masklike, sooty face.

Sometimes twice a day, Coker saw them framed in his window. The man might be in a short-sleeved shirt, with the words "GO BEARS" stamped across the back, or a baseball cap that made him look like a comic bottle stopper. The woman sometimes favored a transparent plastic hood that gave her the appearance of a fabled insect. If the two of them passed Coker on the street, there was no sign from either of them that they had seen him. If the man paused to rest, or to fool with the wagon's load, the woman would be sure to maintain the distance between them. Coker thought a lot about that, but arrived at no conclusions. It did add to his annoyance, however, that the man seemed indifferent to the wobbly wheel.

When Coker's wife asked, "Why Alabama?," since he was free to vacation wherever he liked, he had said something about going into exile. He wasn't sure what he meant by that, but he liked the sound of it.

Back in the fall of 1942, Coker had been sent from his home in Michigan to the Army camp in northern Alabama. What he disliked the most was the weather. The heat was not something he could turn his back on but seemed to surround him like a liquid. The nights presented another kind of problem. Coker couldn't seem to adjust to sleeping in a barracks with a light on. Allen, an Army buddy from Harvard (they were scraping the top of the barrel that season), persuaded Coker to share the expense of a rented car and drive to Oxford, Mississippi, with him. If anything, it would be even hotter there. But Allen had this interest in William Faulkner. He wanted to meet him, to see for himself if Faulkner was real. Coker went along just for the ride, because it would be cooler with the wind blowing on them.

The town itself wasn't much. One thing the Southerners had learned—especially the blacks—was not to get in competition with the climate. Coker and Allen sat at the counter of a drugstore, under a ceiling fan, drinking Cokes. They asked around and found out that Faulkner lived a lot of the time out at his country place, like a farmer. Some of the people they talked to thought he *was* a farmer.

The pharmacist, who seemed to own the drugstore, led them around the corner to the office of J. B. Halsey. He was a lawyer, with a lot of leather-bound law books in his office, but he seemed eager to talk about Faulkner. Right there on his desk he had several books autographed by the author. There was a touch of the scholar about Halsey, a paunchy, gray-haired man, who had gone to Harvard himself. He was like most Southerners back then: what he liked to do was talk. Coker didn't have any literary interests, so he sat there in the light from the window browsing in Halsey's magazines. When it seemed time for the men to go, Halsey suggested that they come home and have dinner with him and Mrs. Halsey. Coker would rather have gone to the local movie, but Allen pointed out privately that this would give them the chance to sample real Southern cooking. And, after all, Halsey was not just a run-of-the-mill small-town lawyer with a side interest in writers; he had been influential in the New Deal and earned the gratitude of President Roosevelt, whom he considered a friend. An autographed picture of the President was there on his desk, too.

Halsey's house was not one of those dilapidated white mansions, Southern style, with pillars at the front and moss hanging from the trees; it was a big, high red-brick structure, like most old school buildings. The large yard was as barren as a schoolyard, with old sheds and outbuildings at the rear, where Coker could see five or six black boys, of varying sizes, seated on the ground with their backs against one of the sheds. When Halsey waved to them, white smiles gleamed in their black faces.

Halsey showed Coker and his friend where the river was; years ago, he said, you could hear the whistles of the steamboats way back here, especially when they were racing. Then he led them past the kitchen entrance and through a side door of the house "so as not to interrupt Mammy Caroline's preparations." Coker noted that the rooms had high ceilings and a musty smell. They went back to Halsey's study, which was not a small room but so crowded with tables and chairs—the chairs strewn with clothes or piled with books, the floor cluttered with boots and unmatched shoes—that Coker and his friend just stood there. And Halsey did not ask them to sit down. Framed and unframed photos, all of them autographed, took up the wall space not occupied by plaques and diplomas. All by itself above the fireplace—and above Halsey, who stood leaning his arm on the mantel—hung a large, dark painting of the bluffs along the river, with the water reflecting the sunset, and a far, deep view across woods and fields to the horizon. It stirred Coker just to look at it, as if he were privileged to glimpse, through a chink in time, an actual moment of the past.

Halsey served his visitors drinks—a thin finger of whiskey each in a heavy tumbler. He was right in thinking they were both inexperienced with drinking, and Coker's eyes watered as he sipped his. Halsey's wife—young for him, Coker thought—came into the study, holding a child she had just finished nursing. She added water to the drink her husband served her, and carried it with her as they moved to the dining room.

Halsey took his place at the end of the table, under a chandelier without bulbs. An extension cord screwed into one of the sockets dangled to a space heater under the table. It was Coker's impression as they sat there, the only sound some subdued laughter in the kitchen, that they were waiting for Halsey or his wife to say grace. Halsey's eyes were lidded, his head raised, and Coker thought his expression was very like that of a smiling Buddha. In this suspended moment the laughter in the kitchen was remarkably suggestive. Were the guests meant to hear it? Coker looked up to see Halsey send him what seemed a conspiratorial glance. Coker was puzzled. About what? Mrs. Halsey broke the spell by rapping on her glass with a spoon.

Halsey remarked that the first Mrs. Halsey—now living in Atlanta, the mother of his three sons and a daughter—had taken exception, over the years, to some of Mammy Caroline's ways, but that the present Mrs. Halsey understood that the past didn't change just to please a few people. Mrs. Halsey confirmed this, laughing shrilly as she dunked her ice cubes with her fingers. They seemed well suited to each other, Coker thought, the way talk seemed to get them both pleasurably excited.

It was some time before Mammy Caroline appeared, in her red bandanna headkerchief, her long skirt concealing her feet as if she came into the room on rollers. She carried a large tureen of soup.

"Lawdy, Lawdy!" she exclaimed, rolling her eyes. "If Ah'd just known these young genmun was coming . . ." She beamed her wide smile on them and placed the tureen before Mr. Halsey, who seemed even more delighted than she was. He interrupted her peals of laughter to tell her that he lacked the bowls to serve the soup in. This got them both laughing harder than ever. Mammy Caroline was so shame-faced to have forgotten the bowls that she stood with her apron pressed to her face, her shoulders heaving. "Lawdy, Lawdy!" she repeated, dabbing at her eyes, but it took her some time to recover her composure, and be reminded that the soup plates were still missing. As she left the room, Halsey again sent Coker a glance he found perplexing. What was it his host seemed so eager to share with him?

Once he was able, Halsey explained that since the war—and
it was the Civil War to which he had reference—it had been difficult to maintain the style of service to which cultivated Southerners were accustomed. Was that a joke? Coker's friend thought
so, and guffawed loudly. Mrs. Halsey called them all to order by
rapping crisply on her glass again. This brought from the kitchen
a young woman Coker would not have thought of as black except
for her hair, which she had greased heavily to reduce the crimp.
The palms of her hands were like coral, the shine of her skin like
pulled taffy. Seeing her, Coker understood the laughter he had
been hearing. Her name was Lena. She had come to inquire of
Mrs. Halsey which of her soup plates she wanted. She was not
full to overflowing with dark, black laughter like Caroline, but
she asked where in the world Mistuh Coker was from, and was
elated to learn that he had lived in Chicago. So had she. For almost
three weeks. Every day she rode somewhere on the elevated. But
she did not really like to be with so many people she would never
know.

"Where you plan to live, Lena?" Halsey asked her. In the way
he put the question, Coker sensed it was like a line in a blackface
routine: white folks with black faces asking leading questions.

"Ah wouldn't live anywheah but right heah, Mistuh Halsey.
Theah's nowheah the folks is so friendly as in Oxford. Theah's
nowheah it's so much like one big famly."

Was it for Coker and Allen they were all putting on this act,
or was it a regular performance? Halsey seemed anxious that his
visitors should miss none of it. When Lena left the room—for the
soup plates, they hoped—Halsey had to take his napkin from its
heavy silver ring to muffle his laughter. Lena was back quickly
with the plates, perhaps so as not to miss Mr. Halsey's good
questions.

The soup, a Creole something or other, seemed a little peppery
to Coker. He resisted a second helping to make sure he had room
for all that would follow. Mrs. Halsey excused herself, handing
the infant to Halsey, to go into the kitchen and return with a small
pot of drip coffee. Three demitasse cups were found on the sideboard, with spoons from the World's Fair in St. Louis. The chicory

blend of the coffee was thick with silt and grounds, sweet as syrup, but Coker drank it. He realized, as Mrs. Halsey lit the candles tilted in two old brandy bottles, that dinner consisted not of what was coming but of what they had eaten. She offered him a peppermint from a tin in her bag of knitting. Halsey rose from the table to go to a window open on the yard.

"Oh, Blue!" he called, as if he meant to croon it.

Feebly, as in a distant echo, a voice replied, "Yessir, Mr. Halsey, yessir!"

"We'd like some wood, Blue. Would you bring us some wood for a fire?"

A fire? The soup had left Coker filmed with perspiration. The setting sun blazed on the high windows. Halsey described Old Blue's life on the river, when he was a cabin boy, back before Emancipation. Old Blue himself interrupted this report, entering like a man peacefully walking in his sleep. On his crossed arms he carried a single piece of charred wood about as thick as a roll of salami. He held it out like a gift to Halsey, who made a little bow as he took it and then went through a well-rehearsed performance of placing it on the grate and cleaning the ashes from beneath it. Blue handed him a piece of crumpled paper from his pocket, and Halsey stooped to ignite it with the table lighter.

"Look how it burn!" crooned Blue. "Look how it burn!," and he extended his hands as if to warm them. The paper flared for an instant, then died, and a draft of air sucked the ash up the chimney.

Were they all crazy, Coker wondered.

Halsey straightened to stand, one arm back on the mantel, as if Coker and Allen had suggested taking his picture, while he patiently explained that at the moment there were nine young black people at the house, four of them women. Every year for the last ten or so, Halsey said, he had given one or two of them money to go north, to Memphis or St. Louis, and enjoy the great life of emancipation. After three or four weeks, every one of them was right back where he or she had started. Halsey would hear the shrill laughter of the girl in the kitchen, or see the boy leaning against the shed with the others. It wasn't that they didn't like it in Memphis; they just liked it better in Oxford. They liked Mistuh Halsey. They loved Mammy Caroline.

As many times as Mrs. Halsey must have heard this story, she encouraged Halsey in the telling. Halsey himself took special pains to spell it all out for Coker, since he could sense in him a reluctance to believe it. Coker did not believe it, but there it was, whether he believed it or not.

Mrs. Halsey excused herself to put her baby to bed. Halsey poured them all brandy in large snifters with chipped edges. Allen called Coker's attention to a collection of commemorative plates on the sideboard, featuring familiar views of Harvard and Cambridge. As Coker admired the plates, he caught sight of Halsey's reflection in the sideboard's oval mirror. He had stepped to the window open on the yard, and stood there with his head cocked, listening intently. Beneath the easy, silken ripple of black laughter, the murmur of mockery was audible. Halsey had been at pains to make sure that his guests appreciated the humor of his situation, but what he overheard now at the window appeared to provoke him to anger. He leaned through the window as if he meant to speak; then, apparently remembering his visitors, he thought better of it. Blue left the room as if in response to an unheard summons.

Halsey followed him, but soon returned with a small mahogany chest, the brass fittings recently polished. He placed it on the table, then tilted back the hinged lid to reveal a row of silver goblets with long stems. The bowl of each goblet was of gold plate, and the silver had the satin softness of worn coins. But, when Halsey offered him one of the goblets, Coker could see that it was useless: it would not stand erect. Halsey gave Coker a moment to reflect on the puzzle. Then he explained that when Mammy Caroline rinsed the goblets, or when she prepared to wipe them, the stems just twisted in her hands before she could help it. Halsey gripped one to show Coker how easily it was done. It was, he said, like unscrewing a tight lid from a jar—something that Mammy Caroline did all the time. She simply underestimated her own strength.

Finished with this story, Halsey doubled up with laughter. Coker could believe his eyes, if not his ears, and waited for Halsey to recover his poise. What was it the man wanted of people like

Coker? As his laughter ran down, they stood facing each other as if they had had some sort of showdown. A film of laugh tears made Halsey's eyes shine. He raised his hands from his sides to turn the palms upward in a "Search me!" sort of gesture that both startled and touched Coker. He averted his eyes from Halsey's palms as if he feared seeing stigmata. Something about Halsey seemed vulnerable, defenseless. He was appealing to Coker so directly—he seemed to demand confirmation of his own self-abasement, to hear from Coker that it was no laughing matter.

"Well, you boys have got a long drive ahead of you," Halsey said, and showed them out of the house.

Coker was anxious to get back to the base, but his literary friend was out of his mind to get it all down before he forgot most of it. As they left the house, Coker was suddenly aware of the voices in the side yard falling silent. He felt the presence of this silence at his back until they reached the street, where the silence was broken by cries of glee so impulsive and infectious he shared them. A wide smile cracked his lips and wrinkled his face in spite of himself. "What's so funny?" said Allen, at his elbow, but all Coker could do was shrug his shoulders.

Back in Alabama, Coker made it a point to see less and less of his Harvard companion, who was soon assigned somewhere in the Pacific. Later, Coker began to wonder if the piece ever had been published. He never got wind of a word of it himself. Not a word. That *did* surprise Coker, since he considered it one hell of a story. Had the Harvard people found it hard to credit? Or had Allen gone off to the wars and simply never come back? All of that was more than forty years in the past now, but it had not led Coker to read any of Faulkner's novels. The truth was he was not prepared for what might turn up.

Coker was there at the window the day the man with the wagon, its front wheel wobbling, stopped to scrounge in the trash at the curb. About all Coker could see of him was his backside, with his shirttail dangling. On impulse—not thinking at all, but on an impulse that had long been building—Coker slipped a bill out of his wallet and hustled from his doorway to the curb, where he tapped the hole worn at the man's elbow.

"Yassuh! Yassuh!" the fellow exclaimed before he straightened up and turned to face Coker. Coker had often plotted this scenario, and just what he would say when the man looked at him: he would explain that when he was a boy he used to have a wagon like the one the man was pulling, and on more than one occasion he had had the same problem with a wobbly wheel. What he wanted the man to do (as a favor to Coker) was to get himself either a new wheel or a new wagon. But now, seeing the man's blank, bloodshot gaze, which hardly seemed to take him in, he said not a word.

He placed the bill on the man's sleeve; it proved to be a twenty. The man stared at it as if puzzled by the sight of so much money. "Take it," Coker said, but in his free hand the man held a bottle half full of some dark liquid.

"Yassuh," he replied, but he did nothing. Before he could make a move, the woman raised her staff and thumped it hard on the pavement. She then muttered something, jerking her head in the manner of a driver starting up a team of horses. The man stood immobile, one hand gripping the bottle, his left arm crooked before him with the bill on his sleeve, as if he were reading the time.

Just then a passing car swirled the air, and the bill fluttered to the ground between them. There it remained as the woman approached and shuffled, unseeing, past Coker. The man had already turned back to pulling the wagon and went up the street ahead of her, the wheel wobbling. Coker might have imagined seeing the downcast gaze of the woman's eyes, her lashes fluttering, but there was no mistaking the smile of triumph at the corners of her lipless mouth. Smiling and nodding, Coker stood at the curb as she passed by.

1984

To Calabria

In the early years of their friendship, in the nineteen-thirties, Hal and Morgan did some cycling in Italy. Their destination was old Calabria, well known to Hal through the writings of Norman Douglas but somewhat undefined for Morgan, whose specialty was the eighteenth-century novel.

Several years his senior, Hal seemed to Morgan an ideal travel companion. They had met at the Berlitz school in Paris, where Hal, a tasseled muffler dangling from his neck, held a collapsible tin cup to catch the fall of his cigarette ashes as he tutored select students in Spanish and Italian. He was the smartest person Morgan had ever met, but a bit short on style. The cape of his olive-green Aquascutum raincoat might be pulled over his head during a downpour, the frayed bottoms of his pants rolled to reveal his bone-white shins. To Morgan's knowledge, he never ran a comb through his thin patch of hair to where the back of his neck was usually raw from the clippers.

For the adventure, Morgan bought a better bike than he could afford—one with three gears, real tubes in the tires, a meter on the front wheel to register the mileage. Hal had picked up a wreck of a bike in Verona, both its wheels so warped that they slapped on the frame like paddles. When they had to walk their bikes into a head wind, Morgan found this racket annoying.

It shamed Morgan, in his authentic lederhosen and rucksack, to be cycling in Italy with a character who wore a blue serge suit, with black-and-white wing-tip oxfords that squished when it rained. Hal's pants cuffs dragged in the grease of the chain, and frequently tangled in the sprocket. Coasting down the grades, the wind puffing out his cape, he looked like a madcap runaway monk. On the other hand, it was Morgan who suffered from blisters under his shoulder straps, and a mysterious rash at his waistline.

From the moment they started down the coast below Pisa, squalls of rain, pouring down their necks, soaked both of them inside and out. Hal seemed pleased with their wet-dog smell. His two-tone shoes discolored his corpse-hued feet, which led Morgan to reflect on the fate of Shelley, who had drowned right there in the sea off Viareggio. On the infrequent occasions the weather cleared, Morgan walked along the beach, skimming stones, while Hal waded in the frothy surf. In a ruined garden in Civitavecchia, Hal read to Morgan from the memoirs Stendhal wrote when he served there as French consul, while Morgan, pantless, hunted down lice in his lederhosen. Morgan's enthusiasm for cycling was dimming. According to the meter on the wheel of his bike, they had ridden less than seven hundred kilometres in three weeks. Somewhere to the south, Calabria was like a sock in the toe of Italy's boot.

A few days later, pushing along toward Amalfi with his head down, Morgan stopped as if a voice had cried *"Basta!"*—his one Italian word. He had had his fill of cycling. Worse, he'd had his fill of Hal—Hal's cheerfulness, his clipped, reddened neck, his baffling indifference to how he looked. Thanks to that haircut, Morgan could see that Hal's ears were dirty. This was not something he could discuss in a wind that blew sea spray into his mouth. What he did say was that he was eager to spend April in Paris.

Spray filmed Hal's glasses and made him look as if he were weeping. This so irritated Morgan that he determined to take himself off fast, before he said something he might later regret. To make it up to Hal, Morgan swapped bikes with him, even Steven. He then pushed Hal's old bike, with its flat front tire, all the way back to Naples, where he gave it to a boy who was tending a goat.

After the war, when Morgan had found a place in the academic world where Hal was already an established Hawthorne scholar, they picked up a kind of friendship again. When they ran into one another at scholarly meetings, it was Morgan who supplied the bottle of sour mash for their late-night talks, or made the early run to the deli. Bicycles, or Italy, sometimes came up, but their aborted adventure seemed remote, and Morgan never actually got around to discussing what he might have missed. Nor did Hal.

It was to Morgan's advantage to be considered one of Hal's cronies, and to receive his coveted recommendations. Yet Morgan was one of the last to hear when Hal married, or when his children were born. Around that time, Morgan was living with one of Hal's brighter ex-students while she finished her thesis on Melville. Both projects came to an end at the same time. Morgan was never sure whether Hal knew about that episode, and may have forgotten to tell him about his own marriage, later, in a university town at the other end of the country.

They were running into one another less by then anyhow. In the sixties, Morgan took two leaves of absence rather than deal with campus agitation. Still, in airport throngs or crowded hotel lobbies he would always keep an eye out for Hal's shabby Pan Am flight bag, or his green Cambridge book sack stuffed with papers to grade. Some of their best discussions were in the public washrooms, while Hal shaved with his spring-wind Swiss razor, his hairless body whiter than his B.V.D.s. His brown hair was still short, trimmed with clippers at the back, his ears red and prominent in the winter; one tasseled end of his forgotten muffler dangled from a sleeve.

Once, in 1975, they crossed paths on the escalators in Penn Station. Hal had just arrived from Stockholm, hatless in the winter, an ash-strewn gray sweater under his raincoat. He looked worn as he puffed his cigarettes. Just chatting with Morgan left him winded. Morgan thought of joshing him a little, asking if he had actually made it to Calabria. But the opportunity didn't come up.

A few years later, around the time his own wife died, Morgan learned from a colleague that Hal had mysteriously vanished. The door to his office stood open, papers and books were piled on his desk as usual, along with the cheap Ingersoll watch that he would set out on the lectern as he talked.

That news transported Morgan, on the instant, to the wind-swept coastal highway south of Pisa where they had plodded along in a downpour, walking their bikes. On a low rise, they had paused to look at the gray, foaming sea, swept by tatters of cloud. In a nearby farmyard, a white stallion, his pelt gleaming with rain, pranced about like a unicorn, tossing his mane. Two small men trailed the beast, waving their arms and hooting. The scene was an allegory Bellini might have painted, but Morgan had been too miserable to appreciate it. That would come almost fifty years later, when he heard that his friend had vanished.

Had Morgan been wrong to let Hal push on alone to Calabria? For all his talents, his air of authority, Hal had always seemed somehow vulnerable to Morgan, as if one day he might do just what he had done: disappear. Nothing terrible had happened to him in Calabria, but on the highway south of Naples, in a gale of sea spray, Morgan had just walked off and left him. Half a century later, the memory of that defection gripped Morgan so intensely that he could not speak to the man who had brought him the news.

Once, in public, Hal had spoken of himself as one of the good starters—think of the notable careers he had helped people launch—and of Morgan as a good finisher. Morgan had flushed with pleasure and embarrassment. What had he ever finished? Or was that what Hal meant to point out?

Over the next few years, unconfirmed rumors reported Hal sighted in many places, his raincoat frayed, his vest strewn with ashes, his green book bag stuffed with cartons of Camels. A colleague recognized him, from a distance, on the deck of a Danube river steamer. One of his old students—now a matron with grown sons—received an unsigned pre-war postcard from Barcelona, where they had both loved the Gaudí buildings. Had he meant to reveal or to obliterate himself?

Among the objects found on Hal's desk was an emptied film packet with Morgan's name lettered on it. One of Hal's daughters had finally got around to sending it along. In the packet, wrapped in a wad of tissue, Morgan found a nickel-plated gadget, a meter with a spiked gear on its side. Numerals were visible through a narrow window. Twirling the gear, Morgan watched the figures change—1746 edged to 1747. He recognized the meter from the front wheel of the bike Hal had pedaled and pushed to Calabria. Had Hal meant the packet as a gift, or a reproach? Was he suggesting that this was Morgan's unfinished business?

With his love for gadgets, Hal had been one of the first to own a sound recorder, with its spools of wire. He had the voices of Eliot and Pound on the same tangled reel. These spools were displayed around his house and office for idle visitors to puzzle over and unsnarl. Short snippets of wire were stored in a shoebox, on the chance that they might one day reveal their message. Looking for coins in the lining of his coats, Hal often found bits of wire he would wind about his fingers as he talked.

Seated in his study, twirling the spiky gear, Morgan found he could advance or reverse the numbers in its small window. Four decades after their pause in Civitavecchia, Morgan had finally got around to reading Stendhal's memoirs, much of which he confused with his own Italian adventure. Was there more, mile by mile, in the meter he toyed with now? He recalled the moment on the road south of Naples when he announced his departure. Sea spray had glistened on Hal's face and glasses, and the possibility that he was weeping had only irritated Morgan. Now it seemed reasonable to him that by reversing the meter he could return to that point overlooking the sea where the white horse pranced about like a mythical beast; or that, by advancing it, he could proceed down the coast to Calabria.

Still spinning the gear, Morgan left his study to stand at his half-curtained kitchen window. Just outside it hung a large bird feeder. Before his wife died, she used to keep the feeder from being taken over by the big, aggressive jays—birds Morgan hated. He could always hear their damned hammering clear back in his study.

After a bit of it, he would come running on the double to throw empty cans at them.

"The poor birds!" his wife would say. "They're only doing what birds do!"

"And I'm doing what I do!" Morgan would shout, as if that settled the matter. The first truce, of sorts, came during his wife's last illness. Morgan would hear the racket, come roaring out of his study, and then, for some reason, would stand calmly at the kitchen window observing the birds hammer the seeds. He still hated their mindless, beady-eyed tenacity, but it came to him that the racket these birds made, like the slap of a warped wheel on a bike frame, was less a stupid personal affront than part of the rising cost of living. Was it costing him more to live than he could afford?

The cashmere sweater Morgan's wife had given him one Christmas was airing on the line outside the window. Morgan had coveted that sweater for years, but now that he had it he felt reluctant to wear it. The moths were getting at it before he did. He actually thought cashmere a bit too elegant for a man whose shirt cuffs often picked up a little egg yolk these days, but that was not what disturbed him. Nor was it the fact that his watch fob often snagged in the fabric. So what was it—his growing aversion to anything new? If he took the sweater over to the Goodwill Thrift Shop, the manager would say, "Why, it's absolutely new! Didn't you ever wear it?"

Morgan stepped outside, took the sweater from the hanger, and slipped it on. The fist that clutched the meter caught in the sleeve.

In the mirror on the bathroom door he considered the cashmere sweater and found it on the loose side but handsome. He had never been at his ease with those young women (his wife among them) who wore their sweater sleeves up on their forearms, stretching the cuffs. His own sleeves seemed to run long, now that he had narrowed somewhat in the shoulders. Eight or ten months ago, he had come home from a hospital stay in a suit that draped on him as on a hanger. The mirror's reflection, then and now, filled him with dismay.

From a shoe bag at the back of the closet he pulled a pair of glove-leather oxfords, of a burgundy color, so supple he could roll them up like socks. They had been shaped to his feet by a *signorina* in Venice who used douses of alcohol from a hair-tonic bottle. The soles were scuffed, but the uppers showed little wear. Years of care and polishing had given the leather a luster like a limousine's waxed sheen. His wife had pointed out that the movement of his toes was visible through the leather.

In the Goodwill shop, where he had stopped recently to look for braces (the old kind), an attractive matron had mistaken him for a celebrity. Where had she seen him, she asked—on TV, on the *Over Easy* program? Or in Florence, or Venice, or Oaxaca? Strangers often took a second look at Morgan, as they did at old cars. That day, he was wearing a loden-green velour shirt, purchased between trains in Salzburg some sixteen years back; the fabric still had the gloss and texture once common to the seats of train coaches. Morgan himself had a quality of old porch furniture, he often thought—of patent-medicine labels, and cars with a leather sling for the crank handle. In his pants watch pocket he carried a train conductor's timepiece—adjusted to heat, cold, various shocks and human affections—with a dial on the face to indicate if it needed winding. That was apt; Morgan considered whether he might be a timepiece that had stopped.

Tucked into the toe of the left oxford, Morgan found a key wrapped in a cocktail napkin. He had always had trouble with keys. Especially one—was it this one?—to an apartment in Brooklyn Heights, near the foot of the Brooklyn Bridge, where, in 1957 or so, another student of Hal's was doing a thesis on Hart Crane. Morgan had been the first to get her up at dawn to watch the sunrise from the bridge span. Hal had met them in the bar of the St. George Hotel, where they had talked for hours about bridges and connections. But what connection? All that vast swarm of people, millions of them daily, passed *under* the river, not over it, most of them hardly knowing the bridge was there. This young woman had sworn she could live nowhere else—she loved to ponder the bridge while she worked—and she had extra keys made for friends like Morgan. A year later, returning from Spain, he found that the lock on the door had been changed. The young woman had taken up with an Irish poet who proved to have a wife and family in Perugia. Morgan had looked forward to discussing with Hal the weakness of bridges as symbols when compared with the actuality of changed locks, but—like the key in the toe of his shoe—it slipped his mind.

One reason that pair of Italian oxfords had lasted so long was that it took a shoehorn to get them on. He couldn't find the horn now, so he slipped on a pair of sandals. Once he was out of the house, he felt better. Debris from the last storm runoff had clogged the street drain, and Morgan took a moment to remove some of the leaves. Buds were already opening on the trees; the view down the street was veiled by a mist of pale green. Three of the neighbor's dogs, now too old and feeble to attack him, barked hoarsely from behind a hedge. It was a morning of the kind that made Morgan think of Italy. Those few times the sun shone, he would wake his friend early to get what Hal called "the bloom of it." With Hal, Morgan had always felt at ease about a step behind; in Italy, though, Morgan was often out front. Something to do with the bikes, perhaps.

At the foot of the incline, the street opened out on a prospect of sheds and small tract houses, stalled and battered old cars, several of them with flat tires, one covered with a sheath of bright green plastic. At a fire station, a man in red suspenders and hip-high boots let a stream from the hose play on the wheels of the engine. Nothing unusual in any of that, but right at that instant all of it danced and shimmered in the radiance of light. Morgan halted, his lips parted. The fingers of his right hand, warm in his jacket pocket, played with the spiked gear on the meter, bringing him with every twirl of the wheel closer to Calabria.

1984

Fellow Creatures

Nothing special, just a leghorn pullet, the pet of children who lived in a nearby trailer, its feathers soiled by too much handling, the little bird had escaped from its pen and found shelter in the garage of Colonel Huggins, U.S. Army, retired. The malfunctioning garage door stood half open, offering a dark and convenient sanctuary that had attracted the pullet at an early hour of the morning. Huggins had been awakened by the mournful clucking. When it persisted, he investigated. In the dawning light, the little bird looked ghostly, but cast a huge shadow in the beam of the flashlight. Her jeweled eye seemed to flash; the clucking became shrill and agitated. Huggins crouched, extending one hand, and the bird, with some reluctance, took a few steps toward him. When Huggins clucked encouragement, the pullet responded. Huggins had grown up in a farmyard cackling with chickens without remarking that they were so expressive. He was amazed to note the range of emotion in the cluck of a chicken. Fear and anxiety soon gave way to a soft, throaty warbling for reassurance. Huggins responded. Soon the little bird pecked at the button on his shirt cuff; then, with a minimum of flutter, she allowed him to slip a hand beneath her breastbone, cradle her on his arm. She liked that, being accustomed to it.

As Huggins left the garage and entered the house, the pullet's cackle was troubled and anxious. Huggins stroked her throat feathers to calm her. The bird was quiet while he dialed the neighbors' number and heard the excitement of the children, their cries of relief. The pullet's name proved to be Lucy.

In a moment, three of the children came scrambling through the brush on the slope, trampling whatever it was Huggins' wife had planted. Had he fed her? they cried. She was probably starving! The youngest of the three hugged the little pullet like a package, and off they all raced, hooting. High on the slope Huggins heard the shrill voice of their mother, a liberated young woman who had set up her trailer in her parents' backyard; she was urging them to thank the nice man.

Was Huggins a nice man? For three years, he had endured the cackling of chickens (originally a flock), the honking of geese (now down to two), the bleating of a goat, and the bloodcurdling cry of a peacock kept in a cage too small to strut in or display his plumage. All of this illegal in an exclusively residential area. Even the trailer the young woman and her brood lived in (the tires now flat) required a special permit she had not been granted. Huggins, that nice man, had said nothing. Over the years, he *had* written several letters, all unmailed, to her father, Albrecht, a prominent figure in the foreign-car business. Huggins wondered how he himself would have handled a grown daughter (a squatter on his property) who had brought a court suit against her own father for polluting the air with his diesel-engine Mercedes. Huggins had never met her. She called her cats, her chickens, her geese, and her children by clapping her hands—a racket he found distracting. The pullet had left bits of dirt and feathers on his sleeve. How light she had been! Like a feather duster. He stood as if waiting for something to happen, plucking at his sleeve.

Huggins' daily morning walk was altered to bring him past the pen where the little pullet did her scratching. With a little coaxing, Huggins persuaded her to take birdseed from his palm. Imported Irish oatmeal also caught her fancy. He inquired in the local pet shop what was recommended to brighten up a young bird's feathers. He added the vitamin mixture to her water. He was caught red-handed by Mrs. Albrecht, the young woman's mother, who appeared with vegetable hulls and cuttings. She, too, had a weakness for chickens! Just in passing, she let it drop that this little pullet was the last of the fryers but hadn't fleshed out like the others—had he noticed? There was nothing to her. For which the bird could be thankful. Mrs. Albrecht (she drove a non-diesel Mercedes) could hardly wait to tell the children that their neighbor, Colonel Huggins, had taken on the chore of feeding their chicken—that's how starved it looked!

Huggins would surely have explained what led him to feed his neighbors' chicken, but the word "fryer" had so unsettled him that he was speechless. Was it new to him that young chickens were *fryers?* Hardly. He had once even barbecued fryers in batches—a *spécialité de la maison,* as he had put it.

A few days later, Mr. Albrecht, a jovial type with a strong, booming voice, called across from his deck to say that Huggins was welcome to the whole damn zoo if he would like it, so long as he took the peacock, too. How did Huggins stand it? Albrecht thought it sounded like some female screaming "Help!"

During the war in Europe, Colonel Huggins had enjoyed the hospitality of a French family proud of their cuisine. He had been instrumental in providing them with hard-to-find gourmet necessities. At war's end, they cooked him a five-star dinner, featuring steak. Huggins had admitted to being a connoisseur of steak.

"So," the host asked him, "how you like?"

His mouth full of the steak, Huggins smiled and nodded.

"A *spécialité, mon vieux—filet de cheval américain!*"

Huggins was calm enough to swallow what he had already chewed. Moments later, however, he was obliged to excuse himself, leaving most of the *filet de cheval* on his plate. He perspired a good deal. A damp towel was applied to his face.

"You Americans!" his host exclaimed. "You like it fine till you know what it is. What you eat is not on your plate, it is in your mind!"

Then there was the time Huggins' wife cried out from the kitchen, "Oh my God!" Fearing the worst, he went to her rescue. But at the door to the kitchen he saw nothing unusual. His wife had prepared a plump bird for roasting with a coat of olive oil that made it glisten.

"Yes?" he said.

She took a moment to slip off the bib of her apron. The she said, almost flatly, "It looks just like a newborn baby!" and left Huggins alone with it.

A cow, somewhat on the small side—not so large that Huggins found her intimidating—was tethered to pasture in a field that Huggins passed on his long daily walk. He was in the habit, when the spirit moved him, of pulling up the grass that grew along the bank where the cow was unable to reach it. When she raised her head to crop the sweet, fragrant offering from his hand, the breath she exhaled smelled of clover. On the instant, Huggins experienced a time displacement, familiar to poets. A boy, he stood in the shadow of a freight car down the tracks from the town, peering into a great vat of sorghum as sweet and thick as Karo syrup. Bees droned in a cloud above it. A thick green scum spotted its surface. He almost swooned at the thought that he might topple into it. So rich and fragrant had been its smell that he felt no need to taste it. The whole great vat of it, swarming with bees, the scum on the top softly undulating, had put him in mind of the old movie serials where if the hero toppled into one of the pits of terror he would be preserved like a bee in a jar of honey.

On occasion, the cow shared the pasture with a swaybacked horse. In the rainy season Huggins might pull up a tuft of the new grass, earth still clinging to the roots, and toss it to where the horse could munch it. The animal showed no interest whatever. The horse's owner occasionally forked hay from the back of a pickup, but he never checked to see what the horse thought about it. He drove in, made his drop, and drove off. Some days Huggins would stand on the bridge over the creek, where he and the animals had a good view of each other; the bare spots on the horse, worn by the harness, were the shiny black of old oilcloth. In bad weather, the beast took shelter in a shed, where Huggins, attentive as he passed, might hear a snort and the stomp of a hoof. Somehow it troubled him that it was a mare. On cold mornings he saw her breath smoke. He thought it especially disturbing that she was both so big and so useless. He had read about pet food, but he tried to put it out of his mind.

Occasionally, this pasture also nourished several black-faced sheep, adored by children. Seen close up, their faces were like felt masks, the heads like carnival toggery on a stick. At no time did Huggins entertain any notion that he and the sheep shared a common doom or aspiration. He did feel the creatures' ill-starred need to be led somewhere, anywhere—even to slaughter. Nevertheless, for no particular reason, Colonel Huggins—a lover of roast spring lamb—passed up the seasonal special called to his attention by Angelo, the butcher, well known for his own hopeless love for steak tartare with three raw eggs.

"So what is new?" queried Angelo, sensing a change.

"Less fat," replied Huggins, patting his midriff. It was old advice he was now moved to take. What did that leave him? Perhaps a mozzarella pizza from the freezer. One day—not today— he would ask Angelo how horses did so well on just hay and cereal.

Escaped or missing pets—now that Huggins had been alerted— were having one of their high seasons. Urgent requests for their return were posted on abandoned cars, telephone poles, and supermarket bulletin boards, citing rewards along with descriptions of their character, identifying marks, the names to which they sometimes responded, or—in the case of parrots—what they would say if questioned. What parrots might say often shocked Huggins; he had always teased them to speak with a mere "Polly want a cracker?," but lately one had told him to buzz off.

One day, a big cottontail rabbit, with feet like snowshoes, hopped from behind a shrub to startle Huggins. The sight of Huggins did not give the rabbit cause for alarm; it hopped so close that Huggins might have seized it if he had not been so unnerved. When he mentioned this incident to his cousin, Liz Harcourt—a woman who had hatched several batches of quail eggs in her kitchen and raised the broods to eat from her plate and nest in her apron pockets—she said, "You should have grabbed him. I love chicken-fried rabbit!"

Some years back, during a rainy season with bad mud slides and considerable flooding, a herd of Holstein cows pastured somewhere behind the ridge had made their way, pursued by a pack of baying dogs, through groves of oak and laurel, through a dense tangle of brush that streaked their hides with red as if raked with barbed wire, to where they exited, mooing distractedly, at the foot of the driveway Huggins shared with the Albrechts. He saw them from his deck, where he was barbecuing spareribs. As they made their mooing way up the driveway, he worried that they would trample his azaleas. Single file, following the leader, they continued up the slope to the Albrecht house (at that time the trailer was not there) and followed the walk around the house onto the deck at the rear. The rail fence around the deck confined them; there they formed an assembly, casually informal, like guests at a cocktail party. Peering down at Huggins, one or two mooed plaintively. He could see the red streaks on their flanks and udders. The bizarre spectacle brought to Huggins' mind a fantastic, fanciful painting. Fear that the deck might collapse—his neighbors were out that afternoon—aroused him to call the fire department for some quick action. The man who owned the cows, a shaggy, bearded fellow who did not trouble to greet Huggins, finally appeared to herd them peaceably back down to the street.

At the time, the incident seemed merely bizarre. But that night, as Huggins put his mind to it, his eyes on the play of shadows on the bedroom ceiling, it came to him that the face of a cow, a craggy primitive mask, was like a piece of the landscape seen in closeup. That congress of cows assembled on a house deck, their gaze centered in judgment on Huggins, had led him to forgo the ribs smoking on his barbecue.

Another day—it had been overcast, with a bit of drizzle, obliging him to plod along with his head down—Huggins heard a raucous clamor above and behind him. A flock of grackles, their wet feathers gleaming, sat along one of the telephone wires. On an impulse, he threw up his arms and hooted hoarsely. The birds rose about him like a leaf storm, scattered for a moment, then gathered on a wire on the street below. Did Huggins detect, as he passed by, a change in the tone of their discussion? Several flew ahead to strut about on a plot of grass. As he approached them they took off, flying in crisp military formation. He wheeled to watch them, blinking his eyes at the pelting stream of their forms. After several orderly strategic flights, they congregated in a tree along the curb walk. The tree itself was not much—a dark clump of leaves without visible branches. It was Huggins' impression, however, as he walked toward it, that the gabble of the birds caused the leaves to tremble, as if stirred by a breeze. He sensed their hovering, inscrutable presence. From beneath the tree, he peered upward just as the flock noisily departed, like bees from a hive. Bits of leaves and feathers rained on him. The agitation Huggins had observed in the leaves he now felt within himself—a tingling, pleasurable excitement. Squinting skyward, he could see strips of sky as if through cracks in leaky shingles. High at the top, perched at an angle, was a single black bird. Either that bird or another just like it—among birds it seemed unimportant—fluttered along with Huggins, its hatpin eyes checking on his interests and curious habits, all the way back to the foot of his drive, where he heard, high on the slope above him, the expectant clucking of the little pullet, and he responded in kind.

1984

Wishing You and Your Loved Ones Every Happiness

"It works!" Charlotte exclaimed as she opened the envelope with her Christmas letter opener. Her habit of using a butter knife, or anything handy, ripping the envelope open like a package, was one of many that Charles found annoying. It was Charlotte who opened and read the holiday mail, being more familiar with her friends' handwriting. She turned from Charles to catch the light on what she was reading.

After a moment he said, "Anything wrong?" Charlotte was silent. "Not Arlene?" he queried. Arlene always wrote to remind them that she hadn't heard from them, and was worried. Charlotte's plan to just answer Christmas cards, rather than send them, had resulted in complications.

"Lee and Olivia," Charlotte said, "I think."

Charles replied, "My God, is he still hanging in there?" For years now they had expected the worst about Lee. He had had a racking, hacking cough for years before emphysema was talked about.

"Did you see my glasses?" Charlotte asked. With the card, she went in search of them.

Olivia had been Charlotte's best friend at Swarthmore, where both Lee and Charles were instructors. Charlotte had thought to take a master's degree in French, with Charles, but instead she had gone to England with Olivia. That was the summer that

Charles, to impress Charlotte, had gone to France to do relief work with the Quakers, but they soon shipped him home with hepatitis. It was so novel in the late forties that his pale saffron color proved to be a mark of distinction.

"I still can't read her writing," said Charlotte. "Can you read it?"

She passed the card to Charles. Olivia's crabbed, chicken-track hand had always been a problem for him. It had been formed by the writing of cribs for her high school Latin translations. Charles could read the card's greeting, however, and read it. "Wishing you and your loved ones every happiness," he said.

Charlotte snatched the card from him (another one of her annoying habits) and gave it a shake as if more words might fall from it. It saddened Charles to think how that had once charmed him. At the time, he had actually been reluctant to ask a classy girl like Charlotte, with her southern exposure, to take a back seat on a double date. Right after the war, few of the boys had cars. Charles and Charlotte would take the train to New York, see a play or a movie, have a late dinner at the Algonquin, then get back to Philadelphia in time to catch the last local to Swarthmore. But when Charlotte came back from England with her Pond's Cold Cream complexion, it had been her idea that they double-date with Lee and Olivia. One thing Olivia had at the time was a car, a Chevy coupé with a rumble seat. They had been on several dates Charles found pretty drafty—Charlotte was not a girl to slouch down and get cuddly—before it dawned on Charles she was sitting up high to keep her eye on Lee, and his eye on her. Up to that moment it hadn't crossed Charles's mind that a smart girl might be sweet on a pretty dumb guy.

"For once it's not a cat picture," said Charlotte, examining the card, "but it's not like her not to say *something*."

That called for a comment Charles resisted. He did not want to get into Olivia and Lee, a long-closed book. Olivia's father, a brilliant, homely Rhodes scholar in the twenties, had come back from England with a bride so stunning nobody could figure it. She starred in local productions of Gilbert and Sullivan while her husband worked nights in the physics laboratory. Their only child proved to be a girl who looked very much like her father. Only Charles could believe it when she caught on to Lee, who looked and smoked like Dashiell Hammett. When was it Charlotte had stopped saying, "At least we know what to buy him for Christmas"?

"Poor Olivia." Charles sighed, then added, "You ever wonder how she happened to get Lee?"

"Have I *ever* wondered? Have I ever *wondered?*" Charlotte looked about her, her lips parted. "She got him because she asked him. He couldn't make up his mind so she made it up for him."

Charles was too startled to comment. Charlotte flushed, her eyes flashed, but Charles was not the object of her anger. How had she known all these years and not told him? She had not told him because right to the last—to that summer in England—she had thought that Lee might choose *her*. And why not? Would he pass over the swan for the duckling?

"*Poor* Olivia!" she cried, mocking Charles. "But maybe I should call her. When did she last call?"

Once, in those early years, Olivia had called to tell Charlotte that it was no go on the twins adoption. A blow. Only a family would redeem the lost time. Olivia had been a sweet, toothy, poo-poo-pah-doo type of girl who did a lot of baby-sitting in college. Babies were what she wanted. At the time, Charlotte had confided, she feared Olivia might steal one.

"I don't know what I'll do if Lee answers," Charlotte said now. "He can hardly whisper. Suppose you call them?"

Lee's husky whisper was the last thing Charlotte wanted to hear. There had been a period, she called it his "blue" one, when he would regularly get plastered and phone them at about midnight. If Charlotte answered, he would ask for Charles; if Charles, he would ask for Charlotte, wheezily laughing. Did he think it was funny? Charlotte could never just lie there and let the phone ring. What if somebody had died?

"Is this a new address book?" asked Charlotte. "Where's their number?"

Charles roused himself out of the recliner, walked to the patio doors. A drizzle fell on a film of water. The runoff was clogged.

Lee used to clear the drains and the runoffs, back when he could breathe. He was Mr. Fixit, and when he and Olivia came to visit he would check out the plumbing. Charlotte flattered him silly, of course. "I just can't tell you what it's like to have a man around the house," she would tell him. Charles had to admit that Lee, for all his godawful habits, was a sweet-natured, superior person. Charles was a smaller, less generous person. And Charlotte knew that. It was also pretty damn big of Charlotte not to bring it to his attention, he thought.

"I'm calling," said Charlotte. "I'll say that not having heard, it had led us to wonder—"

"But we did hear," said Charles. "That's the trouble."

"—it has led us to wonder," continued Charlotte. "If there's anything amiss I'll feel it. There's not an ounce of make-believe in her nature."

Charles watched her dial the number. If Lee had a fault, besides the wheezing, it was his tendency, after a few beers, to belch in the manner of distant thunder or rumbling artillery. He was always shame-faced with embarrassment. Charlotte would always insist there was nothing more natural, and Charles agreed. On one occasion Charles had been in such wholehearted agreement that after a few good burps he had started to hiccup. Swallows of beer or water would not stop them. Charlotte had been so incensed she left the table. Still hiccuping fiercely, Charles had gone for a walk without his billfold. Several blocks away he was stopped by the police who patrolled the neighborhood on weekends. When questioned, Charles hiccuped. He had neither his credit cards nor his driver's license. When he was brought back to the house, Charlotte identified him, but Olivia and Lee had already departed. The next day Lee called to say it had been his fault.

"Lee, darling," Charlotte cried, "Lee, this is Charlotte. Is Olivia there?"

As was his custom, Charles came up behind her. Olivia was speaking. In a shrill voice she cried out that they were overwhelmed, simply overwhelmed. The package had arrived in just the cord it was wrapped in, dangling the torn label, but she knew it was from Charles and Charlotte! If they were only there to help them eat it. Bangers! Why, they've never eaten English sausages. And the unsliced bacon! Didn't they know Lee was forbidden to eat bacon? But Lee did want to thank them for the dehydrated maple syrup he could sprinkle on his cereal in the morning. Powdered syrup. Just imagine!

Charlotte turned to pass the phone to Charles. "Olivia," Charles said, "how wonderful to hear you."

Actually, she had never been hard to hear. He heard her clearly as he passed the receiver back to Charlotte. "You've just got to come, you two," Olivia was saying, "and help us eat it. Lee says he'll make Charles some buckwheat flapjacks."

"We just can't, Ollie," Charlotte replied. "We've both got colds. Charles refuses to drive on the freeway on weekends." She passed the receiver back to Charles, who bared his teeth and waved it away.

"You two there, you hear me? You're either coming up here or we're coming down there. Lee has a cold too. You can comfort each other. You know what they now say? They say sneezing doesn't matter. It's the touching and kissing. We promise not to kiss you. We'll bring some logs. You won't even have to burn your own wood."

There was a silence. Charlotte stood with closed eyes, as if in prayer.

"What should I bring?" cried Olivia. "I've made some real wassail. Charles used to love my wassail. You remember the time they were both so deathly sick from the marjoram he put into the stuffing? They couldn't eat the turkey dinner. They went to bed early, and the two of us played Scrabble. Did we drive to New Haven? Whose play was it? How long has it been since you've seen a real play?"

Were people crazy? Charles wondered. Did they live in their dreams? Back from a sabbatical in England, Lee had been so changed it embarrassed Charles to make small talk with him. Driving him back to Cornell, Charlotte talked shrilly to conceal his wheezing. In the barn of a house they rented in Ithaca, Olivia had had the mumps, dangerous at her age, and Charles offered to prepare the dinner. He ruined the dressing, as usual, with too much marjoram. They ate silently at a table in the kitchen, their backs to the warm draft of air up from the basement. After the meal, at the risk of contagion, Charlotte cuddled up with Olivia on the sofa, reading *Winnie-the-Pooh.* Charles played Olivia's old Gilbert and Sullivan records that featured her mother's voice. Not to trouble Lee, who needed his sleep, Charles bedded down on the couch in the study. He was awakened by shouting, the slamming of doors, and the drumming of the shower on the ceiling, suggesting that one or both of the girls were plastered. It was followed by Olivia's muted sobbing, for her accumulated losses, encouraged by a bottle of three-star brandy. At daybreak Charles found Charlotte in the front seat of the car, their bags packed. They drove clear to Poughkeepsie before they had breakfast at the Smith Bros. Restaurant, an old favorite. It surprised them both to find that they were silent but not bitter. That was the end, except for the call Charles made to Lee on the day Kennedy was shot. Kennedy had meant the world to Lee.

Charles has moved a chair from the table to where Charlotte can sit on it as she listens. For years it had been her habit to sit and doodle, with her fine-pointed pens, on five-by-seven file cards. One of Charlotte's friends, an interior decorator, was the first to "discover" Charlotte. She used her doodles on designs for lampshades, and the collages she transferred to shower curtains. A framed collage of Charlotte's doodles is in the Young Reader Room of the local library, a Gift of the Artist. All of that stopped when her friend went to California, and Charlotte had gone back to twisting a lock of her hair around one finger as she listened to telephone calls. On a visit to New York, after they were married, she had taken a seat on a Broadway bus beside a youth so pale he looked ghostly. He wore a black suit, a wide-brimmed black hat, and dangling coils of hair at his ears, like Charlotte. Charles did not trouble to point this out to Charlotte, but in a few weeks' time she had changed her hair style to something more like a pageboy, short at the back, and had taken to doodling on large file cards. This post-Christmas morning her head lobs to one side as she cradles the phone at her shoulder, freeing one hand to feel about her ears for the curls that are no longer there. The voice of Olivia, vibrant at the thought of old times and new problems, is audible to Charles, as he ponders what it is that matters in a friendship.

"Who would have sent them bangers," Charles says, "was it you?" But Charlotte has turned to other matters.

"They're coming," she says, resting the phone on its hook. "Wouldn't it be just like them to both have colds?"

1985

Country Music

On the previous evening, Durkin and his wife had sat up late to watch *Coal Miner's Daughter* on television. His wife liked the music, but what Durkin liked were the scenes of the coal miner and his family, in some godforsaken hole in Appalachia. Durkin had known hard times himself, on a farm in Missouri, and he liked the way the older girl in the family helped with the young ones, as if it were expected. Instead of having a sister like that, Durkin had had a daddy who liked to whip him, just for the hell of it. In the movie, this older girl, who was about fourteen, married a returning G.I., quite a bit like Durkin, who liked cars and girls. The way she settled right down to childbearing and rearing had both Durkin's wife and his daughter hooting. All she could do to entertain herself and her kids was sing to them. Her husband liked the way she sang, and it was his idea to launch her on a career as a singer. Right at this point, the movie Durkin had liked so much changed as if he had switched channels. Instead of the real hard times, which he found sad but moving, what they had were a lot of trashy good times in Nashville. All they seemed to do together was ride around in a bus and eat junk food. It troubled Durkin that his daughter, old enough to know better, saw nothing wrong with a girl swapping her real family life for a pot of money and a home on a bus. He switched the TV off, but he heard her mother switch it back on while he was brushing his teeth. They didn't give a damn, while they were watching the movie, that the girl singing about a coal miner's daughter was glad to have put all of that behind her.

Durkin made his living installing automatic garage doors, with a home-maintenance service as a sideline. He had the assistance of his daughter, Caroline. She didn't like the work, but he paid her the same as he would a man. Durkin ran the business out of his home. His wife took the calls during the daytime, and Caroline talked her into seeing she ought to be on Durkin's payroll, too. Durkin had never urged his wife to make more of herself, perhaps fearing she might. When he began to date her, he'd felt that she was above his own level, but the truth seemed to be that she didn't know what her level was.

In the garage-door business, Durkin did a lot of waiting, and that was what he was doing now while his wife was marketing and his muffler was being repaired. From where he sat in the mechanic's office, he could see the sheds at the rear, where his green station wagon was up on the hoist. "Forty minutes or I do it for free," the repairman, Haley, had joshed him. Durkin had already been waiting for half an hour.

Another customer, a big, beefy fellow, came into the office and left his Coupe de Ville in the carport at the door with the wipers flapping, the motor idling. He seemed to be less accustomed to waiting than Durkin, and chewed up a lot of toothpicks while he was at it. They weren't the toothpicks you get in a dispenser but the ones that come in a packet, like paper matches. One reason he stood the way he did at the door was to listen to the music on his car radio. Durkin appreciated how the flick of the wipers syncopated with the music. The way his white flannel suit draped on him so loosely put Durkin in mind of Burl Ives. To accommodate his paunch, the big man's coat hung open at the front, like the flaps of a tent. A Greek-type fisherman's cap fit his head so snugly it bushed the gray hair at his temples. Durkin thought the man was probably about his own age, but the skin of his jowls had a spanky firmness. Sideburns grew down to his powdered jawline.

To no one in particular the fellow said, "Where's the boss man?"

"He's out in back," said Durkin. "He's busy."

"I've seen you somewhere," the man said. "You do commercials?"

As he often told his wife, Durkin highly respected a first-class smart-ass. The man turned away from Durkin to catch the voice of the announcer. Without turning back, he said, "My name's Pyle. I do commercials, if I can keep the goddamn appointments."

"You do Rolaids?" queried Durkin. He said it so nice and easy that the fellow was of two minds how he meant it.

Sucking the air between his teeth, Pyle said, "I like to give people around me my own names. You like to do that?"

"What name comes to your mind?" said Durkin.

"Oh, hell," he said, "I just like to name things. I like to name horses. I like to name songs." He paused there as if he meant to sing one. Durkin realized that the voice of the singer on the radio was Digby Pyle. What seemed to be a perpetual smile on his lips was just his way of toying with the toothpicks.

"I'm running behind, Tiger," Pyle said, snapping his fingers, and stepped back into the carport. Durkin watched him toddle, his broad shoulders hunched, through the drizzle to the sheds out back. Durkin's station wagon was still on the hoist. Haley came from beneath it to talk to Pyle, who hung one beefy arm around his stooped shoulders. Now and then Pyle gave him a squeeze, as if testing his bulk. Durkin watched Haley hammer on the rusty muffler, reluctant to be rushed, then turn and wipe his hands on a piece of newspaper as he walked through the drizzle back to the office. He stepped through the door, water running from his hair down his grease-smeared face. He looked beat up. Durkin didn't much like him, so why did he feel a surge of sympathy for him?

"Mr. Durkin," Haley said, "how about it?"

"How about what?" Durkin knew, but he wanted to hear him say it.

"Pyle's running late, it's costing him money. You suppose you could spare him some time on the hoist?"

They were both silent a moment, listening to the singer. He sang a good song.

"Time's money, like you say," said Durkin, "but it's my wife that's got it, not me. She's at the Alpha Beta, doing a little shopping. You want to pay me for what it's worth if I'm late picking her up?"

The muffler man tapped a cigarette from the pack on the counter, lit it up. He ran a greasy hand through his wet hair, the way Bogart did in *The African Queen.* "I'll tell him," Haley said, and walked back in the drizzle to the shed. For some time, Durkin watched the two men stand facing each other like comedians. When Pyle waved an arm, the pearl buttons on his cuffs seemed to leave tracers of light on the shadows. Even the way Pyle argued, it seemed to Durkin, was like that of a man accustomed to TV cameras. This delay was not only costing him money, but the shoulders of his white flannel coat were soggy, gray as underwear, and it warmed Durkin's heart to note that. Pyle waved both his arms, as if he meant to fly; then he took off on the double back to his car and climbed in. He slammed the door, gunned the motor, and the car lurched forward, stopping just short of the hoist. In the fading light the hearse-dark windows of the car looked black. Haley took his time loosening the bolts on Durkin's muffler.

A crackle of background music, interspersed with commercials, came through a vent in the office ceiling. To get away from it, Durkin crossed the street for a cup of coffee. Behind the counter, four or five schoolboys in green-and-white caps thumped into each other as they prepared snack orders. Most of the tables were occupied by girls huddled over containers of soft drinks. The seats outside, under gay beach umbrellas, were swept by windy gusts of drizzle. Durkin sat down to let blasts of rock music pass over his head.

In the dim light of the rain-streaked window, two boys with book bags played a game with coins on the slick top of a table. A coin was finger-flicked to the opposite side, on the chance that it might stop near the table's edge. If it failed to, the boy seated there caught it, then flicked it back toward his companion. Sometimes it fell to the floor and rolled about under the tables. Not all coins, Durkin noted, were worth picking up. The boys hooted and snorted, tilted back on their chairs, waved their arms, swung their legs, and pounded on the table. The game did not focus much of their attention, but it provided some outlet for their energy.

Their play was closely observed by a smaller and younger boy, in a short-waisted windbreaker and knee-length britches. He was seated with his mother, a smartly dressed young woman in a trenchcoat. While the boy was distracted, she skillfully removed the pickles and wilted lettuce from a three-tiered sandwich that he had started to eat before he lost interest.

The game played with the flicked coin had him entranced. He pressed the white knuckles of his hands to his face, shook his head as if it pained him, squealed shrilly. Durkin saw little but his dark, tight ringlets of hair until the boy turned his head to glance at his mother. He was pretty as a girl—maybe prettier than most. Long tangled lashes screened his eyes. In the quick exchange of glances with his mother, Durkin sensed the depth of her infatuation. With her free hand she lightly brushed the curls from his flushed brow.

It pleased Durkin to share in her pleasure, in spite of his envy. He would have liked such a pretty, slender woman for a wife, and a child, preferably a girl, as pretty as this boy, who would turn to glance in that way at her daddy. She urged the boy to eat, putting the sandwich to his lips, but it seemed to repel him. He made a rude, snorting noise, like the boys he was watching, and drew the back of his hand across his mouth. When his mother dabbed at his lips with her napkin, he turned away, clenching his fists. If Durkin had been his father, he would have slapped him. Why would such a beautiful, favored child turn like that on a loving mother? What was the matter with people? Offered love, why would they turn away from it?

A wind-whipped sheet of rain slashed across the window and flickered the lights. The boy seated with his mother shouted with excitement, rolling his eyes. Durkin saw him turn to give his mother the full glow of his attention. She suddenly glanced at Durkin, as if she felt the weight of his gaze. One of the older boys jumped up, thrusting back his chair, and with a gesture of contempt or of triumph swept the paper plates and drink cartons from the tables as he passed them. Some liquid spilled on the smaller boy's bare legs, and he kicked out wildly, shrieking with pleasure. His mother's efforts to calm him increased his excitement. Spurred on by the music, he ran about between the tables. With Durkin's assistance, he was cornered and brought back to the table.

"I feel responsible," the young woman said, stooping for one of the paper plates. "Now, isn't that silly?"

Durkin assured her that boys would be boys. She explained to him—she seemed to feel the need to—that none of this would have happened if it hadn't been drizzling, but she did not say why. She led the boy to the door. An older girl, her books clasped to her front in a way Durkin found appealing, joined them under the awning at the entrance. They stood there while the young mother looked in her purse for her car keys; then the three walked to her car, a bright yellow compact. She had left its low lights burning, so Durkin was relieved for her when her engine started and the wipers cleared an arc on the windshield. Through it he caught a blurred glimpse of the woman's face as the yellow car headed for the turnaround down the road.

He let several minutes pass before he walked through the drizzle for his car. But the station wagon stood to one side, its tail pipe still missing; Pyle's black Coupe de Ville was just coming down from the hoist. Durkin saw Pyle climb in, slam the door, then back into the highway, with a whoosh that slapped gravel onto the carport windows. He couldn't have seen where he was going, Durkin thought, and he didn't seem to care. There was little screech of tires on the slippery pavement, just the grinding crunch of metal and splintering of glass as the yellow compact struck the Coupe de Ville. A pickup loaded with firewood piled into the compact, and a van slammed broadside into the pickup. Above the din, Durkin could hear one of those horns that toot a few bars of music. The clamor eased up, but the horn was stuck. The crushed hood couldn't be raised to get at it. Pyle had run down one of his car's black windows, thrust out his head. He didn't seem to be hurt, and waved off the people who wanted to help him, preferring to sit there out of the rain, listening to his music.

From the shelter of the carport, Durkin could hear the approaching sirens. A highway patrol car, its beacon revolving, was parked to block off two lanes of traffic; its headlights shone on the front of the pickup. The little yellow compact was like a molar crushed between the jaws of the pickup and of Pyle's Coupe de Ville. A clot of people had gathered around it. Pyle sat answering the state trooper's questions. The crown of his fisherman's cap gleamed. Once, he raised his head to look directly toward Durkin, as if for help. A front door of his car yawned open to reveal the dark glow of the cockpit, where red and green lights were blinking. Several white-clad attendants moved through the lights and drizzle, just as they did in war movies.

As he might when he was watching a gruesome movie, especially if it was in color, Durkin turned away. Car lights cast his shadow on the wall of the carport. Durkin's wife was particularly caustic about the way he refused to sit out a sad movie: if he could see it was going to end up sticky, he'd go to the kitchen for a beer, or pay a visit to the bathroom. "Your father can watch grown men clobber each other silly in a football game, but he's just too sensitive to see Meryl Streep break up with Hoffman," she'd tell Caroline.

Durkin turned back to the highway. Someone had raised an umbrella over the trooper so he could write down on his pad all that Pyle told him. If Durkin was questioned, he would say that smart-ass sort of people often tend to be careless, but that's all. Once something had happened, it had happened. There were songs about that. Whatever had happened, Durkin would get it later on the TV.

Durkin waited till the wrecker arrived, its beeper tooting, and towed the pickup off in the drizzle. As he drove to get his wife at the supermarket, he pictured the young mother, in her raincoat, removing the wilted bits of lettuce from the boy's sandwich, and saying to Durkin, in such an open, appealing manner, "I feel responsible. Now, isn't that silly?" Actually, he had thought it silly at the time, but now he wasn't so sure. And say you are responsible, then where do you draw the line?

By the time he found his wife, standing beside her shopping cart, her arms crossed high on her front to let him know she had been waiting, he was thinking of the boy, of the touch of wildness in his nature, and how what you come to love in a person can hurt you the most. One thing Durkin couldn't get enough of about his wife was the way, when she was washing the windows or about to take a shower, she would swoop her hair up off her neck and ears. She stopped doing that the moment she sensed how much he liked it. A tune she liked to hum that drove Durkin crazy was "You Turned the Tables on Me," which he took personally. "Why do you take it so personal, hon?" she would ask him, but he had no idea.

1985

Things That Matter

They made some pair, Enid liked to say—the one like two big scoops of ice cream, the other like a cup of yogurt with the fruit on the bottom. Enid was pint-size to Carolyn's quart, a creature to whom the word "bouncy" readily applied. She was the allegro to Carolyn's stately largo, yet she was more deliberate than impatient—very much her own person, in Carolyn's opinion, given to open-toed sandals with platform soles, and with more of a bark than a laugh. When Carolyn laughed, Enid thought she might be choking and clapped her on the back. No matter what Carolyn said, Enid replied, "You can say that again!"

At war's end, Enid had followed a sailor from Liverpool to a sheep ranch in the outback of Australia, where she had grown to love horses and gramophone music. The sailor hadn't worked out, and on her way back to England she stopped in Reno and settled nearby on a dude ranch, working with horses. Enid liked dude-ranching, but she had to get away and unwind on weekends in Reno. When she was on a roll, men would give her the dice and say, "Hey, baby, you roll 'em." She was in Reno when she met Carolyn in the ladies' room of Harrah's all-night restaurant. Carolyn had spent the night cranking slot machines, and she was pooped. She had come up from Bakersfield on a bus, but she let Enid drive her back in her '57 Chrysler convertible, with the top down, Carolyn so windburned she looked like an Indian. And that was how it happened. How explain to anybody that the un-likely pairings were those that worked out?

Carolyn's house was upwind from the freeway, so there wasn't much noise. She had moved to Bakersfield from L.A. to get away from the smog, and had bought a two-story house with gingerbread scrollwork in the gable at the front and along the eaves of the porch. That was back before the top blew off the real-estate market. Bakersfield was like a furnace compared to Reno, but Enid paid for the air-conditioners in their bedrooms.

When it would start, Carolyn drove the old jeep that was parked under the green pup tent in the side yard. It would not start on unleaded gas, but if pushed it would run, making a racket like marbles in a milk can. Carolyn drove it in the parade on Veterans Day (Enid was there on a white horse named Queenie) to honor her big brother Lee, who was killed in North Africa fighting Rommel. Enid's Chrysler was always parked in the street, but so far from the curb she often got a ticket. Enid knew better, but, short as she was behind the wheel, she had trouble judging where the curb was.

If Enid was really British, or Scottish, it only showed when she talked to her dog, Douglas. She got him on a visit to the local pound, where she was dropping off a litter of unwanted kittens. Douglas was a brindle-colored, mostly Scottish terrier, with big ears but no legs to speak of. Carolyn had to kneel in the grass to pet him, he was so low to the ground. In the rainy season he picked up filth he couldn't reach to lick off, so Enid had to brush him and even use her vacuum-cleaner attachments to clean him. He liked to lie out flat in the draft at the kitchen door, where the bottled-water boy was likely to trip over him. Outside, where the neighborhood kids left their stuffed animals around the yard, Douglas didn't look real until he moved, or the grass had been mowed. Children were Douglas's sort of people, if they were small enough, and on his own level. He didn't like being eye to eye, however, which led him to bark and race around in circles. Douglas scooted when he ran, stirring up leaves and dust, but right at the end of his run he would leap and jump like a windup toy. The children loved it, but it gave Carolyn a fit.

After washing her dark waist-length hair, Carolyn would sit in the yard, weeding dandelions, her hair fanned out on her shoulders to dry. In the blaze of the sun there wasn't a black hair in it; in the swirl at the crown it was bright as the copper in a scouring pad. Enid loved to braid Carolyn's hair in one long heavy rope with a brush at the end. The weight of it drew the skin taut at Carolyn's forehead and sometimes gave her headaches, but it was worth it. "You're a bloody knockout," Enid said, "you know that?" In the shopping malls, men would follow Carolyn the way kids follow big scoops of ice cream.

Enid did the cooking and the laundry. Carolyn did the housekeeping, the out-of-doors, and the lights on the porch at Christmas. She had the assistance of a neighbor, Mr. Dalton, who didn't mind shocks. The lights blinked in a manner that Enid found annoying, but they were important to Carolyn. On a trip to the beach, or into the mountains, or to Reno for the weekend (blackjack was important to Enid), they would use the Chrysler, but Carolyn did the driving; she would make a less flighty impression on the cops than Enid. Carolyn was not at ease with Enid at the wheel on narrow two-lane roads without a line down the center; Enid was prone to switching lanes if the road was empty.

Most of the year, Carolyn wore Army-surplus fatigues with T-shirts not tucked in. She liked the St. Louis Cardinals in baseball, having twice seen them play. Enid's pleasure, besides a weekend in Reno, was to pull on her riding breeches with the suède seat and knee patches, and the purple boots that made her hot and flustered to lace up—beads of sweat on her upper lip, bangs of curls stuck to her forehead, but the boots pointing up her trim ankles and brandy-snifter figure. That left her ready for the County Fair, where she would throw balls, flip darts, toss rings, and shoot automatic rifles until she got a high on. Carolyn was sometimes bewildered by this; she saw it as Enid's way of letting her hair down, while she still had some.

Good-humoredly, Carolyn once said, "You just enjoy being het up, you know that?"

"I got to be somethin'," Enid replied curtly. "I get awfully tired being nothin'."

Carolyn was so hurt by that she just let it drop.

Enid skied, too—not very well, but she got around. She liked the rides on the lifts, the rush down the slopes, the snow down her neck, the fun in the lodge, and the square dancing. Enid was a bouncer. Even young men liked her bounce. When her face was flushed, her eyes flashing, it hardly mattered whether her hair was dyed or just naturally orange. Carolyn knew all that about her, but not her age. What Enid let slip about her past life all took place in countries Carolyn was not up to date on. If they had a tiff, Enid would speak of it as a "contretemps"; when she was young, whenever that was, her father sometimes took her across the Channel to France. It seemed strange to Carolyn that a country like France could be so close. One of their bad tiffs had to do with a play from British television called "The Norman Conquests," Norman being the name of the main character. Enid explained that it also referred to the Norman conquest of England in 1066. Did Enid think that Carolyn didn't know *that*? What else did she think, for God's sake?

What would she think—high-strung as she was, and impulsive—if she knew that, against the day Enid might leave her, Carolyn occasionally filched a few of the little flat pills from Enid's Valium prescription? Would she believe it? Carolyn hardly did herself.

On Sunday, usually, Carolyn cut the lawn, giving the mower a good thump on the laurel, a tree she never liked. She would work around the tree with short, choppy strokes, like a fighter with body punches. Depending on how she felt, she might or might not thump the loose clapboards at grass level on the side of the house. If Enid was upset by this racket, she would go off to shop for imported Parmesan cheese in the gourmet market. There was an olive oil there, too, heavy as motor oil, that she liked to eat on bread smeared with garlic. Enid had no head at all for financial matters, and had to be told over and over that the dollar was now worth almost as much as the English pound.

On balmy days Carolyn sat in the yard weeding dandelions, a floppy-brimmed beach hat shading both herself and Douglas. If she rolled him over, she could see the fleas scoot on his pink belly.

Carolyn's portable radio, tuned to the news, always started with a blast and then tailed off as the recharged batteries ran down. She might forget all about it, and leave it for Enid to turn off and bring into the house.

For money, Carolyn house-sat for local real-estate people or worked part time as hostess at a motel restaurant, wearing the Indian jewelry Enid liked to buy her. Enid had once house-sat, and liked it, but she couldn't talk to people without smoking too much—especially on the phone. Before she lifted the receiver to answer inquiries about the house, Enid had to light up. Partly for the money, but mainly because she liked to, Enid helped with remedial reading at a country day school she could walk to.

People found it hard to say no to Enid, not wanting to hurt her feelings. Enid's mother, who still lived in Liverpool, said that some people—women especially—gave off a glow she could see around them. Enid herself believed in demons and poltergeists. Carolyn had been too astonished at hearing this to show disbelief. Enid confessed that an atomic blast anywhere set off flashes in her head like those in comic-strip balloons—no noise, just flashes. She would see the light first—say, at three o'clock in the morning. Then she would hear about it on the 7 A.M. news or read about it in the paper. When the big boom came, she said, she would be the first to know it, but there would be nothing to read afterward.

In other respects, except for her high blood pressure, Enid seemed normal enough. While she square-danced, Carolyn watched her just to see her snub the men who approached her later. She wouldn't have missed it for the world.

Diagonally across the street, in Enid's direct view from the kitchen window, the seven children of the Francobolli family played in their yard. Mrs. Francobolli, like her husband, was from the North of Italy, where it often flooded. She was a square slab of a woman, with six black-haired *bambini* and then the littlest one with reddish hair and freckles. Mr. Francobolli, a contractor, parked his machinery in the side yard, one of his big dump trucks in the two-car garage. During the summer, the children used the empty space in the garage as a playroom, with a table and little red chairs, like a kindergarten. Enid liked to hear their shrieking, and watched them at play through the kitchen window. When Douglas heard the cries of the children, he would scratch at the door until Enid let him out. How he loved to be with the little Emilia, a playmate his own size!

When Enid whistled Douglas home, which she often had to, Mrs. Francobolli might come along with him, Emilia straddling her hip. Seated on the counter at Enid's sink, little Emilia would dangle her feet in the dishwater while Douglas jumped and barked. Mrs. Francobolli, thick as she was, would lift Emilia and make like a dancer, turning first this way, then that way, passing her to Enid, who would do the same, singing "La di da, la di da, la di da," in her croaking voice, her eyes flashing, her head tilted back so she could gaze into the face of the child, like a lover. In this excitement Carolyn would turn to trimming the hedge, or weeding the lawn, where she was not missed. In the bright sunlight of Enid's kitchen, Emilia's hair glinted with reddish lights, like Enid's. On her pudgy little hands there were orange freckles that would not rub off. How explain it? All her other kids were dark. Mrs. Francobolli herself exclaimed that the child might have been Enid's *bambina.* And why not? There were already more than enough to go around, and another on the way. How they both laughed!

Over the summer—a hot one to Carolyn—Estelle, the mail-person; Sammy, the bottled-water boy; the transients in the nearby trailer, who teased Douglas, were struck by the change in Enid's manner. She would offer rides to elderly shoppers, or buy lottery tickets for shut-ins. The Jehovah's Witness people, often a family with babies, or two earnest young women discussing points of doctrine—all gentle, decent folk of the sort Enid detested—were asked to come into the house for a cup of coffee, or mint tea if they objected to stimulants. Over the previous five or six years she had always argued with them through the bathroom window. Now, sometimes with Emilia riding her hip, Enid would smilingly listen to their message.

Over this same summer, when Enid whistled for Douglas he might not come home from the Francobolli garage. He hung back.

He hid under the children's table. Emilia would have to bring him, tugging at his collar, and receive a reward from Enid that she would eat while sitting on the counter. Carolyn could testify that Enid sometimes called her Yum-Yum and fed her yogurt. Nor did it please Carolyn to see the way the little girl clung to Enid's neck, hugging her for dear life as she hung up the laundry. Enid was not disturbed by Carolyn's feelings of jealousy. She paid to have Carolyn's old piano tuned so she and Emilia could play "Chopsticks."

The clincher for Carolyn, after a summer of losses, was Enid's sudden decision not to go to Reno with her in October. Going to Reno together (they both hated Las Vegas) was one of the things they always did. What Enid said was that a dog like Douglas shouldn't be left to himself in a kennel. Carolyn suspected that she couldn't bear to be apart from Emilia for so long. If Carolyn yielded to something like that, where would it end? She took the bus to Sacramento, then got on the Gamblers' Special over the mountains to Reno—a train of boozers and high rollers, most of them half crocked before they even got into the mountains. The man in the coach seat next to her took alternate swallows of Coca-Cola and Four Roses whiskey. He insisted on sharing with her his packet of Sen-Sen. The way he rubbed the smeared window with his coat sleeve put Carolyn in mind of her father.

Big as Carolyn was, she didn't have the knack of dealing with men. This one draped his arm along the back of her seat and toyed with her hair. "A big broad like you," he said, finding her unfriendly, "can't lose anything but her luggage." She excused herself and went to the washroom, where she stayed until the train reached Reno, the floor slippery with water that had sloshed from the sink.

That evening she won forty-eight dollars on the slot machines, but not a nickel of it gave her any pleasure. The person she sat down beside at the counter in Harrah's was one of the bag-packers in her supermarket at home. He had a double room, with nobody else in it, which he offered to share with her, gratis. During the night, from her own room, she listened to the revelry in the adjoining suites. She was strongly tempted to call Enid and tell her about the silly invitation, but it would be like Enid to say, "Well, why didn't you?"

The next night, after losing all she had won and then some, the sight of her face in the bathroom mirror gave her a shock. Her lips were black. Her hands had a shine from the coins that wouldn't wash off. To get herself clean she took a long, soaking bath in the tub. That night she wanted to phone Enid so badly that she woke up thinking that she *had* called her, and even remembered what she had said. The next day she took her meals in her room and watched TV. Unable to sleep that third night, she called home. The phone rang and rang, but no answer. Before daylight Sunday, Carolyn packed her bag and sat in the bus depot until morning. Would Enid know how close she had come to despair?

The mountains always made her feel she was watching a movie, but she began to feel better down on the freeway, with the cars whooshing by. On the long ride home she napped on and off. Not to trouble Enid, she took a taxi from the bus terminal. Where Enid's car was always parked too far from the curb, the bottled-water boy had parked his truck, with the engine running. Mrs. Francobolli, her hair wrapped in a towel, stood in the street holding the hand of her oldest daughter, Alma. They were ringed by four or five boys with skateboards. What had happened?

It was not easy to determine. In her excitement, Mrs. Francobolli mixed up her English and Italian. From Alma, Carolyn learned that Enid, Douglas, and Emilia had flown the coop. Alma had seen them go; Enid had waved. Mrs. Francobolli was now so exhausted she appeared to be calm.

Carolyn entered the house, where she found Enid's TV still blinking. She went first into her own room, then into Enid's, then into the kitchen, where Enid often left a note held by a magnet to the door of the refrigerator. There was no note. Just the heads of the pussycats on the magnets. Actually, Carolyn preferred finding nothing at all to what a person like Enid might put into writing.

Hearing Mrs. Francobolli's voice at the window, Carolyn turned on the water at the sink and let it run. Over the half curtain at the window, she saw that she had left her overnight bag at the curb. How abandoned it looked! The lid had been closed on a wad of her nightgown. Everything about it testified to somebody's departing, not arriving.

Carolyn's eye was caught by the erratic behavior of a small, plump boy on a large bicycle. Rather than riding it in the proper manner, he had thrust a leg through the frame in order to pedal it sidesaddle. Carolyn had not seen a boy do that since she was a child. This one, a brown-faced boy, used the bike to run errands for the druggist, but he was not accustomed to this way of riding. The front wheel wobbled, the cycle zigged and zagged as he tried to get the hang of it. Teetering crazily, he came along to where he would surely strike Mrs. Francobolli; then he veered about, the front wheel spinning, and went zagging off in the direction he had come from. The bottled-water boy turned off his truck blinkers and drove away. The big boys pirouetted on their skateboards, their knees flexed, their arms flung wide like surfers', putting on a show for Mrs. Francobolli's daughter in her confirmation dress and white stockings.

Carolyn put off until it was called to her attention the overnight bag she had left at the curb. Her mind was on other matters. Why would Enid, who disliked cats, have bought magnets with pussycat heads? Were the things that really mattered the things that Carolyn had never understood?

1986

The Origin of Sadness

There is a plain in Kansas where the advancing ice sheet once spread itself thin on the earth's surface, the cutting edge rolling before it balls of turf the size of cart wheels. A few are still visible today, and deceptively resemble the playthings of giants. Who is to say they were not? Several of these wheels lie embedded in the yard of Dr. Klaus Schuler, in Osborn County, whose son, a big, shy, pensive boy, transformed them into snowmen in the winter. Not the usual sort of cheerful Santa Claus–type figures, topped with a red stocking cap and muffler, but hulking, jut-browed creatures that might have crawled from a cave and found no place to hide. A bookish sort of boy, he might have seen such creatures in books.

A progressive, forward-looking citizen of the new world, with reputable old world connections, Dr. Schuler had come west from Ohio to be on the frontier of human advancement. He had good books in his study, as well as a globe of the world that his reading had led him to feel might be wobbling. He was the first of the doctors in the county to use a gas buggy to make his house calls, and he considered this machine, a Dodge coupé with yellow wheels, to be the one thing he had in common with his son. The boy was soon big enough to reach the pedals, and more than strong enough to steer, but it seemed to terrify him to shift the gears. Nothing would persuade him to try to crank it. Neither could he, big as he was, catch or throw a ball in the prescribed manner. He had to toss it, awkwardly underhand, in the way of girls. With the exception of Fox and Geese, which was played in the snow, where his big feet found secure footing, he watched most games from the sidelines or one of the schoolhouse windows. A friend of sorts, a dark-skinned Indian boy who might turn up in the shirts that Schuler had outgrown, sometimes stood with him watching the others play, but they did not talk much.

To the north of the Schuler house, perhaps a half-mile walk, a tributary of the Solomon River appeared to be little more than a crack in the plain's undulating surface. Soon enough, however, Schuler found it. Sometimes shallow as a gully, it was deep as an arroyo after the flash floods of spring and summer, and he found crevices in the walls large enough for a creature or a boy to curl up in. Scoured clean by the water, fossil fragments trapped in the rock folds emerged as if from hiding. The impressions of plant forms were like the flowers pressed between the pages of a book. To a boy of Schuler's brooding, expectant nature they were more wondrous than puzzling. Perhaps nature herself spoke in this manner to those accustomed to listening. It was also characteristic that Schuler kept these revelations to himself. Explanations, however clever they were, would surely fall short of his expectations. And why would he reveal secrets known only to himself? These findings were forms of buried treasure that persuaded him to keep his own counsel. Deep within himself Schuler was drawn toward secret agreements, and pacts of silence.

With his moon-faced Indian friend he concealed and fed a litter of coyotes found in the arroyo. All but one soon turned up in steel traps. This pup, with a trap-maimed paw and a pelt that was short and coarse as a doormat, survived to slink around the house like a mongrel dog, an enemy to everyone but Schuler. The creature was of a cowering, suspicious nature, preferring to scavenge the garbage in the town dump rather than eat the food offered by Schuler. But in the late afternoon, sometimes unobserved, it would cunningly join him on the long walks to the arroyo, stirring up along the way the nesting birds and rabbits, or going on ahead to wait for him in the canyon. In this wild defile, like Schuler, it felt at home.

One early March, returning from Kansas City, Dr. Schuler was caught in a fierce spring blizzard. He left his stalled car to make his way to a farmhouse, but several days passed before he was found buried in a deep drift with several hundred head of cattle. The Dodge coupé, still as good as new, was stored in the rear of the livery stable until young Schuler—it was hoped—would prove to have an interest in it.

Mrs. Schuler took for granted that her bookish son would be a doctor, like his father. He often read at the table while eating his meals, glancing up only when he wanted something. She considered this somewhat rude, but she found it less disturbing than his bemused gaze. What his thoughts were she couldn't imagine. What she came to miss even more than she missed her husband was the shrill chatter of women occupied with house chores. Young Schuler sometimes tunelessly whistled, but he seldom talked. Thinking he might be musical, she employed a young woman to teach Schuler the piano, but after some months of fruitless instruction she came to the conclusion that he was tone deaf. These handicaps did not trouble his mother as much as something in his nature, his self-absorption, that was more that of a grown man than a teen-aged boy.

To keep her company in the large empty house, one of Mrs. Schuler's sisters, Ilse, came to spend the long winters with her. A slender, very erect, decorous young woman, who had felt her true calling to be in church work, she showed little or no interest in sewing, cooking, or house chores, but she was patient and understanding with Schuler. Ilse was the first, and she proved to be the last, to take pains with his contorted left-handed writing, which was so clear and sensible in meaning if one could only read it. She was gentle but firm. She did not like to be hurried. What was it that appealed to her in a boy who could not line up the buttons of his shirts with the buttonholes?

Young Schuler was not unfriendly, but he did not seem to feel a need for friends. With boys of his own age he was shy, but he was at ease in the company of adults. At a gathering of teachers or parents he often managed to make himself useful. Dr. Gulden, who had taken over his father's practice, sometimes found the boy in his office pondering the human skeleton that hung in the closet. Dr. Schuler had used it to entertain and frighten other children, but his son was more respectful. Did Dr. Gulden know, Schuler asked, whose bones they were? Gulden thought it a curious question from a prospective doctor. If a patient appeared with a broken limb, or a severe and bleeding cut, he observed that Schuler recoiled. Big and strong as he was, he seemed to lack certain masculine components in his nature, but Gulden was tactful in his comments to his mother. In Dr. Gulden's opinion a country doctor needed to be more outgoing with women, and less squeamish about blood.

It was Schuler's Aunt Ilse who divined that he was not cut out to be a doctor or a lawyer. There was surely no future for him in Junction, but if he lived in Topeka, with his Aunt Myrtle, he could attend the Teachers College. No one would question that he had the scholar's turn of mind. He had once spoken out, clearly and at length, on the subject of meteor showers, leading her into the yard on a chill November night to observe what he described as a "rain of light."

In Topeka he was fitted with horn-rimmed glasses that gave him the look of a goldfish. The casually slurring remark of a classmate, who may have envied Schuler his head of curly black hair, led him to ask the local barber to use the clippers on all but a tuft of hair on the crown. His mother never forgave him for it, but of course she saw little of him. His curly hair had been the one thing he had from his father of which she approved.

He helped support himself with part-time work at a chicken hatchery, where he sat up half the night turning the eggs and checking the temperature of the incubators. The helplessness of such creatures, hardly more than puffs of down, yet once hatched chirping for dear life, elicited from Schuler both sympathy and admiration. Chicks that were deformed, or felt themselves to be outcasts, he would slip into the front of his unbuttoned shirt, where they would huddle while he got in some reading. In the dim nocturnal glow of the sheds he felt at home.

A history teacher, Professor Alexander, early noted the drift of Schuler's mind for the time that preceded history. The vanished, relatively timeless past, most of it buried beneath the earth's crust or entombed in its rocks, enflamed his imagination. Alexander was the first to point out to Schuler that the remote past, if it concerned *living* creatures, continued to be part of the present. This simple observation overwhelmed him. In a few weeks it diverted him from the study of rocks and meteors into the labyrinth of evolution, where in time—in the fullness of time—he would surely come up with the answers. These were the feelings he shared with Bernice, a cousin three years Schuler's senior. They may have spared him, if not her, the torment of romantic attachments, as she gave to Schuler freely the respectful attention that he both needed and took for granted.

A very plain young woman (in his mother's opinion) with a substantial figure and expansive nature, she willingly cowered in the loft of the barn where the bats hung upside down, awaiting twilight or, in the predawn darkness, awaiting the first glow of light. Later, having passed this initiation, she sprawled on the floor of the screened-in porch to register, on her perspiring forehead, the movement of air created by their wings as they entered and exited a hole in the screen. He had persuaded her, although she trembled with fear, to corroborate his own observations: bats did not seek to tangle themselves, even when given a chance, in the hair of women. This shared world opened horizons to Bernice that were not, somehow, apparent to Schuler. Her large eyes fastened on his animated face; his lips parted to show his uneven upper teeth. A gap, where an incisor was missing, made him reluctant to smile.

All by himself, in the arroyo near his home, Schuler had found (so he believed) some of the missing pages of evolution, and had begun to decipher bits of its passage. Further pages, perhaps even the missing link, were there to be stumbled on or excavated. Schuler might himself be the one to unearth it, or, more likely, the one to recognize it. It pained him to watch the blade of a shovel or a pickaxe disturb what had been millennia in the making. But, once the deed was done, Schuler was the first to come eagerly forward. The open, expectant face of Schuler was the place to look for what had been discovered.

His temperament proved to be well suited to both nourish and contain his excitement. He passed the gray days of winter in the library, the radiators hissing and pounding, and the long nights in the glow of the incubators, an environment peculiarly supportive of his ceaseless, wakeful dreaming. Work was found for him at nearby diggings for fossil remains. A shovelful of earth might rouse in Schuler puzzling, troubling sensations. He was not above certain common superstitions, and took pains to stay clear of gravesites. He *was* a bit of an odd one. When he took one of his walks, God only knew where he was off to. It did stretch the minds of those who had them to visualize the vast plains as the bed of a sea, and later a swamp where dinosaurs waddled, but once it was envisioned, as in a diorama, Schuler found it as real as what he saw around him. No, make that *realer.* He did not find the immediate and shifting flux of time present real at all.

One of his students, a young woman from Oklahoma, shared with Schuler both his passion for bones and his talent for silence. Doreen Oakum often sat, her hands idle in her lap, while Schuler stood as if entranced at the window of his office, seemingly unaware that he had fallen silent. Below the window a large parking grid occupied several acres, ending where weeds and the shed of chicken farmers sloped down to a creek, dry most of the year, with leafless shrubs clinging to its banks. Beyond it a patch of gone-to-seed victory gardens, a gully cluttered with trash, old stoves, iceboxes, and stripped car bodies, from one of which smoke often curled where a tramp was camping. And then, without space or transition, spread a field of sprouting winter wheat, chaste and green as a lawn, soon to be concealed by the first snow of winter.

As he turned from this scene Schuler would glance at Doreen as he would at a wall map, to get his bearings. Part Cherokee Indian, on her mother's side, Doreen Oakum was a square-shouldered, slab-flat young woman with plain features that somehow proved to be striking. She was dark, with large prominent eyes, a wide, full mouth, her complexion like that of a dull penny. Her manner was impassive, her face without expression as she listened to Schuler's ponderous soliloquies. His own feeling was that she was *all* Indian, but ashamed of it. His impression of her, in his mind's eye, was one of extraordinary unrelieved flatness, like that of figures sculpted in low relief. Her arms hung straight from her wide shoulders to swing free of her narrow hips. In his office she sat erect with her knees pressed together, a clipboard with yellow paper face up in her lap. He learned to be at ease with her impassive manner, since he sensed that it concealed strong emotions. She was bright enough, as a student, but it surprised him to learn that she had an unusual talent for drawing. She was able to contribute to her own support by making drawings of plant forms for textbooks. Their accuracy astonished Schuler, who had observed such details closely. Had she, he asked her, thought of branching out? He needed reproductions of fossil remains for the research papers he hoped to publish.

On his desk Schuler kept samples of fossil remains as delicate in their details as the veins of a leaf. Could she capture such details? She made no comment. He gave her several pieces to try her hand on, and she soon returned with drawings as accurate as rubbings, with the flawed or missing details restored. Schuler was flabbergasted. He took pains to explain to her that the imperfect fragment was the one he wanted; the perfect restoration would arouse suspicion. Her gift, like the fossils themselves, was a matter of shared but secret communications.

For her own pleasure, when she could find the time, she made watercolor sketches of the stuffed birds with the most exotic and brilliant plumage. The delight she seemed to take in the colors and the feathers he felt to be a part of her Indian past. He was not aware, for some time, of the extent he had grown to rely on her presence. Glancing up from his reading, or letting his gaze pass over a classroom, it was often for her he proved to be looking. Some days before the summer freed him of classwork he drove her to her home in Claremore, Oklahoma, where they were married by a justice of the peace. They had not planned it. He could not say with assurance that marriage was what he wanted. But on the long drive south he had experienced an urge to be free of his self-perpetuating obsessions, the rocks left for him to find, the bones left for him to classify, the truths left for him to discover. To all of that he knew there would be no end. He felt compelled to share with her his entrapment. He had stopped the car, asked her to be his wife, and she had not objected. He had never courted her. He had seldom actually desired her. But at that moment he had acted with deep assurance and satisfaction, as a person might feel at his conversion. Her response was so low-keyed he was not really sure she had accepted his proposal. While he mumbled his proposal (he had left the motor running, as if ready for flight if speech failed him) her hands fingered the clasp of her handbag, but the silence between them, as they both knew, was a form of assent.

In no way whatsoever did Schuler prove adequate to the intimacies of marriage that could not be avoided, but his wife gave no indication that anything should be more or less than she found it. They drove to Carlsbad Caverns for their honeymoon, where they watched the sky darken with clouds of bats that left the cave in the evening, then returned in the morning. They then drove to his home in Kansas, where his mother accepted the news without comment. Ilse, away on a visit, later sent the bride a gift of a silver-backed comb, brush, and mirror set, profoundly pleasing to a woman who spent time each day grooming her hair. Such a gift would never have crossed Schuler's mind. His mother had thought it hardly appropriate for a squaw.

They settled into an apartment near the campus, feeling no need for larger accommodations. He frequently carried a bag lunch to his office to avoid the crowding in the school cafeteria. Schuler's interest in food proved to be for anything easily prepared and quickly eaten. He liked canned grapefruit better than fresh, and never tired of peanut butter spread on white toast. They took their meals in the breakfast nook, which was actually too small for

Schuler, the dishes and cups rattling noisily when he tried to seat himself or make his escape. He ate silently, fully absorbed with eating, as if he feared the food might be taken from him. If he happened to like something he would glance up for a second helping, but it did not cross his mind to comment.

Each evening, while waiting for his supper, seated at the table with its piece of green oilcloth, Schuler would recite the events of the day he thought to be of interest. While he talked she set the table, or stood for a moment at the door to the kitchen, her presence being all that was necessary in the way of a comment. Administrative problems might require that Schuler, in fairness, present both sides of a question, which he would do at some length, then wait for her glance to confirm his judgment. This done, he might turn to the headlines of the paper. The comics he reserved until last. It disturbed him to miss the happenings of *Gasoline Alley* or *Out Our Way*.

For two weeks of the hot summers Schuler would take Doreen to the Lake of the Ozarks, where the nights were cooler, and the days slipped by as he rowed her about in the shallows of the shoreline, since she feared deep water. One could understand Schuler's delight in water, seldom having seen more of it than a tubful, but the quantity of it was crucial. Lake Michigan, for example, with its rimless horizon and intimations of floods and returning ice sheets, depressed him. Ponds were ideal, as were bodies of water that consisted of miles of shoreline. The sight of boats, water dripping from oars, and sounds and voices carried across water, aroused Schuler the way a small boy might be stirred by band music and parades. In the shallows near the shoreline he would rock the boat to grope around in the muck for crayfish. As Doreen squealed, tucking her skirts beneath her, the usually solemn, mirthless Schuler would giggle like a tickled small fry, holding between two fingers the little monster with its waving antennae and huge snapping claws. Doreen's pleasure came in the evening, with the music and dancing, the lights across the lake reflected on the water, Schuler contentedly slouched at her side eating ice cream spooned from a carton. He loved ice cream.

A crucial incident in Schuler's life was a visit he made to Philadelphia while his wife went home to her people. He had come to see the zoo. The strangeness and exuberant variety of living species overwhelmed him. The confidence he felt in the great theory of evolution, as sublime as he found it, was shaken. Although species existed with startling reality, their evolvement was often sketchy or missing. Why did only the giraffe grow such a long neck, and the elephant a trunk? They appeared to him like creatures in a dream or a fanciful painting, out of time and history. On the other hand, his feelings of man's brotherhood with the ape were strengthened. The meeting of Schuler with the great ape Massa, a huge and somber gorilla, was a memorable confrontation of his life. He felt for this creature a profound and close kinship. Bluish black in color, his hands like patent leather, he crouched like a Buddha to peel and eat the ripe bananas Schuler brought him. He did this with delicacy and refinement. Man and ape exchanged glances that caused Schuler's hands to tremble. Greater than the unspoken kinship, the shared captivity in a world not to their liking, Schuler divined the ape's despair at his place in a cul-de-sac of evolution. No exit existed. His awareness of this entrapment seemed as obvious to Schuler as man's awareness, seen in his effort to escape the planet and inhabit space.

From Philadelphia he brought his wife a parrot, rather small in size but with brilliant, iridescent plumage. The bird's head was red as a ripe tomato, its beak like the tusk of a saber-toothed tiger. It was there in the apartment when she returned from Oklahoma, and it pleased him to see that it awed her. Their voices, as she spoke to the bird, sounded like those of a loving teacher and a slow pupil. It led him to recall his mother's complaint that what her home lacked was the voices of women. The bird, whose name was Georgia, learned to say many things, but it disturbed Schuler to find that Doreen did not clearly distinguish the bird's mimicry from human speech. There were things she said to it, for example, only in Schuler's absence. A deep superstition surfaced in her conviction that it might well speak for a departed spirit. Why not? Why would *he*, of all people, take exception to that? He took exception to that, as he felt obliged to, so that she would maintain crucial distinctions, but in this matter her large dark eyes seemed to observe him from a distance. There was no quarrel, but the invisible bonds that joined them noticeably slackened. Over the winter Georgia began to lose plumage, exposing the thin neck in the ruff of feathers, the clouded eye that it fastened on Schuler so dull it appeared to be lidded. The relief that he felt on the bird's death filled him with shame.

What Schuler loved about his wife, besides her glistening black hair, the scalp bone-white where the hair parted, was her detachment from the world that hummed and buzzed around her, her attachment to the invisible world within her. The problem with earthly attachments, as the parrot had demonstrated, was that they were all made to be broken. It pleased Schuler to note that she did not suggest having the bird stuffed.

When a question was put to him in a public lecture, as to what it was he was really seeking, Schuler had gazed long at the chalk dust powdering his fingers, then replied, "What interests me is the origin of sadness." That they could believe. Heavy-jowled, less solemn than somber, sometimes given to an appealing melancholy, the normal impassive set of his face was that of a banished warrior who knew himself to be doomed. Impressionable students felt he practiced black magic with the skulls and bones he kept in a closet. Both those in awe of Schuler and those who were intimidated by him remembered with affection his love of cough drops, noisily slipped from his pocket during lectures. He often brought to his oral examinations the petrified tusk of a saber-toothed tiger, one he had himself found in the bluffs west of the Missouri. In the posture so familiar to his wife and students—the palm of one hand, the fingers splayed, pressed firmly to his forehead—he might or might not ask the student to enlarge on the subject of tigers in Kansas.

In late November, although feeling poorly (a complaint that Schuler associated with women), Doreen returned to Oklahoma to visit her ailing mother. Some days later—he did not know how many—one of her older female relations wired Schuler to say that she had passed away. He had assumed that the wire referred to her mother, but it proved to be his wife. Schuler managed to be there in time for the service, held in an open field that was gray with a dusting of snow, the earth beneath it packed hard as a playground. In the long day he felt little but disbelief. An older brother of his wife, a harness and saddle maker, as white-skinned as Schuler and talkative as a barber, proved to have the shiftiness of the mixed-breed and tried to blackmail money from him. He believed that an evil spirit, the property of white men, had possessed and carried off his sister.

An old woman who had lost an eye, the empty socket like a heel's bruise in the earth, followed Schuler about rattling a gourd to which a long whisk of horse-tail hairs was attached. Only Schuler seemed attentive to her presence. Muttering to herself, a cigarette between her lips, she would fiercely wag the rattle at him whenever she attracted his attention. Back in the privacy of his hotel room he had examined his body for signs of her stigma, but he also believed, whatever her intent, that he merited her disapproval. He thought her a witch.

From Oklahoma he drove north to his birthplace, the winter landscape bleak and sunless. The stands of trees planted by the settlers were dying. In the sweep of his car lights the barkless branches rose up before him like tongues of flame. All of his anguish and suppressed grief chose this moment to overwhelm him. On a road of gravel, under threatening skies, the sight of a patch of road weeds, whipped by winds that blew to no purpose, just to be blowing, filled him with a tearful and burning despair. He had to slow the car and pull to the side of the road. Low sweeping black clouds seemed intent on clearing the plain of all living creatures, and Schuler sat in wonderment at the deep satisfaction this spectacle give him. Whose side, in the name of God, was he on? He did not know.

At the Junction intersection, visible for miles, a sign that resembled an exploding rocket rose from the roof of a truckers' diner. All about it was the squalor of wrecked and stripped cars, and the stench of burning rubber tires. In the deafening clamor of rock music the blonde waitress watched a TV movie. If Schuler lidded his eyes he could detect the moist crack of her gum.

The dirt road leading up to his home was blocked by a house that was being moved. In the flicker of the car lights he saw the glitter of a cat's eyes at one of the windows. The rays of reflected light pierced his own like lasers. It reassured Schuler, more than it disturbed him, that these encounters were like visitations, the confirmation of his disordered feelings. A voice speaking from on high would not have surprised him. In the winter sky the stars were dazzling, and on the balls of his eyes he could feel the prickling rain of light.

In a room with drawn blinds, the air moist and rancid with the odor of dying house plants, he found his mother asleep in a wheelchair facing the glare of a silent TV. He did not disturb her. Ilse, her flaxen hair in long braids, one hand clutching the robe at her throat, reassured him that his mother's mind was "clear," and her spirits good. Ilse herself seemed at peace with a life that left her no option but self-negation. In her calm resignation he felt a palpable aura of sainthood. "There is so much we have to be thankful for," she said, meaning that they were caretakers, not patients. A matter of fact. Was not Schuler one to appreciate the facts?

In the morning, when he stooped to kiss her, his mother's eyes showed little sign of recognition. Her face resembled an unbaked cookie, the eyes like sunken raisins. She thumped the floor with a stick to get Ilse's attention. During the day she was wheeled from window to window, following the sun, but the TV provided her view of the world.

Laundered sheets and underclothes hung on the sagging lines that criss-crossed the kitchen, the water dripping like rain on the Kansas City papers Ilse lacked the time to read. She lacked the strength to care for the dying house plants that grew in a wild tangle on the sun porch, but new life sprouted from the seeds in the jars at the kitchen window.

On the radio, just before her stroke—Ilse mentioned it in passing—his mother had heard of an organization that would freeze her body, just before life left it, then preserve it by refrigeration until medical science could restore her to health. At that moment she would be thawed and returned to life. Ilse had been of two minds concerning this project, which she personally viewed with some skepticism, but before his mother could look into the matter she had suffered the stroke.

What in God's name was it, Schuler wondered, that his mother had been so determined to hold on to? Her soul? She scoffed at religion. What she seemed compelled to preserve was her body. But he felt he detected in Ilse's recital, and in her calm acceptance of such a bizarre project, that he, Schuler, the eminent scholar and expert in the recovery of what had vanished, had had more than a little to do with his mother's fascination with her own survival. However infrequent his visits home, and however remote his investigations, his preoccupations had seeped into the minds of those who knew him.

Why did he find all of this so unusual?

In his love of fossils, of images trapped in rocks, was he not obsessed with a similar passion? Survival in one form or another? A blind refusal to accept extinction? A somewhat bookish and fanciful effort to hoodwink time?

Schuler might indulge in such speculations on his afternoon walks. Big flakes of snow, falling like bits of torn paper, clung to his face and sleeves like ashes. He heard little but his own hoarse breathing. A carpet of flakes whitened the furrows as he crossed a field of stubble. He stooped to scoop up a handful, as light and dry as the remains of the parrot. As the flakes brushed his face and pricked his eyes, melting when his breath sucked them into his mouth, the idea, no, the *image*, unforeseen and unbidden crossed his mind. He saw that he need not wait for the ice to come to him, since it was there, ready and waiting, at the polar ice caps. A vast quantity of ice, inexhaustible, with more than room enough to store the planet's exploding population. A natural deep-freeze—the white cliffs of ice honeycombed with dormant bodies—at the thought of it he laughed aloud, a boy's gleeful chortle at some grisly bit of human behavior. Not merely safe storage and preservation, but in due time, surely, restoration. In due time? There would be no more due points in time. In the time warp of preservation, time, as man conceived it, would have a stop. For a brief, giddy moment Schuler experienced an unearthly lightness, a buoyant elation. Time's bitter hug—was he free of it? A gulp of air too cold for his teeth brought him back to where he stood in the furrow. The deep freeze of all freezes was time itself.

He plodded on, puffing clouds of vapor, to be stopped by a fence he dimly remembered. Back then he had scuttled beneath it. Now, with some effort, he spread the strands of rusted barbed wire and squeezed through. A tangle of brush and weeds slowed his progress. What he had thought to be shrubs, suddenly thickening before him, were the tops of trees in the arroyo. Overeager, as he approached the rim he took a misstep that sent him sprawling, scuffing his knees. But that, surely, was to be expected. Recent floods and runoffs had scoured the rocky slopes and removed all traces of former footholds. Predictably, as he began to get his bearings, the arroyo seemed less deep than he remembered, but it was also much wilder. It pleased him to realize that he had been such an adventurous child.

On the slow climb downward he repeatedly fell, sometimes skidding and sliding, but he was indifferent to such discomforts. In the debris at the bottom, under the covering of snow, he found the familiar fossil fragments. Many lay weathered and exposed. In all these years had no other curious, snooping child been here? Down on his hands and knees, feeling his old excitement, he stuffed his pockets with rock fragments. The falling snow, like a swarming cloud of moths, concealed the rim of the arroyo when he glanced upward. It also muffled the sound of his movements. He might pause, as he began the climb upward, to hear the rocks he had dislodged tumble to the bottom. The creature he had become, grossly heavy and awkward, an intruder in these once familiar surroundings, was now bringing ruin and disorder to one of time's orderly niches. That saddened him. Where a jutting ledge crumbled under his weight he found fossil forms, like a packet of letters, undisturbed since the moment of pressing. His elation at finding this treasure gave way to a numbing pang of loss. His wife had received more from these disclosures than he did, and by that token she had been less destructive. Did that make him careless?

Anxious to bring to a conclusion what he had started, his full weight on a root extending from the rock face, he reached upward just as it snapped beneath him. He had a short free fall, touching nothing, that was over before he felt the climber's chill of terror, then he landed on his side, facing inward, feeling little but immense relief. The climb had been so steep, his breathing so heavy, he felt the light-headedness of hyperventilation. Snow fell about and on him. He succumbed to a creature's drowsy contentment—no throb or stab of pain until he moved. When he cried out he heard no echo. The pain at his hip—he could pinpoint it, as he so often had for his appreciative students—concerned the ball and socket of the hip joint, one of nature's most remarkable engineering triumphs. This point now radiated heat. Schuler lay on his side where he could reach and touch the detritus in an old bed of ashes. Had they been of his own making? Had he come here to slip time's noose? The find seemed appropriate to the fold in the rock where Schuler, his pockets full of fossils, creating his own time warp of dismaying proportions, would be unearthed with delight and con-sternation by those who probed for anything, and everything, but what they would actually find. It pleased Schuler to reflect that perhaps the ice would get to him first.

1984